The Absolution

Also by Yrsa Sigurdardóttir

The Thóra Gudmundsdóttir novels

Last Rituals
My Soul to Take
Ashes to Dust
The Day is Dark
Someone to Watch Over Me
The Silence of the Sea

Standalones

I Remember You
The Undesired
Why Did You Lie?

The Freyja and Huldar Series

The Legacy
The Reckoning
The Absolution

About the Author

Yrsa Sigurdardóttir works as a civil engineer in Reykjavík. She made her crime fiction debut in 2005 with *Last Rituals*, the first instalment in the Thóra Gudmundsdóttir series, and has been translated into more than 30 languages. *The Silence of the Sea* won the Petrona Award in 2015. *The Absolution* is her twelfth adult novel and the third in the Freyja and Huldar Series.

About the Translator

Victoria Cribb studied and worked in Iceland for many years. She has translated more than twenty-five Icelandic authors including Arnaldur Indriðason, Ragnar Jónasson and Sjón. In 2017 she received the Orðstír honorary translation award for her services to Icelandic literature.

The Absolution

Yrsa Sigurdardóttir

Translated from the Icelandic by Victoria Cribb

HODDER &
STOUGHTON

First published in Great Britain in 2019 by Hodder & Stoughton
An Hachette UK company

First published with the title *Aflausn* in 2016 by Veröld Publishing, Reykjavík

Published by arrangement with the Salomonsson Agency

1

A CIP catalogue record for this title is available from the British Library

Hardback ISBN 978 1 473 62160 2
Trade Paperback ISBN 978 1 473 62161 9
eBook ISBN 978 1 473 62162 6

Typeset in Sabon MT by Palimpsest Book Production Limited, Falkirk, Stirlingshire

Printed and bound in Great Britain by Clays Ltd, Elcograf S.p.A.

Hodder & Stoughton policy is to use papers that are natural, renewable
and recyclable products and made from wood grown in sustainable forests.
The logging and manufacturing processes are expected to conform to the
environmental regulations of the country of origin.

Hodder & Stoughton Ltd
Carmelite House
50 Victoria Embankment
London EC4Y 0DZ

www.hodder.co.uk

Pronunciation guide
for character names

Huldar – HOOL-dar
Freyja – FRAY-a
Gudlaugur – GVOOTH-lohgur
Erla – ED-la
Stella – STELL-la
Adalheidur – ATH-al-HAY-thoor
Haukur – HOH-koor
Saga (as in English)
Baldur – BAL-door
Fanney – FANN-ay
Helgi – HELL-ghee
Ævar – EYE-varr
Davíd – DAH-veeth
Ásta – OW-sta
Thórey – THOHR-ay
Ósk – Ohsk
Sól – Sohl
Kjartan – KYAR-tan
Bogi – BAW-yee
Mördur – MUR-thoor
Jóel – YOH-el
Egill – AY-idl

Ásdís – OWSS-dees
Thorgeir – THOR-gayrr
Bjarney – BYAD-nay
Arnar – AHD-narr
Laufhildur – LOHV-hild-oor

Chapter 1

The women's toilets on the lower ground floor were deserted. The sinks were dry and the doors of the empty cubicles stood open a crack. The place was in the sort of state you'd expect after all the queues earlier that evening. Bins overflowing with used paper towels. Empty Coke cups littering every surface. The contents of a large box of popcorn strewn over the floor and trampled by the women hopping desperately from one foot to the other in the queue.

Stella assumed the same chaos must reign in the gents and felt thankful that it wasn't her job to clean them. The mess was unusually bad as two films had sold out and the others had attracted pretty big audiences as well. There had been such a crush at the kiosk in the foyer before the films began and during the intervals that the popcorn machine hadn't been able to keep up, even though they'd made loads in advance, and the Diet Coke had run out, much to the disgust of the customers. Stella had had to bite her lip to stop herself answering back when they blamed her. Like it was her job to buy the stuff in or keep track of stocks!

She paused in the doorway, suddenly conscious of being alone down there, the only person in the entire building.

The silence was absolute. No muffled booming from the auditoriums, no chattering voices of the girls she worked with. She had offered to close up as usual so they could catch their bus, and stood watching through the glass wall of the foyer as they vanished into the snowstorm. No sooner had their shapes receded into the thick veil of white than she'd begun to regret her generous offer. Not that her motives had been purely unselfish. In reality, she hadn't been able to resist showing off that she'd got a boyfriend – a boyfriend with a car. No messing about on buses for her.

For some reason her thoughts suddenly returned to the Snap she'd received just after the last interval. She hadn't a clue who the sender was – it wasn't anyone she'd added. Of course she should have changed her settings ages ago and blocked strangers from messaging her, especially now that old people had started using the app. Not content with ruining Facebook, they were taking over Snapchat as well. She bet it was some old bag, maybe one of her mum's friends or a relative she'd forgotten about. The username didn't ring any bells: *Just13*. Maybe it wasn't some old person after all; maybe it was a kid who'd just turned thirteen. That would explain the weird message.

The Snap had been a photo of her, in the act of serving popcorn to a customer. It wasn't a flattering picture: she was making a face and her body, the little that could be seen of it, was caught at a stupid angle. No pose, no smile. The caption had been as puzzling as the Snap itself. All it said was: *See you.* Whoever the sender was, they'd obviously been at the cinema but hadn't come over to say hello. Maybe it was some shy little boy who didn't have the guts to talk to her. Well, it was lucky for him because she'd have told him where to go. She had zero interest in meeting creeps and only a creep would send a Snap like that uninvited.

The door swung to behind Stella. The hydraulics were

broken, so it closed slowly at first, before suddenly gathering speed and slamming shut with a loud bang. The noise reverberated around the tiled space, echoing in her head, drawing attention to the silence. She'd been feeling a bit uneasy upstairs but it was a lot worse down here on the lower level. At least in the foyer you could see out of the windows, or as far as the thickly falling snow would allow. It must have been the weather that had driven people to the cinema in hordes. Stella had seen all the films that were showing so she knew they sucked. Still, while you were watching them you could forget the Arctic conditions outside.

Now, though, the snow seemed infinitely preferable to the deserted cinema. Stella couldn't wait to be safe in Höddi's car. So what if it was a wreck and the heater was broken? It was still better than the bus. A bit like Höddi. He wasn't exactly a fairytale prince but being with him was better than being single. He'd do for now, while she was looking around for someone better. Someone fit, with a car that was cool enough to turn her friends green with envy. That's the kind of boyfriend she wanted. Not someone like Höddi who always had to be out of focus in the pictures she posted on social media.

Stella chose the furthest cubicle and hurriedly shot the bolt. Opposite the cubicles was a row of sinks with a huge mirror running the length of the wall. She didn't particularly want to see herself right now: tired, looking like shit, in need of a haircut, highlights and an eyebrow pluck. The roots showed dark along her parting, like the go-faster stripe on the bonnet of Höddi's car. Gross. Before coming downstairs she had paused by the cardboard cut-out of a ghost advertising the horror film being shown in screen one. She'd meant to send her friends a Snap of her standing beside it, but changed her mind because she didn't want them to see how crap she looked. It was kind of creepy standing beside the grisly display, too, though she knew it was nothing but a huge piece of cardboard. She'd take the pic another time when she was looking hot and there were other people around. Her pay had better arrive on time because she'd made an appointment for the moment the salon opened on the first of the month. Shame it was so fucking expensive to keep your hair looking good.

Stella pulled down her knickers and peed, crouching above the seat. God knows what germs the cinemagoers might have left behind on it. There was no way she was going to be one of those sluts who catch an STD. You never lived that kind of thing down.

Over the tinkle of urine she heard the door of the toilets open. The skin prickled on her naked thighs and her throat constricted with fear. Who the hell could it be? Had one of the girls come back? If so, how did she get in? Had they forgotten to lock the door behind them? Her thoughts flew to the Snap again. Surely it couldn't be *Just13*?

A loud bang indicated that the door had closed again. Stella held her breath, straining to hear if the person had come in. Maybe it was just the security guard, arrived early, checking all areas. But no such luck. The creaking of shoes warned her that she wasn't alone.

Her trickle had dwindled to a few drops that fell in time to the footsteps. It must be a woman. Had to be a woman. What would a man be doing in the ladies' loos in an empty cinema at this time of night? It wasn't like the gents was full. Stella bit back the impulse to call out and ask who it was.

4

Reaching for the loo paper, she tore a few sheets off the roll as quietly as she could, dried herself, then stood up, pulling up her trousers. She felt a little better, or at least not quite as exposed. But this feeling soon evaporated.

Two shoes appeared beneath the cubicle door. They looked like boots, broad enough to belong to a man. Stella clamped her hands over her mouth to stifle a scream. Why was he standing there? The feet didn't move; their owner just stood there as if it was a front door and he was thinking of ringing the bell. Which wasn't far off the mark because next minute there was a loud banging on the door. She stared helplessly at its blank surface as if it could show her what was going on.

Just then her phone buzzed and she took it from her pocket with a trembling hand, nearly dropping it when she saw that she'd got another Snap from *Just13*. Before she could stop herself, she had touched the screen and opened the message. She bit back a scream when the picture appeared: it showed a closed door like the one to her cubicle. It had to be the same door, the only thing now separating her from the sender. There was no caption.

More loud banging. Stella recoiled, backing so hard into the toilet bowl that her knees buckled. 'Who's that?' No answer. She'd blurted out the words before she could stop herself. Her voice sounded feeble, pathetic, unlike her. Stella was used to being the leader of the pack. Strong. Determined. Showing no mercy to wimps who sounded like she did now.

This time the banging was so hard that the door shook. Stella's eyes dropped to the flimsy bolt and she saw at once that it would offer little protection. Her head was spinning as she glanced round frantically for something, anything to save her. The toilet roll and holder. A plastic bin with a lid. The wall-mounted toilet that she might be able to swing at the man's head if he forced his way in. Except she'd never be able to wrench it off the wall. Then she remembered the phone she was clutching in her sweaty hand. Should she ring the emergency services? Or Höddi? If he was already on his way, surely he'd be nearer than the cops?

She was spared the decision. The man hurled himself at the cubicle door, the lock broke and the door slammed into Stella's head, knocking her backwards to sprawl, dazed, on the toilet seat. Fighting off nausea, she forced herself to look up into her assailant's face. At first she thought it was hidden in shadow, it was so black. It took her a moment to work out that she was looking at a shiny Darth Vader mask under the dark hood of his anorak. Eyes were watching her through the almond-shaped holes but she couldn't read their expression. A gloved hand reached out and snatched her phone. As the man started fiddling with it, Stella prayed he was a thief. He was welcome to her phone. To the contents of her pockets. To all her pay at the end of the month. Her bag. Anything. So long as he left without laying a finger on her.

'Well, well.' The man's voice was strange, not unlike Darth Vader's. Rasping, as if his throat was lined with sandpaper. The mask must have come with a cheap voice-changer. He aimed the phone at her as if to snap her sitting on the loo. Tears began to trickle down her cheeks. What was he doing? Why would a thief want a video or photo of the phone's owner? 'Now, I want you to give it all you've got.'

'What?' Stella slid back on the toilet seat until her spine was pressed against the wall and the feel of the hard, icy surface through her thin jumper only made her shivering worse.

6

'Say you're sorry.'

She didn't even try to resist but did her best to apologise, in spite of the sob that forced its way up her throat.

'Aw. That wasn't good enough. Not convincing at all. You can do better than that.'

She tried. And tried. Repeated the word 'Sorry' until it began to ring oddly in her ears, as if it wasn't a real word. But nothing seemed to satisfy the man.

And for that she would have to pay the price.

Chapter 2

'We need a bigger screen.' Finally one of the officers in the incident room blurted out what everyone else was thinking. Ever since the playback had started, the group had been edging their chairs closer to the wall where the footage from the cinema's CCTV cameras was being shown on a ridiculously small screen.

Erla, who was perched on the table closest to it, glanced round irritably. 'Try to concentrate. The quality's so shit that a bigger screen wouldn't help. But if it bothers you that much, you can put a request in the suggestion box.'

The man was silent and Huldar knew why: Erla rarely took it kindly if one of her team answered back. She was an OK boss in many ways but not too hot at the human relations side of things. He didn't for a minute believe that the wish for a decent screen in the incident room would find its way into the suggestion box; they'd all learnt the hard way that it was nothing but a graveyard for complaints.

'Look. Here it comes.' Erla had turned back to the footage. 'There. Watch the cardboard cut-out of the ghost or whatever the hell it is.'

All eyes were glued to the corner of the screen dominated by the advertising display. The girl had walked past it a short time before, pausing to pull faces while she fiddled with her phone, took a few selfies, then continued out of the frame.

According to Erla, that was the last time she appeared upright on any of the recordings. There were no security cameras on the lower level where the toilets were, or by the stairs that led down to them. Judging by the time display on the recording, and on the video clips sent from the girl's phone, she must have headed down to the ladies at this point.

A shadowy figure suddenly materialised from behind the cardboard cut-out and everyone rocked forwards simultaneously to get a better view. It had to be the perpetrator. The quality was fuzzy, as Erla had pointed out, but once the entire figure was visible they realised that this was irrelevant; it would be impossible to identify him even if the picture had been in HD. He was wearing a bulky, dark anorak with the hood pulled up, and a Darth Vader mask. Apart from that, he had on dark-coloured trousers tucked into black boots, and dark gloves. The man vanished out of the frame in the same direction as Stella.

'And there we have it. He hid behind that stupid advert and lay in wait for the girl.' Erla paused the recording. They were left staring at the frozen image of the cardboard ghost and the empty foyer. 'We need to go over all the recordings from when the cinema opened, to try and work out what time he arrived. At least we can be pretty damn sure he wasn't wearing the mask when he turned up.' Erla rose and faced them. 'It's not going to be easy. According to the cinema, they sold just over sixteen hundred tickets yesterday. They opened at two, like every Sunday, and there's no knowing when the man entered the building. He could have turned up for the first screening and hidden until after closing time, and not necessarily behind that cut-out. Someone needs to study the recordings to establish a time frame.'

Everyone ducked their heads, Huldar included, silently praying the task wouldn't fall to them. From where Erla was standing, they must look like a bunch of kids playing musical statues. She frowned. 'Someone needs to go through the ticket sales too. It's not that common for people to go to the cinema on their own, so we'll need a list of all those customers who bought single tickets. If we can find out when our man arrived, we may be able to narrow it down by checking who bought a single ticket from the box office at that time. As long as he paid by card. If he paid with cash, we're screwed.'

'He could have bought the ticket online. In advance.' As usual, Gudlaugur turned pink the instant he had spoken. He was sitting beside Huldar, who nodded encouragingly at him. They formed their own little team within the team, sitting across the desk from each other in the open-plan office, and were usually assigned the same jobs. There were times when Huldar would have preferred to be partnered with a more experienced detective, but he'd learnt to appreciate the young man's qualities. He could be perceptive when he didn't let his low self-esteem and diffidence get in the way. 'I mean . . . tickets aren't only sold on site. You know . . . so . . .'

Huldar interrupted as Gudlaugur started to flounder. 'If the attacker bought them online he could easily have got two tickets to make himself less conspicuous. He must have realised we'd check the ticket sales, especially the single ones. But if he did buy online, he'll have paid by card, which is a plus. Or it will be, once we've got the names of some potential suspects.'

This intervention did nothing to soften Erla's frown. When she spoke, it was to Gudlaugur, not Huldar. That was nothing new; their relationship had been strained ever since they were dragged through the internal inquiry into allegations that she'd sexually harassed him. Although no further action had been taken, the experience had left a bad taste in both their mouths. Since then she had behaved as if he didn't exist, never looking in his direction or speaking to him first if she could help it. He didn't know whether she was afraid their interaction might be misinterpreted or she just couldn't stand the sight of him. Personally, he'd found the whole process excruciating, though in hindsight perhaps it had been worth it. There was no denying that he was relieved to have dodged the consequences of shagging her. No need now for the awkward conversation in which he broke it to her that their night together had been a mistake.

Erla's scowl deepened. 'I *know* tickets are sold online. The total I mentioned included online sales. But if the perpetrator's not a total fuckwit, he'll have paid in cash. We'll work on that basis for the moment, though of course we'll go through the online payments too. Happy now?' Erla's eyes bored into Gudlaugur, who squirmed in his seat. He nodded. 'Fine. If not, you can come up here and take over the meeting.' Everyone except Gudlaugur and Huldar laughed.

Erla didn't so much as crack a smile. Picking up the remote, she selected the next video clip, then pressed 'Play' again. 'Here he is, leaving the building. As you can see, it's unlikely we're looking for a living victim.'

A different view appeared on screen. This time they were looking at a pair of glass doors that Huldar recognised as the cinema's emergency exit, used mainly by smokers like him during the intervals. The officer who'd gone through the recordings with Erla earlier that morning made a face that didn't bode well.

The dark-clad figure appeared in the frame, his back to the

camera, dragging Stella's motionless body by the ankle. Her arms trailed behind her head, her long hair fanning out between them. Her jumper had ridden up in the process, revealing her bare midriff and a glimpse of bra. The man paused by the exit, dropping her leg, which landed heavily on the floor. He was about to lift the big steel bar that secured the door, when he hesitated and darted a quick glance back at the girl.

'Whoa!' A detective in the front row pointed at the screen. 'Look! She moved.'

Erla paused the recording. If her face had been grim before it was positively haggard now. 'We believe the girl made a noise. Maybe she was coming round. Unless it was just her death throes. Anyway, it's immaterial. Watch.' She pressed 'Play' again.

The team watched, collectively holding their breath, as the man stepped closer to the girl and prodded her with his right foot. Her bare stomach quivered slightly as if with a cramp, and the fingers of one hand twitched convulsively. The man swung his head around, surveying his surroundings, then made straight for a fire extinguisher fixed to the wall, detached it and carried it back to the girl.

'Shit.' Huldar didn't care that he'd sworn aloud. He steeled himself not to look away. Next to him, he saw Gudlaugur screwing up his eyes to slits; but, like the others, he kept watching as the man raised the heavy cylinder and brought it down with brutal force on the girl's head. A violent spasm shook her body. After that she didn't move again.

The man opened the door, grabbed the girl by the ankle and dragged her to the opening, where he took the time to pause and wave at the security camera. Then he vanished into the falling snow, towing the girl behind him.

The door was left open. On the floor was a broad dark slick.

Gudlaugur got up from his computer, running his hands through his fair hair. 'I'm going to get a coffee. Want one?' His face was ashen and Huldar didn't blame him. Despite being an old hand himself, he still found it hard to stomach extreme violence and murder. Some officers became desensitised, others never got used to it. Time would tell which group Gudlaugur belonged to.

'Yes, please. Black.' Though in truth he could have done with something stronger.

Gudlaugur made no move to fetch the coffee. Perhaps he didn't really want it either. 'Do you think he knew her or was it a random attack?'

'He probably knew her, judging by the way he made her beg for forgiveness. But we can't take anything for granted. Maybe she just got his order wrong at the kiosk.' Huldar didn't need to explain: Gudlaugur knew as much about the case as he did, having seen the horrific Snaps that had been sent from Stella's phone to all her followers. After watching the CCTV clips, the inquiry team had been shown the Snaps; short videos of her saying sorry over and over again, with rising desperation, though what she was apologising for was anyone's guess.

The last Snap, which Huldar could have lived without, showed Stella's head being repeatedly bashed against the toilet bowl. The only glimpse of the attacker was his gloved hand gripping her by the hair. Fortunately, the resolution in these clips had been even grainier than the CCTV footage, since they were films of videos playing on a small phone screen.

The police had been forced to resort to this method for now because apparently it was impossible to save Snapchat messages once they'd been viewed. Efforts were under way to get hold of the original clips directly from Snap, the company behind the messaging app. Only then would it be possible to see them in full resolution. Even so, the poor quality did little to mitigate the girl's piercing screams and moans, or the way they became progressively fainter until finally she went quiet. No way would Huldar be volunteering to watch the high-res versions when they finally arrived.

Until the brief introduction earlier, he'd known next to nothing about the app. If he understood correctly, each Snap, like the ones sent from Stella's phone, could only be viewed twice by the recipient, and once it had been seen by all the recipients, it would self-destruct. So if you wanted to watch it twice, you had to do so immediately. After that, the Snap was gone forever and there was literally no way of retrieving it. Not even when it was a police matter or a question of national security. It was pure luck that so many followers had received the videos from Stella's phone. The police had managed to track down some of her friends that night, asked if they followed her on Snapchat, and confiscated their phones if they did. It had been crucial to ensure that not all her contacts viewed the Snaps, so they wouldn't auto-destruct. Stella's own phone hadn't turned up yet. There was no sign of it on the network and the police assumed the perpetrator would dispose of it. Since he appeared to be no fool, it was unlikely he'd hang on to it, let alone switch it on and risk being traced.

'How do you think her boyfriend felt after watching that?' Gudlaugur still hadn't moved, his offer of coffee apparently forgotten.

'Devastated. No wonder he's in shock.' The young man had been on his way to pick Stella up when the Snaps started arriving. He had viewed one while waiting at the traffic lights and taken it for a sick joke. Then he'd started thinking maybe she'd been cheating on him and this was her way of apologising, though he couldn't work out why she'd do it in the toilet like that.

By the time the final Snap arrived, the boy had twigged that it was neither a joke nor an apology. By then he was nearly at the cinema, so instead of wasting time calling the police, he had driven the rest of the way like a maniac, leapt out of the car and started hammering frantically on the doors at the front entrance. According to the timeline the police were drawing up, at this point the perpetrator must have just left the cinema via the fire exit at the side of the building. When the boy had finally got round to circling the cinema in search of another way in, he had found the emergency exit open, seen the bloody trail and immediately rung the emergency services.

Gudlaugur turned away from Huldar to stare out of the window. There was nothing to see: just a grey sky louring over an equally grey city. The heavy snowfall dumped on Reykjavík by the blizzard yesterday evening was turning to brown slush under the wheels of the morning traffic. Faced with this depressing view, Gudlaugur quickly turned back to Huldar. 'What can she have done to the man to deserve that?'

'Nothing,' Huldar said flatly. 'Nothing could justify it. She was only sixteen.' But Gudlaugur already knew this. 'Still, our mission today is to find out. The sooner we start looking into her background, the sooner we're likely to dig up a motive.' He pulled over his mouse, ready to get stuck in. The background check had been assigned to them. It might not be the most exciting task but it was infinitely preferable to having to sit in on Erla's conversation with the girl's parents. Spotting them crossing the open-plan office in the direction of the small meeting room, he'd hastily dropped his eyes. He wasn't the only one. The mother had been clutching her daughter's laptop to her chest like a shield to protect herself against further shocks.

The laptop was now sitting on Huldar's desk, waiting for him to go through the contents. In stark contrast to the standard black office hardware, it was white and decorated with ladybird stickers; the computer of a teenage girl barely out of childhood. The conversation with her parents must have been gut-wrenching. Since Stella hadn't been found yet, they were bound to be cherishing a faint hope that she would turn up alive, despite what they'd been told. One of the grim facts that Erla had to make clear to them was that their daughter was almost certainly dead.

Huldar's gaze was drawn inexorably to Erla's office, the office that had once been his, though he didn't miss it for a second. The parents had left and she was standing by the glass wall, arms folded, her demeanour as uncompromising as it had been in the incident room earlier. Their gazes met for a split second before skittering apart.

Gudlaugur hadn't noticed. He seemed as preoccupied as Huldar, though not for the same reason. Eventually he heaved a sigh and showed signs of going to fetch the coffee. But first he asked, without apparently expecting an answer: 'Why the hell did he take her body with him? However hard I try, I can't think why he'd do that.'

He wasn't the only one.

Chapter 3

'What do you know about teenage girls?'

No hello, hi, good morning or how are you? No introduction. Not that there was any need. Though Freyja hadn't seen or heard from Huldar for months, she recognised his voice instantly; far too quickly for comfort. Typical. She never got phone calls out of the blue from anyone she wanted to talk to.

'Good afternoon,' she said coolly. The moment she'd spoken, she regretted it. Why hadn't she disguised her voice and pretended to be someone else? Told him Freyja would be out of the country for the next month? Whatever it was Huldar wanted, it could only lead to trouble and bruised feelings. She'd been there too many times before.

'Oh. Hi. Sorry. It's Huldar.' He left a gap for her to respond. When she didn't, he added: 'I was wondering if you could help me. We've got a case involving a teenage girl and I wanted to ask your advice.'

Freyja instantly made the connection and felt intrigued in spite of herself. She forgot her original intention of ending the call as soon as possible. Since lunchtime, news had been coming in of a brutal assault on a teenage girl the previous evening and her disappearance from the cinema where she worked. As usual the police weren't releasing any details, so the media's main sources at this stage were the girl's friends and classmates, who had been sent phone messages containing video clips of the attack.

Although descriptions of the content had been kept deliberately vague, reading between the lines you could tell that the videos weren't for the faint-hearted. The young people interviewed so far had appeared to be in shock. Like the rest of the public, Freyja was impatient for more information, not from a morbid desire to wallow in the grisly details but from concern about what had happened to the girl and what could possibly have motivated her attacker. Though it was hopelessly naive to think they'd ever really understand it, since nothing could explain or justify such a savage assault. 'Is this to do with the attack on that girl?'

'Yes.' She heard Huldar take a deep breath. 'I don't need to tell you how urgent it is that we find the girl and catch her attacker. Any chance you could come down to the station today? Preferably ASAP.'

Much as she wanted to, Freyja couldn't bring herself to say yes straight away. Her grubby little kitchen table was littered with textbooks and sheets of paper covered in her failed attempts to solve the maths problems she was supposed to hand in on Wednesday. Long before the phone rang she had been forced to face the fact that however often she tackled the questions, the result would be the same: a jumble of numbers and symbols that refused to relate to one another. Her decision to go part time at the Children's House and enrol in a business studies course at the university had turned out to be a terrible mistake. The course had done nothing whatsoever to cure her existential crisis or improve her life. If anything, it had made things worse. 'It's my day off.'

'I know. I rang the Child Protection Agency first to ask if

I could borrow you, and they passed me on to the Children's House. The director told me you were at home but that I should ring anyway. She said you could take your day off later.'

'Really?' Freyja was disconcerted. Her request to go part time had not been popular with the management. Up to now, far from accommodating her, they had thrown all sorts of obstacles in the way of her coordinating her work and studies. 'She said that?'

'Yes. After offering me various other psychologists. But I said I didn't want them, I wanted you. For this job, I mean,' he added hastily.

Two contrasting emotions did battle inside Freyja. On the one hand, she was pleased Huldar had expressed his preference for her over her colleagues to her boss; on the other, she was irritated that he didn't seem to have got the message and given up pursuing her, despite having learnt from bitter experience that they just weren't meant to be together. They had originally met out clubbing, tumbled into bed together and had a great time, but then he'd ruined everything by doing a runner in the morning. Their acquaintance should have ended there, but their paths kept crossing through his job in the police and hers at the Children's House. It had gone from being acutely embarrassing at first to being merely annoying. He was just so maddening. He kept giving the impression that he was eager to renew their acquaintance, then couldn't resist the temptation to sleep with other women when she didn't immediately lie flat on her back.

Huldar was bad news: it was as simple as that. It was a pity he was so attractive – in a scruffy way – and so good in bed too. But that wasn't enough. Sadly, she had to face it: Huldar was the wrong man in the right body.

But at this moment he offered a welcome escape from her maths woes. 'If I do come, what is it you want me to do?'

'Help me interview some teenage girls who knew the victim. The school thought it would be better for them to come to us than for me to go over there. The parents have given their permission, on condition that there's a representative of children's services present to make sure we don't overstep the mark. Which is ridiculous as it's not like they're suspects. It's only a formality really. Anyway, I'd be happier if I had someone there who understands girls their age. I don't even know if teens require the same handling as younger kids – you know, whether questions can accidentally influence their testimony, that kind of thing. Because it's vital that doesn't happen. The sooner we can build up a picture of Stella's life, the better. They reckon her attacker knew her.'

'Why are you referring to her in the past tense? Has she been found? Is she dead?'

'No, she hasn't turned up yet.'

Freyja noticed that he dodged her other question, which was a bad sign. 'I can be with you in half an hour.' The moment she'd spoken, her gaze fell on Molly, who was lying on the kitchen floor, guarding her bowl. She did this out of habit, though if anyone were ever foolish enough to steal her food, the result would be a foregone conclusion. Dogs didn't come much larger or more menacing than Molly. Whenever Freyja took her out, she noticed the owners of small dogs stopping for friendly chats with one another, while she was doomed to walk alone. On the other hand, the deterrent effect was ideal for the dog's real owner, Freyja's brother Baldur, who was currently doing a spell inside. Having to look after Molly was one of the many downsides of living in his grotty little flat. But these were more than outweighed by the bene-fits, the most important of which was that she had a roof over her head and wasn't reduced to sleeping on a bench in the park. Iceland's unprecedented boom in tourism had created a chronic housing shortage in Reykjavík and there were no signs of things improving any time soon. Baldur was nearing his release date, and then she would have to find her own place, but luckily she still had a few months left to sort it out.

The dog closed her eyes and turned away sulkily. She'd obviously interpreted Freyja's tone as meaning that the prom-ised walkies would be cancelled. Freyja was flooded with a familiar sense of guilt. It went with having a dog, this constant feeling that you were failing in your duties – to take her out more often, give her better food . . . But it was dictated by affection really, because although her relationship with Molly wasn't perfect, she did care about her.

'Actually, I won't be able to make it for another hour. Is that OK?'

The teenage girls looked totally out of place at the police station. There were five of them, so similar in appearance that Freyja immediately forgot their names. Long blonde hair, wide blue eyes thickly framed with mascara, and unnaturally black eyebrows. To make it even harder to tell them apart, they seemed to have coordinated their outfits: dark skinny jeans, white trainers and waist-length jackets in similar colours. They all had their hands buried in their jacket pockets and, as a finishing touch, they all wore virtually identical scarves draped over boyishly skinny bodies that barely betrayed so much as a swell of the hips. Freyja knew this was the last year they would still be teetering on the edge of childhood, or would be so uniform as a gang. Come the autumn they would go to sixth-form college and start developing their own individual tastes; a stage of development Stella had been denied, if Huldar was right about her fate. She was doomed to remain forever an adolescent in the memories of family and friends.

Freyja had been given a quick briefing when she arrived, but it hadn't added much to what had already appeared online, apart from the detail that the police believed Stella was dead and the fact that the killer had been caught on film dragging her body away. Huldar had asked her to keep this information to herself and her nod was good enough for him. They'd worked together in similar circumstances before, so he knew she could be trusted.

'Right,' said Huldar, once Freyja and Gudlaugur had taken their seats on either side of him, with the five girls lined up in a row facing them across the conference table. They had huddled their chairs as close together as possible, almost as if they wished they could pile onto each other's laps.

Freyja studied Huldar discreetly. He was looking good, much better than the last time she had seen him. The black circles had almost gone from under his eyes, he was clean-shaven and his hair had recently been trimmed. He was in fantastic shape, too. Too bad he was such an idiot. She was glad she'd taken the time to put her make-up on after walking Molly. It would have been infuriating to have to sit next to him, conscious that he was looking better than her. As it was, she reckoned they were pretty evenly matched.

'Did you all get the Snaps sent from Stella's phone last night?'

Three of them nodded, one said yes and the other raised her hand, then quickly lowered it when she realised she was the only one.

'All of you, in other words.' Huldar pushed a pen and pad of paper in Gudlaugur's direction. 'Would you mind taking notes?' Gudlaugur nodded and scribbled something down. Huldar turned back to the girls. 'Which of you watched them?'

This time the girls weren't so ready with their answers. They shot glances at one another, either too shy to take the initiative or silently agreeing on how to reply.

'I'd like an answer, please. Did you see them?' Huldar leant forwards over the table, smiling thinly.

The girl who had grabbed the middle seat answered first. 'Yes. I did.' Although she had been the boldest of the five, her voice came out barely above a whisper, as if she were admitting to having watched porn.

Huldar looked at the rest and prompted: 'What about you lot? Yes or no?'

One after the other they muttered, 'Yes.' The girl who had answered first spoke up again. 'I didn't know what it was. Stella was always sending Snaps. If I'd known, I'd never have watched it.'

'So you only looked at the first one?' Freyja knew the answer to that already. Before the interview, she'd learnt from Huldar and Gudlaugur that the girls had watched every single Snap. As Stella's best friends, they had been among the first people the police contacted in an attempt to get hold of phones on which the messages hadn't yet been viewed. They were too late, though, as the first girl to see them had immediately rung round the others to tell them to watch.

'No. Yes. I mean . . . No.' The girl lowered her eyes to the table. 'I watched them all. First I thought it was, like, a joke and kept waiting for the funny bit? Then I realised it was serious but by then I couldn't stop. I wanted to know how it was going to end.'

'And the rest of you? Same story?'

The other four nodded. Their eyes shot to the girl in the middle, who Freyja took to be the leader. Given how unconfident she seemed in the role, Freyja guessed that Stella had been the queen bee. This girl must have been Stella's best friend, since the others seemed to take it for granted that she would take over the role.

'It's all right, girls. You haven't done anything wrong.' Huldar leant back again. 'We didn't get you in because you watched the videos. We called you here because we're hoping you can help us find the person who did this to your friend. OK?'

They all nodded in unison and Huldar continued: 'Can you think of anyone who might have had it in for Stella?' This time there was a concerted shake of the head. 'Quite sure? No secret boyfriend? Someone older than her, maybe?'

'She's got a boyfriend. He's older than her. He's got a driving licence and everything.' Again it was the girl in the middle who spoke up. Cue more nods from the others.

'You mean Hördur? Hördur Kristófersson?'

'I don't know. She calls him Höddi. She hasn't let me meet him yet so I've only seen a photo. And he was only half in the picture.' The girl made a face. 'Stella said he hated having his picture taken. Maybe he's, like, you know, a bit of a weirdo.' Her eyes widened. 'Was it him?'

'No. Höddi's not a suspect. What about someone else, someone older? Not necessarily a boyfriend – maybe a man

who was interested in her, who sent her messages, that kind
of thing?'

They all shook their heads again.

'Would Stella have told you if there was someone?'

The group hesitated, exchanging quick glances, lowering
their eyes.

'Yes or no? Did she talk to any of you about private stuff?'

'Yes. Me.' The girl in the middle sat up straighter as she
said this. Freyja was pleased that her instinct had been correct.
'But she never mentioned anything like that. We're all, like,
really careful about not accepting friend requests from strange
men on Facebook? They're all paedos. Stella knew that. If a
creep was stalking her, she'd have told me. Definitely.'

'Are you absolutely positive about that? She didn't let you
meet her boyfriend. So it's possible she kept other things from
you as well, isn't it?' Huldar's voice was cold.

The girl glared at him, in a sudden foreshadowing of what
she'd look like as an adult. 'She was going to introduce me
to Höddi. But, you know, she was busy. Like, she was always
working? At the cinema.'

'All right.' Huldar changed the subject. 'I've looked
through Stella's computer.' The girls' eyes popped at this
and they seemed to stop breathing. The ringleader's expression went from annoyed to alarmed. Freyja prodded
Huldar's thigh under the table in case he'd missed their
reaction. She knew from experience that interpreting other
people's feelings wasn't his strong point. 'And what do you
think I found there?'

The girls stared at him dumbly, their eyes round. Huldar
smiled again. 'Nothing.' The girls' shoulders relaxed. He went
on: 'Nothing exciting, anyway. Half-finished homework

exercises. A load of photos, mostly selfies. Illegal downloads of films and music. You lot get up to that as well, do you?'

They blushed guiltily, each muttering 'No,' in turn.

'Good.' Huldar's gaze raked their faces. 'But judging by your reactions, I reckon I should take another look, because I get the feeling I've missed something. Maybe you could give me a clue what I should be looking for? Or just tell me straight out?'

None of the girls spoke. Their apprehension was obvious. Huldar, sensing they weren't going to open up, changed tack and started bombarding them with questions about Stella: what sort of person she was, her likes and dislikes, what she did after school, who her other friends were, both male and female, and other details about her life. Gradually the girls' tongues began to loosen.

Nothing of interest emerged, as far as Freyja could tell. Stella appeared to have been a singularly boring, if popular, teenage girl, interested in pop music, celebrities, boys, make-up and fashion. The more her friends told them, the more Freyja was inclined to think that Stella had been a bit of an air-head. But maybe that was unfair, maybe in time the girl would have blossomed and developed into a person of more substance.

When their descriptions started getting repetitive, Huldar asked about the weekend instead; about when they had last seen or heard from Stella. It turned out none of them had laid eyes on her since they'd said goodbye after school on Friday. The girl in the middle had chatted to her on the phone and online, but Stella hadn't wanted to meet up because she was working at the cinema on Friday evening, all day Saturday and Sunday afternoon until late in the evening, when the attack had taken place. The girl added that Stella had been moaning about her hair, which was why she didn't want to go out on Saturday night. None of this sounded as if it would provide the police with any leads.

An hour or so after they'd entered the meeting room, Huldar brought the interview to a close. The girls were visibly relieved. They zipped up their jackets and buried their hands in their pockets again before scurrying out of the room. Huldar, Gudlaugur and Freyja watched from the window as they left the police station and gathered in a knot outside, apparently engaged in a heated discussion. Then they peered around and one of them stole a quick glance up at the building. Freyja and Gudlaugur recoiled from the window but Huldar stood his ground and waved at her with a chilly smile.

He turned back to the others. 'Well, what do you reckon? What are they hiding?'

Freyja shook her head. 'Who knows? An older boyfriend, perhaps. You should also consider the possibility that Stella was having sex for money. It's not unheard of, as I'm sure you're aware. Judging by their reactions, it's something bad. Mind you, what looks bad to them may seem trivial to us in the circumstances. But what really struck me was something else.'

'What?' Huldar studied her face.

'It's less than twenty-four hours since they learnt that something terrible's happened to their friend, yet not one of Stella's so-called mates showed any signs of grieving. Not one of them had the red-rimmed eyes, puffiness or blotchy cheeks that you get from crying.'

Chapter 4

Freyja took a big mouthful of coffee and felt a little better. She'd tasted worse, though the barista's clumsy attempt to draw a leaf in the milk froth looked more like a child's idea of a Christmas tree, stripped of all its needles. It wasn't a café Freyja usually patronised; she'd wandered in after leaving the police station, in dire need of a caffeine boost. Once the girls had left, Huldar had shown her the Snaps and CCTV footage, which had turned her stomach. She understood now why he was referring to Stella in the past tense. But she couldn't give him any insight into the man's motives, or read anything from his actions, other than to say that the police were dealing with an insanely violent individual. Which Huldar was perfectly capable of working out for himself.

Coming face to face with Erla on her way out had done nothing to improve her day. The look she'd sent Freyja would have caused most people to quicken their pace, but Freyja had reacted with studied nonchalance, deliberately smiling and saying a friendly hello. It had the desired effect. Erla's face darkened and Freyja didn't envy Huldar when she summoned him with an angry bark the moment Freyja had turned her back. Although the brief encounter had left a bad taste in her mouth, it did at least feel like she'd won a small victory in their pissing competition. How it had started was still a mystery to Freyja. Erla had taken an instant dislike to her the first time they'd met and Freyja had been quick to reciprocate. Ironic that the two people who really rubbed her up the wrong way should work at the same place. Come to think of it, it was appropriate that Huldar and Erla should have ended up in bed together, though she hated to think what their offspring would be like if they ever reproduced.

If Freyja was honest, her craving for coffee wasn't all down to the encounter with Erla or the sickening videos: the interview with the teenage girls had stirred up ghosts from her own past. Looking down at her cup, she realised that it was nearly empty. By tipping her head back she managed to coax a few more drops out of it. For her, the taste of coffee was the taste of adulthood. It reminded her that she was a grown-up, nominally in control of her own life, and that, whatever happened, she'd never be a child again.

The saucer clattered as she put down the big cup more heavily than she'd intended. She didn't like dwelling on the past. It never did any good. She and her brother Baldur had had an unconventional upbringing at the hands of their God-fearing maternal grandparents, which had left them with few happy memories except when it came to each other. Freyja's teens had been particularly difficult. It wasn't the shortage of money so much as her grandparents' rigidly old-fashioned views on how to bring up kids. The commandments by which she and Baldur were supposed to live their lives would have been familiar to Moses' offspring. OK, she hadn't actually been forced to dress in a habit and sandals, but her clothes had been conspicuously unfashionable compared to those of other kids her age. Even her packed lunches had been different.

No wonder she'd had trouble fitting in, forbidden as she was to own the same toys and clothes or get up to the same sort of things. As a result she couldn't really relate to the in-crowd, to kids like Stella's friends. On the other hand, she'd had plenty of practice in watching cliques like theirs from the outside. She could easily identify the leader and her deputy, and the girl who was on the verge of being ejected, who lived in terror of saying or doing the wrong thing, which would pitch her out into the cold. And she recognised the girl who was there as padding, who laughed in the right places and missed no opportunity to flatter the queen bee.

But this didn't bring her any closer to guessing what it was that Stella's friends were concealing.

The waiter took her cup and asked if she wanted a refill. Although she could easily have downed two more, Freyja said no thanks and asked for the bill.

The café was heaving and the only place she'd been able to find a seat was right at the back. As she was squeezing her way out between the tables she couldn't help noticing that all the other customers were foreign tourists. Maps or brochures were spread on every table, backpacks hung from the chairs and everyone was better equipped for the great outdoors than your average Icelander. She moved faster for fear of being asked what country she was from or if she'd mind taking a photo or, God forbid, performing the Viking football chant.

Outside, the sky was the same unrelieved grey as it had been when she arrived, but then she hadn't been there that long. She wrapped her coat more tightly around herself and wished she had a scarf like the girls earlier. She could do with one inside the car too: the heater had stopped working again but she'd already had it repaired twice and felt that taking it back to the garage for a third time would be a waste of money.

Her phone rang as she was walking. It was the director of the Children's House to inform her that they were lending her services to the police for the next few days. Freyja stopped dead in astonishment. The woman went on to say that Freyja needn't come in for the rest of the week. The police needed a child psychologist on call while they were interviewing juveniles in connection with the girl's disappearance, and she was the obvious choice as she had already attended one interview and they'd rather not have to share sensitive information about the case with anyone else. A likely story, Freyja thought: this had Huldar's fingerprints all over it. But her pleas for mercy on the grounds of coursework and lectures fell on deaf ears. By the end of the conversation she found herself committed to being on standby for the rest of the week.

By the time she reached her car, Freyja's anger had largely evaporated. All things considered, it could have been a lot worse. She could still attend her classes as long as she kept her phone on the desk, ready to slip away if summoned. And when she wasn't helping the police, she could focus on her studies, something she couldn't normally get away with at the Children's House where work required her undivided attention. Perhaps this would enable her to make up some lost ground. She could start by going home and trying to make sense of her maths exercises.

But Freyja had no sooner formed this intention than her plans were thwarted. Her phone rang and this time it was Huldar, demanding to know if she was far away because her presence was required again. He couldn't hide his pleasure.

The teenagers had piled into the rows of seats at the very back of the assembly hall, as if expecting a flamethrower to be trained on them from the stage. It seemed nothing had changed since Freyja's day. The aim was still to sit as far as possible from the grown-ups. Only a few scattered individuals sat near the front, mostly adults, who Freyja took to be teachers, and four pupils. Two boys, one obese, the other weedy enough to look as if he'd wandered in from the local primary school by mistake, and two girls who, in contrast, looked very ordinary, their brown hair tied back in ponytails, their shoulders drooping like players who've just scored an own goal in a cup final. All four kept their eyes carefully lowered and looked as if they hardly dared breathe. Freyja recognised that posture: she herself hadn't sat up straight until she went to college. It was surprising she hadn't developed a hunch.

Huldar leant over and murmured: 'Keep an eye on the kids. If you notice anything interesting, give me a nudge. Then we can have a chat with the kid in question.'

Freyja nodded, letting her eyes roam over the assembled teenagers again. She, Huldar and Gudlaugur were standing at the side of the hall. While she had been drinking coffee with the tourists, they had been changing into uniform, presumably to underline the seriousness of the occasion. As the pupils filed into the hall, all eyes had been drawn to the two police officers, and the principal emotion had appeared to be surprise. No one had stopped dead or shiftily averted their gaze, but then it was extremely unlikely that any of them was the perpetrator. From the footage, it appeared the police were looking for an adult male, not a gangling adolescent.

On stage, the headmistress tapped the microphone. Her opening words were drowned out by a deafening screech. She moved a little further away and started again, her voice sombre as she informed the assembled pupils of what they already knew, that they were there to discuss what had happened to Stella. She went on to thank them for coming in outside school hours and the chair of the student council for suggesting the idea.

Freyja turned from the stage to watch the audience reaction. Most of the teenagers were leaning forward, eager not to miss a thing. Only in one or two places did she see the blue glow of a phone screen.

'We're aware that many, perhaps most, of you received the Snapchat messages from Stella's phone, which the police believe were recorded and sent by her attacker. Many of you have watched some or all of them. Now, of course we can't undo that, but I would urge those who haven't yet watched them not to do so. By watching them, in the full knowledge of what they contain, you'll only be doing what her assailant wanted. And it won't make you feel any better. I want to remind you all – whether or not you've seen the videos – that these messages are not from Stella herself. The videos have nothing to do with the Stella we know, who'll be in all our thoughts in the coming days, so it's best to focus on remembering her as your friend from school. Hold on to that thought. Try not to dwell on the images in the videos. The police have the recordings, so you won't be helping the investigation by watching them.'

That wasn't quite right. From what Huldar had told Freyja, he wanted to ask the kids if anything they'd seen or heard in the videos rang any bells. So she wasn't surprised to see him grimacing at the headmistress's words. The teenagers caught it too, since they'd automatically glanced at him and

Gudlaugur when the head mentioned the police. Distracted by this, they probably didn't even take in what she said.

'Now, I'm aware that journalists have been trying to contact some of you, and although your form teachers have already been over this, I want to stress yet again that no one is to talk to the press. If you have anything to say that you think might be relevant to the inquiry, you're to speak to the police. Not, under any circumstances, to a reporter. Is that clear?'

The group mumbled 'Yes.' Whether their promise would mean anything in practice was another matter. They were only kids, and experienced journalists were experts in winkling stuff out of people. They wouldn't necessarily bother, though. They'd already milked everyone dry; lurid accounts of the recordings and the kids' statements had been plastered all over the online news sites. Tomorrow they'd be clamouring for new revelations from the police.

A girl in the back row stuck up her hand and waved it to attract the attention of the head, who didn't look particularly pleased at this interruption. 'The police took my phone. And Björg's too. When'll we get them back? Being without a phone's a nightmare. Isn't it, like, against the law or something?'

The head's gaze shifted to Huldar and Gudlaugur. 'That's for the police to decide. But I don't imagine they'll hang on to them any longer than necessary. However inconvenient it may seem to you and Björg, it's not actually illegal to deprive someone of their phone.'

The girl slumped back in her chair, looking sulky. The headmistress went on to enumerate Stella's virtues and to point out how incomprehensible and unfair it was that she should have fallen victim to a violent criminal. The woman reminded them to think about their own safety at all times and also to look out for each other, then went on to express the heartfelt wish that Stella would be found soon, safe and sound. As she said this, Freyja caught a movement as one of the girls sitting near the front of the hall raised her head and looked at the stage for the first time. Her expression was harsh, as if she wasn't particularly concerned about Stella's welfare. Then she dropped her gaze again, unaware that she'd been observed. Freyja got the impression she was smiling. She nudged Huldar, pointing unobtrusively at the girl, but he had no chance to study her because at that moment the headmistress introduced him.

As he walked up to the stage, Freyja noticed that something had distracted the kids' attention. They were nudging each other and the blue glow of screens proliferated along the rows until they all appeared to be glued to their phones, apart from the four pupils isolated at the front.

Huldar seemed to realise that he had lost his audience. He stood in silence, watching them until one by one they tore their eyes from their screens. Finally, a boy stuck up his hand rather diffidently, as if undecided about whether he should speak. Huldar nodded to him.

'Er . . . we just got a Snap?' He held up his phone with the screen facing Huldar, as if he thought he'd be able to see it from the other end of the hall. 'From Stella.'

For an instant, in defiance of the facts, Freyja believed Stella was alive. No doubt she wasn't alone in experiencing this momentary rush of relief. But clearly not everyone felt the same way. The girl Freyja had been watching stole a rapid glance over her shoulder.

There was no mistaking the look of disappointment on her face.

Chapter 5

The girl's way of walking was familiar. Eyes down, coat clutched tightly to her chest, taking long, rapid strides, without quite breaking into a run. Everything was aimed at making a quick getaway without attracting attention. *I'm not here.* Freyja used to walk like that herself as a teenager. If called on to describe the corridors of her school she would be at a complete loss because she used to keep her head permanently lowered. She would recognise the floors, though. The person who had stuck up the homemade poster on the noticeboard, advertising help for the victims of bullying, would have done better to stick it to the floor. Mind you, she noticed that one of the phone numbers at the bottom of the poster had been torn off. Evidently, someone had raised their eyes from the floor long enough to spot it.

Freyja reminded herself not to project her own experiences onto a stranger. There might be some other reason for the girl's subdued manner. She might be naturally introverted or depressive, have Asperger's or some other related syndrome. Freyja would soon find out, if only she could catch up with her. Two boys paused to look at something on a phone and Freyja almost cannoned into them. Dodging round, she hurried on but a gap had opened up between her and her quarry. It was a pity Gudlaugur and Huldar had been urgently called away, as the kids would probably have stepped aside for them without being asked. She could have done with their company too as the surroundings were getting her down; they were too powerful a reminder of her old school.

Really, it was surprising she didn't begin every day by falling to her knees and offering thanks for the fact that the ordeal of her teenage years was behind her. Normally she did her best not to dwell on past miseries, but now she had been forcibly reminded of them, partly by this case, partly by the e-mail from a former classmate – one of the most spiteful back in the day – announcing a reunion. She had ignored it, amazed that any of them could have forgotten how they'd treated her. But perhaps the bullies remembered things differently. Anyway, who cared what was going on in their heads? As far as she was concerned, they could shove their invitation where the sun don't shine.

Though Freyja had survived her own schooldays and done her best to put them behind her, she couldn't help worrying about her niece Saga. Like seagulls, kids tended to pick on those who were different. All you had to do was paint a red line on a bird for the rest of the flock to turn on it. And although Freyja loved the little girl more than life itself, her love wasn't blind. She was painfully aware that Saga was unlikely to fit in. She was too odd, in character, appearance and family circumstances. Her face was set in a perma-scowl and she showed little interest in learning to talk. Although Freyja had long ago abandoned the hope that Saga would grow out of her sullenness, she did think there was a possibility her circumstances might improve; that her father wouldn't always spend more time in jail than out. But for that to happen, Baldur would have to make a big effort to turn his back on a life of crime. He'd failed to do so for his own sake but he had a duty to reform his ways for his daughter. And if he didn't realise that himself, Freyja would point it out to him in no uncertain terms. Surely he wouldn't want Saga to end up like the poor kid Freyja was trying to catch up with, a mere shadow of a girl, jeered at by her classmates. Saga, the child with the perma-scowl, whose dad was a con: it was a recipe for disaster.

'Excuse me! Could you wait a minute?' Freyja broke into a jog. Her shouts were ignored, either because the girl's thoughts were miles away or because she assumed Freyja was talking to someone else. 'Hello!' Freyja kept having to dodge round the other kids who'd been at the meeting, while trying not to lose sight of the girl. Unlike her, the others walked in groups or pairs, deep in discussion about what had happened to Stella. It wasn't every day they found themselves caught up in a major news story.

'Excuse me . . . excuse me . . .' Freyja pushed some teenagers politely aside and was rewarded with the disgusted looks of those who believe the earth was created for them. Finally she managed to grab the girl's shoulder. Feeling the delicate bones through the shabby coat she slackened her grip so as not to hurt her. The girl looked round, eyes wide, as if fearing a blow. Freyja removed her hand, smiling awkwardly. 'Sorry, but I couldn't have a quick word, could I?' They were standing in the middle of the corridor while the other pupils streamed past, shooting them looks and whispering to one another. 'We should find somewhere quieter. It won't take a minute.'

The girl opened her mouth to object, then closed it and let Freyja steer her out of the throng. Clearly she had decided it would be better to talk to this stranger in private than to stand there arguing with everyone watching.

They went through the first door Freyja spotted. It opened into a classroom, crammed with chairs and desks. The white-board was covered in equations that someone had forgotten to rub out and Freyja felt a stab of guilt about the neglected homework waiting for her on the kitchen table. The girl took up a position behind the most solid piece of furniture in the room, the teacher's desk, and stood there, her gaze flickering up to Freyja, then back down to her feet.

'You may not have noticed me at the meeting earlier. My name's Freyja and I'm helping the police. I'm a psychologist – a child psychologist, actually.' This additional piece of information obviously didn't go down well. The girl may have been socially isolated but she clearly shared her peers' delusion that they were almost adults. 'What's your name, if you don't mind my asking?'

'Adalheidur.' The girl seemed a little less timid now that they were alone and it was clear that Freyja wasn't planning to spring any nasty surprises on her. She met Freyja's eye as she introduced herself and her face was properly visible for the first time. In contrast to the girls at the police station earlier, she wore no make-up, not even mascara. It made her look younger, more innocent than them. Her unhappiness was evident not only in her rounded shoulders but in her mousy hair that hung lank and lifeless.

'Hello, Adalheidur.' Freyja smiled. 'Why don't you take a seat?' The girl shook her head. 'OK, no problem. This shouldn't take long.'

'What? What shouldn't take long?' The girl darted a glance at the door. 'Why do you want to talk to me?'

'To have a little chat about Stella. We're not having much luck building up a picture of her.' Freyja had to concentrate to stop herself accidentally slipping into the past tense. Stella's classmates were still under the impression that she was alive. 'The police have spoken to her parents, friends and teachers. And to the girls who work with her at the cinema. They all paint the same picture: Stella's a lovely girl, popular, fun. Which doesn't give us much to go on. But I noticed you at the meeting earlier and thought maybe you could tell me a bit more about her – things the others either can't see or don't want to admit.'

The girl snorted.

'It won't go any further and none of the other kids need ever know.'

Adalheidur stared at Freyja, her face inscrutable. 'I don't really know her. You'll have to talk to someone else.'

'Really? You don't know each other?'

'No.'

'But you're in the same class, aren't you?'

Adalheidur's lips tightened.

'Aren't you?'

Adalheidur remained stubbornly silent for a moment longer, then said reluctantly: 'Yes. But, like, I don't go around with her. We're not friends. She sits at the back; I sit at the front. Talk to someone else – someone who actually, like, hangs out with her.'

Freyja ignored this. 'I thought I saw you smiling when the headmistress was talking about Stella. Was I right?'

Adalheidur shrugged but Freyja persisted: 'Are you enemies?'

The girl dropped her gaze to her feet again. Freyja noticed her fingers properly for the first time as Adalheidur clutched her coat defensively around herself. The nails were bitten down to the quick. 'I already told you: she's not my friend.'

'Not being mates is one thing. Being enemies is another. Which are you?'

The girl looked up. Finally there was a spark of life in the eyes now glaring at Freyja. 'Enemies, OK? Will that help your investigation?'

'We'll see,' Freyja said calmly, and gave the girl a moment to recover from her flash of anger. 'So you don't share Stella's friends' opinion that she's a lovely person?'

'No.' It was curt, unwavering.

'Do you know if she's embroiled in something that might explain what's happened to her? Whether she associates with people older than her, for example?' Freyja's use of longer words was deliberate. When talking to children or young people who were being stubborn or difficult, you could some-times jolt them out of their sulkiness by confusing them.

'Embroiled in?' Adalheidur frowned. 'What do you mean?'

'Does she mix with people older than her? Dodgy types?'

'I dunno. I haven't got a clue who she mixes with.'

Freyja smiled. 'No. I don't suppose you do. But tell me something: how come you're enemies? She seems very popular. Did she do something to upset you or was it the other way round?' When Adalheidur didn't answer, Freyja went on: 'Look, I promise this won't go any further. But if you've got information that the others are withholding or aren't aware of, you could help us find Stella or her attacker. The perfect picture we've been given so far isn't helping us at all. Your opinion may not be any use either, but we'd like to hear it.'

The girl's face darkened again. 'You want to hear? Seriously?' She put her hands on the desk and leant forwards, as if to reduce the distance between them. 'People like you are always coming out with stuff like that but you don't mean it. Nobody wants to hear. Not really.' Her eyes were suddenly brimming with tears. 'The school knows exactly what that bitch and her mates have done to me. Yet they try and make me pretend I'm sorry she's missing. Drag me into that stupid meeting. Make me listen to crap about trauma counselling and how Stella's in all our thoughts. Yeah, right. I've told them and told them but they won't listen. Any more than you will.'

'Fire away. I promise I'll listen.'

Adalheidur sighed and shrugged but took Freyja at her word. And Freyja kept her face carefully blank as she heard the girl's story. It was no different from countless other tales of modern bullying. Ugly, cruel and humiliating, and the girl's voice was filled with bitterness as she told it. She'd repeatedly begged the school authorities to intervene, but their feeble response had not only failed to improve things but had actually made them worse. Stella had put on an innocent face, denied everything and turned the accusations back on Adalheidur, with tears in her eyes. Only to take a vicious revenge afterwards. Adalheidur's parents' attempts to intervene had been no more successful. Every time they tried to stop the bullying, it got worse. The hate page set up on Facebook, which was taken down when she complained, kept popping up under a new name as soon as the previous one disappeared – with even nastier content. It was like using lighter fluid to try and put out a fire. Adalheidur couldn't be bothered to complain any more, no matter what happened. She just kept a low profile, avoided social media and spent her time counting down the days until she was old enough to leave the country.

After the girl had finished her story, Freyja stood there thinking. Some people clung on to their sanity in situations like this by finding some core of inner strength that helped them get through the ordeal unscathed. Others weren't so lucky. They carried the bitterness Adalheidur was nursing well into adulthood. Freyja herself was somewhere between these two extremes.

There was nothing she could say, no way of getting across to the girl that better times were around the corner. Realistically, to have any effect, Freyja would need to see her regularly for counselling sessions over a long period. Just telling her it would soon sort itself out would sound like an empty platitude. Talking about the future was no comfort when it was the present that was crushing a person's heart and soul. Especially when it came to teenagers, for whom the future was what happened next week. You couldn't take it for granted, either, that things would get better. Some people were eternal victims, bringing out their fellow human beings' baser instincts. And workplaces were as fertile a breeding ground for bullying as any school, though at least you could change your job.

In spite of this, Freyja decided to share her own experiences with Adalheidur, in the hope that they might provide temporary relief from her misery. 'You know, I went through the same sort of thing at school, though not quite as bad. In my case things got better as soon as I went to college. New environment, new kids. You'll probably find the same thing.' She glossed over the fact that it hadn't been quite that simple; she'd had to take a Saturday job to earn money for nicer clothes, a phone and a computer. And then there had been the mirror she'd hung up in the cycle shed of the block of flats where she lived, so she could put on her make-up before school without being denounced as the whore of Babylon.

Adalheidur snorted again, then gave Freyja a challenging stare, her mouth set in a hard line. 'Don't think I'm going to help you catch that man.' She pushed herself upright again, holding her chin higher than before. 'I bet Stella showed her true colours and someone finally noticed.'

The outburst was to be expected and Freyja didn't rise to it, just continued in a calm voice: 'I can tell you one thing, Adalheidur. Though you may not believe it now, sooner or later you'll change your mind. I don't know the exact details of what Stella did to you, but nothing can justify what's happened to her. It's easy to think all kinds of things when you're upset. But over time your attitude will soften. It's human nature. Hopefully it won't be long before Stella and her mates stop mattering to you. Hold on to that thought and don't let yourself get bogged down in hating them or yourself. You never know, it might make your current situation a little easier to bear.'

The girl's voice shook with rage as she answered: 'I'm not trying to make things better or fix them. I'm just telling the truth. Anyway, I'm going. I've got nothing more to say to you, and my dad's waiting.'

There was no point detaining her any longer. She'd described a different side of Stella from the one the police had been told about so far. Stella wasn't just the nice, popular kid; she was capable of acting with astonishing cruelty, with a total disregard for other people's feelings. In other words, she was two-faced, like so many people. Of course, no one label was ever adequate to describe the mass of inconsistencies that made up an individual, any more than a single stroke of a brush could constitute a painting. It was hard to see, though, what connection there could be between Adalheidur's story and the attack. The victims of bullying rarely took revenge. Quite apart from which, the girl was far too small and skinny to be the person in the CCTV footage. But she was bound to have male relatives who were bigger and stronger. Her father, for example. Perhaps he'd been driven to distraction by the way his daughter was being treated? It wasn't entirely implausible.

'Of course you're free to go. But you may be contacted again. The police may want to hear for themselves what you have to say. Do you have a phone?' An absurd question; Freyja might as well have asked if she had a head. There wasn't a teenager in Iceland who didn't have a phone.

Adalheidur gave Freyja her number, then went to the door, her shoulders as hunched now as they had been when Freyja was pursuing her down the corridor. Before leaving the room, she paused, looked round and said, so quietly that Freyja wasn't sure she'd heard right: 'I hope Stella's dead.'

Then she turned and walked away, her head held high.

The door swung shut and Freyja was left standing there, staring blankly at the equations on the board. Then, remembering the girl's father, she hurried after her, keen to get a look at him.

Adalheidur didn't notice her; her head was hanging once again. It wasn't far to the main exit and once the girl had gone through the large glass doors she headed straight for the car parked outside, almost breaking into a run. Freyja remained inside, watching. From what she could see, the driver was middle-aged and his face was set in harsh lines as he sat staring straight ahead. Freyja couldn't see if it softened when he turned to his daughter as she got into the car, as the back of his head didn't convey much. But when he faced the front again the grimness was still there. He drove off, faster than necessary, and when Freyja stepped outside to watch, she noticed three pupils jumping out of his path to avoid being run over. The man didn't slow down. It seemed Adalheidur wasn't the only member of her family consumed by a justifiable but no doubt corrosive sense of bitterness.

Chapter 6

Flashing blue lights lit up the snow outside the house, making the scene appear almost Christmassy, though there was nothing else particularly festive about it. Squad cars were lined up in front of the drab, single-storey terraced house. Police officers were fanning out around the property. Neighbours stood silhouetted in doorways, watching intently; one couple even had a bowl of popcorn.

Huldar stamped his feet and blew on his hands, sending clouds of vapour streaming out through his fingers. His police parka and uniform, which he hadn't had a chance to change after visiting the school, were stiff with frost. He would have given anything to go indoors, but the odds of that happening any time soon were virtually nil. Erla was responsible for deciding who went in with her to talk to the stricken occupants and who stood guard outside, and he wasn't in her good books. Relations between them had soured still further when he'd involved Freyja in the inquiry without asking Erla's permission. She'd given him hell for that; his protests that the school had insisted and that Erla herself had been busy talking to Stella's parents at the time had cut no ice. To make matters worse, the school had rung to request that a representative from children's services be present whenever the police spoke to any of their pupils, preferably a child psychologist, in case it all proved too much for them. Management had agreed, effectively making Freyja one of the team, to Erla's even greater vexation. She seemed to believe that Huldar had plotted the whole thing, which couldn't have been further from the truth: he wasn't that cunning. He had merely set the ball rolling.

He extracted a cigarette from the crumpled packet and pushed it back into his jacket pocket. As always, the first drag warmed him up a little and he wondered idly why this was. If he voiced the question aloud, Gudlaugur, who was standing beside him, was sure to look up the explanation on his phone. But Huldar doubted he'd like the answer: online searches never threw up anything positive about smoking. Besides, Gudlaugur appeared to be busy admiring the shapely backside of a young woman from Forensics, who was bending over some footprints in the snow with another technician. The assumption was that the prints belonged to the person who had shoved Stella's phone through the letterbox. Huldar gestured at the young woman with his cigarette. 'Reckon she's taken?'

Gudlaugur blinked at him in surprise. 'I wouldn't know. Why don't you ask her?'

'I was thinking about her for you. She looks like your type.' Huldar took another drag, taking care not to blow the smoke in Gudlaugur's face. 'My type's not that friendly; wouldn't give us a sweet smile like she did. I tend to go for snarky women. Or moody ones.' He omitted to mention that the snarkiness and moodiness didn't usually become apparent until after he'd got to know them. To begin with, they were all smiles. Or most were. Though, of course, going home with a stroppy cow could have its moments. 'Anyway, how about it? Want me to introduce you?'

'Er, no, thanks.' Gudlaugur tried to blow some warmth into his numb fingers. If his cheeks hadn't already been scarlet with the cold, no doubt he'd have blushed: it didn't take much to set him off. 'She's not my type either. Anyway, I'm perfectly capable of pulling without your help.'

Huldar didn't comment on this. He knew Gudlaugur better. The young man was crippled by shyness and the few times they'd gone out on the town together, he hadn't once plucked up the courage to approach any women. Even when they'd obviously been checking him out. But if he didn't want advice, Huldar wasn't about to force it on him. When it came to relationships, his advice was better avoided.

'Is he sending us a message by dumping the phone here?' Gudlaugur asked in a transparent attempt to change the subject. They'd already tossed this question back and forth between them without coming to any conclusion.

'No idea – any more than I did earlier. But I'm beginning to think the location must be significant. Maybe he was passing. Maybe he lives in the area. Maybe he's the guy next door with the popcorn.' They both glanced at the couple with the bowl and watched as the husband shovelled a handful into his mouth.

Huldar shook his head and turned back to the garden. The chill was creeping into his bones again; the nicotine had stopped working. 'When's Erla going to call it a day? We might as well be in the office, doing something useful. Like eating.' He pinched out his cigarette butt and carefully put it back in the packet so Forensics wouldn't pluck it out of the snow and send it for analysis. 'It must be clear by now that Stella's not here.' The over-the-top response to the tracing of the girl's phone had stemmed from their belief that her body might turn up nearby, but the two tracker dogs from the K9 unit had scoured the area and drawn a blank, swiftly extinguishing that hope. Yet, in spite of this, no one appeared to be leaving. The dogs, bored, had just cocked their legs on the wheels of the vehicle that had brought them there.

The door of the terraced house opened and a detective came out. It was Helgi. Past his prime and with his coat unzipped to reveal a big belly straining at his shirt. He'd certainly embraced middle age: too much food, too many beers, not enough hair. Although Helgi was no great mate of his, Huldar tapped Gudlaugur on the shoulder and jerked his head towards him. He knew Helgi would love this chance to wallow in his superior knowledge but he didn't care. He was fed up with being kept in the dark. All he and Gudlaugur knew was that the phone had been traced here after a picture had been sent an hour ago to all Stella's Snapchat followers.

Huldar had been the first police officer to see the picture, having leapt down from the stage in the assembly hall and snatched the phone from the first teenager who hadn't yet viewed the Snap. The photo showed the fully dressed body of a girl. Her head wasn't visible – mercifully, as it was unlikely to be a pretty sight after being bashed in with the fire extinguisher – but the clothes looked like Stella's. Whether it had been taken at the cinema or afterwards was unclear. The caption, written on a black strip across the picture – *Cruelty has a human heart* – sounded like a quotation, but Huldar didn't recognise it. Mindful of the tutorial he'd been given on Snapchat, he took a screenshot of the photo before it could self-destruct, then reported it to the station and confiscated two more phones on which the Snap hadn't been opened, much to the disgust of their owners.

'Hey, Helgi!' Huldar sped up, determined to catch the other man before he got to his car.

Helgi turned, his face registering displeasure when he saw who it was. 'What?' He screwed up his eyes, shielding them against the glare of the flashing lights.

'What's happening in there? Are they nearly done?' Huldar stopped at the end of the paved path that led from the front door to the drive, and Gudlaugur came up beside him, blocking the exit.

'Yes, nearly.' Helgi's annoyance at being cornered evaporated when he realised he had the upper hand: he was in possession of information they wanted. 'Why are you in uniform, lads? You must be freezing your balls off out here.' His face split in an evil smile. 'Won't Erla let you in or are you just scared she'll feel you up?'

'What did you fucking say?' Huldar advanced threateningly almost before the words were out of Helgi's mouth. Attack was sometimes the best form of defence and he was keen to discourage any further comments along these lines.

'Keep your hair on.' The whites of Helgi's eyes showed as he glanced round for an escape route. Ever since Huldar had stubbed out a cigarette in the eye of an arrested suspect he'd gained a reputation as a bit of a psycho. He made no effort to quash the rumours as there were advantages to keeping his colleagues on edge. Pity the incident was fading from people's memories and he kept having to bang the table, so to speak, to reinforce his image.

'Do I have to ask again? What's happening? Is there any link between Stella and the people who live here?'

The smirk had vanished and Helgi's tone was almost civil as he answered: 'No – or none they're admitting. They know who she is from the news but they're not relatives and they claim not to know her or her family.'

'Who are they?'

'A couple of lezzies.' Helgi's nasty grin returned. 'One's a doctor, the other a nurse. They're married or partners or whatever it's called.' He winked at Huldar and Gudlaugur, who stared back expressionlessly. When Helgi went on, Huldar couldn't decide if he'd misread their reaction or was even more of a fool than he'd thought. 'They're both pretty tasty, I can tell you. I wouldn't hesitate if they invited me to join in, know what I mean?' He winked again.

'I think you've misunderstood the basic concept, Helgi.' Huldar made no effort to hide his contempt. 'They're into *women*. They wouldn't touch the likes of you with a barge-pole. So spare us your pathetic fantasies.'

Helgi's jaw sagged a little as his brain cast around furiously for a comeback, but Gudlaugur got in first. 'Look, can we stick to the point? Have they got any kids Stella's age?'

Helgi looked relieved at being thrown a question he could answer without sending his brain into overdrive. 'No. Two little girls: one's just started school, the other's still at nursery. No links, like I said.' He shivered and tugged at his coat, which he had to hold closed over his gut. 'The kids keep interrupting the interview. Makes no difference if you shoo them back to their room. The moment your back's turned they've got their heads round the door again. It's obvious they don't get visits from the police every day.' He sighed. 'One of them's cross-eyed, looks a real freak. It gives us the willies every time she appears.'

'For Christ's sake, you're talking about a child, you stupid twat.'

Gudlaugur intervened before it could escalate into a full-blown row. 'So, do they reckon the phone was dropped through their door by chance?'

Helgi turned to the younger man, glad of an excuse to avoid Huldar's contemptuous glare. 'No. Erla doesn't buy it. The person who dumped it deliberately walked up to their front door and stuck it through the letterbox. He didn't just chuck the phone in the garden as you'd expect if he'd wanted to get rid of it. That's why it's taking such a long time. Erla keeps grilling them in the hope of finding a connection to Stella, but so far we're not getting anywhere.'

'They didn't see who brought the phone?' Gudlaugur gestured towards the door.

'They say not. They came in via the garage and didn't check what was in the box.'

'Box? You mean the phone wasn't lying on the floor?'

'No. Apparently the previous owners had a dog that used to wait by the door and shred letters and papers as they came through. The postman's fingers, too. So they fixed a box inside to prevent it. When we turned up and knocked on the door, the phone was still inside, so they may well be telling the truth. They certainly seemed surprised.'

It wasn't only Helgi whose brain was working sluggishly. The frost seemed to have paralysed Huldar's ability to think. The questions that had crowded into his head while he and Gudlaugur were on guard wouldn't come back to him now. If he couldn't think of anything else to ask, he'd have to let Helgi go as he couldn't just stand there staring into his vacant, watering eyes much longer. 'Any news about the phone? Have the tech team managed to unlock it? Have they found any prints?'

'No idea. We haven't heard yet.' Helgi shuffled his feet impatiently and Huldar stepped aside to let him pass. Now that he'd come out, presumably Erla and the other two officers would be following him any minute.

As Helgi's car door slammed, Gudlaugur muttered: 'I can't stand that bloke. He really pisses me off.'

'You're not the only one.' They resumed their post in the garden, silently watching the young technicians from Forensics bending over more tracks in the snow. Huldar toyed with the idea of ringing Freyja on the pretext of wanting to hear what had emerged from her conversation with the girl who'd reacted oddly during the head's speech. But before he could pull out his phone, his attention was caught by a movement in one of the windows. The cheerful pink curtain was pulled aside to reveal a child's face – the elder daughter, Huldar guessed. In the illumination of the blue flashing lights, her eyes were wide and inquisitive, and one of them was pointing off to the side. The girl had a bit of a squint; she wasn't cross-eyed like that idiot Helgi had claimed. When she saw Huldar, their gazes locked for an instant before she dropped the curtain back into place.

Huldar was still staring at the window when the front door opened and Erla came out with her retinue in tow.

Chapter 7

The top of Davíd's head was just visible over the back of the black sofa. His blond hair was unusually tousled, a few tufts standing up on end. Ævar remembered the first time he ever saw his son's head and thought how much his hair had changed from the black strands that had been plastered over his scalp when the midwife invited him to see it emerging, just before the final push. The sight had etched itself on his memory, horrible yet beautiful at the same time. Feeling faint, he had dashed back to Ágústa's side. His dizziness was caused not by the sight of the blood or his wife's unnaturally stretched vulva, so much as by a crushing sense of the responsibility that was about to land on his shoulders – a responsibility he meant to take seriously. Had he known then how things would turn out, he might have surrendered to his faintness and keeled over on the floor of the delivery room.

Ævar closed the laptop on the kitchen table. He couldn't read any more, couldn't take any more of the ugliness. He focused instead on the back of his son's head.

It was a small flat, smaller than he'd have liked, though bigger than he could really afford. There had been embarrassingly little property to divide up when he and Ágústa divorced. The flat had an open-plan kitchen and living area into which he had crammed a small table, a sofa and a television. Although their old house hadn't exactly been palatial, at least it had been possible to make coffee without being able to reach out and adjust the TV controls at the same time. But the compactness had its advantages, one of which was the enforced intimacy with his son. Davíd had a tendency to shut himself away, but that was impossible here since his room was little more than a windowless broom cupboard and all the floor space was taken up by his bed. He preferred using his PlayStation in the living room to sitting on his bed, staring at the blank walls.

Armed men were involved in a shootout on screen, in a game Ævar knew was not intended for children of Davíd's age. Ágústa would disapprove, but she had no say here. Besides, Davíd would be fourteen soon and he had a feeling that content banned for under sixteens was allowed if an adult was present. Or, if the rule didn't exist, it should be invented. There must be plenty of kids like his son, kids who needed a safety valve, an outlet for their feelings that a more sedately educational game wouldn't provide. He briefly considered joining Davíd to see if he could find any relief himself in blasting away enemy soldiers from a sniper's lair, but he doubted it.

Ævar turned and stared out of the window. He couldn't bear to look at the fair head as he asked: 'How's the new school?'

Davíd didn't answer immediately. The quality of the noise altered as the relentless rattle of gunfire ceased. 'It's all right.'

'Have you got to know any of the other boys yet?'

Again, that hesitation. 'Sure.'

'Are they nice?'

Another perceptible pause, followed by: 'Sure.'

'What are their names?' Ævar watched a bus drive by,

56

slowing down to edge past the bank of snow that had encroached into the road after repeated ploughings. 'Your new mates, I mean.'

This time the silence lasted longer. Davíd was a good boy; he didn't like lying. 'Can't remember.'

Ævar wanted to put him on the spot, wanted to yell that if you had friends you knew what they were called. But he couldn't do it, any more than he could bring himself to mention the names of the kids who had sent his son all those hateful messages on Facebook. He didn't know if Davíd had already seen them and felt a despairing impulse to confiscate his laptop and replace his phone with an old push-button model. But it wouldn't do any good. Davíd had read plenty of similar abuse directed at him; it was nothing new. And he had a wretched enough time at school without being forbidden to use the internet at home. Ævar didn't want to make his daddy weekends a miserable experience, so he bit his lip to stop himself asking any further questions. After a brief interval, the rattle of gunfire started up again.

Ævar turned from the window to study the back of his son's head. 'Ever wanted a real gun, Davíd?'

The boy twisted round to his father, looking surprised and bemused. 'What?'

'Just wondered.' Ævar couldn't explain why he had felt compelled to ask. Perhaps he had wanted to sound out his son's attitude to real-life violence; find out if his desire to kill was limited to the figures on screen. Davíd's reaction made it clear what he thought of the idea. Ævar should have known: such a thing would never have crossed his own mind once. But these days he'd become hardened, a consequence of all those endless, unsuccessful attempts to put a stop to the mental torture his son had been forced to endure since his very first day at school. It was only surprising he hadn't felt like resorting to violence sooner. They'd tried everything else. But despite everyone's apparent eagerness to help, nothing had changed.

The school system had let them down every time, in spite of repeated attempts to implement the Olweus Bullying Prevention Programme, which had been held up like a crucifix against the Antichrist. At meetings with him and Ágústa, the school authorities had spoken of the programme as the gold standard, which would provide a solution to the whole problem, but it had proved totally ineffectual in practice. And the psychologist Davíd was seeing had turned out to be full of hot air. Whatever they tried, nothing worked. Instead, the unspeakable situation got steadily worse. He had lost count of the phone conversations he'd had with the parents of Davíd's classmates, who had all, without fail, let them down as well. At first they appeared willing to take firm steps to deal with the situation but when that didn't work, their enthusiasm quickly waned. By the fifth phone call to the bullies' parents, they all, almost without exception, turned against Davíd and started listing his faults and issues that were, in their view, at the root of the incidents. In other words, the problem lay with Davíd. Ævar should concentrate on sorting his son out, then everything would be fine and they could all go and get an ice-cream together.

Even his and Ágústa's friends and families had lost patience over the years. They listened to his tales of woe but no longer had anything to contribute, just waited for the conversation to move on to a more uplifting topic. Even worse, their children, who had been drafted in to play with Davíd outside school hours, were now bored of the situation and had started making excuses about how they were too busy to help. The little shits.

Davíd had returned to his game. Ævar watched the figures toppling, shot either through the heart or the head. They all died instantly; no death throes, no convulsions. As unrealistic as what you saw on TV or in films. Presumably the gamers had little interest in pretending to take part in a real war; as little as his son had in using a real gun. Which was strange in light of what he was going through, but probably just one more symptom of the boy's lack of self-esteem. He didn't feel he deserved anything but crap from other kids. Davíd had stopped noticing what was glaringly obvious to Ævar: that there was nothing wrong with him. The problem lay entirely with his tormentors.

Ever since social media had entered Davíd's life, the situation had got totally out of hand. The stuff that had happened before seemed almost laughable in comparison, though it had felt like hell at the time. Now Davíd had nowhere to hide. The abuse pursued him wherever he went, into his room, into bed. And it was getting worse. If the other kids at school had been spiteful to him face to face, there were no limits to what they could do now. Moving to another school had made not the slightest bit of difference since his old enemies had hunted him down in cyberspace and spread their poison to his new classmates. Some of the messages were so cruel and hurtful that Ævar could hardly bear to read them. He wanted to hurl the laptop out of the window, send it crashing onto the pavement three storeys below, but he curbed the impulse. The computer was valuable because it enabled him to access his son's Facebook page without Davíd knowing. He'd let the boy use it from time to time and at some point Davíd had unwittingly ticked the 'Save password' option. Ævar might not be so lucky again.

He bit back the mocking laughter that threatened to burst from him. Luck. A phenomenon that had vanished from his life long ago. As a boy he'd had it: he'd won at the school bingo, made lucky guesses on various exam questions and scored goals in football that had had less to do with skill than fluke. But these days he wouldn't be able to win the lottery with the help of a crystal ball. Not that he had any interest in a financial windfall. All he wanted was for something to go right occasionally. Something for Davíd. Like making a friend. Just one. An acquaintance, even. At least that would lighten the burden he himself carried as a result of his son's sufferings.

But such dreams had long ago gone sour. Davíd was alone and isolated and there was no prospect of the situation changing. The dreams Ævar consoled himself with these days were of a different kind. Old Testament justice, that's all he had to cling to. An eye for an eye, a tooth for a tooth. Without descending to the same level as his son's abusers. No, he preferred a different take on the old adage. A blow for a tear. One for every tear Davíd had shed over the years. One for every tear he himself had shed. And one for every tear of Ágústa's. That would make for a hell of a lot of blows. Enough to pulverise those bloody kids as if they'd been put through a blender. If that was good enough for God, it must be good enough for him.

The messages his son had received had etched themselves on his retinas. They felt like acid injected into his skull.

Kill yourself.
Hang yourself.
Kill yourself.
I hate you. We all hate you.
Pig. Dirty pig.
Fuck off and die.
You faggot.
Do us a favour. Cut yourself.
No girl will ever want you. You ugly freak.
Fuck off out of our school. You ruin everything.
Kill yourself.
Hang yourself.
Kill yourself.

Ævar looked at Davíd's head and the game on screen. The bullets were still blasting, muscle-bound soldiers falling like flies. He hoped they were the bad guys; grown-up bullies who had wrecked the lives of other children when they were kids. If so, they deserved it, and worse.

Ævar ground his teeth, then rubbed his face to clear away the hate-filled expression it wore more and more often these days. When he reckoned he looked normal again, he stood up. 'Right. Time to turn that thing off. How about we go out and get a burger?'

Davíd obeyed immediately, putting down the controller, switching off the screen and getting to his feet. His good, obedient, clever, beautiful boy. Ævar smiled warmly so Davíd wouldn't be able to see the ugly thoughts running through his head.

Kill
Hang
Cut

Chapter 8

The girl was dead. There could be no doubt about it. She was lying on her side at the back, and the trail of blood that led from the door was dry and brown. So was the blood masking her smashed face. He tried to avoid looking at it, tried to shut out the horror and the sickening smell. Instead he concentrated on what he'd come here to do.

Laying his torch on the floor to free up his hands, he spread out the sheet of clear plastic beside her, then, holding a gloved hand over his nose and mouth, took a deep breath. He didn't want to have to inhale when he bent over her. After this he edged round behind her with difficulty, bent down and started rolling her over onto the plastic. This turned out to be harder than he'd expected and he was grateful that the girl was so slight. Corpses weren't like living people; they provided no more help than a sack full of sand. Twice he broke off to stand up and gasp for breath, face averted, but in the end he succeeded in manoeuvring the girl's body onto the sheet. Now it was easier to roll and he wrapped it in the crackling plastic, fastening it with tape here and there, then straightened up.

After switching off and pocketing his torch, he took several more deep breaths, then began to drag the bundle towards the door, praying the plastic wouldn't tear and that no one would see him. The mere thought made his heart contract. What would happen if he was spotted? But there had been nobody around when he arrived and it was unlikely anyone would be outside now. Opening the door, he peered out into the darkness and was relieved to see that the place was still deserted. It was going to be all right.

As he was lugging the body outside he wondered why no explanation had appeared online or in the media yet. Was it possible that the newsdesks had forwarded the letters to the police rather than using them to boost their circulation? Or hadn't they realised what they were? They must get a ton of stuff sent in by the public and probably dealt with it in the order they received it. That had to be the explanation. They just hadn't read the letters yet. But the blog must have been posted; it had been prepared ages ago and the postings were timed to appear automatically. He didn't dare check, though, since that would leave behind a digital trail. As long as he was careful he had no need to worry; everything apart from the publication of the material in the media had gone according to plan. He needed to focus on that instead of worrying about minor details that had gone awry.

If he made it through the next few days without being spotted, he would get away with it. Holding on to that thought, he made for the car with the bundle rustling along behind him like a giant plastic tail.

Chapter 9

Photocopy of a handwritten letter, entry no. 1 – posted on blog.is by a blogger going by the name of Laufa.

Now that I've made up my mind I feel good. It's strange. I can hardly remember what that feels like because usually I feel bad all the time. It's not like I'm relieved or cheerful or happy, exactly. More like I'm contented. It reminds me of a berry-picking trip we once went on when I picked more than anyone else. That was just before everything started to go wrong.

I want to repeat that I feel good. I'm not in a state, I haven't tipped over the edge. You need to remember that when you try to understand what I've done. I finally know what it's like to feel contented.

But I want there to be a record of why I did this. It should help you come to terms with what's happened. Perhaps the kids from my class will see it. If they do, it would be good for them to be reminded of what happened. Though things will probably look very different to them. I expect their memories of what school was like are like mine were before the boy sniggered at my name. The nice smell of a new eraser, the shiny stickers the teachers used to put in your exercise books, the fun we had during storytime, lunchtime and break. How lucky they are, though I don't suppose they realise it – that's what being lucky means. I'm not one of them.

The Absolution

I remember when it all began, where we were and who started it. I was eight years old. We were only in the same class for that one year, then he moved away and I haven't seen him since. Perhaps it's just as well because I don't know what I'd say to him if I saw him now. Nothing, probably. He wasn't to know what effect his words would have. I mean, all he did was repeat my name after the teacher called it out, then snigger. That's all it took. He'd often heard my name, so had the others. They all knew me. But they giggled too, like he'd said something unbelievably funny. My name's not even that strange.

After that I became a laughing stock. Every time someone said my name people would crack up. Their laughter was spiteful – it had nothing to do with being happy or having fun. It was like the laughter of someone who treads on a spider just to be mean. First it was my name, then it was other things. My hair was stupid. My clothes were stupid. My shape was stupid. Everything I said was stupid. Everything I did was stupid. I was stupid. Useless, ugly, boring, uncool and dumb. It didn't matter if it was true or not. The group had decided and that was that. Sometimes the truth is just what everyone else decides it is.

I still remember it vividly.

The boy's eyes opening wide in his freckled face as he thought about my name before repeating it.

My lunchbox on the desk in front of me; the untouched sandwich my mum had made me, forgetting that I didn't like cucumber any more.

The carton of chocolate milk I'd just started drinking from when the giggling began.

My friend beside me, laughing along with the rest.

65

The sweet milk turned sour, and, although I didn't realise it then, the same would happen to my life. From the moment he opened his mouth, my nice life turned sour and was ruined. And just as there's nothing you can do about milk once it's gone off, the same was true of me. My life turned bad from then on.

Chapter 10

The sandwich tasted off; the bread was stale and the shrunken lump in the middle was unrecognisable as tuna salad. Come to think of it, the sell-by date had been illegible, and Huldar wondered if the shop owner had deliberately rubbed it off. He scrunched up the wrapping and chucked it across the room. The ball flew in a high arc over a colleague's head and landed in the bin – well, admittedly it was the green bin, but never mind. 'Ta-da!'

Gudlaugur, unimpressed, barely looked up from his screen. He himself had taken his packaging over, conscientiously separated out the plastic and paper and disposed of them in the appropriate bins. 'What do you think of this e-mail from Freyja? Worth looking into?'

'Maybe. It's not like we've got anything else to do.' Huldar opened the message and read it again. She'd tried to ring but he'd forgotten to unmute his phone after leaping off the stage in the school assembly hall. Which was ironic, given how much time he spent waiting in vain for her to call. He'd rung straight back but she hadn't answered. 'She does point out that it's unlikely to have any connection to the attack since there's no way Adalheidur could be the assailant and she's so socially isolated it's difficult to see how she could have got anyone to help her. I know Freyja says the father's a possible suspect but I don't agree. If he was waiting outside the school during our meeting with the pupils, he can hardly have put the phone through the women's door. There wouldn't have been time. I remember seeing a car like the one Freyja described parked outside the school. It was there when we arrived and still there when we left.'

'An older brother, then?' Gudlaugur fiddled with his mouse. 'Or her mother?'

'It's possible.' Huldar frowned. 'How would you react if your daughter was being bullied like that? It says here that Stella took a picture of her in the shower after gym and sent it to everyone. She also set up a Facebook page, the latest version of which is called "We hate Adalheidur". Have you seen the crap she and the other kids posted?' Gudlaugur nodded. The page was public and Freyja had sent them the link. Huldar had failed to notice it when he was going through Stella's laptop. That suggested there might be other things he'd missed, but then he was no IT expert. Just as well the laptop was now with Forensics, who would examine every last byte of information on the hard disk. Huldar went on: 'And that's not including all the other abuse she subjected her to. Might you be driven to beat up a girl who'd made your daughter's life a misery?' Since they were both childless, neither of them was in a position to answer. After a moment, Huldar asked: 'Do you think it was the Facebook page that Stella's friends were scared we'd find?'

'Maybe. If it's worse than that, it must be bad.' Gudlaugur sighed, then added: 'Still no reply from Erla?' Huldar had forwarded Freyja's e-mail to her, partly for her information and partly as a reminder, in case she'd forgotten, that he and Gudlaugur were still part of the team.

'No.' Since returning from the house where the phone had

been found Erla hadn't even glanced in their direction, so they were still sitting there twiddling their thumbs while the others gradually drifted off home.

'Maybe we should get going.' Gudlaugur rattled his empty yoghurt pot as if hoping it would magically fill up again. 'I've run out of things to do.'

'Me too. But if we sit tight, Erla might give us something.' Huldar knew it wasn't going to happen but he was childishly determined to hang on until Erla was forced to acknowledge his presence. He didn't want to have to sit there on his own, though. 'Maybe there'll be news from Forensics. They have to finish checking her phone and laptop soon, surely? There'll be plenty to do after that and it would be a pity if Erla was the only one left in the office.'

'Yeah, maybe.' Gudlaugur sounded doubtful.

The man over whose head Huldar had chucked the sandwich wrapper switched off his computer, stood up, stretched and removed his jacket from the back of his chair. He left without saying goodbye; a fair indication of Huldar's popularity in the department.

The muffled sound of a phone ringing came from Erla's office and, instantly alert, they watched through the glass wall as she answered. 'You see,' Huldar leant back in his chair, arms behind his neck, 'I reckon our wait's over.' Erla was on her feet, one hand on top of her head. She drew it slowly down her face, stretching out her features. Huldar knew that gesture: it meant something was about to happen.

The phone call ended and Erla emerged from her office. She surveyed the empty desks. Apart from Huldar and Gudlaugur there was only one detective left, a long-serving officer nearing retirement. His name was Kári and he was on crutches following an operation on his ankle. According to office gossip, he was losing his marbles as well. Erla beckoned him over, looking disgruntled. When she took in Gudlaugur and Huldar still sitting in the corner, she looked even more annoyed, shaking her head over the unfairness of it all. Huldar couldn't hold back a broad grin when she told them to get their coats on, but it was wiped off his face again when he heard why: Stella's body had been found.

The lingering taste of stale tuna did nothing to improve the situation. Huldar had never been good with blood or other bodily fluids; or with vomit, open wounds, corpses . . . all the things associated with the aftermath of violence or suicide. Still, looking on the bright side, the smell wasn't that bad in this instance since Stella had been dead less than twenty-four hours and was lying in the open air. Nevertheless, he could detect the metallic odour of blood and the whiff of decomposition that would only get worse. He couldn't bring himself to scrounge some menthol ointment from Erla to smear under his nose but sooner or later he would be forced to swallow his pride. Either that or step aside and puke up his sandwich. It wasn't an uncommon reaction. When an officer threw up, he or she generally got a pat on the back and a kind word, but Huldar knew he couldn't expect that sort of consideration. Aware that his reputation couldn't take any further knocks, he swallowed hard, determined to tough it out.

Stella was lying on her back on the wet tarmac of a small car park behind one of the last old-fashioned convenience stores in the city. These days people went to supermarkets for their sweets and canned drinks, and petrol stations for their hot dogs. Although the owner of this shop had refused to give in, the chocolate turning white under the glass counter and the dusty sweet packets on the shelves bore witness to the fact that he was losing the battle. Yet however depressing the surroundings, Huldar would have given anything to be allowed to stand guard in there. Contemplating dusty gummy bears easily beat staring at a dead body. Sadly that role had been allocated to the hobbling Kári since it meant he could park himself on the chair that the shop owner had conjured up. It had been obvious too that Erla wanted Kári out of the way, driven demented by the fact that, ever since they'd arrived, he had been prattling on about having a powerful sense of déjà vu. He didn't say a word about the actual scene, just kept muttering about a confused memory of something that had probably never happened.

The shop owner had stumbled on Stella's body when he took out the rubbish. He swore it hadn't been there when he'd arrived for the evening shift at five. She was lying halfway between his car and the two dustbins that stood by the fence, so if she'd been there he would unquestionably have seen her when he drove in. He'd reported the discovery just before eight, so logically Stella must have been dumped at some point in the three-hour interval. Huldar would have bet that it had been at around 7 p.m., when the traffic was at its quietest. But no one asked his opinion: Erla acted like he wasn't there and Forensics were more likely to look through a microscope for answers than ask him what he thought. Sadly, there was no sign of the nice, pretty girl Gudlaugur had been eyeing up earlier.

The shop owner, who had been much too distressed to answer any questions when they tried to interview him, stubbornly refused to go home, insisting that he had to stay open;

the locals depended on him. Yet it was half past nine now and only one customer had come in the whole time they'd been there. On the other hand, the forensic technicians and four detectives had all purchased snacks, and Huldar suspected this was the real reason the owner was sticking around. He himself had bought a bottle of Coke, then another when one turned out not to be enough to quell his nausea. After watching the pathologist stick a thermometer into Stella's liver, it was time for a third.

Huldar's stomach curdled and threatened to rebel. He cursed the location and the weather. Because the car park wasn't overlooked from the road, there was no need to erect a tent over the body while they were working on it. If only there had been a little precipitation or wind they would have had to cover it, but no: for once it was still and the sky was clear.

Huldar closed his eyes, trying desperately to focus on something positive. But however hard he tried to concentrate on trout fishing or the Icelandic football team, Stella's battered head kept intruding into his thoughts. He couldn't even face a smoke, which was saying something. He longed to turn his back on the activity around the corpse and stare out of the narrow drive that he and Gudlaugur were supposed to be guarding. He felt like a wuss beside his younger colleague.

The pathologist stood up, tugging off his latex gloves and shoving his hands into the warm pair of mittens that an assistant was holding out to him. Like the other members of the forensics team, he was wearing a white plastic overall, but due to the cold he had a padded jacket on underneath, which made him look like the Michelin Man. He waddled over to Erla and they exchanged a few words.

Gudlaugur bent towards Huldar. 'What's going on?'

'No idea. I'm going to see – wait here.' If they both went over, Erla would snap at them to get back to their post. But since no one had tried to enter the car park so far, it would be unreasonable to insist they both remained on guard. Huldar carefully averted his gaze from the body as he passed, but the powerful floodlights meant he couldn't help catching a glimpse out of the corner of his eye. The childlike shape in the familiar, skimpy, indoor clothes; the chalky skin and fair hair fanned out around the unrecognisable pulp of her face. Like a battered doll abandoned by a disturbed child.

There wasn't much Erla could say when Huldar appeared at her side. The pathologist was bound to have heard the gossip about her being investigated for sexual harassment, so, in the circumstances, she wouldn't want to betray any hint that their relationship was strained. Or that was what Huldar was banking on as he waded in: 'Found anything interesting?'

'Yes and no. It's her all right.' The pathologist glanced in Stella's direction. 'But she hasn't been here the whole time. Which, I gather, fits with the shop owner's statement. The lividity – the pooling of blood under her skin – indicates that she must have been lying on her side in the period immediately after her death. But there's no evidence of further pooling underneath her. As she's still in the rigor mortis phase, you can also see from the alignment of her body that her present position doesn't match the flat surface of the tarmac. Then there's the fact that it snowed last night and again at midday, and although the tarmac's underheated in the parking spaces, so any snow on the ground would have melted, her body ought to be covered by a thin layer or at least by traces of snow if she'd been lying out here since last night. But there isn't a single snowflake to be seen. Hopefully the picture will become clearer once I've got her on the slab.'

Huldar felt the blood draining from his face and hoped the others wouldn't notice. He had been forced to attend a few post-mortems and had witnessed what happened on the slab. He felt a rush of pure gratitude that this was now Erla's job. 'Any chance you'll find something on the body that could help us nail the killer?' Normally he'd have asked about the cause of death but this time there was no need: they'd all witnessed the killing on CCTV.

'With any luck. She was clutching some hairs in her fist. They were short – too short to be hers, I think. The follicle's intact on several, so we should get some DNA and – if our luck's in – a match in the CODIS database.' The pathologist stared over at the floodlit area. 'That may mean she was still alive after she was dragged out of the cinema, contrary to what we concluded from the CCTV footage. If I remember correctly, her fingers were splayed out after her convulsions, which suggests she may have clutched at him unconsciously at a later stage, perhaps while he was heaving her into his car. Assuming he'd taken off his mask by then.'

'We haven't found anyone who saw him,' Erla said. 'And we're unlikely to get any witnesses coming forward now. We followed the trail of blood to the car park behind the building; it was late, there was a whiteout and the place was deserted. So we can't be sure he'd have taken the mask off.'

'But he would hardly have driven away still wearing it?' The pathologist looked thoughtful. 'Let's say you're right, though, and the hairs aren't from when she was being loaded into the car. There's a chance she tried to defend herself during the attack at the cinema and the hairs got caught in her fingers, but I can't quite picture it. They're too short. Unless her hands were sticky, like so many women's. All those bloody hand creams, you know. Her fist could have closed later as a result of rigor mortis.' Erla's eyebrows drew together at his comment about hand creams, but the pathologist carried on, oblivious. 'Then again, it's possible the hairs don't belong to him at all. They could have stuck to her hands while he was dragging her along the floor. Or they could have been in his car, in the boot or on the back seat. The fact he moved the girl from the murder scene doesn't exactly help. Christ knows where the body's been in the interim.'

'Anything else?'

'Not yet, though of course I'll be examining the body more thoroughly. I wouldn't get your hopes up about the results of the post-mortem, though. The killer was wearing gloves in the recordings and probably had the sense to be careful, in spite of those hairs. I'm assuming he didn't rape the girl and it's usually only in those cases that we get something water-tight. There's a chance he might have assaulted her before he started taking those pictures in the toilet cubicle but I doubt it. She was properly dressed, not as if she'd pulled her clothes on in a state of shock after that kind of attack. And there's no indication that he molested her after dragging her out, then put the clothes back on her dead body.'

Erla grimaced. 'I suppose we should be grateful for that, though watertight biological traces would have been welcome.'

'There's still a chance we'll find something.' The pathologist gestured at the white-clad technicians bending over the body. It would be removed shortly, after which Forensics would take charge of the scene. They had already scoured the cordoned-off area in search of evidence, without much to show for it, though they could tell from the marks on the thin layer of snow in the drive, where the geothermal heating system had broken down, that the body had probably been dragged to the site from the road. There were also two distinct sets of vehicle tracks leading to the car park, one of which matched the treads on the shop owner's car. They were now checking the tyres of the car belonging to the woman he had taken over from at five. As it was highly unlikely that Stella would have been dragged far, they were also examining and recording vehicle tracks in the road outside. These were unlikely to lead them to the perpetrator but could help them make a case against him when he was found. *When he was found.*

Gudlaugur let two men past carrying a stretcher. They went over to the body and began to ease it up with help from two of the technicians. It wasn't the girl's weight that required four people but the necessity of transferring her from the ground to the stretcher with the least possible disturbance to the body or the ground beneath. While they were searching for the best grip, the others watched in silence.

One of them counted to three, at which point Stella's stiff body rose slowly into the air. Then the men hesitated and looked as if they were going to lower her again. The man directing the operation turned to the pathologist and called: 'There's something underneath her. What should we do?'

The pathologist and Erla hurried over, Huldar following in their wake. He couldn't get a clear view as they were in front, but he thought he saw something white on the ground where Stella had been lying. It was only when the pathologist had his latex gloves on again and ordered the men to lift her onto the stretcher that they could get a proper look. Lying on the worn tarmac was a sheet of white A4 paper.

The assistant, ever ready, handed the pathologist a pair of tweezers.

He and Erla read what was written on the paper.

Erla sighed explosively. 'What fucking bullshit is this?'

Huldar moved closer so he could read over their shoulders. Printed in a giant font on the paper was a number:

2

Chapter 11

For once the question of the day was simple. It didn't concern the timeline, the motive, the perpetrator or the evidence, simply what, if anything, the number two could possibly mean. Although the pathologist thought it likely the paper had been deliberately placed under Stella's body, they couldn't take this for granted. It could theoretically have been lying there when her body was dumped. That's what most members of the investigation team hoped, because otherwise the only logical conclusion was that Stella was victim number two. Which meant that victim number one must be lying out there somewhere, as yet undiscovered. While there was no better explanation available, they would have to work on that basis and do everything in their power to prevent the nightmare scenario of a member of the public – especially a kid Stella's age – stumbling on another body. And, what was worse, a member of the public who would *inevitably* have a camera on their phone. If that happened, there was every likelihood the pictures would find their way onto social media, and from there spread to every home in the country. They'd be lucky if the person who posted the pictures had the decency to pixelate the face and any other sensitive areas – assuming the victim was still identifiable.

'Nothing?' Erla sounded uncharacteristically shrill. 'Not a single missing person?'

The police officer who'd been tasked with checking the missing-person reports shook his head. From his disappointed expression, he'd obviously have preferred it if half the population had gone AWOL. 'Nope, nobody. A few old reports relating to people who still haven't been found, but no one Stella's age. Mostly just mountaineers or presumed suicides.'

'Presumed suicides?' Erla was still hitting high C. Huldar doubted she had got much sleep. He himself was bleary and unshaven after getting home late and coming in early. When he'd left she'd still been hard at it and when he'd arrived this morning she had already been at her desk. It was quite possible she hadn't been home at all.

'Er . . . yes. The person who gave me the reports put it like that. People who are presumed to have committed suicide by walking into the sea.'

Erla groaned. 'OK. How old is the most recent report?'

The officer scrabbled around among his papers, looking stressed. 'Er . . .' He raised his eyes to the ceiling, muttering, then looked back at Erla. 'Eight months. By my calculations.'

Erla waved him away but instead of moving, he asked what he should do with the copies of the reports. Erla appeared to be on the point of saying something regrettable but thought better of it and snapped at him to leave them on her desk. Then she turned back to the detective she'd been talking to. Since he sat near Huldar and Gudlaugur, they were in a good position to eavesdrop.

It was a welcome opportunity to find out what was happening. Although they'd attended the scene yesterday evening when the body was found, today they'd been relegated to the bottom of the heap again. While other members of the department were bustling around, they were sitting almost

79

empty-handed. It was absurd given how much donkey work needed to be done.

From what passed between Erla and the guy at the next desk, it was clear there was a ton of information that needed sifting through. Experts from Forensics had examined Stella's laptop and phone overnight, and passed on copies of any material they found interesting. Records of Stella's social media activity were also available, which meant there were hundreds if not thousands of posts that needed skimming through. The CCTV footage from the cinema required further attention since the first viewing hadn't produced any results. The crowds that had gathered in the foyer before the screens opened and poured out of the auditoriums during the inter-vals had made it incredibly difficult to spot potential suspects. The results of the post-mortem were also due any minute, along with a preliminary report on material found at the scene where the body was dumped. The latter shouldn't take long to read as Huldar had gathered from the forensics team yesterday evening that evidence had been thin on the ground in the car park, apart from the sheet of paper with the number two on it.

On top of all this, the police had a long list of people who needed interviewing, some for the second time – particularly those, like Stella's parents, who had been too traumatised the first time round. Huldar pricked up his ears when he heard this, hoping it would involve more interviews with adoles-cents, which would give him an excuse to bring in Freyja. But Erla didn't mention any. He only hoped she wouldn't let her hostility towards Freyja have an adverse impact on the inquiry. Certainly she hadn't said a word about Freyja's e-mail or the bullying angle yet. But perhaps she was working up to it.

'If I had unlimited manpower I'd send someone for another chat with the two women whose letterbox the phone was dropped through.' Erla exhaled irritably. 'One of them was definitely behaving suspiciously. I didn't manage to catch her out but she was nervous. Unnaturally nervous, I reckon.'

'Gudlaugur and I can cover that,' Huldar cut in, betraying the fact he'd been eavesdropping. 'It might make sense for someone different to have a word with them. To get a second opinion.'

Erla's head snapped round. Gudlaugur was bending over his computer, pretending not to listen. 'What? You two?'

'Sure. Why not? We've got nothing else on. Or have you got another job for us? We're all ears.' Huldar's smile earned him a grimace. For a moment, meeting her contemptuous look, he missed the days when they were mates. Back before they'd slept together, before internal affairs had ripped and chewed their way through the tatters of their friendship. In the fraction of a second before Erla answered, he wondered if they'd ever be mates again.

'OK. Go ahead.' Erla put her hands on her lean hips, a malicious grin crossing her face. 'And take Kári with you. It'll be good to get him out of my hair as well as the pair of you.'

There was a snigger from the detective Erla had been talking to. Huldar didn't give a damn. He'd actually succeeded in prising an assignment out of her. Holding Erla's gaze, he asked: 'Which was it?'

'Which was what?'

'Which of the women was jittery? The nurse or the doctor?'

'The nurse, Ásta. The doctor's called Thórey. You'll find her details in the report. It's in the case folder on the server.

And mind out for Kári's ankle.' She turned back to the man she had been talking to, presenting Huldar with the uncompromising line of her knobbly spine, jutting through her tight shirt.

The nurse, Ásta, looked like the type who goes jogging or mountain walking every day after work and cycles hundreds of kilometres every weekend. She positively glowed with vitality. Though it was December, her thick blonde shoulder-length hair appeared sun-kissed and she was healthily tanned. Huldar suppressed a sigh over the injustice of it. But any further such thoughts were nipped in the bud when he recalled his colleague Helgi's sleazy comments about lesbians.

Ásta was reluctant to let them in. She blocked the doorway for as long as she could, as if hoping they'd change their minds. When they persisted, she reluctantly made way for them. Yet it wasn't as if they'd turned up unannounced. Huldar had rung ahead, assuming both women would be at work and that he'd have to speak to them in some quiet corner of the hospital. Or outside in the car, maybe. But the one he was interested in, Ásta, turned out to be at home.

'I don't know what else you want from me,' Ásta protested. 'I told the police yesterday that we don't know the girl. Nothing's changed since then.' She led them into the kitchen and gestured to the chairs but didn't offer them any coffee. Not even a glass of water. Like the rest of the house, the kitchen was neat and unpretentious, though everywhere you looked you could see signs that they had kids. The fridge was covered with drawings by their two daughters. Some were little more than crayon scribbles by a very young child who was just learning to draw people. Circles with eyes and mouth,

82

stick limbs. The other pictures were better executed and the people in them had hair, bodies and clothes. Most were drawings of the family: four smiling figures in dresses, two big and two small, all holding hands. Each figure was clumsily labelled: 'Mummy', 'Mummy', 'Ósk' and 'Sól'. It was lucky the girls had such short names as there wouldn't have been room on the paper for any more big, wobbly letters. From the back of the house came the screeching soundtrack of a cartoon. It seemed the small artists were at home.

'We've just got a few more questions.' Huldar pulled out a kitchen chair. 'It won't take long. Sometimes things come back to people after we've left, so we do a routine follow-up.'

Ásta propped herself against the kitchen unit as the three of them took their seats and Kári laid down his crutches. He grunted as he lowered himself into a chair.

'What happened to you?' Ásta gestured at Kári's plaster cast sticking out from under the table. Huldar doubted her interest was genuine: she must get enough of sick people at work. Personally he had zero interest in maintaining law and order during his free time. He guessed her question was no more than a delaying tactic.

'I broke my ankle.' As Kári embarked on the tedious tale of how he'd injured himself, Huldar thought Ásta looked pleased at the temporary respite this offered from their questions. He and Gudlaugur had already been subjected to the story in the car. Still, at least it wasn't as boring as Kári's droning on about his déjà vu in the car park. Huldar broke in before he could move on to that.

'Anyway, I suppose we'd better get down to business. The sooner we do, the sooner we'll be out of your hair.' Ásta immediately showed signs of being on edge again, reaching for a cloth by the sink and starting to wipe down the already spotless work surface. Huldar went on with what he was saying, pretending not to notice. Erla had been right: the woman was definitely nervous. He reminded himself that he never used to doubt Erla's instincts and that there was no reason to do so now, just because they'd fallen out. 'Yesterday you told my colleagues you didn't know the missing girl, Stella Hardardóttir. Have you had time since then to search your memory for any possible connection?' Rising to his feet, he laid a blown-up photo of Stella on the worktop in front of her, then sat down again.

'The answer's still no. I've never met her.' Ásta didn't pick the picture up or appear to give it more than a fleeting glance.

'Are you quite sure?' When she nodded, Huldar persevered: 'Could you have nursed her at the hospital?'

'I doubt it. I work in the cardiology ward. We don't tend to get children or teenagers in there.'

'You haven't done any extra shifts at the Children's Hospital? Or as a school nurse?'

'No.' Ásta started cleaning the worktop again, avoiding Huldar's eyes. She wiped around the photo, as though reluctant to touch it. 'You can ask all the questions you like: I don't know the girl. And I have absolutely no idea why her phone was put through our door.'

Huldar wasn't giving up that easily. 'Could you have come across her at the cinema where she worked? Taken your daughters to a film and exchanged a few words with her in the interval maybe?'

'No. How often do I have to repeat it? I don't know her.'

Huldar couldn't deny that in spite of her strange behaviour and obvious tension, the woman sounded convincing. He cleared his throat. The police were going to issue a press release about the discovery of the body before the midday news. As it was already ten o'clock, he saw no reason to withhold the fact any longer. 'I'm going to let you into a secret. We've found the girl. She's dead. Murdered. So perhaps you'll understand why we have to keep repeating the same questions. It doesn't get any more serious than this.'

The cloth stopped moving on the worktop. Ásta's knuckles were white. 'Will you catch the person who did it?'

'Yes. Of course.'

She seemed relieved. If she was mixed up in Stella's case, he was willing to bet it wasn't through any involvement with the killer. But her behaviour was definitely odd and it was hard to imagine what else she could have to hide. 'What about the phone? Did it look familiar?' Huldar had seen a photo of it and, apart from the decorative case, it had looked like pretty much every other teenager's phone in the country.

'The phone? No. I'd never seen it before.' Ásta wrinkled her brow, puzzled. Her gaze, no longer lowered to the worktop, was fixed on Gudlaugur. 'Do I know you?'

'Me?' Gudlaugur blushed and looked shifty. 'I don't think so.'

'I could have sworn I've met you before.' The woman appeared to be genuinely struggling to remember, though Huldar suspected this was just another ruse to change the subject. 'Have you ever been to Cardiology?'

Gudlaugur shifted in his seat, turning away from her. 'Me? No. I don't believe we know each other.'

'I expect he's got one of those typical Icelandic faces that you always think you've seen before,' Kári volunteered, apparently failing to notice Gudlaugur's peculiar reaction.

'Maybe. But I don't think that's it.' Ásta studied Gudlaugur's red face thoughtfully. 'I've definitely seen you before. It'll come back to me as soon as I stop trying to remember.'

Gudlaugur stood up with a loud scraping of his chair. 'Could I use your toilet?'

She told him where to find it and Gudlaugur fled the kitchen. Huldar tried not to let this development throw him off track, but it was hard. What the hell was going on? 'If you find it easier to remember things when you stop trying, do you think it might come back to you later? Where you've encountered Stella before, I mean. Perhaps we could drop by this afternoon and have another go.'

'That's different, because I'm positive I never met her. So there's nothing to remember. But I know I've seen your colleague before. What's his name again?'

'Gudlaugur. Gudlaugur Vignisson.'

'Doesn't ring any bells.'

'Anyway.' Huldar returned to the matter at hand. He'd have plenty of opportunity to interrogate Gudlaugur later. 'What about your wife, Thórey? Has she remembered anything?'

'No,' Ásta said flatly. 'She doesn't know the girl.'

Huldar decided a slight change of tactics was in order. 'All right then. Tell me, what do you know about bullying?'

'Bullying?' Ásta repeated the word as if she'd never heard it before. 'How do you mean?'

'Bullying. Have you ever been bullied? You, or your daughters, or your wife? Or, let's put it another way, have you or any member of your family ever bullied anyone?' Huldar wondered if he should mention her daughter's squint in this context but decided against it; no need to put her back up any further.

86

Her eyes dropped again to the cloth in her hands. 'No.' Shaking her head, she said again: 'No.'

'Quite sure?'

'Yes, quite sure.' But she didn't look or sound it. Her face hardened. 'I'd rather not answer any more of your questions. They're getting ridiculous. Surely your time would be better spent investigating something that's actually relevant? My time's precious too, you know. I'm on duty this evening and I hadn't bargained on wasting half my day.'

'You can't always tell what is or isn't relevant at the beginning of an inquiry,' Kári offered sagely, looking smug. He was right, of course, but Huldar hoped he wasn't about to become overconfident and start muscling in on the conversation.

Kári lapsed back into silence, though, and Huldar was able to go on questioning the woman until he'd run out of things to ask and was becoming as fed up as Ásta was. Her answers were all along the same lines: *no, no, I don't know* or *I've already said no*. Every time she opened her mouth she sounded more resigned, yet she stuck to her guns. While this was going on, Gudlaugur returned from the toilet and sat down again, this time on the other side of the table. He didn't seem himself, contributed nothing to the interview and gave the impression of counting down the minutes until they could leave. Before they did, Huldar decided to copy his ploy and see if leaving the three of them alone together would achieve anything. 'I couldn't use your loo as well, could I?'

Ásta looked surprised. 'What, don't you lot have any toilets at the police station?' When Huldar merely smiled, she muttered her consent.

On the way there he passed the room from which the cartoon voices were emanating and, peering round the door, saw a large TV on a low stand, showing blue cartoon parrots rolling around on a beach. The two daughters were sitting on the sofa. Neither looked like Ásta. Perhaps they took after their other mother. Certainly, they bore a striking resemblance to each other, as though they were the same girl in different sizes, apart from the eye patch worn by the elder sister. Both had rosy cheeks, slightly protruding ears and big blue eyes that were now regarding him in surprise from under wavy, mouse-coloured fringes. 'Who are you?' the elder girl asked while her little sister snuggled against her. The patch made her look like a sweet little pirate. Huldar wouldn't have been surprised if one of the parrots had flown out of the television and perched on her shoulder.

'My name's Huldar.' He smiled at them, injecting as much warmth and likeability into his voice as he knew how. 'Shouldn't you two be at school?'

'We've got the day off. It's teacher training day. And Sól was allowed to stay home because I'm here. She doesn't go to school yet. She's at nursery.' The girl lifted up the patch.

'I *do* go to school. *Nursery* school.' After this brief outburst, the younger girl ducked behind her sister again.

Ignoring her, the elder girl let her patch fall back into place. 'Are you a cop?'

After a moment's hesitation, Huldar decided to answer honestly, though he'd rather have said he was a plumber to forestall the inevitable questions about what he was doing there. 'Yes, I am.'

'I know. I saw you out of the window yesterday. You were wearing a uniform. Why aren't you wearing a uniform now?'

'I only wear it sometimes.' He waved goodbye and turned to continue down the hall.

'You made Mummy cry.' It sounded matter-of-fact rather than accusatory.

'Me?'

'Not you. The police. That woman. Mummy cried a lot. After you all went home.'

'Oh, sorry, I didn't know. We didn't mean to.'

'Nobody knew. Only me. She hid in the bathroom so Mummy Thórey wouldn't see.' The girl paused and frowned. Lifting up her nose a little, she wound a strand of hair between her fingers. 'Has Mummy done something bad? Are you going to put her in prison?' The little sister's head popped up again, staring at Huldar with wide eyes.

'No. Of course not. The police often have to talk to people who haven't done anything wrong. That's why we're here. There's really nothing to worry about.' He pointed at the TV. 'Except how that parrot fight's going to end.'

The girls turned back to the screen and Huldar made his escape. He couldn't be bothered to keep up the pretence of going to the loo, so he went straight back to the kitchen to fetch Gudlaugur and Kári. They might as well leave. The woman wouldn't provide any answers, however long they grilled her, and she'd already betrayed the fact that there was something funny going on. As he left, he placed his card on the kitchen table and asked Ásta to call him if she remembered anything. He didn't for a minute believe she would.

On the way back to the station Kári started boring on about his ankle again. Huldar tightened his grip on the steering wheel, threw Gudlaugur a sideways glance, and asked, not caring that he was talking over Kári: 'What exactly was going on back there?'

'Going on?' Gudlaugur kept his eyes straight ahead; you'd have thought he, not Huldar, was driving. He was sitting bolt upright, as if his seat back had been cranked up too far. 'In my opinion she knows something she's not letting on. But it's anybody's guess what it is.'

'I wasn't talking about that. I meant what was going on between the two of you? Where does she know you from?'

'She was mistaken. I've never met her before.'

'You do realise you sound about as convincing as she did when she denied knowing Stella?' Huldar snatched another glance at Gudlaugur, then returned his eyes to the road. The young man was looking as twitchy as he had in Ásta's kitchen. 'Come on, where does she know you from?'

'Look, I haven't a clue, all right? I've never met her before in my life.'

Huldar gripped the steering wheel even harder and drove on without asking again. In the back seat Kári was still gassing away, completely oblivious to the undercurrents in the front.

Chapter 12

The phone rang and Freyja wondered whether to pick up. She'd have been better off ignoring the calls she'd received earlier that morning for all the pleasure they'd brought her. One was from an old classmate wanting to know if she'd got the e-mail about the reunion. He seemed oddly keen that she should go along. After racking her brains for a moment, she remembered who he was: they'd bumped into each other recently at the supermarket. He'd behaved like an idiot and couldn't stop exclaiming over how great she was looking. So she got a kick out of telling him that yes, she had got the e-mail but had forgotten to reply. Still, now that she had him on the line she could save herself the bother: no, she wouldn't be going. She rang off, punching the air with her fist.

The second call had had more of an impact on her day. Saga's mother had rung to ask if Freyja could collect her from nursery as the little girl had a stomach bug. Since she herself had used up all her sick days, she'd be grateful if Freyja could stand in for Baldur. And of course, as always, she said yes. If she could look after his dog, it was both her duty and her pleasure to shoulder some of his responsibilities towards his daughter. Though when she'd originally signed up to be one of her niece's carers, she hadn't really given any thought to vomiting bugs.

As she picked up the phone, Freyja glanced over at the child asleep on the sofa. Saga's mouth was turned down, even in sleep, traces of vomit still clinging to the corners. Freyja made a face, then, checking the screen, saw that it was Huldar. She dithered, unsure whether to answer. What if he asked her to come down to the station and help him interview more minors? She could hardly take Saga along, especially when she was throwing up. But she had no choice as she was officially on call.

'Have you heard the news?' As usual Huldar jumped straight in the moment she said hello.

'Is this some kind of police technique? Never introduce yourself, just start talking as if we're already in the middle of a conversation?'

'No. Sorry. It's Huldar. Have you seen the news?'

'No, I haven't looked at it yet.' Before being landed with Saga, Freyja had spent the morning with her nose buried in her course books. The maths problems, meanwhile, lay unsolved on the kitchen table, a situation that seemed unlikely to change any time soon. Oh, well, that wouldn't be the end of the world. 'What's up?'

'Stella. Her body's been found.'

'Found?' Freyja blurted, sounding foolishly surprised, though deep down she'd known ever since seeing the CCTV footage that Stella was dead.

'Yes. So it's officially murder.'

Freyja was silent while casting around for the right words. If she'd been clinging to a faint hope that the girl was still alive, what must it have been like for her parents? They must be utterly distraught. 'That's terrible. Her poor parents. They were notified before it was made public, weren't they? Please tell me they didn't have to learn it from the news? Have they been offered grief counselling?' As always when she got bad news, she couldn't stop herself pouring out a stream of point-less questions.

'They didn't want any. And no, they didn't read about it online. The police contacted them yesterday evening. They're . . . they're in shock. As you'd expect.'

Freyja bit back any further questions about the poor couple. For Stella's parents, life would never be the same again. Right now it must feel as if the future was stretching out before them in an eternity of emptiness and grief. She only hoped for their sakes that they had other children to keep them going, force them to take part in the daily business of living, however much they might long to take to their beds and never get up again.

'One question,' Huldar went on. 'If I say the number two to you, what immediately springs to mind?'

'Two?'

'Yes. What are the first things you think of?'

'Umm . . . Well, a couple . . . a silver medal, a sequel. Someone who takes second place. Nothing else off the top of my head. Why do you ask?'

'It doesn't matter. That's not the reason for my call.'

'Oh?' Freyja frowned, her eyes straying to Saga. What was she to do if he needed her to come into the station? 'Are you conducting more interviews?'

'No. Not right now.'

Freyja couldn't hold back a sigh of relief.

'What?' It hadn't escaped Huldar.

'Nothing. Go on.'

'As there are no interviews planned for today, I was going to ask if you could do a bit of research into bullying for me.

I have a hunch that the incidents you mentioned could be linked to the case, so we'd be grateful for anything you can dig up on the subject, especially any evidence that it might drive someone to commit murder.'

'I'll take a look but the answer to that is fairly obvious. In the worst-case scenarios, all conflicts can potentially drive people to violence. I'm not saying everyone would be capable of murder, but being subjected to that kind of ordeal over a long period can tip some people over the edge. Especially if they're under the influence of alcohol or drugs. You must be familiar with that from your job.' Saga stirred on the sofa and Freyja lowered her voice, got up and moved towards the door.

'Yes, I am.' Huldar dropped his voice too.

'You don't need to whisper.' Freyja stopped and leant against the doorframe, from where she could keep an eye on Saga, who appeared to be sound asleep again. 'I'm only whispering because I've got a sleeping child here. But don't worry, I can still look into it for you.'

'A sleeping child?'

'My niece Saga, Baldur's daughter.'

'Oh.' Huldar's voice resumed normal pitch. 'Isn't he due to be released soon?'

'Yes. He's got a place at the halfway house after Christmas.' Freyja fell silent. She preferred not to discuss her jailbird brother with Huldar. It felt like a betrayal. 'I was wondering if I should talk to Stella's headmistress; find out if Adalheidur's father has shown any signs of being violent. Subtly, of course. I could say I'm concerned about the pupils Stella came into contact with. She may have picked on other kids as well. Has anyone looked into that?'

'No. To be honest, we're not actually exploring the bullying angle. Not yet. But we're going through Stella's computer and social media activity and I understand quite a lot of ugly stuff has turned up, which fits in with the info you gave us. So they're bound to start taking that aspect more seriously soon. Anyway, I can't see any reason why you shouldn't do something for us. We've only got you for a few days, so we'd better make good use of you. By all means talk to the head. But remember, you're not interrogating her, just putting out feelers. If it looks like there's something to be gained from it, we'll organise a formal interview. Tread carefully.'

'Will do.' Freyja lowered her voice still further as Saga murmured in her sleep and rolled over. A string of drool dribbled out of her downturned mouth, washing away the remnants of the vomit – onto the sofa. Oh, great. 'One question: have you found anything that could explain why Stella's friends were so alarmed when you mentioned her computer?'

'Well, we found a hate page she set up, directed at Adalheidur. It's nasty, vicious stuff but I doubt they'd be that bothered about being exposed, seeing as they all seem to have posted the abuse under their real names. Maybe there's worse to come. Like I said, we're still going through her computer.'

'OK.' Saga stirred again and Freyja had to dash over to the sofa to prevent her from rolling off. 'Listen, I've got to go. Do you want me to call if I find out anything interesting?'

He said yes and, as Freyja was about to say goodbye, added quickly: 'Any chance you're free this evening? Could I maybe invite you out for supper? You can bring your niece, if you like. Just for a meal. You could fill me in on what you find out today. Save yourself a phone call.'

Freyja rolled her eyes. She'd have refused the moment he

asked if she could have got a word in edgeways but he spoke in such a rush that he was almost stumbling over the words. Just because she'd given up on Tinder, that didn't mean she was desperate enough to go out with Huldar. Though maybe she'd have thought differently if he'd rung her during her last Tinder date. The man in question had had to abandon her in a hurry since he was wearing an ankle tag and had to be home by ten. He'd rushed out of the restaurant in the middle of dessert, leaving her with the bill and the question about what he'd been charged with still on her lips. 'No, Huldar. Thanks all the same.'

He sounded crestfallen as he said goodbye.

Saga sat on the floor playing with the wooden bricks Freyja had given her for her first birthday. Saga's mother Fanney, feeling that the bright primary colours didn't quite go with her tastefully muted decor, had sent them home with Freyja the next time she came to collect the little girl. Although Freyja had been rather offended, the bricks had subsequently proved so useful that she'd forgiven the woman. They bought her a little peace while Saga was playing with them, even if the little girl's technique wasn't quite what the manufacturer had had in mind. The bricks now formed a long wobbly line across the sitting-room floor. It was the only game Saga would play with them. She could amuse herself for hours. Freyja doubted she got as much pleasure out of any of the other toys she'd received at her tasteful birthday party: the dolls, tea sets and small horses in pastel colours, each featuring huge eyes or a cute flowery pattern. After two parcels, Saga had lost interest and her mother had had to open the rest while her daughter entertained herself by kicking off her tiny patent leather shoes. Despite the guests' valiant efforts to hide the fact, they were obviously unimpressed by her behaviour and sullen expression. Fortunately, her mother had seemed oblivious to this. And Freyja herself had been preoccupied with wondering if she was the only adult in the room who didn't write a lifestyle or food blog.

Freyja reread the e-mail, then pressed 'Send'. When Saga had used up the final brick, she would have to get up, collect them all and put them back in the bucket so the little girl could start again. Alternatively, Saga would lose interest and Freyja would have to find something else to keep her occupied. Still, Freyja had made good use of the peace and quiet after Huldar's phone call to read everything she could find online about bullying, though most of it wouldn't be much use to the police. It consisted mainly of news items, blogs and interviews that didn't shed any real light on the problem except to show how widespread it was and how difficult to stop. Huldar could have looked that up himself. Nevertheless, she noted down the names of any potentially interesting individuals, though the name of the victim was usually withheld.

Next, she turned her attention to academic articles and found two that gave her a more in-depth insight. Neither was concerned with violence, though. She was acquainted with the author, Kjartan Erlendsson, since he'd studied psychology with her at university. His name had kept cropping up in the news reports and articles she'd read as the media's go-to expert. Every issue had its specialist and it seemed that he had cornered bullying. She tapped his name into a search engine and saw that he had specialised in this area after his undergraduate degree, later opening a clinic offering counselling for the problem.

In the hope of speeding things up, she decided to e-mail him and ask if they could meet for a chat. Short though the message was, she found it tricky to write due to the necessity of leaving Stella's name out of it. Her biggest worry, however, was that he might think she was trying to renew their acquaintance for something other than professional reasons. She didn't want to look foolish in the eyes of a former fellow student and there were few things more uncool than flirting by e-mail. Deciding that the final version just about passed muster, she sent it off, only to be struck immediately with doubts. If only she'd reread it one more time.

Before closing her laptop and starting to pick up Saga's bricks, she checked the screen again in the hope that he might have answered. No such luck. Pity her e-mail didn't offer the same feature as her messaging app, which would have shown whether he'd opened it and maybe also three moving dots to indicate that he was writing a reply. Then again, there was nothing worse than watching those dots only for the anticipated answer not to materialise.

Freyja dropped the bricks back into the box while Saga sat on the floor, legs outstretched, watching her. Molly was lying beside her. The two of them had formed an alliance and there were times when Freyja almost felt they were whispering about her behind her back, though of course neither of them could speak.

Once the last brick was back in the box, Saga embarked on her line-building again. Guaranteed a quarter of an hour's peace, Freyja hurriedly tried the headmistress again. She'd rung her immediately after saying goodbye to Huldar but the woman had been busy.

This time she answered on the second ring. Freyja introduced herself as the psychologist who had accompanied the police the day before, and this immediately secured the head's interest. She even seemed pleased to hear from her, despite being upset by the news about Stella. While she talked at length about the tragic business, Freyja watched the minutes ticking away and the number of bricks in the box dwindling. At this rate, by the time she finally got a chance to ask about Adalheidur and Stella, she would be forced to cut the conversation short. The instant the woman paused for breath, Freyja jumped in. 'Now we know for sure that Stella's dead, I was wondering if there were any pupils in particular you'd need to keep an eye on.'

'Well, yes. I expect so.'

'Apart from the obvious ones, like her friends.'

'I'm sorry, I'm not with you.'

'I gather there was bad blood between Stella and one of the girls in her class. I'd advise you to include her when you're offering trauma counselling.'

'Adalheidur, you mean? I don't think you need worry about her. I know it's not a very nice thing to say, but I wouldn't be surprised if Stella's death makes life easier for her.'

'I wouldn't be so sure of that. She may struggle with her feelings. If my information is correct, relations between them were still bad at the time of Stella's death, which means there can never be any showdown or reconciliation. That's not good for Adalheidur. And there's a risk, too, that Stella's friends might take out their grief and anger on her. Feelings like that tend to seek an outlet.'

'To be honest, that hadn't occurred to me. But they're good girls really, so I don't think you need worry.'

Freyja watched as Saga attempted to place a bright-red brick next to a green one. Despite her fierce concentration, her short, fat fingers struggled to complete the task. Her perma-scowl deepened with frustration. Freyja clamped the phone between ear and shoulder and smiled at her, silently clapping her hands to forestall any tears. In her limited experience, bringing up children consisted on the one hand of preventative action, like constantly saying 'no', and on the other, of forcing them into things against their will: clothes, shoes, hats, gloves, car seats, pushchairs and the child seats in shopping trolleys. She would never have believed how difficult it was to get a toddler dressed. It was as bad as trying to pull your clothes on when you're wet from the shower.

Freyja focused on the conversation again, hoping the short pause wouldn't prompt the head to return to the subject of Stella's death. 'I do think you should bear it in mind. How serious was the bullying, by the way?'

'Bad enough for Adalheidur to attempt suicide. She was off school for a month. After that, serious efforts were made to resolve the situation and, as far as I know, it had improved. At school, anyway. Unfortunately it's harder to monitor what happens outside school hours. That's when things can really escalate, on social media.'

The news of Adalheidur's suicide attempt rendered Freyja momentarily speechless. The matter was far graver than she'd thought. 'I had a quick word with Adalheidur after the meeting and understood from her that Stella had still been giving her grief.'

'I'm very sorry to hear that. But please believe me, it's not from any lack of effort on our part. The solution in these cases doesn't lie entirely with us. We can't control what happens outside school, on the internet. That's a matter for the bully's parents. All we can do is speak to the kids when we hear about this type of incident. And urge their parents to take action, which is what we did in Adalheidur's case. We talked to Stella's parents and to all the girls in her circle of friends. I really believed we'd made progress in tackling that particular problem.'

'Temporarily, perhaps. But I gather Stella had recently circulated a photo of Adalheidur naked in the shower after gym, with the sole purpose of humiliating her. The photo was taken at your school.' Freyja broke off, realising that she was no longer motivated by the interests of the police inquiry. What was she thinking of, talking about a newly deceased girl like this? 'I hope it doesn't sound as if I'm accusing you of anything. I know schools have few options and that this problem is almost impossible to stamp out.'

'What's this photo you mentioned?'

'A picture of Adalheidur naked in the shower, taken without her knowledge or permission, and posted on the internet.'

'It's the first I've heard of it. As far as I'm aware, Adalheidur hasn't made any complaints for several months. And I understood from Stella that she was making a real effort to be nice to her.'

It was obvious what had happened: Adalheidur had given up. The victims of bullying often said that when it proved impossible to get help, they lost the will to go on fighting. What was worse, the perpetrators often reacted extremely badly to being reported and only upped the level of abuse. Adalheidur had mentioned that herself. The fuss around her suicide attempt had probably provoked the gang of girls to behave even more spitefully. Teenagers didn't like it when parents got involved in what they regarded as their private affairs. Especially when it showed them in a bad light. 'No, apparently the photo was recent. According to Adalheidur, the bullying hadn't stopped.'

'Well, I'm very sorry and shocked to hear that. There was a period when her father used to turn up here constantly and, stupidly, I assumed he'd have started coming again if the bullying had just continued. But we haven't seen him in a while. It *must* be a misunderstanding.'

'Well, possibly.' Freyja changed the subject. Now that Adalheidur's father had come up, she wanted to keep the woman on the phone. 'Understandably, parents get very upset by this sort of thing. Was he noticeably worked up? I've heard of some quite serious incidents involving angry parents.' This last bit was an invention; Freyja hadn't heard of any such thing but had an intuition that before this case was over, that would have changed.

'I don't know how to put it politely but there were times when he was beside himself with rage. You can't imagine how relieved I was when he stopped coming in and I thought the matter had been solved. I found being alone with him quite nerve-racking. Sometimes us staff could do with trauma coun-selling too. Or a bodyguard.'

'I can believe it.' Freyja reached out a toe to push a brick back into place where Molly had knocked it out of line. Luckily Saga had been fetching another brick at the time or she would have made her feelings powerfully clear. 'Did Stella pick on anyone else apart from Adalheidur? Bullies aren't usually satisfied with just one victim.'

'Well, actually there *was* another girl Stella had it in for: Hekla. She and Adalheidur used to be friends but then they fell out. The last I heard, Hekla was part of Stella's gang. I was hoping the same would happen with Adalheidur; that they'd make up and become friends before the end of the year. But of course there's no chance of that now.'

Freyja saw through this immediately. One of the aims of bullies was to isolate the victim, which was best achieved by luring away the few friends he or she had. 'I see.'

'I hope you understand that we take bullying extremely seriously here. We have a zero tolerance policy and do our best to crack down on any incidents. But it's not easy.'

'I know.' After trawling the net for information, it was clear to Freyja that schools were in an unenviable position. However firmly they dealt with the problem, circumstances worked against them. The bullies had unlimited access to the victim in cyberspace, so separating the kids at school achieved little. Nor did the staff have any means of tackling the lies and declarations of innocence and the claims that it was all a misunderstanding. Bullies were cunning at hiding their vicious side, girls especially.

Freyja kept the woman on the line for a little longer but she was running out of things to ask. Before ringing off, she reiterated the necessity of keeping an eye on Adalheidur, then asked what her patronymic was.

The phone call had not been a complete waste of time. She'd learnt about Adalheidur's attempted suicide, and that her father, Haukur, had become intimidatingly angry with staff about the things Stella had done. Freyja reached for her laptop again to see if Kjartan had replied.

Chapter 13

Kjartan needed a holiday. He should get his secretary to move his existing appointments, then book a hotel and a flight somewhere warm and sunny with enticing green golf courses. Preferably somewhere far away in the southern hemisphere where it was summer.

There was a distinct lack of beer and shorts in his life. Office coffee and too many clients were no compensation. Especially not clients like the one presently sitting in front of him. The man, whose name was Bogi, was achingly dull and inclined to be querulous, and Kjartan found it hard enough to focus on what he said when he met him in the mornings, let alone late in the afternoon like now.

'Boring Bogi' was little better than his other middle-aged client, 'Moaning Mördur', who did at least have one redeeming feature: he knew a lot about computers. He'd agreed to create an online appointments system for Kjartan and the other psychologists in the practice – in return for a generous discount on his fee, of course. Kjartan would have to cancel his discount soon; it wouldn't do to make it a permanent arrangement. After all, it wasn't as if the appointments system had been offered for free. Come to think of it, though, Mördur had missed his appointment earlier that day, so perhaps he would stop coming altogether. Kjartan knew he was unlikely to be that lucky, though. You could never shake off clients like Bogi and Mördur.

Bogi: a man who was all work and no play, who lived a life of unrelieved monotony. If Kjartan didn't do something about it, he risked turning into Bogi in middle age.

He tried not to let these thoughts show in his face, reminding himself that he was much better-looking and more interesting than the man with the weak, sloping shoulders sitting in front of him. Not that this was anything to boast about.

Bogi droned on: 'It's not a problem I can do anything about. It's all in the past. I don't know why I keep brooding about it. I haven't a clue how to deal with my thoughts. You're the expert – what would you have advised me to do if I'd come to you when I was young? What advice do you give your other clients? I'm sure lots of the kids you see are facing the same issues.'

'I'm not discussing my other clients with you, Bogi. Any more than I'd discuss your problems with them.' Kjartan looked up from his notes. 'And I don't know where you get your information from about who else I see.'

Bogi's head jerked back. Perhaps Kjartan had spoken too harshly.

'I'm just going by the people I see in the waiting room. They're usually kids.'

Kjartan nodded. 'Anyway, going back to you. Perhaps your obsession with the past is a smokescreen. Perhaps the problem doesn't really lie in the past at all but now, today. By constantly dwelling on what happened then, you're avoiding dealing with the issues confronting you now. Why don't you run through the things that are bothering you at the moment, for a change? You know how it helps to put your feelings into words. If you face up to what's going on in your life now, perhaps the past won't loom as large in your thoughts.'

Bogi had been seeing him for eight months; Mördur for two years. Neither seemed to be making any progress. They were constantly ruminating on the same problems and Kjartan had begun to suspect that they only came to see him out of loneliness. They had few friends, were rarely invited out to dinner or to parties and when they were, he guessed they had a habit of buttonholing the other guests, who would listen and nod, while desperately seeking a way of extracting themselves from the conversation. It wasn't something he was familiar with himself. The instant he mentioned his job, people were intrigued. Particularly if he mentioned the sort of cases he specialised in. Everyone had a good story to share about bullying.

As Bogi embarked on a monotonous account of what was troubling him, Kjartan pretended to listen while letting his mind drift.

'. . . and I can't get over my frustration with myself for not reacting differently. We might be married today if only I'd told her how much I liked her. Happily married. But of course that's absurd. We were young. We'd probably have broken up like other teenagers. Maybe I should visit her, though?' Bogi looked enquiringly at Kjartan. 'What do you think?'

'It sounds to me as if you're dwelling on the past again. I thought you were going to talk about what's wrong with your life today. Once we've done that, we can discuss whether this visit is a good idea.'

Bogi beamed. But his smile faded a little when Kjartan closed the file and put down his pen on the desk. Funny that the man still hadn't twigged what it meant when that note of finality entered Kjartan's voice. 'I'm afraid our time's up.

ment. You say you're unhappy at work. Why don't you talk to your boss, listen to what he has to say and let him know how you feel? Don't argue with him. It's better to avoid conflict. And next time we can discuss how it went.'

With this advice under his belt, the man said goodbye and left. Hopefully in a better frame of mind than when he had arrived, though Kjartan doubted it. Adults weren't his forte. Their problems were more often than not so ingrained that the kind of psychological plasters he provided would be of limited use. You couldn't wait for them to grow out of it, either, as they'd already been moulded by life and rarely managed to change much.

Since his next client hadn't yet arrived, Kjartan turned to his computer, though he usually left this until after his final appointment of the day. He made it a rule to deal with all his e-mails before leaving the office, as a way of ensuring that he didn't take his work home with him. And since he invariably booked more appointments than he ought to, this meant he usually got home late. Too late to have a proper life. That needed changing. He could make a start by taking on fewer new clients. Looking at his diary, Kjartan saw that his next appointment was Davíd Ævarsson. The boy was struggling with cripplingly low self-esteem as a result of chronic bullying and Kjartan had been seeing him for almost a year, with little sign of improvement. Unlike Bogi and Mördur, though, the boy was an interesting subject.

But not as interesting as the message waiting in his inbox.

It was from Freyja Styrmisdóttir, a fellow psychologist he remembered clearly from their university days. He'd hit on her once when he was drunk at a student party but she hadn't so much as looked at him, just headed out into the night with somebody else. After reading her e-mail, he looked her up online. To his disappointment, she shared her landline with a man called Baldur Fransson, but Kjartan cheered up again when he saw that this Baldur didn't have a mobile registered to his name. Perhaps he was her son? The address was in a rather downmarket area too, which would make sense if she was a single mother. Perhaps she would be less picky now than she had been in the old days. Smiling, he replied to her message, saying he would be happy to meet up. He suggested a bar that was neither aggressively trendy nor mentioned in the tourist guides, where they should be able to chat in relative peace. By way of underlining his qualifications, he added that he was the Icelandic expert on bullying, to make sure she wouldn't back out.

Kjartan pressed 'Send' just as his next client entered: Davíd, a teenage boy with the hunched shoulders and drooping head of someone who felt he hardly had any right to walk on God's green earth. Prepared to reveal every detail of his miserable existence to a sympathetic ear. As always, Kjartan felt a rush of sympathy for the boy and wondered how his tormentor was feeling at that moment. He couldn't help hoping that he was having the day from hell.

Chapter 14

It wasn't even seven in the evening but there wasn't the faintest gleam of light; the sky was uniformly opaque. In the unrelieved darkness, the large garden seemed desolate. The outdoor lights they'd installed when they moved in had stopped working, just like they did every winter. 'Sealant's letting in water,' was the electrician's verdict every year when he came out to fix them – only for the lights to fail again the next time it snowed. Not that it mattered, since the garden's only function, once the nights started drawing in, was to provide a toilet for the dog. Egill peered at what he could see of the wide lawn and the tiled terrace his parents had put in at the same time as the outdoor lighting. The terrace didn't go with the house; it looked like it had been stolen from a beach hotel and plonked down in the middle of an Icelandic suburb. The fact became even more glaringly obvious once autumn arrived, though Egill's parents didn't see it that way. In an attempt to make better use of it, they'd added a couple of patio heaters, still with their price tags on. But no one wanted to sit out there with freezing feet and a scorching head.

Egill edged past the smart garden furniture shrouded in the specially designed covers that he had put on in the autumn – not out of choice but because he'd been ordered to. He hadn't got any thanks either. And if one of the covers came loose and blew away in a gale, he knew who would get the blame. Personally, he couldn't give a shit about the furniture. It wasn't like his parents ever invited him to the parties they held out there in the summer. That privilege was reserved for their swanky friends – if you could call it a privilege. The parties made him cringe: all those tragic forty-year-olds, deluded enough to think they were still young and hip, playing compilation CDs from the year he was born.

'For fuck's sake, get a move on!' Egill yelled at the dog. It was sniffing the bush where it had urinated yesterday, as if convinced that some other dog had invaded its territory. 'Just get on with it and piss, you stupid animal!' The dog didn't even look up. Perhaps he'd have more luck attracting its attention if he called it by its name, but he couldn't bring himself to. It was so lame he was embarrassed to say it aloud. Anyway, he got a kick out of yelling abuse at the fucking loser. If the strong couldn't take out their frustrations on losers, what were they there for?

The dog belonged to his sister, who had left it behind when she'd moved out that autumn. She had swapped their big, posh house for a crappy little student flat where pets weren't allowed. Unlike Egill, she loved the dog, but her love hadn't been as strong as her desire to leave home. He could under-stand that. Of course, he wasn't happy about her going, since this left him to bear the brunt of their parents' moaning, but he'd have done the same in her shoes. They weren't particularly close, never had been – and never would be now. When she did come home, it wasn't to see him, and her visits to the dog were becoming less frequent with every month that passed.

The animal disappeared inside the bush and Egill gave an explosive sigh. The stupid fleabag was so shaggy it was bound to get tangled up in the branches. It wouldn't be the first time.

An empty plastic glass that had caught on a twig – a relic of his parents' last barbecue of the autumn – was knocked loose by the dog and blew away over the hard-packed snow. Unbelievable how much noise an empty plastic glass could make. The irritating rattling would persist until it got caught in the bushes again, which could take days, even weeks, but it didn't cross his mind to go and pick it up. His bedroom window faced onto the street, not the garden. He glanced round at his parents' window with a nasty grin: it was their problem.

He turned back to the garden: his parents' darkened windows were a depressing reminder that he would be alone at home tonight. If it had been the weekend, he couldn't have been happier, but on a weekday there was no chance of inviting a mate to stay over. Like him, all his friends were in deep shit; they had Christmas exams coming up and it was clear to their parents that they'd been slacking this term. 'Fucking stupid dog! Come here or I'll leave you outside all night.'

His dad had really taken his poor performance at school to heart, whereas his mum obviously couldn't give a shit. But then all she cared about was her next teeth-whitening appointment, her exercise class, gossiping with her friends and shopping for clothes. The only times she'd spoken to him in months were when she wanted him to pass her something. She never asked Egill about school, never took any interest in his life. The last question he remembered her asking him was whether her eyeliner was even. He'd answered yes, though it wasn't true. Actually, she *had* shown her face the last time his father had laid into him about getting his act together, nodding in all the right places when she wasn't glued to her phone, messaging her friends. He didn't blame her; his dad's lecture hadn't exactly been earth-shattering, just a boring rant about how his son would end up as a road sweeper or a cleaner if he didn't pull his finger out. Which was ironic, seeing as his father made his money out of selling cleaning services. He reckoned his dad's employees wouldn't be too pleased to hear that he held them up as examples of wasted lives.

Not that Egill was about to tell them. He appreciated his family's comfortable financial situation, and any dissatisfaction or resignations among the staff risked putting a spanner in the works. Anyway he only saw one employee regularly, the woman who cleaned their house, but she spoke no Icelandic and it wasn't like he had anything to say to her. Pointing was enough: at the sticky Coke spillage in the sitting room where he'd overfilled his glass, at the dirty clothes heaped on the floor of the shower room, the packaging from the latest computer game littering the TV room, the pool of piss from when he couldn't be arsed to take the dog out, and so on.

Fucking animal. He couldn't see any sign of it. There was no movement from the bush, so it must have either crawled along the flowerbed to a new spot or fallen asleep out there. Unless it had dropped dead. Jesus wept.

Egill would have to fetch it. He should have let it piss indoors. The cleaner was coming tomorrow so it wouldn't have mattered. And his parents wouldn't have known. They never spoke to the cleaner either, just let her in and locked the door after her. According to his mum, if you were too nice to the home help, they started taking advantage.

Egill hesitated momentarily before stepping off the snow-free, underheated terrace in his slippers. It had been drummed into him that he had to wear outdoor shoes in the garden; an unbreakable rule.

But there was no one home to object, so, a smirk on his face, Egill walked out onto the snowy lawn, his open-toed indoor sandals slipping on the frozen surface. He picked his way gingerly over to the bush and shook it hard, but the dog didn't come running out and there was no bark from among the tangle of branches. For all he knew it could still be in there, though, as it was too dark to see anything much. There were no lights on in the neighbouring gardens either.

Although Egill wasn't particularly afraid of the dark, he had no desire to linger out there so he shook the bush harder in the hope of flushing the dog out. Nothing happened. He moved along the hedge, shaking that as well. He had to find the bloody animal, despite his threats of leaving it out there all night. After all, the dog's company was better than nothing. Although he did have the internet. He quickened his pace, longing to get back to the computer and his mates. They were supposed to be studying but he knew they'd be online. He himself was always telling his parents that he needed his computer to do his homework.

'I'm writing an essay. I'm going through slides. I'm reading the news because I've got to find something to talk about tomorrow. The Danish teacher said the best way to learn the language was to read Danish websites.' His parents would swallow any old lies.

One of his feet broke through the frozen surface into the soft snow beneath. It was deep enough to wet his sock up to the ankle. Egill whipped out his foot and shot a quick look over his shoulder, half expecting to see his dad standing in the doorway, ready to give him a bollocking. But of course he wasn't there; he was abroad. Egill turned back to shake the last section of hedge. If the dog wasn't there, it could sod off. So what if he was alone in the house? It would serve the stupid animal right if it had to whine at the door all evening. He'd let it in just before he went to bed. That way the dog would be punished for its disobedience and Egill would have its company once all the lights were out.

All of a sudden, Egill had the creeping sensation that he wasn't alone; that someone was watching him. He spun round but all was quiet. The big sheet of glass in the sliding door was as blank as it had been before.

He turned back to the hedge, suppressing an urge to jerk his head round again. It was like the feeling you got on the football field, the nervous habit of constantly checking the stands. And always being disappointed. When he first started training as a six-year-old, his dad used to turn up to every game, proudly watching his son outplay all the other boys. Scoring endless goals as though it was a handball match. But as he grew up, his teammates had gradually caught up with him and his dad had begun to lose interest. When Egill looked over at the stands, he would often be talking on his phone or chatting to the people next to him. Then he started missing games and eventually he stopped coming along altogether. Egill hadn't realised at first. He kept hoping his dad would turn up unexpectedly. By the time it finally sank in that he wasn't going to, it was so long since his dad had last come to watch that he couldn't even remember how he'd played that day. Badly, probably. By then Egill was hanging entirely on the coat-tails of his former glory. He wasn't the best in the team any more; he was barely average. His burning enthusiasm had gone and nowadays he mainly turned up for the company. He didn't want to lose touch with the boys and end up like one of those sad fucking losers who were nothing but a waste of oxygen. Whose sole purpose in life was to provide him and his mates with a punch-bag.

He heard a sharp bark from behind him. Egill whirled round. 'You piece of shit! Where have you been? Eh?' The dog crouched down, whimpering in the snow. 'Get the fuck inside.'

Egill picked his way back across the white lawn. The dog kept up its whimpering as it trailed after him. He assumed it was because the mutt had understood his threat to leave it outside. But even as he was thinking this he was brought up short by the sight of the sliding door. It was open. He was sure he'd closed it behind him. Another unbreakable rule: always close the door to keep in the warmth.

The plastic glass came rattling over the snow and caught against Egill's feet as he stood staring, transfixed, at the open door. In vain he tried to remember if it had been open or closed last time he looked round.

He must be mistaken. He must have left it open.

Egill stepped up onto the terrace, trying to decide what to do. His phone was lying on the sideboard by the door. The sensible thing would probably be to reach inside for it, then wait and listen. If he heard the slightest sound, he could leg it over to the neighbours' house. But if he didn't hear anything, it was probably fine.

He walked over to the open door and stepped inside. Hearing nothing, he breathed easier and reached for the phone, then slid the door shut behind him. Outside the dog whined pathetically. He noticed that he'd received a Snap in his absence and opened it. It was from a user he didn't immediately recognise: *Just13*. That didn't tell him much; he followed too many people to know them all individually and loads of people followed him. Opening the message, he stared at the screen. It was a photo, so dark you couldn't see what it was. Or could you? He zoomed in on a faint differentiation in colour and peered at the grainy image. The resolution was just good enough for him to work out what it showed: the lighter colour in the foreground was one of the covers on the garden furniture. The black area was the garden and the grey shape in the middle was him. Egill looked up quickly from the phone and peered through the glass, down the dark garden. The dog was still whining outside but that was tough: he wasn't going to open the door. Instead, he reached out and locked it.

His phone buzzed. Another Snap, from the same sender. Egill bit his lip nervously but couldn't resist the temptation to open it. He saw himself on the screen, standing in the sitting room. With his back to the camera and the phone in his hand.

He turned, with dreamlike slowness, as the dog began barking hysterically outside.

Chapter 15

The evening shift in the cardiology ward generally grew quieter the later it got. Things were hectic between six and eight when they did the rounds, taking blood pressure and so on, but after that there was time to breathe. The patients dozed and there were fewer acute cases than during the day. You could take the weight off your feet for a bit instead of constantly dashing around. Still, working nights wasn't popular. Time passed more slowly when it was quiet. And although you got paid more per hour, each hour felt longer.

'I'm falling asleep here.' The nursing assistant who was taking the shift with Ásta made a face and got to her feet. 'Do you want a Coke? I'm going to pop down to the vending machine.'

Ásta declined the offer. She didn't like fizzy drinks, though she wasn't going to tell the girl that. It would sound as if she thought she was better than her. Like when she said she didn't drink coffee or eat meat, sugar, dairy products or gluten, or touch alcohol. By the time she got to the last item on the list, most people had her down as a recovering alcoholic. She didn't usually bother to correct this impression when she read it in someone's face. It sounded so lame, like she was in denial. It was different on the rare occasions when someone asked her outright. Then she could put them straight.

She watched the girl disappear in the direction of the lifts, her rubber soles squeaking. Once the doors had swung shut behind her there was no other sound but the low bleeping of monitors. Usually Ásta found it relaxing but this evening it had the same effect on her as the squeaking. Wrapping her arms around herself, she thought about calling Thórey and trying to patch up their quarrel. She was feeling so miserable, and it would be much easier to sort it out over the phone than face to face. Thórey knew her through and through, too well to believe her lies. But she might be able to fool her over the phone.

Having pulled the mobile from her pocket, she lost her nerve. What could she say? Thórey had been so angry when they parted that she was unlikely to have cooled down yet. She rarely lost her temper but when she did, it took her ages to get over it. The last thing Ásta needed right now was another row – more harsh words about lying and betraying people's trust. Thórey was the cleverest person she knew, a fact that was to Ásta's disadvantage right now. Thórey had immediately guessed that the police's interest in them wasn't simply due to the phone turning up at their house. That detective, Huldar, had rung her at work shortly after he and his colleagues had left Ásta. When Thórey came home, she had wanted to know why most of their questions had been about Ásta rather than the phone. Ásta had given evasive answers. Telling the truth was out of the question. It was too late for that.

No, she wouldn't call yet. The perfect moment would be after Thórey had put the girls to bed and was sitting alone in front of some crap on TV. Give her time to start missing her. Thórey would be a softer touch then and more likely to believe her explanations. Ásta shoved the phone back in her pocket.

The bleeping was still coming from all sides. There were thirty-four beds on the ward and every one of them was occupied. Ásta was far from being alone. In addition to her, there were seven registered nurses and five nursing assistants on the evening shift. Yet she felt jittery. The fact that she knew why didn't help. If anything, it made it worse. She tried to reassure herself that she wasn't in any danger, but she couldn't tear her gaze from the doors at the end of the corridor or shake off the fear that sooner or later someone would come through them with one aim in mind: to take her life. Complete rubbish, surely? But the girl at the cinema would probably have dismissed the idea too and look what had happened to her.

Ásta was still standing rooted to the spot when the doors at the end of the corridor swung open. Her heart lurched and she gasped, then breathed out in relief when she saw that it was one of the other nurses, her arms full of disposable kidney dishes. They'd only discovered that they'd run out because a patient kept having to spit. He'd probably started that this morning, which would explain why all the dishes in the cupboard had been used up.

'This should do for now.' The woman handed Ásta the stack. 'Would you mind putting them away? I'm going to check the vital signs of the patient in room seven and take the temperature of the woman in room three. If she's still running a fever I'll have to call the doctor on duty.'

Ásta took the trays from her, grateful for a task that excused her from having to tend to the patients. She wasn't in any fit state to face them this evening.

The doors to the ward opened again and the nursing assistant waltzed in carrying a can of Coke. Two nurses emerged from another room and suddenly the ward didn't feel so deserted any more. Ásta immediately felt better. If she concentrated on the task at hand she might even manage to stop dwelling on the nightmarish dilemma she was in. She went into the storeroom and arranged the dishes on the shelf with exaggerated care. Then she returned to the nurses' station and waited for the time to pass.

The other nurse reappeared, sat down and jotted something on the notes belonging to the man in room seven. She exchanged a few words with Ásta as she did so, appearing not to notice when Ásta barely responded: '. . . prepare to move him to Oncology tomorrow morning. Did they mention that during the handover?'

'What?' Ásta tried in vain to remember what the last shift had told her.

The other woman looked up from the notes. 'Did they say anything about moving the man to Oncology? It says in his notes that he's not eligible for a bypass. He's in too bad a state, so there's no point putting him through it. According to this, he hasn't responded to radiotherapy or chemo. He's on his way to palliative care, so he shouldn't be taking up one of our beds. Is he going to Oncology or to one of the nursing homes?'

'I don't think they discussed it.' It was perfectly possible that they'd gone over it in minute detail without Ásta taking in a single word. She had been relying on the ward sister in charge of the shift to know what was happening, but the woman had gone home earlier with an upset stomach. The nurse who had stepped in for her was now sitting in front of Ásta, waiting for answers. 'No. They didn't mention it.'

'Strange.' The woman raised her eyebrows, then bent over the notes again. 'Poor man.'

'Yes,' Ásta said automatically. She reached for a glass of water and took a sip in the hope that it would revive her.

'Have you spoken to him much?'

'No. Hardly at all.'

'Neither have I. After all these years I still find it hard to talk to the ones who've been given a death sentence. Like him, and that man last week. Everything you say sounds so inadequate somehow.' The woman closed the patient's file and put it back in its place. 'I just hope that when my time comes it'll be sudden. Alive one minute, dead the next.'

'Yes, maybe that would be best.' Ásta's reply was a little hesitant. Not just because this description usually applied to those who died prematurely but because she herself was no longer sure she wanted to go that way. Now that she was afraid for her life, old age with all its ailments, hospital stays and lingering death appeared in a different light. She didn't know if the patient in question would agree with her, though, and she wasn't about to ask him. Perhaps he'd have chosen to go several days ago when he'd had a heart attack right in front of her. But she doubted it. And even if he had, she'd still have reacted by giving him CPR. Her job was to heal people, to nurse them; not to make decisions about who should live and who should die.

But somewhere in Reykjavík there was a man prepared to do exactly that. He had already killed one person, a teenage girl, and he hadn't finished yet. Ásta realised she dreaded finishing her shift. Dreaded walking alone through the empty hospital corridors, crossing the dark car park. She probably wasn't the only woman feeling jumpy tonight, given the endlessly repeated news reports about the murder, which kept hammering home the point that the police still hadn't made any arrests. Unlike most people, though, she had a genuine reason to be afraid.

Chapter 16

Another morning progress meeting passed with no mention of the bullying angle. Stella was still the sweet, popular kid who'd never hurt a fly. All that distinguished her from your average Disney princess was the fact that her mother was still alive. A number of other ideas were kicked around, including the possibility that the killer might be a geek, based on the fact that he used a *Star Wars* mask. When this theory gained little traction, the person who came up with it added defensively that anyone else would have opted for a clown mask since killer clowns were in fashion.

In the absence of any solid leads, the rest of the meeting was spent going over who had already been eliminated from the inquiry, including close family members, boyfriend and friends. They either had watertight alibis or their physical build didn't match that of the attacker. The list of people who'd bought cinema tickets had also been weeded out considerably, a process that had taken an inordinate amount of time and only resulted in a tiny handful of possible suspects. The individuals in question now needed to be looked at more closely.

Huldar had debated whether to put up his hand and mention Freyja's point about bullying, but decided it wouldn't be appropriate. Stella's behaviour towards a classmate was unlikely to have any bearing on her murder. Afterwards, he regretted his decision to keep quiet. There was no logical explanation for the brutal attack on the girl, so why not at least consider the possibility that it might have been motivated by revenge? It was too late now, though. He could hardly stand up in the middle of the office and start presenting this theory to his colleagues, who were all immersed in the tasks they'd been allotted. All except him and Gudlaugur, that is.

He had sat patiently on the hard plastic chair, waiting to hear their names called out, assuming some deadly boring assignment would be dumped on them last of all. But Erla had finished without so much as mentioning them. He had gone up at the end of the meeting and pointed out her over-sight. Instead of slapping her forehead and saying it had slipped her mind, Erla had given him a look of pure malice and said she wanted them on hand to deal with any other matters that came up. The country's criminals weren't simply going to down tools so the police could focus on the murder inquiry.

As Huldar stormed back to his desk, it occurred to him to go over Erla's head and complain to her line manager. But even through the red mist of rage, he realised this was unlikely to achieve anything. For one thing, her comment about other crimes was, on the face of it, true. For another, he hated telling tales.

'This is a complete joke.' Gudlaugur was no happier than Huldar. 'Are we seriously expected to sit here, waiting for someone to break into a car and steal a shopping bag or something?' He glanced over at the neighbouring desk where their colleagues were poring over CCTV footage from the area around the convenience store. In Huldar's opinion, their task was as futile as his and Gudlaugur's thumb-twiddling, since the nearest cameras were several streets away from the site where Stella's body had been found and few, if any, pointed at the traffic. But no stone unturned and all that.

'If they really believe there's a second victim out there, this is a total disgrace.' Gudlaugur scratched his head in exasperation, causing his usually sleek blond hair to stand up on end.

'You think the two of us could solve it if we got the chance?' Huldar grinned at Gudlaugur, though he wasn't amused. He was annoyed that Gudlaugur was still claiming not to know where Ásta had recognised him from. Whenever he raised the subject, the young man looked shifty and, much as Huldar longed to shake the truth out of him, he decided to let it lie. For now.

'No. Not necessarily. But we could at least do our bit.' Red spots of anger had appeared on Gudlaugur's cheeks, but now the colour deepened and spread down his neck.

Jóel, who was, in Huldar's opinion, the most obnoxious member of the team by a long chalk, had emerged from Erla's office and was heading their way. He was holding a folded piece of paper and wore the beatific expression of a man who has just been ordered to deliver bad news to his worst enemy. He and Huldar had gone through police training college together, started work at the same time and more or less kept pace with each other through their careers. They had failed to hit it off from day one and their relationship had only deteriorated since.

A couple of years ago, when Huldar was promoted to head of the department, Jóel must have felt like wearing a black armband to work. When, shortly afterwards, he was demoted, Jóel's schadenfreude had known no bounds.

'Hey, you guys! Lovebirds!' Jóel spoke deliberately loudly so the rest of the office could hear. 'I've got a job for you from Erla.' Her choice of messenger wasn't accidental: she was well aware that they loathed each other. God, Huldar was going to make her pay for this.

He ignored the jibe. Reacting would only play into Jóel's hands. Gudlaugur's jaw tensed and he suddenly became very interested in his computer screen.

'Either shut up or spit it out.' With an effort, Huldar kept his voice level. 'Or are you having trouble reading what it says? Why don't you just hand it over?'

'Ha ha,' said Jóel dryly. Unfolding the note, he read out the morning's task in ringing tones. 'A cleaner called to say she couldn't get into the house where she's supposed to be working this morning. The family dog has been locked out and she's afraid something's wrong.' Jóel's face split in a broad grin, exposing the crooked teeth he usually tried to hide. Huldar itched to rearrange them with his fists but controlled himself and allowed Jóel to relish the moment. 'Oh, yes, and she doesn't speak much Icelandic. Erla wanted to know if you have enough data allowance left to talk to her via Google Translate?' He placed the note on Huldar's desk. 'The rest of the information's there.' Unable to resist the temptation to linger a moment, Jóel drew a long breath, as if savouring the demeaning nature of the task. Then he smirked again. 'Obviously, this is urgent, so don't let us delay you.' As he sauntered away, Huldar gripped the arms of his chair until it hurt.

'Jóel's a total prick. Don't let him get to you. I'm pissed off enough for both of us.' Huldar drove into the residential street where – he hoped – the cleaner would be waiting for them. He thought that's what they'd arranged when he spoke to her on the phone, but communication had been tricky. 'Don't let it ruin your day. Erla'll stop messing about sooner or later and give us a proper job.'

Gudlaugur was staring out of the window. The thin-skinned type, he'd taken the whole thing personally. Perhaps he was considering asking for a transfer, either to another department or a different desk. Preferably as far away from Huldar as possible. It was understandable; the boy was paying the price for being associated with him. 'If you ask to be moved, you'll be left in peace by that arsehole, and the rest of them too. You'll get better assignments as well. I wouldn't blame you.' Huldar kept his gaze fixed on the road ahead, resisting the urge to check Gudlaugur's reaction. The last thing he wanted was for the young man to move; he'd miss him. Despite his relative inexperience and his shyness, he could be perceptive when it mattered. And it was uncertain who, if anyone, would take his place. Huldar was glad he hadn't started grilling him about Ásta again this morning – that could have been the final straw.

Gudlaugur didn't reply, either because he wanted to think about it or because their destination had appeared ahead. 'There.' He pointed to a large, concrete, single-storey house on what was evidently the more exclusive side of the road. It backed onto the lava-field. The place had clearly been done up: freestanding concrete walls had been added here and there, with an overall eye to creating an angular aesthetic; the roof trim had been removed, and the typically Icelandic corrugated-iron cladding had been replaced with standing-seam copper panels. The front garden had been paved over too. The same applied to most of the neighbouring houses, though on the other side of the road the occasional building had been allowed to retain its original features and was even painted in something other than white or shades of grey.

'Reckon that's her?' Gudlaugur gestured towards a skinny woman hanging around by the front door. She wore a brightly coloured anorak made of some thin material and looked as though she was cold, though not as cold as the small dog huddled at her feet. She wasn't wearing a hat and her thin, shoulder-length hair kept blowing over her face. No sooner had she pushed it back, briefly revealing her hollow-cheeked features, than the wind whipped it over her eyes again. Huldar parked in the drive beside a small, rather beaten-up car. He diplomatically averted his eyes when he saw that the MOT was badly out of date.

The path to the front door was lined with low posts containing outdoor lights that were currently switched off. The posts were covered in a layer of rust so uniform that they must have been designed that way. Huldar wondered casually how much the occupants had had to fork out for the rust effect. The property certainly gave the impression of being home to people with seriously deep pockets.

They introduced themselves to the woman and shook her bony hand. She told them her name in a Slavonic accent, then pointed at the door and gesticulated to indicate that it was locked. 'Not home.'

Huldar just stopped himself raising his eyes heavenwards. How long had Erla spent sifting through the notifications before she hit on this one?

The woman now pointed to the dog at her feet, then waved towards the corner of the house. 'Dog. Outside. Cold.'

'Yes, right.' Huldar searched for simple words that she could understand; for some way of getting it across to the woman that these things happened but they weren't a police matter. Stray dogs were the responsibility of the local council. But before he could say another word, the woman bent down, scooped up the dog and showed them its front paws.

'Blood. Much blood.' They bent to examine the reddish-brown stains on the dog's hairy legs. 'Blood. Much a lot blood.' She waved at the corner of the house again.

Huldar and Gudlaugur exchanged glances. What would this woman consider a lot of blood? More than could be found in the veins of a small dog? There was no visible wound on the mutt but its shaggy coat could be hiding it. 'Can you show us?' Now it was Huldar's turn to point to the corner of the house. The woman nodded and put the dog down. They had only taken a few steps when Huldar flung out an arm to stop them, turned to the woman and asked: 'Can we get round the other side?' He waved at the opposite corner of the house. She nodded. Before they went back, Huldar drew Gudlaugur's attention to a track in the snow, half a metre wide, which ran from the house across the garden in the direction of the road. It was too irregular to have been made by a sledge and there were no marks left by runners. Here and there they could see pink stains on the snow. It wasn't unlike the pictures they'd been shown of the scene behind the cinema where Stella had been dragged into the car park by her killer. Chances were that it was a coincidence. Nevertheless, Huldar didn't want to trample all over what could turn out to be the scene of a far more serious incident than a locked-out dog.

Gudlaugur had taken out his phone and was tapping it

frantically as they walked round the back of the house. 'According to já.is, a family of four lives here.' He went on tapping. 'The father's a CEO, the kids are still in full-time education and the mother has no job title. Want me to call them?'

'No. Hang on.' Huldar could have kicked himself for failing to ask Gudlaugur to look up this information on the way. It would have been normal procedure. But his anger at Erla and Jóel had clouded his thoughts. No doubt they had covered this sort of thing on his anger-management course but, ironically, he had been too angry at being forced to attend to take much in.

Behind the house was a much bigger garden with a large terrace, partly fenced in by low concrete walls. The garden furniture had been packed away for the winter, its lines softened by the covers, rendering it out of synch with the general rigidly geometric effect. Also out of place was the dark trail that led from the big glass sliding door, across the terrace and down onto the snowy lawn, before vanishing round the corner of the house on the opposite side. 'Shit.' Huldar held up a hand to stop Gudlaugur and the woman.

'Much blood.' The woman shook her head sadly. 'Much blood.'

Although the terrace had underfloor heating that kept it free of snow, the red streak was no less conspicuous on the pale stone tiles. Here and there they could see dark paw prints, suggesting that the dog had been investigating the scene. From where Huldar was standing, it looked as if the red trail had been licked in a couple of places. As if to confirm this, the little dog suddenly darted through their legs up onto the terrace and began lapping at the broad streak.

'No!' Huldar bellowed, but the dog didn't even look round, so he had no choice but to fetch it. Taking the longest strides he could, he snatched up the animal, which was as light as thistledown, and carefully retraced his steps. There was no longer any question of what this meant. A blood-stained trail. But humans weren't the only creatures that bled. It was just possible that the owner of the house was a hunter.

'What's the husband's number?'

Gudlaugur read it out as Huldar, the dog clamped under one arm, tried it. From the tone of the ringing, it sounded as if the mobile phone was abroad. No one answered. He had no more luck when Gudlaugur supplied him with the numbers of the wife, daughter and son. The son's phone immediately switched to a recorded message saying that it was either turned off or not reachable at the moment.

Gudlaugur tapped Huldar's shoulder. 'What's that in the window?'

Huldar glanced up from his phone and peered at the large sheet of glass beside the sliding door. The low sun was shining directly on the window, making it hard to see what Gudlaugur was referring to. Then he spotted it. There was a piece of white paper stuck to the inside. He turned to the woman while trying to keep hold of the wriggling dog.

'Are you sure you don't have a key?' he asked roughly and the woman shook her head, frightened. As if she expected to be arrested for having either forgotten or lost it, or simply not being trusted with one in the first place.

'Take the dog.' Huldar handed the shivering animal to Gudlaugur, in whose arms it immediately seemed happier. Then he went over to the window in as few strides as possible, stepping over the bloody trail on the way.

Behind him Gudlaugur called: 'Does it say anything?'

'Yes. Well, the writing's on the other side, but I can see it.' Huldar shifted to prevent his shadow falling on the paper. As he did so, a shaft of sunlight illuminated it enough for him to see right through.

Printed in a giant font on the paper was a number:

3

He took out his phone again and dialled Erla. This wasn't the call he had envisaged making when they set off. Grim though the news was, he couldn't help gloating a little at the trick fate had played on his boss.

Chapter 17

He'd forgotten to bring a torch so he had to use the one on his phone. Although it didn't shed much light, he could see, with a sickening sense of shock, that the boy wasn't quite dead. His skin was grey, like an old fish, and he stank to match. He was lying where he had landed, but then he was in no condition to move. At least one of his arms looked broken, his head was badly battered, one of his ankles was bust and so was his knee.

Yet, in spite of all this, the boy wasn't dead. It had been different with the girl. She'd given up the ghost more or less immediately, without causing him any trouble, her manner of dying so very different from the way she had lived.

He knew he should put the boy out of his misery. One powerful blow to the head ought to do it, with something heavy like that fire extinguisher. But there was nothing suitable to hand. Maybe it was just as well, because at least it meant he wouldn't have to get any closer to the boy and that nauseating smell which seemed to be some sort of harbinger of death. He could barely cope with it from a couple of metres away; God knows what it would be like if he was standing right over the body.

The boy was lying on his back, staring upwards. Whether he could actually see or not was unclear, but there was no way he would be capable of finishing him off with a blow to the face. Not after seeing what it had done to the girl. A blow to the back of the head, now he reckoned he could manage that, but it would mean having to roll the kid over, which was unthinkable.

It had to end soon. The kid couldn't survive much longer in that state, on nothing but air. If he couldn't bring himself to smother the boy or pull his clothes off and drag him outside into the freezing cold, it could take him three days to die. Or maybe a bit less, seeing how much blood he'd lost. His clothes were covered in stains, long since dried and no longer red.

His senses screamed at him to get out of there. It wasn't just his nose and eyes; the sporadic rattling from the boy's throat tortured his ears as well. He couldn't face touching anything in there and there was a horrible, iron taste on his tongue, which made him long to spit. But that was a complete no-no; he mustn't risk leaving any biological traces behind.

Another low rattle came from the boy on the floor. It was such a pitiful sound, like the murmurs of a newborn baby. Totally incongruous in this grim setting. For an instant he regretted the whole thing, asked himself why the hell he was in this position. Then he reminded himself fiercely that the boy had deserved it. But somewhere at the back of his mind, doubt sprang up: was it really true? He pushed the thought away: it would be utterly futile now to start thinking it had all been a mistake. A terrible, fatal mistake. It could never be undone. So there was nothing for it but to make the best of the situation. For now, that meant waiting. Which wasn't that complicated, and demanded nothing of him.

The boy emitted another rattle and his head rolled slowly sideways. His eyes closed briefly, then opened again, staring straight ahead. The stare was horribly uncomfortable. Thank

God he'd brought the mask along as a precaution, in the unlikely event that the boy might be rescued. Though even if he could see, there was no guarantee that the image before his yellow eyes would be transmitted to his brain. Especially given the trauma he'd received to the head.

He couldn't have long left. He just couldn't.

The boy's dry, cracked lips moved. What the hell? He'd come here to fetch his body, not to look him in the eye or hear him talk. The fact he could force out a word couldn't be a good sign.

What emerged was a weak puff of air, though you could make out sounds, different sounds, like words. Was it possible?

There was only one thing for it: he would have to edge closer. What was the boy trying to say? Was he begging for mercy? For help? If so, he obviously had no memory of what had happened before he lost consciousness or he would have known that he could expect no mercy.

The stink wasn't that much worse close up. The boy seemed to sense the presence of another person. Staring blankly at the black mask, he went on whispering. But he was struggling to hold his yellow eyes open; the lids kept drooping, one of them swollen and purple.

Thinking he could distinguish words, he bent closer, turning his ear towards the boy's face. These might be the kid's last words. Perhaps they would matter to his family.

Or maybe the boy just wanted to beg for forgiveness. Hopefully he'd mean it this time. But it was too late.

The boy raised his eyelids again, slowly, and kept struggling to speak. In an effort to hear, he bent closer until his mask almost touched the grey skin of the boy's face. There were no breathing holes in the mask but even so he sensed it when the boy opened his mouth and began his breathy whispering again. The stench was like nothing on earth; the stench of mortality. But the voice faded before it could say anything and now the boy seemed to have come to the end of his strength.

Then his eyes slid sideways, closed and didn't move again. Straightening up, he looked down at him dispassionately. The boy's chest was moving up and down in spasmodic jerks.

Better leave him to it. Things were going the right way. He couldn't have long left.

Once he'd made up his mind, there was nothing to do but get out of there and lock the door. He'd come back later. Clearly, he wouldn't have to worry about the boy calling for help or managing to attract any attention. He would be left to die in peace.

The moment he was outside he tore off the mask and took great shuddering breaths, drinking in the clean, crisp night air. It was like ice-cold water when you were parched with thirst.

Then, after warily scanning his surroundings, he headed back to the car.

Chapter 18

The quiet residential street had been transformed. Police officers, forensic technicians and the pathology team had congregated at the house, while dogs from the K9 unit had been brought in to search for the occupants' son, who'd turned out to be missing. They drew a blank.

The police made countless phone calls. Some were a waste of time, others led to further calls, and a couple resulted in information that could be used to piece together what had happened. They had a time frame now. Or so Huldar gathered from the comments he overheard. The moment Erla had turned up with her retinue, she had sent Gudlaugur and Huldar packing, regardless of the fact they'd been first on the scene. Now she was back at the station too but in no mood to praise them. She had gone straight into her office and shut the door, without so much as a glance in their direction.

Erla was on the phone in her glass cage when Huldar knocked. She pretended not to hear but he let himself in anyway. She seemed to be talking to either the father or the mother of the missing boy. When he tried to catch her eye, she avoided his gaze. Finally she ended the call by asking them to let her know when their flight was due in. She hung up and stared at the phone for a moment, perhaps trying to imagine what it was like to be stuck in another country while your child was missing, feared dead. Then her expression hardened and she looked up at Huldar. 'What do you want?'

'I thought I'd look in and see what jobs you have for me and Gudlaugur. We're fed up with having bugger-all to do.' This was no lie. They'd been kicking their heels ever since they'd got back to the station. 'As far as I can see, there's more than enough to go around. More than we can handle. So why aren't any tasks coming our way? We know the background. We've done the least overtime of anyone, so it makes sense to use us. Or do I have to remind you that we're good detectives?'

Erla's mouth twisted in a scowl. She had thrown him a fleeting glance when he started talking, then returned her gaze to the computer screen. Huldar didn't doubt for a minute that there were any number of e-mails, reports and forms awaiting her attention as head of department, as well as all sorts of tasks linked to the current investigation. But it didn't take a genius to see that she wasn't actually reading them. Her eyes weren't moving, her jaw was clenched and her cheekbones were unusually sharp. 'I haven't got round to it yet. You'll just have to wait, like everyone else.'

This lame reply only made Huldar angrier. 'Correction. Nobody else is waiting.' He shifted to the front of the chair, which he had sat down on without waiting for an invitation, and reached out to turn the monitor away so Erla couldn't pretend to be looking at it. 'If we don't get a job to do in the next fifteen minutes, I'm going home. This is a joke. You only sent us out this morning because you assumed it was a time-waster.' Huldar's voice was cold, his face unsmiling.

Erla cleared her throat. 'That was a mistake. Everyone makes mistakes.' She said nothing for a moment, just pulled her screen back to face her. 'A lucky mistake as it turns out. If younger, less experienced uniforms had been sent to the scene, they might have missed the signs. It's started snowing and the evidence would soon have been covered up. Outdoors, anyway.' Inside they had found an awful lot of blood, from what Huldar had gathered, and, according to the pathologist, the person who had lost it must have been very seriously wounded. There was a large pool of it on the kitchen floor and splashes halfway up the walls. So far, they'd been unable to ascertain what kind of weapon had been used. If it was still in the house, it must have been cleaned and replaced. But if the killer wasn't a complete idiot, he'd have taken the weapon away with him.

'You had no way of knowing what would come out of it. You just wanted to waste our time.' Huldar stood up.

As he reached for the handle, the door opened to admit Erla's boss. He was looking uncharacteristically pleased for someone who habitually walked around wearing the morose expression of a man who had last smiled when he'd blown out all the candles in one go on his sixth birthday cake. He was the kind of old-school bastard who gets his way by throwing his weight around, a method that had got him to where he was now. And he couldn't care less how many people he trampled over on the way, so long as it smoothed his path to his goal. But he wasn't rising any higher; he was due to be pensioned off soon. Given his massive unpopularity, his leaving party was sure to be packed out with colleagues keen to toast his retirement.

Acting as if Huldar wasn't there, he addressed Erla. 'Good work this morning.'

Erla's forehead puckered in a puzzled frown. It wasn't every day that her boss or any of the other senior officers praised her. 'Sorry?'

As usual her boss ploughed on without listening. 'Plenty of people would have overlooked that phone call from the cleaner. You're pretty sharp.'

Erla was silent. She may have wanted to say something but as Huldar wasn't budging it was hard for her to agree and she was unlikely to tell her boss the truth.

'Anyway, my time's nearly up and I've been asked to nominate possible successors. I have to say I'm pretty underwhelmed by most of the internal candidates but I like your style. Keep it up and I'll put your name at the top of the list. I just wanted you to know.' His gaze fell on Huldar and the familiar morose look descended again. 'The only problem will be finding someone to fill your boots. We're not exactly drowning in talent.'

Huldar beamed at him. The jibe didn't hurt. Didn't even smart. The last thing he wanted was to do Erla's job again.

The man turned back to Erla. 'Remember – I've got my eye on you. We're under a lot of pressure to get a quick solve. The sooner you find the culprit, the better. The longer it drags on . . .' He left the sentence unfinished. 'Well, best of luck.'

After he had gone, there was dead silence. Huldar thought it only natural that Erla should be the first to speak about what had just happened but she merely stared at her wonky screen as if he wasn't there.

'Right.' Huldar gave her a chance to react but she didn't; didn't even mutter a grudging thanks for holding his tongue while she received praise she didn't deserve. He shook his head. 'OK. Like I said, I'm off home.' He stalked over to the door, desperate now to get out of there, away from her, into the fresh air. Desperate for a cigarette that he would suck down in four deep drags.

'Huldar.' This came just as his hand grasped the door-handle. He didn't turn, doubting he would be able to hide his contempt if all she offered him was an insincere apology. 'I'll find something for you two to do,' she continued. 'Come back with Gudlaugur in ten minutes.'

He walked out without a backward glance or a word of thanks. He shouldn't have to thank her. It was her job to keep him supplied with work.

The coffee tasted much better now that Huldar had a purpose again. The assignment they'd been given wasn't exactly thrilling but at least it was connected to the inquiry and didn't involve pets. Erla had even brought them up to speed on the investigation, so he was no longer burning with questions – questions he couldn't ask his colleagues without risking mockery and the usual crap from those who believed they had the upper hand. There had been a complete turnaround in his fortunes. Now he had a hold over Erla, which meant no one else in the department could touch him. He was going to milk what he could from the current situation. As soon as she started thinking straight she'd realise that Huldar would never report her or correct the misunderstanding, no matter how angry he was. And then they would be back to square one.

'Would you like a tissue?' Gudlaugur drew a small packet from his jacket pocket and handed it to Egill's sister, Ásdís. Huldar admired his thoughtfulness. His own pockets contained cigarettes and lighter, coins, house keys and an empty packet of Ópal liquorice that he hadn't got round to replacing.

Nothing he could offer this young woman. Perhaps this difference between them could be traced to the fact that Gudlaugur had been a boy scout, whereas Huldar had gone in for *glíma* – traditional Icelandic wrestling – as a means of self-defence against his sisters, and built makeshift dens, neither of which had prepared him for the present circumstances.

Ásdís extracted a tissue, dried her tears and blew her nose. Not that it did much good. She'd no sooner put it down than she needed another one. 'Sorry. I didn't think I had any tears left.' She regarded them with swollen red eyes. 'Do I have to stay here? Tonight, I mean?' She lifted up the small dog that was lying in her lap and kissed its rough fur. There were still traces of blood on its paws but she didn't seem to have noticed and they weren't about to draw her attention to them.

'Yes. They think it could help. You see, there's still a chance the blood might not have been your brother's, though we're having trouble tracking him down. If he rings home, we need someone he knows to answer the phone.' Huldar placed his hands on the arms of his leather-upholstered chair. Gudlaugur was sitting in a matching chair beside him. Between them was a small glass table of the kind he'd seen in the pictures of celebrity homes in glossy magazines. He wouldn't be surprised if this three-piece suite hadn't featured as well. These were the kind of furnishings that usually appeared under headings like 'Designer Paradise'. 'It's also just possible that the person who abducted your brother – if he was abducted – might call. In that case it would be better for you to answer than one of us.'

'But what am I supposed to say?' The young woman's red-rimmed eyes widened with fear.

'Just answer the questions he puts to you. And listen to

what he says. It's highly unlikely that anyone will ring, but if they do, there'll be two female officers here to assist you. You've got nothing to be afraid of.'

'How can you say that?' Ásdís's gaze swept round the living room, which showed clear signs of a visit by Forensics. 'My brother wasn't safe here.'

'No. But he was alone. You'll have two police officers with you.' Huldar watched her pull out another tissue to staunch the tears that had started pouring down her cheeks again. 'With any luck your parents will manage to catch a plane this evening and be home by midnight. They'll need you here.' Huldar watched as the dog closed its eyes, content to be in its owner's arms again. It appeared indifferent to the upheaval but hadn't left Ásdís's side for a moment since Huldar and Gudlaugur had arrived. 'Let me stress that it's not certain your brother has been the victim of an attack. There may be another reason for his absence.' The police were also looking into the possibility that it was Egill himself who had beaten someone to a pulp in the kitchen, then removed the body. But there was no need to tell his sister that. No Snaps had been sent from the boy's phone, but then it still hadn't been found and couldn't be traced. If it hadn't been for the message on the sheet of paper in the window, there would have been no reason to connect his case to Stella's.

'Do you think Egill's OK?'

'We don't know. But of course we're all hoping he is,' Huldar lied smoothly. Few, if any, of them believed the boy would be found alive, though of course it wasn't impossible. He turned to the questions they'd been ordered to put to her while waiting for the female officers to arrive. Ásdís had already been interviewed once but she had been too distressed to provide any coherent answers. She had got the news when she came out of a lecture, switched on her phone and found a message to ring the police immediately. Afterwards, they had gone to collect her from the university where she was still standing outside the lecture room, leaning against the wall, rigid with horror.

'Are you close? You and Egill?'

'Yes.' The girl focused on the dog, as if to avoid looking at Huldar and Gudlaugur.

'Was your brother a friend of yours on Snapchat?'

'Er . . . yes, I think so.' She reached for her phone, which was lying on the coffee table, and fiddled with it briefly. 'Yes. He's there.' The implications of this question didn't seem to have struck her.

'You're five years older than him, aren't you?'

'Four and a half.'

'So you don't share the same friends?'

'No.' Ásdís raised her eyes. 'Why would we? He's my little brother. You don't think one of his friends did this, do you?'

Huldar didn't answer. He was the one asking the questions. 'Can you think of anyone who had it in for your brother? Anyone his age he didn't get on with, or an adult, even?'

Ásdís appeared to give this some thought. 'No one I can think of. Of course, I know less about what's going on in his life now I've left home, but before that there was nothing wrong, as far as I know. He's gone around with the same group of friends since he was six. They don't fight much. I'd be surprised if that had changed.'

No one spoke for a few moments as Huldar tried to think of a tactful way of asking whether her brother had ever bullied anyone. The question wasn't on the list he'd been provided with but he felt it wouldn't hurt to ask. Maybe it would be best to get straight to the point. 'Do you know if Egill ever took part in bullying?'

'Bullying?' Ásdís looked perplexed, as if she'd never heard the word before. Perhaps problems of that kind were not part of her world, since in spite of her bloodshot eyes and puffy face, it was clear that this young woman had everything going for her in life. She was clever, pretty, in good shape, and her clothes, phone, bag and the car parked outside were all well beyond the budget of your average university student. Judging by the constant buzzing of her phone, she had plenty of friends too. Her demeanour was that of someone who'd never had to struggle in life. Her phone buzzed yet again, as if to emphasise the fact. Every time it made a noise, her eyes automatically darted to the screen, even when she was in floods of tears.

At first Huldar and Gudlaugur had reacted the same way. Every new alert could be a notification that she'd received a Snap. And every new Snap could be what all those working on the investigation were dreading: a photo or video sent from Egill's phone. Now that she'd confirmed she was on his list of contacts, they automatically glanced at the phone again. They hadn't seen any reason to take it from her yet. In the unlikely event that Egill rang her in tears, she'd need it to hand. But they'd confiscated the phones of Egill's closest friends so they could take screenshots of any Snaps that might be sent. The pressure on the police switchboard had been greatly reduced since they'd returned the phones to Stella's friends, but it would soon be jammed again by another set of teenagers begging to have their phones back, and their grateful parents calling to beg the police to keep them.

'Yes, bullying. Has your brother been mixed up in anything like that?'

'Er . . . no. Not that I'm aware of. I find it very . . . unlikely.' Her hesitation told a different story. 'Egill's been in trouble at school but that was for slacking. He's bright but lazy. If he's not at football practice, he's on his computer. School's always bottom of his list. But as far as I know, the complaints have been to do with his laziness.'

Huldar's phone rang. 'Excuse me.' Seeing that it was Erla, he waved at Gudlaugur to take over the interview.

Erla didn't beat about the bush. 'Take the girl's phone. Now. She mustn't see what's just come through.'

It seemed no phone call could be expected from Egill after all. Not today, not this evening or ever again. Huldar did as he was told.

Chapter 19

The last video ended. Huldar looked away from the screen to avoid seeing the frozen final frame. It wasn't only the consequences of violence he abhorred; witnessing the deed itself was just as horrific.

The phones taken from Egill's friends had all received the same series of messages, sent at short intervals on Snapchat. Some showed several versions of the same scene: Egill begging for forgiveness for some unspecified transgression. Exactly like Stella. But the police still hadn't managed to find any links between the two teenagers. They were born in different years, lived in different areas, weren't related, weren't friends on social media and had never met, as far as could be established. So the thing they were apologising for could hardly be something they had plotted together. Nevertheless, Egill bore an uncanny resemblance to Stella: the tears, snot, despair and incomprehension had stripped their faces of their maturity, making them appear much younger, like the children they had been until so recently.

The videos were filmed in the kitchen at Egill's house. Before being screened in the meeting room, they had been arranged in chronological order. In the first, Egill was on his knees, clutching a bloody hand to his chest. In later clips he was huddled against the kitchen unit, as if seeking refuge. He kept repeating the word 'Sorry', just like Stella, until in the end, like her, he didn't seem to know what he was saying any more, and the word came out increasingly garbled. Now and then a wooden club appeared in the frame, either jabbing hard at the boy or striking him. Although the weapon was never visible in its entirety, there was no doubt in anyone's mind that it was a baseball bat. But they couldn't get a proper look at the handle to see how the attacker was holding it. In Huldar's opinion, there was little to be gained from watching the sequence since there was nothing to see or hear that could possibly help them find out who had done it.

He found it particularly hard to understand what the last clip was intended to achieve, apart from hardening their resolve to catch the man. It showed Egill's last moments as his head was repeatedly battered with the club. The boy fell to the floor at the first blow and after that Huldar found it almost impossible to watch any more, regardless of all the fights he'd been involved in himself or the countless occasions when he'd had to overpower members of the public in the line of duty. Those tussles had been quite different. They hadn't involved weapons and the violence had ceased as soon as the subject had been subdued. You didn't hit a man when he was down. Let alone a child, an adolescent or anyone else weaker than you.

He couldn't imagine what it must be like for Egill's family and friends to have to watch this. The Snaps had been sent to a long list of people, mostly teenagers, and, according to Erla, there was no sign of the notifications drying up. The police were powerless to stop it: an officer had been given the task of fielding the phone calls, writing down the callers' names and their connection to Egill, offering them trauma counselling, asking them not to talk to the media and not to open any further messages from Egill. In the case of minors, their parents were alerted, with the warning that more Snaps might be sent.

The worst phone call, though, was to Egill's parents, who were still abroad, waiting for their flight home. When the Snaps started arriving, it was a few minutes before it occurred to anyone that the boy's parents might be among his Snapchat contacts. The officer who drew the short straw and called to notify them realised immediately that it was too late. Although it was Egill's father's number he had rung, it might as well have been his mother on the line, so loud were her screams. She had received the videos. It was impossible to establish whether she'd watched them all but the officer advised her husband to snatch her phone away, and in the end he threw it on the floor of the air terminal and stamped on it. While all this was going on, the police officer had been listening at the other end. He was still pale and silent, and could probably have done with a bit of counselling himself.

The police had scoured the area where the phone had popped up on the network but found nothing; apparently it had been switched off and the battery removed as soon as the Snaps had been sent. At the time, it had been located on Smidjuvegur, in a retail park on the way to Kópavogur, the town immediately to the south of Reykjavík. But none of the people working in the nearby businesses had noticed anything untoward and there were no CCTV cameras in the area. The tracker dogs failed to find any trace of Egill either. They just circled round their handlers, hoping to be rewarded with biscuits. The only positive element was that no body had turned up, so they could still cherish the hope, faint as it was, that Egill might be found alive.

'The parents have got a flight.' Erla broke the silence that had descended after they'd watched the videos. No doubt she could read the minds of the assembled detectives, who were all male. The only other female officers in the department were both at Egill's house, keeping his sister company. The powerful odour of competing aftershaves was already getting to Huldar. 'They're due to land just after midnight. I'd like a couple of you to pick them up from the airport. We've spoken to Customs and their luggage will be taken aside as we can't expect them to hang about by the bloody baggage carousel. The staff also offered to collect them from the gate and speed them through the arrivals hall, so whoever volunteers will need to turn up at Leifsstöd well ahead of time in case the plane's early. Any takers?'

The silence grew even more oppressive. Clearly no one was keen to share a car with the distraught couple for the forty-five-minute drive from Keflavík to town. Huldar raised his hand. He'd rather do that than man the phones. 'I'll go.' Beside him Gudlaugur raised his hand as well. Erla nodded distractedly and carried on with the briefing. Huldar and Gudlaugur lowered their hands. Neither had been expecting praise or thanks.

'We'll continue to monitor the phones we've confiscated. If things develop in the same way as in the Stella case, we can expect the phone to turn up after maybe one more Snap. And following that, the body. Until then we're going to have to work round the clock to catch the perpetrator. There's nothing to indicate that he's finished and don't forget that we're still missing number one from his series. The third victim could be just around the corner – or the first, I should say.'

While Huldar was debating whether to stick up his hand again and mention Freyja's theory about a possible link to bullying, Jóel jumped in without bothering to ask permission to speak. 'Where are we supposed to start? There's no common ground between the two victims. No connection.'

Erla narrowed her eyes angrily. She hated being interrupted during these progress meetings, clear evidence that she found them a strain. She'd prepared what she wanted to say and didn't like having her train of thought interrupted. Any discussions could take place afterwards. 'Of course they've both got a bloody connection to the perpetrator. Maybe not through family or friends, but we can be sure this fucker didn't choose his victims at random. If he had, that whole business of forcing them to apologise wouldn't make any sense. We have to work on the basis that they both crossed paths with him at some point and pissed him off big time.'

Jóel wasn't about to give up so easily. Erla's harsh tone obviously rankled with him. 'What if it's a terrorist? A member of IS? In that case their only crime would have been that they were born in this country, so they could easily have been chosen at random.'

'Did we not just watch the same fucking videos?' snarled Erla. 'Did you hear anyone shouting "*Allahu Akhbar*"? Because I didn't. All I heard was "Sorry". So let's not have any more of that bullshit.' She leant forward on the meeting table, surveying the assembled officers, every muscle tense in her lean body. 'Don't you dare fantasise for one second that we're looking for a terrorist. The guy we're after is a sick fucker, who the entire country expects us to arrest within the next twenty-four hours. If anyone else has any crackpot theories, you can bring them to my office. Just don't waste everyone's time by blurting them out here. We can't afford to lose our focus.' She straightened up. 'Is that fucking clear?'

Huldar reflected that it was a good thing he hadn't raised the subject of bullying. All those present nodded meekly, even Jóel, who was squirming in his chair, his face dark red. Huldar, on the other hand, had rarely felt better.

There was complete chaos at Leifsstöd. People were pouring through the double doors into the arrivals hall, but it wasn't hard to tell the locals from the foreign tourists, who all seemed to be dressed to man the weather station in Antarctica, and wandered in bemused circles, trying to work out which way to go. The Icelanders, on the other hand, made a beeline for the exit or the queue for bus tickets. The tourists' luggage was different too, consisting of rucksacks or battered holdalls, while the locals' trolleys were piled high with enormous designer suitcases and duty-free bags. A number of planes had landed at around the same time, and the one carrying Egill's parents had been one of the last. The couple were due to appear any minute but Gudlaugur and Huldar had to use their elbows to remain at the front of the waiting crowd. They'd studied pictures of the couple online before setting out, so they shouldn't have any trouble recognising them, and besides they would be escorted by customs officials.

When they did come out, Huldar thought they might as well not have bothered to look them up, since they were unrecognisable. In the pictures he'd found online they looked like those glossy types forever snapped holding wine glasses at cocktail parties or leaning smiling on ski poles on foreign pistes under a brilliant blue sky – no shivering on the local slopes at Bláfjöll for them. Not a hair out of place or trace of lipstick on their white teeth. Even their designer ski-suits looked freshly cleaned and ironed.

Now, though, they presented a very different picture. The woman's face was puffy with weeping, and any make-up had long worn off. The man's eyes held an almost crazy glint, like the expression Huldar remembered from drugs busts, back in his days in uniform. Their clothes were a mess; his shirt was buttoned up wrong, her dress was creased and there was a ladder in the front of her tights. Their coats looked crumpled and grubby too, as if they'd slept in them. And her bag was hanging open from her shoulder, revealing the contents to anyone who cared to look. They looked like a couple who'd been caught up in some natural disaster.

He and Gudlaugur shook their hands, and thanked the customs officials, who seemed glad to get away. Then the four of them walked out to the car park in the bleak, icy surroundings of the airport, having completely forgotten their original plan that one would fetch the car while the other waited inside with the couple. They couldn't ask these people to wait in the terminal, being bumped and elbowed in the crush.

The car doors had no sooner slammed shut than the woman broke down in tears, not with a loud sobbing but quietly, almost politely.

'You must be hungry and thirsty. We got you some sandwiches and drinks.' Gudlaugur passed back a plastic bag from the shop in Arrivals. He and Huldar had spent ages dithering over what they'd want to drink and in the end had opted for soda water as the most neutral option. As Huldar pulled out of the car park, he heard the bag rustle.

The woman's quiet weeping had stopped. Instead, she asked

hoarsely: 'How could you think for one minute that we'd have any appetite?'

'No need to have them if you don't want to. We just thought you might not have eaten much. Or that you might have forgotten to drink.' Gudlaugur sounded mortified. It had been his suggestion and Huldar had thought it a good idea. He heard the hisses as the bottles of soda water were opened, so obviously it hadn't been such a bad one after all.

'Thanks.' The husband sounded as hoarse as his wife. 'We're not quite ourselves. I hope you understand.'

'Of course, no problem.' Huldar pulled out onto the Reykjanes dual carriageway. 'We understand what you're going through.'

'Did you see the videos? On Snapchat?' The woman didn't sound quite as husky now that she'd had a drink.

'Yes.' Huldar turned on the wipers to brush a few white flakes from the windscreen. There was heavy snow forecast for the drive back and it wouldn't be long before they got caught up in it. 'It's better if we don't discuss them.'

'Why not? I can't think about anything else. If I shut my eyes, they're all I can see. If I open them, too. It's going to be like that for the rest of my life.' The woman started crying again, with low gasping sobs this time.

Neither Gudlaugur nor Huldar said a word. The sobbing ceased after a minute or two and the woman sniffed. 'Thanks. Thanks for not saying anything.' She didn't sound sarcastic. Her husband was silent and in the rear-view mirror Huldar saw that he was staring out at the dark lava-fields lining the road.

'That's OK.' Huldar turned up the wipers.

'I can't stop thinking about when Egill was little. When he

was three. He used to have nightmares about a bad man. A bad man hitting him. We got so fed up with being woken in the middle of the night. Perhaps he remembered that when the man finally turned up – how we used to lose our tempers and tell him to shut up.'

'They don't want to hear about that.' Her husband kept his face turned to the window as he spoke. Huldar thought he'd closed his eyes.

'All right, I'll shut up.' The woman hung her head and her sobbing started up again, in short, dry gasps that trailed away into silence. But this didn't last long before she started talking again. 'Have they caught the man who did it?'

'No.' It was Gudlaugur who answered. 'But we're pulling all the stops out to catch him as soon as possible.'

The man laughed contemptuously. 'All the stops. Right.' In the mirror his face was drawn in harsh lines. 'Is that what they teach you to say at training college? I suppose you're going to add that it's a "heinous crime". And that you'll "leave no stone unturned"?'

Neither Huldar nor Gudlaugur rose to this. They weren't offended. They'd encountered any number of grieving people and knew that their anguish could take a variety of forms.

'I'm sorry. That was uncalled for.' The man turned from the window, slumping against the backrest. Only now did Huldar notice that husband and wife were sitting pressed against the doors at opposite ends of the seat, as if to keep as wide a space between them as possible. He remembered that they hadn't held hands or leant against each other as they walked to the car. He put it down to yet another strange manifestation of grief.

To reassure the man that they weren't affronted, Huldar

said: 'I don't know if you were told but there are two female officers waiting at the house with your daughter. You'll be offered a police guard for the rest of the night if you want it.' Ahead the snowstorm closed in and he took his foot off the accelerator as they drove into the sudden darkness. 'No need to decide now.'

Neither gave any sign of having taken in what he'd said. Nor did they seem alarmed that the police thought they might need protection. Right now they probably couldn't care less what happened to them.

'I never wanted to go on this trip.' The woman appeared to be addressing the back of the seat in front of her.

'Sure you did.' The man sounded as if they'd had this conversation before. Many times. Huldar hoped they'd had a row to themselves on the plane. He pitied anyone who'd had to sit next to them.

'Did you remember to fasten your seatbelts?' Gudlaugur's attempt to calm the waters seemed to work, as the couple relapsed into silence.

For the rest of the journey, they repeated this exchange from time to time, sometimes in different words, sometimes the same. By the time the police car passed the endless grey walls and red-and-white towers of the aluminium smelter at Straumsvík, signalling the beginning of the built-up area, the couple appeared to have sheathed their swords. For the time being, at least.

Huldar turned into their neighbourhood. The sight of the familiar houses and streets reduced the husband to tears, not decorously like his wife but with gut-wrenching howls. She didn't know how to deal with it and started talking aloud, though it wasn't clear who to.

'I never dreamt when we drove out to the airport that our homecoming would be like this.' She laughed sardonically. 'My worries about Egill then seem like a joke now. Laughable. Utterly trivial. Like worrying about whether you'll get a parking space in town.'

Before leaving the station, Huldar and Gudlaugur had been given clear orders not to question the couple on the way. That could wait until morning when the interview would be conducted under the proper conditions. But Huldar couldn't resist this chance. 'What were you worried about?'

The woman snorted. 'School.'

'Wasn't he doing OK?' Huldar halted at a stop sign and grabbed the chance to turn the mirror to reflect the woman's face. She looked like a deflated balloon as she sat there with drooping shoulders and hanging head. Her weeping husband was huddled at the far end of the seat.

'Sometimes. When he could be bothered. But the school had given up ringing about that. No, it was some rubbish about his behaviour towards another pupil. I was supposed to discuss it with him. I was going to wait till we got home. Didn't think there was any rush. Now I'm glad. At least our last conversation wasn't a negative one.'

The man stopped crying. 'What *was* your last conversation about? Can you tell me that? I seriously doubt it.'

Huldar coughed. 'What kind of behaviour?' He met the woman's eye in the mirror. 'Are you talking about bullying?'

She nodded.

Chapter 20

Wednesday evening and the bar was practically empty. The few customers in there had spread themselves out, and were talking and laughing more loudly than usual. The sound system was cranked up too loud as well, pumping out obnoxiously upbeat dance tunes, the kind designed to make you wave your arms in the air with a beer in each hand. Annoying as it was, the music did have its advantages. No one would be able to overhear their conversation, though Freyja didn't imagine that they would be discussing anything sensitive. She wasn't going to ask Kjartan to reveal his clients' secrets, and anyway he had a duty of confidentiality. Of course there were limits to how far this duty went, but the police inquiry had uncovered nothing as yet to justify a relaxation of the rules.

Freyja contemplated the Coke she had bought before sitting down. The bartender, all geared up for more expensive purchases that required cocktail shakers and the creative use of his chopping board, had been unimpressed by her order. She didn't want the drink, wasn't even thirsty, but she'd wanted to get in her order before Kjartan arrived. That way she wouldn't have to make excuses if he offered to buy her a drink. He had tried to pull her back when they were students and she didn't want the embarrassment of having to turn him down if he was still interested. She had a suspicion he might be, based on the alacrity with which he had agreed to meet her. No questions, no difficulties. His answer had been pretty much: *I'll be there.* Of course, there was always a chance that he was genuinely interested in what she wanted to discuss, but she doubted it. After a long day's work at the Children's House, the last thing she would be in the mood for was meeting a former fellow student to talk about child abuse, and the same must be true of Kjartan. Why would he seek out the company of someone who wanted to discuss bullying after spending the whole day dealing with its fallout?

Despite her suspicions, Freyja had made an effort to tart herself up for their meeting. It wasn't because she was in two minds about whether she was interested in him; it was purely out of habit. If she was dressed up and looking good, no one would doubt for a minute that her life was perfect. She reached for her glass. The neon-green straw and the parasol the bartender had balanced on the rim with a mocking flourish were in laughable contrast to the drink itself. One sip was enough to discover that the Coke was flat.

The door opened and for an instant the gloomy bar was lit up with a harsh, dazzling glare, not from the sun, which had set hours ago, but from the powerful floodlights outside the entrance. It was so strong that all Freyja could see of the newcomer was his silhouette until the door swung shut behind him.

It was Kjartan, wearing an overcoat, with snow on his shoulders. He stamped his feet before coming any further inside, and dusted the snow from his hair by ruffling it with his hands. She was pleased to see that he was looking good: slim, fit, still with all his hair. She had been prepared for something different since he had started university late and was older than her, old enough to have fleshed out into a tubby teddy bear in the intervening years. If anything, he was better-looking now than he had been as a student. Well dressed too, his clothes neither too formal nor too casual. She reckoned she could see through his choice of outfit: though it was intended to convey the impression that he had 'just thrown something on', it had in fact been carefully chosen, like her own.

Kjartan came over and they shook hands. Before sitting down, he announced that he was going to get a drink and couldn't hide his disappointment when Freyja indicated her glass. As she watched him walk over to the bar, she felt a twinge of regret at having been so calculating. The fact was, he was looking bloody good, from the back as well as the front, and she was long overdue a one-night stand. This might be her best chance for ages – if he turned out to be single, that is. A quick glance had established that he wasn't wearing a wedding ring, so if he bought another drink and offered her one, maybe she'd accept after all. She took another swig, bigger this time. If the chance arose, it would help if her glass was empty.

'I have to admit, I'm curious. Are you getting bullying cases at the Children's House now?' Kjartan sat down, placing his beer in front of him. 'That's what it sounded like from your e-mail. Unless the problem's personal?'

'No, neither, actually.' Freyja smiled. 'I don't have any children. I make do with being an aunt. My brother has a girl who's eighteen months.'

Kjartan's smile faded. 'Oh, I heard somewhere that you had a son.'

'No, I don't know who could have told you that. I don't have any kids.'

'Oh.' Kjartan looked as if he wanted to ask a question but didn't know how to put it. 'Yet more proof that you should never believe what you hear on the grapevine.' He smiled again, not quite as genuinely as when he'd first sat down.

They briefly exchanged news on what they'd been up to since graduation, but since neither seemed particularly interested in what the other had to say, Freyja quickly got down to business. Never mind how good Kjartan was looking; it was information she was after. 'I'm assisting the police with an inquiry that may involve bullying. I can't go into any details but that doesn't matter. I just wanted to know if it was worth their investigating this angle – whether bullying cases can lead to violence, I mean.'

'Against the targets? Yes. Against the bullies themselves? Also yes. In the worst cases, bullying can lead to situations where neither side shows any mercy.' He sipped his beer and wiped the froth from his upper lip. 'You have to remember that bullies tend to be completely devoid of pity for their victims. And the sufferers are on such an emotional rollercoaster that they can resort to desperate measures. That said, they're more likely to harm themselves than their tormentors. Much more likely.' Then he corrected himself: 'Rollercoaster's probably the wrong word, since they go up and down, whereas if bullying's allowed to continue unchecked, the victim's situation can only go downhill. It doesn't improve by itself, only gets worse. Sadly, when it's bad enough, anything can happen. And violence is an easy way to vent your feelings.'

'I see.' Freyja didn't have to work in the area to be aware that bullying could be serious. She knew from personal experience the mental scars it could leave you with, and her online research yesterday had shown that she wasn't alone in this.

She was amazed by the extent of the problem. All the published material had one thing in common, however: it was from the point of view of the victims, whether named or anonymous. There was nothing from the bullies' perspective. Perhaps some of them had sat down with the intention of explaining their actions, only to realise that there was no way they could justify them. 'Are you aware of any examples of bullying resulting in a death?' She didn't want to mention the word 'murder' in case he twigged that she was talking about the Stella case.

'Yes. Sadly, suicide's not uncommon. The youngest person to commit suicide in Iceland as a result of bullying was only eleven.' He paused and Freyja allowed the silence to hang between them. He took a deep breath and went on in full lecturer mode: 'These are ugly cases. Ugly and challenging. After all, the point of bullying is to hurt and humiliate people, both physically and mentally. And the damage is often lasting. Those who witness the incidents tend to side with the bully, usually to ensure that they themselves don't end up as the next victim. This strengthens the perpetrator's position within the group and earns them respect. It can be difficult for kids like that to step down off the pedestal as it's not only adults who are reluctant to relinquish their hold on power.' Freyja watched Kjartan take another swig of beer, much larger this time. He put down the glass and carried on. 'Speaking of violence, it's not unknown for victims to turn on their tormentors. It's rare but the fallout can be dramatic.'

'Such as?'

'The Columbine High School massacre in America. Thirteen people lost their lives, in addition to the two boys responsible.

They killed themselves afterwards, so a total of fifteen people died. The boys had been bullied and socially ostracised. Not that it excuses what happened – it's just one of the facts of the case.'

'But what about here in Iceland? Do you know of any instances where victims have used violence against the people who bullied them?'

'No one's been killed, if that's what you mean. But it occasionally leads to fights. Generally between boys, at the beginning of the bullying process; while the victim's still labouring under the illusion that they can stop it.'

'What about adults? Any examples of them going for the kids who've been picking on their children?' From the video clips, Freyja knew that the assailant in Stella's case was no child or adolescent.

'No serious cases, no. Just parents swearing at kids and grabbing them by the collar, that sort of thing. They can lose the plot when the system fails them and start trying to take matters into their own hands, but it doesn't do any good. It only complicates things and distracts attention from the main issue. An adult attacking a child is taken a lot more seriously than peer-on-peer violence.'

'Yes.' Freyja told him about the material she'd found online. 'I have to admit the problem's much nastier and more widespread than I'd imagined before I started reading up on it.'

'Yes, it's a disgraceful situation. Perhaps we'll manage to limit the problem eventually but at the moment we're more or less helpless in the face of online abuse. The phenomenon's changed and evolved like everything else.' Kjartan drew a quick breath and ploughed on. 'Everyday bullying, like the kind we remember, was more contained. It was only visible to those who were present. It consisted of taunting and name-calling, and sometimes physical injury or damage to the victim's property. Whereas cyberbullying involves comments and pictures designed to hurt, humiliate and damage the target's reputation. It's not constrained by any limits because the perpetrator doesn't have to look the victim in the eye. He or she doesn't even need to know who you are. It's easy for people to hide behind anonymity and give free rein to their basest instincts.' Kjartan took another deep breath and carried on. 'As if that wasn't bad enough, the material posted on social media can be seen by anyone at any time. The victim is left imagining an endless number of people laughing at them. He or she can't simply avoid the abuse by staying away from the bully. There's no refuge; they're hounded round the clock.'

'That fits with what I read.' Freyja watched a group of women downing shots together and slamming their glasses on the bar. 'I can't help asking myself what the hell motivates these kids.'

'For many of them, abusing some poor child provides a vent for their own feelings. But the main perpetrators in bullying cases tend to be individuals who already demonstrate some form of antisocial behaviour. In my opinion, the system ought to focus much more on the bullies. But it's not always obvious what's causing their behaviour.'

'It sounds as if you haven't exactly chosen an easy field.' The moment she'd spoken, Freyja realised she was hardly in a position to talk. The cases that found their way to the Children's House were often harrowing in the extreme.

'No. It's a challenging area. But there's a comfort in being able to help.' A new song started booming over the sound system, even more aggressively upbeat than the last. The message was unsubtle: dance, dance, dance. Hardly a very appropriate background to their conversation.

'Is it mainly the victims who come to see you, then?' Freyja took another sip of Coke, trying to block out the noise. The ice cubes had melted, diluting the flat drink still further.

'Mainly, yes. Though I do get to see the odd bully. Parents as well. Of victims and bullies. And occasionally adults who were bullied as kids or at work. I see a lot of lasting emotional damage, I can tell you.' Kjartan laid one arm along the sofa back, his fingers resting close to Freyja's shoulder. The move was calculated to appear casual, like his choice of clothes, but she saw through him. She didn't shift away, though. 'But over ninety per cent of my clients are victims.'

'Are bullying cases the only kind you take on?'

'No. Surprisingly, there aren't enough of them. Even though countless children experience bullying and I'm the only specialist in the country. And then there are all the perpetrators. *They* need counselling too, if they're to be stopped. But like I said, people tend to leave it too late to intervene because parents cling to the hope that it'll all blow over. They don't seek counselling in time, if at all. Most expect to wake up one morning to discover that everything's fine again. But it never works out like that. Not in the serious cases.'

'Have you seen any parents, or other relatives, who you judged to be at risk of resorting to extreme measures, like violence?'

Kjartan looked at her in surprise. 'That's funny.'

'What's funny?'

'Well, it's funny you should ask, because yes, I have had cases like that. The father of one of my clients was flirting with the idea of retaliating against the kids who were picking on his son, but he had the sense to unburden himself to me. And I can save you the effort of asking the next question because the answer is no: to my knowledge, none of my clients have acted on their impulses.' He looked thoughtful. 'Anyway, what is this inquiry you're assisting the police with? I have to admit I'm curious.'

'It's confidential, I'm afraid. I can tell you that it doesn't directly concern bullying. But the subject came up and I thought it worth looking into as the consultant psychologist. After all, you never know.' They were interrupted by gales of raucous laughter from the group of women at the bar, which briefly drowned out the music. Suddenly conscious of how inappropriate the venue was for the subject they were discussing, Freyja decided to leave it at that. If it became apparent that bullying was the motive for the attack on Stella, Kjartan would almost certainly be willing to help her. Her thoughts suddenly flew to little Saga. 'If I came to you as the parent or guardian of a child who was being bullied, what would you advise me to do?'

Kjartan knocked back his beer. 'Get a lawyer. Activate all the elements of the school's intervention programme, but sue the bully for compensation as well. It's not hard to prove the damage you've incurred. The victim's parents invariably have to miss work as a result of all the trips to the school to collect their weeping child. Vandalism of property is common too. And then there's the child's diminished quality of life. The kids targeted often suffer permanent emotional scars. It affects their performance at school, and so on.'

Kjartan put down his glass and wiped the froth from his lips. He smiled at her before continuing. 'Though in practice you probably wouldn't have to go that far. After all, if the child's a minor, it's the parents who'll have to cough up. And they'd be a lot quicker to intervene if they stood to lose out financially. Seriously, that would be your best move. And it wouldn't hurt to come and see me as well. I can help with the emotional fallout. But there's nothing I can do on my own to combat the problem itself.'

'I'll bear that in mind. Has anyone done it? Tried suing, I mean?'

He shook his head.

'Why not?'

'I don't know. I can't imagine schools would encourage the idea. But it'll happen sooner or later.'

Freyja nodded. She prayed that Baldur would never need to take that kind of action to protect Saga. 'Can you recommend any articles or studies on violence linked to bullying?'

Kjartan reeled off the titles of several research papers, saying he'd e-mail her a fuller list later. Then he drained his glass, banged it down on the table and asked bluntly: 'Are you seeing anyone?'

'No, not at the moment.' Freyja held his gaze as she answered, taking care not to break eye contact or blush like a coy little girl. 'Why do you ask?' Might as well make him work a bit. Stealing another glance at his hands she noticed a paler mark on his ring finger. That didn't bode well. She hoped he wasn't the kind of idiot who'd slip his wedding band in his pocket before coming out.

Kjartan didn't answer. 'Who's Baldur, then?' He added, a little embarrassed: 'I looked you up in the online directory. Saw that you and some guy named Baldur are listed at the same number.'

The fact that he'd looked her up didn't annoy Freyja. There was nothing wrong with doing a little homework. 'Baldur's my brother. I'm staying in his flat at the moment. He's . . . living somewhere else.' She looked at him curiously. 'Who's your wife? Anyone I know?'

'I'm getting divorced, actually.' Kjartan glanced around the room. 'It's a pity for the kids' sake but we both agree our relationship's over.' He smiled and she returned it. So the mark on his finger had a legitimate explanation. 'What do you say to moving on and getting something to eat? On me.'

'I say yes please.' Freyja was just reaching for her Coke when his offer came. Instead of draining the glass, she pushed it away. 'What are we waiting for?'

Chapter 21

Erla was chalk-white apart from the dark circles under her eyes that had grown even more pronounced. Her shirt was creased, there was a coffee stain on one sleeve and a small red mark on the collar, possibly ketchup. It was getting on for half one in the morning and she was still at work. Huldar wouldn't be surprised if she had a sleeping bag rolled up in the corner of her office. When the pressure was on, she had a tendency to drop anything she regarded as inessential, and he was fairly sure that her drive home would come under that heading. If they'd still been friends, he would have advised her to go home, get eight hours' kip, and have a proper breakfast before coming back to work. It was a more effective method than continuing to run on empty, becoming ever more tired until you couldn't think straight any more. She wouldn't have listened, though.

'Do you think that's wise?' Huldar nodded at the newly topped-up coffee cup in Erla's hand. He was holding a full mug himself and had lost count of how many he'd downed over the course of the day. Then he remembered that it was well past midnight, which meant a new day had started and he could begin again with a clear conscience. 'If you cut yourself, you'll bleed caffeine.'

'Sod off.' The weary way she said it suggested she was just about done in. She took a big slug of coffee, probably larger

169

than intended, to convey the message that he should stop interfering: she'd only do the exact opposite of what he recommended. He made a mental note of this for later use. On reflection, it had been a bad move to suggest they consider bullying as a possible motive. With Erla in this contrary mood, it would have worked better to flatly dismiss the theory in her hearing.

'It *is* something they have in common.' Huldar watched her roll her eyes. They were sitting facing each other across a small table covered with brown rings that would disappear when the cleaners turned up at six. Another four and a half hours. 'It's not as though we've uncovered any more promising leads.'

'Bullying?' Erla took another sip, her eyes wandering around the empty cafeteria. Huldar had followed her downstairs and taken a seat opposite her. He was determined to give it another go; see if she'd be more receptive now than she had been earlier, when he got back from the airport. Instead of heading straight home, he'd swung by the office, guessing Erla would still be there. On the way, he'd dropped Gudlaugur off at home, feeling resentful with him for refusing to open up about the Ásta business. Huldar didn't want to fall out with him and knew that the wearier he was, the greater the risk that he'd take it out on Gudlaugur.

'It's no more far-fetched than any other angle.' Huldar turned the mug in his hands, watching small rings forming in the liquid. 'It's led to mass shootings abroad.'

'You're talking about bullying carried out by kids. It was no kid who killed Stella or attacked Egill.'

'Adults can get drawn in.' He'd learnt that this afternoon from the e-mail Freyja had sent, summarising the information she'd dug up on the subject in general and on Stella in particular. None of it was conclusive evidence, but she'd promised a more substantial report in the morning. He hadn't been surprised that she chose to e-mail rather than talk on the phone. Obviously she wanted to avoid another of his clumsy attempts to ask her out. He cringed at the memory.

'The kids' parents are affected too. Often badly.' Huldar kept his voice level in an effort not to provoke Erla more than necessary. He was hoping to use this unforeseen opportunity to improve their professional relationship. Admittedly, rubbing it in that the information came from Freyja would do nothing to restore their friendship, but he was coming round to the idea that the bullying theory might be key. And solving the case mattered far more than making it up with Erla. 'Some parents are capable of anything when it comes to their kids.'

'Oh, please.' Erla shook her head wearily. 'Can I just drink my coffee in peace? I've already told you I think it's bullshit but I promise to consider it anyway. Later, though. Not right now. I've got more than enough on my plate.'

Huldar nodded. He'd wait until she'd had a few hours' sleep, then renew the attack tomorrow. 'Anything I can do to ease the burden?'

Erla snorted. Then, seeing that his offer was genuine, she mellowed a little. 'Two, three . . . What about one? If you could tell me that, I'd be happy.'

'Are you sure about that?' He didn't need to explain. Ever since the department had learnt about the note with the number three on it, the same question had been preying on all their minds. Who – and where – was victim number one? Of course, they couldn't be certain that the numbers were part of a series beginning with one. It could be a code, or the key to a combination lock, for example. The officer detailed to look into the numbers angle had contacted a mathematician who had been unable to help, pointing out that if it was a series, he'd need more numbers to work from. However, he had ignited a faint hope by saying that theoretically there was no reason why a series shouldn't start at two rather than one. Apparently he had been very curious about why the police were asking about these two numbers, but the officer hadn't enlightened him.

'I'm not sure of anything. It's one big fucking mess.'

Huldar was silent a moment, then asked: 'Is there anything I can do before I head home?'

'Nope.' Erla smothered a yawn.

They sat in silence for a while, listening to the humming of the fridge. It was oddly soothing and Huldar realised his eyelids were drooping. 'Can I give you a piece of advice?'

'No.' Erla drained her cup and heaved herself up, slowly and stiffly, like an old woman.

Against his better judgement, Huldar went ahead and said it anyway: 'Go home. I promise you won't regret it in the morning. Get eight hours' sleep in your own bed.' He shouldn't have mentioned her bed. They were both instantly embarrassed, looking anywhere but at each other.

'See you tomorrow.' Erla appeared to be addressing the fridge. He doubted she would take the blindest bit of notice of what he'd said.

Instead of following her, Huldar decided to stay where he was for a minute or two. He didn't want to come across like a dog, constantly trailing after her in the hope of a pat or a titbit. So he was still sitting there, gazing unseeingly into his mug, when a uniformed policeman came in. 'Is Erla not here?'

'No. She went back upstairs. What's up?'

The man hovered in the doorway. He was holding a piece of paper that flapped as he waved his hand. 'We've just had a call from the Red Cross. The message was a bit weird but I thought you lot should take a look at it.' He hesitated, then added: 'Is she in a bad mood? Should I maybe wait and let the morning shift deliver it?' Erla's reputation had obviously spread.

'Dunno. Depends on the message.' Huldar knocked back the last of his coffee and prepared to listen to some nonsense. The Red Cross wasn't usually a source of important tip-offs.

The policeman read out the handwritten note. '"One, two, three."' He looked up, embarrassed. 'That made me think it could have something to do with your case.' He dropped his gaze to the paper again and continued. '"You" . . . in other words, us, the police . . .' Huldar gestured at him impatiently to get on with it. '. . . "should look into Lauga's case."'

Huldar leapt to his feet, his drowsiness banished in an instant.

Like Huldar, Erla had been instantly revitalised by the message. She sat bolt upright, her eyes properly open and the colour returned to her cheeks. Even the black shadows under her eyes seemed to have receded a little. After bringing her the news, Huldar had had to dissuade her from ringing round the entire team.

The message had been delivered via the charity's helpline, 1717, a telephone service offering a listening ear to those with problems. Although it was supposed to be confidential, in this instance the man who rang had specifically requested that his message be passed on to the police. Fortunately, the person manning the phone had taken him at his word rather than giving in to his first instinct, which had been to put the call through to the emergency reception at the psychiatric unit. According to him, there had been something odd about the man's voice, which had made him take his request seriously. It transpired that the call had been made from Egill's mobile. When Erla learnt this, she raced round to see the technician on duty in Forensics, who was supposed to be keeping an eye on the boy's phone in case it reappeared on the network. Huldar dashed after her, no longer giving a damn if she thought he was following her around like a lapdog. It was worth it, if only to see her bawl out the technician, who they found slumped across his desk, snoring.

If she had anything to do with it, by the time spring arrived he'd find himself back in uniform, shepherding ducklings across the road in the town centre.

'Who the hell's Lauga?' Erla stared at the note that she had been clutching in her fist throughout all the frantic activity of the last hour.

'Search me.' Huldar had typed the name into the Police Information System as well as their more informal database, which, despite being unauthorised, contained the names of almost all those who had ever set foot in a police station.

A search for 'Lauga' had failed to return any results on either system but then, as well as being a name in its own right, it was short for no less than thirty-six Icelandic women's names ending in '-laug' and two that began with 'Laug-'. Both databases threw up countless results, the most common names being Áslaug, Sigurlaug and Gudlaug. 'It'll be a hell of a lot of work to sift through all these women. Not impossible, though. The majority of the entries relate to minor offences, and, more often than not, they're witnesses. There's the odd driving under the influence, one theft and a burglary. Nothing that stands out. All the cases were closed long ago. I can't find any still open in which the woman's a victim or a suspect.'

Erla sighed, burying her face in her hands. When she looked up again, Huldar went on, in the hope of forestalling a stream of invective that he was too tired to see the funny side of. 'Could the caller have said Laugi? Maybe it's a reference to a man's name. You've listened to the recording. Is it possible?' The name that had instantly sprung to mind was 'Gudlaugur', but he wasn't about to tell Erla that. The suspicions that had been roused by his partner's inexplicable caginess over his link to Ásta came flooding back.

'No. It was muffled and the man was obviously using a voice-changer, but the name definitely ended in an "a". You're welcome to listen for yourself. I can forward the file to you.'

'No thanks. I'm too knackered to do any more now.' He held out the two lists to Erla without moving from his seat in front of the computer. 'If you like, I can go over this. Preferably not till tomorrow, though. I can't concentrate now.' He grinned. 'Unless you'd care to nick me some speed from the property office.'

It provoked an answering grin from Erla – a rare sight at the best of times. 'Dream on.' Her grin vanished. 'You know what this means.'

'The message? No, I can't say I do. Maybe I'll be more on the ball tomorrow.'

'Not the message itself. The "one, two, three" business.'

Huldar nodded slowly. 'Ah, that. Yes, it means we're definitely missing a victim.'

Erla groaned, her face flattening out with exhaustion. 'Jesus Christ, I can forget about that promotion. I'm more likely to be out on my ear.'

She was right. If a third body was found and it turned out to be another teenager, she really would be for it. Although she was unlikely to be sacked, her career would take a nose-dive. Maybe she'd be given Gudlaugur's job if he put in for a transfer. 'It's not your fault. No one else could have done any better.' Huldar was hit by a sudden craving for nicotine. 'I have a hunch things are going to start moving now.'

His words did nothing to cheer her up. 'Let's hope so.' Erla drew a deep breath as if preparing to plunge into a swimming pool. 'Where's Gudlaugur?' She seemed to have only just noticed that Huldar was alone.

'He went home to crash. He'll be in tomorrow morning.' He made an effort to sound normal. The last thing he wanted was for Erla to detect from his voice that there was any tension between them.

Erla nodded absently. 'Go home. It's late.'

Huldar stood up, seeing no reason to protest. 'You should take your own advice.'

'I'm going to wait for the cars to get back, then I'll go.' Four officers in two squad cars had been dispatched to the spot where Egill's phone had briefly popped up on the GSM network. They'd called in, saying there was nothing to report at first glance but they were going to take a closer look. 'I've got to be here if they find . . . him.'

'They'd have called by now if they had.' Egill's phone had been traced to a footpath on the western slopes of Öskjuhlíd hill. The margin of error was eight metres, which meant the search area was a rough circle with a diameter of sixteen metres. 'Four men couldn't fail to spot him, whatever the terrain.'

'Yes, well, I'm going to hang on anyway. They should be back any minute.' She folded her arms, yawning. 'Or else I'll just have to fetch that speed from the property office.'

Huldar smiled and said goodnight. In spite of his tiredness, he was pleased. The investigation had gone up a gear, Erla had temporarily thawed towards him, he was about to have a ciggie and soon he'd be in bed. Life was as close to perfection as it could get in the middle of the night at the police station.

Chapter 22

Photocopy of a handwritten letter, entry no. 2 – posted on blog.is by a blogger going by the name of Laufa.

Every year things got worse. Every year I thought I'd hit rock bottom. I kept telling myself the other kids would soon have a change of heart. They'd feel bad and come to say they were sorry. Say they couldn't understand what they'd been thinking of and that I didn't deserve it. That we could all be friends again. But, sadly, nothing like that happened. Whenever I pictured the scene, it always ended the same way: I'd throw out my arms and say I didn't hold it against them. That we could all be friends. Forever, starting right now. Looking back on it, it seems ridiculous.

From the moment I suddenly became the target of all my classmates' cruellest instincts until I moved up to secondary school, time passed slowly. I had no social life and dreaded having to go to school every day. I spent the weekends shut in my room, dreading Monday morning. When I tried to get to sleep at night I used to pray to God for a volcanic eruption in Reykjavík like the one in the Westman Islands in 1974. When that happened, all the islanders were evacuated to the mainland and their children were sent to new schools. I still wonder if any of them were in the same situation as me and welcomed the fact they were forced to leave. Welcomed the chance of a new start with a different lot of children who wouldn't constantly pick on them.

I suppose I should have complained, should have said I didn't want to live in the area any more and insisted on being allowed to change schools. But I didn't want to make life at home any harder or Mum any sadder than she already was. Or Dad. I put on an act to hide the fact that I didn't have a social life. Pretended nothing was wrong and invented all kinds of lies so I didn't have to explain why my life was so different from the lives of other girls.

For example, I used to pretend I'd been invited to parties by people in my class. I'd leave home carrying wrapped-up parcels that I threw in the bin as soon as I was out of sight of the house. Then I'd hang around alone on the swings at the playground behind one of the blocks of flats until it was safe to go home. If it was raining or snowing, I'd wait in the bus shelter, terrified of being spotted by one of the kids from school. Every time I saw a bus coming I'd walk away so it didn't stop.

I only invited the other kids to my birthday party once. That was the year the whole thing started. Nobody came. I lied to Mum that I'd forgotten to hand out the invitations. Then I said I didn't want to hold it the following weekend because most of the girls would be at a handball match, so there was no point. The next year I claimed I didn't want a party because they all had flu. After that I think Mum believed I didn't want to invite anyone round out of consideration for her. Her health had got a lot worse by then and she couldn't be expected to do any baking.

I did try to go along to social events with my class but it was awful. I was mocked and humiliated, though never in a way that adults would notice. Like at school. My teacher just thought I was antisocial. She never once asked me if anything was wrong. Not even when my marks started going down and I handed in my homework late and in a mess. If she'd asked, I could have told her that this was because it was always getting stolen. Sometimes they'd sneak it back into my bag with red scribbles all over the work I'd taken so much trouble over. Or with the hurtful names they liked to call me scrawled all over the exercises I'd carefully written out at home. I think the teacher knew about Mum's illness and thought I was down and couldn't concentrate because of that. It's better than thinking that she just didn't care. Because the fact is, I was boring; I never said a word unless I was asked. Whereas the other kids used to brighten up when she was around. They sucked up to her and were as nice to her as they were horrible to me.

I could describe so many hurtful incidents. I know the story behind every tiny crack in my heart, behind the ones that grew so big they eventually split it in two. There was this one time I was dragged up to the blackboard to recite a poem we'd been told to learn by heart, and the whole class pulled faces and stuck out their tongues at me. I knew the poem but I was so stressed I forgot everything except a few words. And because the teacher's eyes were on me, she couldn't see what was going on behind her back. She didn't say a word when the other kids laughed at me. Just told me off when I finally gave up.

Or the time the boy who sat behind me cut off my pony-tail. I went home and lied that I'd done it myself because I'd wanted short hair. It wasn't true but I ended up with a boy's haircut anyway. The other kids in my class thought it was hilarious.

Or the time a pot of jam from the canteen was emptied into my school bag.

Or the time I was pushed over during gym and broke my nose. The games teacher told me off for being clumsy.

And all the other times. Each one worse than the last. No one would do something this drastic just because of one incident. But when you can't count on the fingers of both hands all the things that happen to you every day, you start to lose your grip. And when it's gone on for years and years . . .

In secondary school it started up again, even though we were all mixed up into different classes. I'd believed the situation couldn't get any worse but it did. The comments grew increasingly bitchy, and more and more kids seemed to enjoy tormenting me. Then, one day, an incredible thing happened: a new girl started at the school. She was shy, an outsider like me, and we became friends. Suddenly the other kids stopped mattering to me. They could say what they liked. It didn't get to me any more. My life was no longer worthless.

Chapter 23

Freyja woke up to the smell of vomit. All the scouring and scented candles had been in vain. The stench had hit her when she'd got home yesterday evening, so she had fetched the candles from the cupboard and placed them around the flat. They were gifts she'd received over the years but never found a use for. Candles were for putting around the bathtub while you wallowed in a mass of bubbles, champagne glass in hand. But Baldur's flat didn't run to such luxuries; all it had was a leaky shower cubicle.

She'd never have gone to sleep leaving the candles burning if she'd been sober but after all the wine she'd drunk with Kjartan, her inbuilt safety threshold had been lowered. Now, as she sat on the side of the bed, rubbing her aching forehead, it came back to her that it was because of the smell that she hadn't invited Kjartan home with her – not necessarily to share her bed, though clearly that had been on the cards. He'd shown all the signs of being up for it but explained that they couldn't go back to his house, so it had been hers or nothing. Which meant nothing, on this occasion. The smell, Molly, the dingy little flat – none of them were ideal for a first date. She was banking on there being a second date, though, assuming that next time he'd make sure his children were staying with their mother.

'Jesus.' Freyja stood up, head swimming. She bumped into

the bedside table and a burnt-out candle in a glass holder fell on the floor and rolled under the bed. Molly watched her lugubriously. When she saw herself in the bathroom mirror she understood why. Red eyes, wild hair and yesterday's make-up smudged all over her face as if she'd invited Dieter Roth to use her skin as a canvas. 'Christ.' She had a lecture in an hour. In the mirror she caught the movement as Molly poked her head round the door and seemed to nod disapprovingly.

A hot shower, breakfast and a brisk walk with Molly worked wonders. By the time Freyja left the flat, closing the door on a rather pissed-off dog, nobody would have guessed she'd drunk too much red wine the previous night. On the outside she looked like someone who'd just done a session at the gym, followed by a healthy carrot smoothie. Inside, she was still horribly hung-over, with a pounding headache and acid curdling in her stomach.

The snow that had been falling when she got out of the taxi the previous night now crunched underfoot. She had a sudden flashback to herself standing out here, head tipped back, mouth open and tongue sticking out to catch the snowflakes. Embarrassed at the memory, she stole a glance up at the building, hoping that none of her neighbours had witnessed the incident. All the windows were dark but that was of little comfort; the occupants were mostly night owls, so someone was bound to have seen her.

She made a vow never to drink again. Or at least not that much, and certainly not in the middle of the week.

The wind snatched up the loose snow as Freyja scraped it off the car, blowing it away. When she got in and slammed the door, a whole drift tumbled off the roof onto the windscreen.

Instead of getting out and scraping it again, she let the wipers do their best.

Her bag on the passenger seat contained the maths exercises that she was intending to hand in, despite having missed the deadline. She'd sat down and gone through the whole lot after coming home last night, though both handwriting and workmanship showed signs that her concentration had been a bit blurred. No doubt her solutions would be marred by the same lack of focus, but she meant to hand them in anyway. It wasn't as if she'd have a sober version to deliver any time soon. If she was going to persevere with the course, it was better to hand in nonsense than nothing. At least she might get half a mark for effort.

The car started at the first attempt and Freyja smiled, taking it as a sign that things were looking up, whatever happened with her studies. For the first time in ages she had gone out with a man she liked. OK, maybe she wasn't head over heels, but that could change. During their date, she'd kept being distracted by thoughts of Stella, her mind's eye presenting her with screenshots of the horrific scenes in the cinema. That was a hard obstacle for Kjartan to charm his way past. And he'd smacked his lips while eating, which had made her shudder. She preferred her dining companions to down their food as silently as ninjas. Still, on the plus side, he hadn't been wearing an ankle tag and he was keen to meet her again, as soon as possible. So the jury was still out on whether this could be the beginning of something.

One of the things she remembered discussing with him was the bullying she herself had suffered as a teenager. It had felt good to open up to someone, since she hadn't let on to a soul at the time. Baldur would only have beaten up the kids responsible, and her grandparents would have fallen to their knees and prayed to the Almighty for an answer – that same Almighty Lord who had proved worse than useless when Freyja needed him. Having no shoulder to cry on, she'd kept her unhappiness to herself. Until now.

Her pleasure at having got this weight off her chest was clouded only by the fact that she'd gone and told Kjartan about the class reunion at the weekend. He'd urged her to go along and take him with her. With him at her side for moral support, she'd soon realise that her former tormentors weren't worth wasting any more anger on. Yesterday evening this had struck her as a brilliant idea but in the harsh light of morning it seemed terrible. Alas, though, when she'd waltzed in the previous night, she had sent off an e-mail to the reunion organiser, announcing that she'd be there after all. With her partner. So Kjartan had better make good on his promise.

Freyja had just put her maths assignment in the tutor's pigeonhole when her phone buzzed. It was Huldar, asking her to come to the station later as they were interviewing some minors. So much for her plan to spend the day in the library. But luckily she'd be able to fit in her lecture first.

Which turned out to be a complete waste of time. Freyja couldn't begin to keep up with the PowerPoint slides as they flew by. Although her hangover was receding, she'd been unable to get her head round the graphs and lengthy definitions before they were gone. Right now she couldn't give a damn about the impact of supply on demand and vice versa. The only demand she could think about was her own craving for a Coke.

That bastard Huldar seemed to understand at a glance what kind of state she was in. Instead of the usual coffee, he had offered her just what she'd been dying for – a sugary Coke. How he knew was a mystery. Before going up to his floor, she'd popped into the loo to check her reflection in the mirror and touch up her appearance. She hadn't done a good enough job, obviously. 'Down it. You'll feel better right away. I should know.' Smiling, he handed her the bottle. 'Good night, was it?'

She mumbled an inaudible reply. He left her with Gudlaugur while he went to fetch the kids. The waiting was a little awkward; she drank her Coke and the young detective ventured some pointless small talk about the weather. Cutting him off mid-flow, she asked: 'Who are the kids?'

'Friends of Egill. One's bringing his mother.'

'Who's Egill?'

'Hasn't Huldar told you?' Freyja's blank look answered the question. 'Oh. Well, the case has taken a turn for the worse. All the indications are that Stella's killer has now abducted Egill Pálsson, the boy who's been reported missing.'

Freyja hadn't paid much attention to the news since yesterday afternoon but she had a vague memory of a head-line and the photo of a missing teenage boy. She'd simply assumed he was one of those kids who'd got sucked into the world of drugs and kept running away from home. 'Has the press got wind of the connection?'

'Yes, but in the interests of the investigation, they've agreed not to publish anything until tomorrow morning. I doubt it'll stay under wraps, though. Unfortunately, too many of his friends know. All it takes is one kid to mention it on Facebook or some other social media platform and the press will no longer feel bound by their promise.'

'When did he disappear?'

'Tuesday evening. But no one found out till yesterday morning.'

'And he hasn't turned up?'

'No.' Gudlaugur shook his head.

'So he could still be alive?'

He hesitated, then answered with little conviction: 'Yes, theoretically.'

Freyja's queasiness returned at the thought of the violence the boy might have suffered; might still be suffering. 'Were the same kind of Snaps circulated?'

Gudlaugur nodded. 'Just as brutal as the ones in Stella's case. Though the attacker waited longer this time. We're expecting more but we haven't a clue whether there'll be any because he doesn't seem to be following the same pattern. Egill's phone popped up on the network last night but it was switched off again immediately and we didn't find him at the location. This time it was used to make a call, not send a Snap, but we're still expecting a final message, if the perpe-trator's following the same M.O. as in the Stella case.'

Freyja pushed away the images conjured up by her imagi-nation. Huldar's reappearance accompanied by three teenage boys and a woman – presumably the mother – proved a welcome distraction.

It wasn't immediately obvious which of the three boys was the woman's son. She had chestnut hair and a hard face, with pronounced cheekbones and a sharp nose, unlike the childishly rounded features of the boys, who were all blond. One was noticeably taller than the others, but carried himself as if all these extra centimetres had arrived unexpectedly in the night. The woman stared grimly at the backs of the boys' heads, deliberately ignoring her surroundings. Paying a visit to a police station was not on most adults' wish list. But the boys turned their heads excitedly this way and that, exchanging whispers.

Once they were all sitting round the large table in the meeting room, the boys' excitement diminished. There was nothing of interest to see in there, just a single black screen on the wall, a recorder, a wireless keyboard and a tangle of computer cables leading to a small cupboard. The white-washed walls and ceiling were bare and featureless.

Huldar laid his hands flat on the table in front of him. 'Right. I should probably begin by reminding you that you're only here to help us with our enquiries. None of you are suspected of any involvement in Egill's disappearance.' He met the eye of the mother who was sitting at the other end of the table. The boy next to her was leaning as far away from her and towards the other boys as the arm of his chair would allow. Her son, presumably, mortified that his mother had insisted on accompanying him, when the other boys were allowed to come alone. 'Freyja, here, is a child psychologist. She'll make sure we don't overstep the mark. She can offer you advice too, if you'd like.' His gaze returned to the mother. 'It would be best if you didn't interrupt too much while we're asking the questions, though of course we can't stop you.' He gave the woman an on–off smile and she looked down her nose disapprovingly.

Huldar turned back to the boys. 'How are you doing, lads?' They mumbled something inaudible but it didn't matter, the question was only an introduction to the more serious business that was to follow. Huldar proceeded to run through all the same questions he'd put to Stella's friends. Once or twice he brought Freyja in to reassure the kids that it was perfectly normal in the circumstances to feel upset or frightened. But she didn't ask any questions herself, leaving that side entirely to Huldar. Gudlaugur took no part, merely sat and observed. Freyja couldn't work out his role. Perhaps he was just there as a witness, in case the mother or one of the boys made a complaint about Huldar.

It took a while for the boys to get into gear but when they did finally open their mouths, it turned out they had little of interest to say. Their answers chimed more or less with those Stella's friends had given. None of them knew anything of significance. Egill had no connection to anyone or anything that could explain his disappearance. They were keen to stress that he didn't smoke and wasn't on drugs. When Huldar asked if he drank, their answers became evasive and they swapped furtive glances. They would probably have been more forthcoming if the mother hadn't been present. Two of them had seen the videos and the third seemed rather disappointed to have missed them.

'If I say the number three to you, what's the first thing that springs to mind?'

The boys' reactions made it clear that they were surprised by Huldar's question. They started asking what he meant: three of something in particular or just three of anything? Huldar had to cut in and repeat his question. 'What's the first thing you think of?'

'Er . . . left back. Er . . . a triangle. Er . . . Eric Bailly. Er . . . injury time.' Apart from revealing their obsession with football, the answers weren't very enlightening. Though for all Freyja knew, the question might refer to football. She remembered him asking her something similar on the phone, but surely that had been about the number two? She noticed that the mother was becoming increasingly restless and she checked her own impulse to steal a glance at her phone to find out the time.

The mother snapped to attention when Huldar's questions suddenly changed tack. Freyja pricked up her ears as well. 'Egill was bullying a boy at your school called Davíd. Tell me about that.'

'What?' The boys looked even more surprised and confused than they had when he'd asked about the number three.

'Egill's mother received a complaint from the school about her son's behaviour towards a boy in the year below you. As his best friends, you must have been aware of the bullying – maybe you even took part in it?'

'My son's never bullied anyone.' Bristling, the mother turned on Freyja. 'Aren't you going to say anything? It sounds to me like my son's being accused of something. We were promised that this interview was about Egill – about helping the police find him. I can't see what this question has to do with his disappearance.'

No one said anything after she'd finished, they just let the silence hang in the air; an effective response to bluster. Freyja had the hardest time holding out, since the woman had addressed her directly, but she managed not to cave in, and the woman didn't insist on an answer, seeming content merely to glare at her. When Huldar eventually spoke, it was to the boys, as if he hadn't heard the mother's outburst. 'What do you say, lads? How bad was it?'

They shot sidelong glances at one another. In the end, it was the smallest of them who replied. 'It was no big deal. It was only banter. You know, just jokes.'

The mother shifted impatiently. 'This is outrageous. Boys, you don't have to answer.'

'As your mother says, you don't have to answer—' Before Huldar could finish, the boy in the middle interrupted.

'She's not *our* mum. She's his.' He jerked his thumb at the boy sitting next to the woman.

'Thanks.' Huldar turned to the boy in question. 'What's your name again, son?'

'Uuuh . . . Thorgeir. Thorgeir Atlason.'

Huldar picked up a sheaf of papers from the table in front of him and began leafing through them under the boys' wary gaze. Finding what he was looking for, he read out: 'Die, you piece of shit. Hang yourself, or I'll do it for you.' Huldar raised his eyes to meet those of the boy who had turned bright red. He carried on reading: 'How about I shove a broken bottle up your arse?' He looked back at the boy who had dropped his gaze. 'Does that sound like "only banter" to you?'

The mother slapped her hand on the table. 'What the . . . ? How dare you read out that disgusting stuff in front of my son? And his friends?'

Huldar looked up. 'Oh, I've hardly got started.'

'I'm speechless. And you . . .' The woman looked daggers at Freyja. 'What kind of child psychologist do you call yourself? Or are you just here for decoration? I insist you put a stop to this. May I remind you that they're only fourteen and fifteen years old!'

'If they're old enough to write it, surely they're old enough to hear their words read aloud?'

'What are you on about?' The woman was wrong-footed. 'Who wrote that?'

'Your son, Thorgeir.' Huldar's gaze moved on to the other boys. 'I could read the same kind of messages from you two to this Davíd. He's a year younger than you. Prefer to pick on the little kids, do you?' None of the three answered or dared meet his eye. The mother sat there open-mouthed, trying to work out what was going on. 'I'm waiting for an answer.' Huldar lifted up the papers as if to go on reading. It was enough to prompt Thorgeir to speak.

'Don't keep reading it out. It sounds really bad when you do that. It's, like, totally different on screen.' He stole a glance at his mother, who ignored him.

Freyja decided to dive in at this point. 'I don't agree. It's no better reading messages like that on screen, alone in your room.' She stopped herself, afraid of breaking into a long, angry rant and saying a lot of things she'd only regret later. She was here as a representative of children's services, not on behalf of the teenage girl she once was. Her own emotional baggage was unimportant in comparison to the urgent hunt for a missing boy – and a murderer. 'I recommend you answer the police's questions without any more evasion. You've been given a chance to make up for your appalling behaviour. I'd grab it, if I were you.'

'Do you send messages like that to girls, too? A girl called Adalheidur, for example? Are the messages anything like the ones you've been sending Davíd? "It's a shame you're too ugly to be raped." Oh, or this one: "Hope you get AIDS and die, you stupid twat."'

'That's enough!' The mother unhooked her bag from the back of the chair with trembling hands. 'I'm not listening to another word of this. It has nothing to do with Egill's disappearance. There's something else going on here.' She rose to her feet, slinging her bag over her shoulder. 'Thorgeir, you're coming with me. It's up to your friends what they do.' The boys didn't wait to be told twice. They almost tripped over each other in their haste to push back their chairs from the table and stand up.

The most confident of them hesitated a moment as his friends hurried out after the woman. He mumbled quickly, without meeting anyone's eye: 'That David's dad's a weirdo. I'd arrest him if I was you. I bet he's taken Egill.' He darted after his friends before they could ask him any further questions, only to pause again in the doorway. With his back to them, he added: 'I'm sorry about the David stuff. We didn't really mean it. It was just bants, you know.'

He left.

They sat there, aware that, wherever he was now, Egill was unlikely to be laughing at his friends' banter. He was unlikely ever to laugh again.

Chapter 24

The atmosphere in the meeting room was no better now that Erla was sitting there in place of the mother and the three boys. Huldar felt a certain satisfaction, though. He took the fact that she'd expressed a wish to talk to Freyja as a sign that she must be thawing towards her. He had decided to sit in, on the grounds that it would be better to have a third party present to keep things civilised. Erla may have been thinking along the same lines, as she had brought along Jóel, who was now lounging in his chair, eyeing Freyja up – much to Huldar's chagrin.

'Do I understand you correctly that there are no precedents for an adult using extreme violence against a minor in connection with bullying?' Erla was forced to tone down her sneer in order to get the words out. As a result, she looked almost like her normal self. 'In that case, why should we even consider the possibility?'

Huldar jumped in before Freyja could speak. He was feeling sorry for her. He'd clocked at once that she was suffering from a bad hangover, and knew from experience that this could make it hard to answer succinctly. 'Because all else has failed,' he said quickly. 'All our other leads have turned out to be dead ends.'

As he'd expected, Erla flared up at this. 'I was talking to her, not you. She's supposed to be our go-to expert.' She turned back to Freyja, who was looking pale.

'The fact there are no precedents doesn't mean it can't happen,' she replied. 'But it's up to you whether you investigate this angle. It's no big deal to me either way. I just felt it was right to draw your attention to the possibility, especially given what the headmistress had to say about the father of Adalheidur, the girl Stella was victimising.' Freyja's chin jutted briefly, then lowered again.

'Are you implying that every dad who loses his temper with his kid's headteacher is a potential murderer?' This was beneath Erla but Huldar knew there was no point telling her so.

'I don't see how you manage to interpret my words like that.' The blood flooded into Freyja's pale cheeks, making her appear suddenly healthier. 'But the answer's no. Of course not.' She licked her lips and, out of the corner of his eye, Huldar caught Jóel's leer. 'Anyway, I included all the information you're asking about in my two e-mails. Perhaps you haven't seen them yet. I was under the impression they'd been forwarded to you.'

Erla unfolded her arms and pushed the printouts towards Freyja. 'I read them but I can't say I was too impressed. When we shell out our limited resources on a consultation, I expect a proper report, not a couple of scrappy e-mails.'

Huldar could sense the chill emanating from Freyja even without looking at her. She answered before he could leap to her defence again. 'Excuse the misunderstanding but I thought it was urgent, so I decided to update you immediately, rather than keep you waiting for the final report I'll be delivering in due course.'

'Anyway.' Huldar picked up the thread the moment Freyja stopped talking. 'Leaving aside reports and e-mails, isn't the question we're all longing to ask: what do we do now?'

There was a lengthy silence while the two women got a grip on themselves. Jóel had started pointedly clearing his throat when Erla put an end to the awkwardness. 'We looked up Adalheidur's father on our system.'

She paused again, as if intending to withhold the results of the search. Huldar guessed this meant they'd found something. 'And?'

'It threw up an incident.'

'What kind of incident?' So that was why Erla was interested in hearing what Freyja had to say.

'A complaint from a neighbour.'

'What about?' Huldar tried to control his impatience. Why couldn't she just spit it out?

'Noise. Shouts and howling. The person who rang thought someone was being murdered. Two uniforms went to the address but there was nothing to see. No bodies, no victim.'

'When was this?'

'Just over a month ago.' Erla's lips tightened. She added that she'd show him the report after the meeting; this wasn't the time or place to go into details. Huldar didn't object, though he was itching to hear more. Instead, he sat quietly while Erla interrogated Freyja, politely for her. She was mainly interested in the perpetrator's probable state of mind and the type of behaviour that could be triggered by chronic stress, in the worst-case scenario. Freyja answered all her questions like a true professional – namely, with endless provisos that diluted the content to such an extent that in the end all she'd really said was that anything was possible. Despite this, Erla and Jóel didn't look too disappointed. They hadn't been expecting her to stick her neck out and express an opinion as to who could have attacked the teenagers or why. The most she could do was provide them with a new avenue to explore, even if it proved to be another blind alley.

'If I've understood you, it's highly unlikely that a parent or other adult relative of a bullying victim would retaliate using violence?'

'Yes. Well, minor scuffles aren't unheard of. But an incident serious enough to cause death is unlikely.' Freyja paused and Erla flicked a look at Huldar, irritably shaking her head. But she snapped to attention again when Freyja went on: 'But, as I'm sure you know, there's a big difference between unlikely and impossible.'

Erla adopted a poker face as she digested this. When she spoke again, she didn't betray any opinion of this statement. 'Has the name Lauga cropped up at any point in connection with Adalheidur or during your research?'

'I wouldn't really dignify it with the name of research. But no, I don't remember coming across that name.'

Erla's face remained impassive. Huldar couldn't work out whether the meeting had done the trick or whether she was going to rule out any further investigation of this angle. Erla stood up. 'We're going to need to interview more minors, so make sure you're available. We'll give you plenty of notice. I may also ask you to be present when and if I decide to interview Adalheidur's father. It wouldn't hurt to hear your opinion of the man's mental state.'

She walked out of the room without another word. Jóel was left sitting there like a spare part, gazing pointlessly at the blank page in front of him. All he'd written on it was the date. He'd lacked the mental agility to keep up with the quick-fire exchanges between the two women.

Huldar sat tight, enjoying Jóel's discomfort. Freyja didn't

budge either. After a moment or two, catching Huldar's mocking grin, Jóel snatched up his blank notepad and got to his feet. Before leaving the room, he fished for his card and handed it to Freyja with a smirk, saying she shouldn't hesitate to get in touch if she needed anything. It didn't have to be about the investigation. He gave her a wink and was rewarded with a frosty stare. Huldar could have kissed her when she put the card down on the table and left it there as they vacated the room.

'The hairs didn't belong to the killer.' The lab had agreed to fast-track the DNA analysis of the strands of hair that had been found in Stella's hand. Erla slammed the report on her desk. 'Fucking hell.'

Huldar reached for it and soon spotted what had prompted this reaction. The hairs belonged to a woman. He slid the report back to Erla. 'Is that a hundred per cent certain? Should we maybe check the CCTV footage again and check it's definitely a man? That could explain why no one's managed to spot a likely match for the killer among the cinema crowd.'

'Yeah, maybe.' Erla rubbed her eyes. 'You do it, will you? By the way, we've finally got the files from Snapchat, so the quality's much better than the first videos you saw. You can have a look at them too, though you can only see the killer's arms. Anyway, by all means go and study the cinema footage. The guy who's been working on that has worn his eyes out looking, but maybe you'll spot something. That hair has buggered things up because they were keeping an eye out for blokes with grey hair, which turns out to have been a sodding waste of time.' Erla tapped the report containing the results of the DNA analysis. Sighing, she went on: 'The ticket sales haven't provided any leads either. Though maybe that'll change once we get hold of a suspect. *If* we do.' Erla rubbed her hands down her face. 'This investigation's making us look totally incompetent.'

Huldar didn't contradict her. You only had to look at the news sites. Now that Egill's disappearance had been made public, the police were coming in for heavy criticism. It was only natural since there had been no arrests, despite dozens of people being interviewed. In addition to friends and family, the police had pulled in a number of individuals with a history of violence. None of them had turned out to be likely suspects and most had provided solid alibis, though their number was known to include psychopaths who made very convincing liars, so some of their names remained on the list. But a closer inspection of these people had turned up nothing. And, despite a major search of Reykjavík and the surrounding area by the police and rescue teams, not a trace had been found of Egill. His phone hadn't reappeared on the network either.

'OK, I'll do it,' Huldar said. 'I reckon it would be worth paying a visit to Adalheidur's father too. The report's a strong indication that something happened at his house. The uniforms who attended the scene say there had been a struggle of some kind. And his explanation's clearly bullshit.'

'No one ever brought charges. I checked. So maybe he was telling the truth.'

'What, that a feral cat got into his house and went for him? Give me a break. Blood spatters on one of the walls? How would you draw blood from a cat during a fight? And how would you get a bruised face? You'd expect him to be scratched, not punched. According to the report, his eye was swollen. How could a cat possibly have done that?'

'Of course it wasn't a cat. But maybe he had a punch-up with a friend or a member of his family. How the hell do I know?' Erla ran her hands through her hair and let out a heavy sigh. 'But someone needs to talk to him. What have we got to lose? We've spoken to everyone else.'

She waved Huldar away and bent over her piles of papers again.

The video clips of Stella weeping in the toilet and the brutal scenes that followed were not improved by being viewed in high res. Nevertheless, Huldar forced himself to go through them in case he'd missed something the first time round, but to no avail. After that, he watched the CCTV footage of the killer leaving the cinema, towing Stella's body, but learnt nothing new from that either, beyond being fairly convinced it was a man. He was too tall, too burly, too strong for a woman, and didn't show the slightest hint of feminine softness in his movements. If the hair did belong to the killer, it would have to be an exceptionally big, hefty female.

Despite his lingering suspicions of Gudlaugur, he'd roped him into watching the recordings of the cinemagoers with him. There was such a throng in the foyer that a second pair of eyes wouldn't go amiss. They sat side by side, faces almost pressed together over the computer screen, scrutinising the recordings from the intervals, which required so much concentration that they had no problem blocking out their colleagues' bitchy comments. But the longer they watched without seeing anything of interest, the more their concentration wavered.

'The guy's not there. Or if he is, he's wearing a different coat.' Gudlaugur paused the video and peered more closely at the corner of the screen. 'I can't understand how he smuggled the anorak into the cinema. There were no lone men carrying bags in the foyer before the films started.' He pressed 'Play' again, muttering under his breath: 'Where are you, you bastard?'

After the final interval, the customers trickled back into the screens again until only the girls working at the kiosk remained. They watched Stella fiddling with her hair, taking out her phone and drawing her finger down the screen while the other three were tidying up. Huldar reached for the mouse and clicked on the footage of the interval from the other camera, which showed the emergency exit and the area by the stairs down to the loos. None of the figures passing the camera looked likely to be the man they were after, though they couldn't be sure. 'Unbelievable how few people smoke nowadays.' Huldar pointed at the emergency exit. 'There are several hundred people in the cinema but only fifteen went out for a puff.' He'd counted them. It had helped him stay awake.

Gudlaugur didn't take his eyes off the TV, watching intently until all the customers had drifted back into the screens. 'Sixteen. There were sixteen smokers.'

'No. Fifteen. I counted them.'

'I just counted them coming in and there were sixteen.'

Their eyes met and Huldar quickly rewound to the beginning of the interval. Fifteen people went outside. Sixteen came in. Huldar shot back his chair and went to fetch Erla. They'd caught their man on film. He hadn't bought a ticket after all; the bastard had sneaked in during the last interval.

Chapter 25

Adalheidur's father Haukur looked nothing like the man caught on CCTV. He was too short and slight, though of course someone's build could be disguised with padding. Frustratingly, the police still had no idea what the killer's face looked like, as the man had taken care to keep it hidden when he'd sneaked in with the smokers. He hadn't been wearing a hood or a Darth Vader mask or it would have been spotted immediately on the recordings. Instead, he had walked in close behind a much taller man, so all he needed to do was keep his head lowered to be sure his features wouldn't be caught on camera. He was wearing a coat, seemingly on top of the anorak he'd worn for the attack. They assumed he must have hidden the mask under his coat as well, since he wasn't carrying a bag.

'I don't know how this works,' Haukur said. 'Should I offer you a seat in the living room or the kitchen? Would you like a coffee? Just say the word.' He stood back to allow Huldar, Gudlaugur and Freyja inside. Clearly he had just got home himself since he still had his coat on and all the lights were out in the flat apart from the one in the narrow hall. When Huldar rang, Haukur had opted to dash home from work to meet them there, presumably so they'd be finished before his wife came back. That in itself suggested he had something to hide.

'It would be best to sit somewhere we won't be disturbed. And we don't need any coffee, thanks.' Huldar was careful not to tread on Freyja's toes as they all crowded into the hall and bumbled about, trying to remove their snowy shoes. In the process Freyja was pushed up against him and Huldar felt encouraged that she didn't immediately jump away, unless it was simply because there was no room to move. He preferred to think it was because she didn't mind the proximity. He was disappointed when Haukur showed them into the living room and the moment of intimacy was over.

They sat down, Haukur and Gudlaugur in chairs, Freyja and Huldar on the sofa, which turned out to be less comfortable than it looked. 'I can't think why you want to see me but let's get it over with. I know nothing at all about what happened to that girl, as I told you over the phone.' He glanced from Gudlaugur to Huldar, unsure which of them he had talked to.

'We have to speak to a lot of people as part of our routine enquiries. Sometimes it turns out they know things they didn't realise were important.' Huldar studied the man as he spoke. Haukur was sitting bolt upright, hands on the arms of his chair, clasping the rounded ends, as if he were strapped into an electric chair. He was still wearing his coat, which was green and not unlike the killer's anorak. He hadn't invited his visitors to take off their outdoor clothes either. 'We know what was going on between your daughter and Stella, so we'd like to ask you a few questions about that.' The man's grip on the chair arms didn't relax at this news. Huldar went on. 'Who were you having a fight with when the police were called round here last month?'

The man looked astonished. 'What's that nonsense got

to do with Stella? I thought you were going to ask about her.'

'I've got a number of questions to put to you. It would be best if you just answered. Who were you having a fight with?'

'I wasn't having a fight with anyone. I was chasing out a cat. A stray.'

'Your neighbours – the ones who called the police – claim they heard shouting. As far as I know, cats don't shout. Not even strays.'

'*I* was shouting. At first I thought I could chase the animal out by yelling at it. The whole thing was a misunderstanding. My neighbour didn't realise it was me making all the noise. It's not like I'm in the habit of it. Look, I told all this to the policemen who came round at the time. Didn't they write a report? Or do you lot only make a note of things when it suits you – like when it's to the disadvantage of us ordinary citizens?'

Many of the people Huldar interviewed in the line of duty referred to themselves as citizens. It wasn't something he encountered outside working hours. He took it as a sign that they wanted to distance themselves from their private identity and become part of a larger whole – like vanishing into an imaginary crowd. 'If I've got this right, your neighbours reported hearing you and another man having a violent argument. How do you account for that? Are you saying you put on different voices in your attempts to get rid of the cat?'

'My neighbour was mistaken. Like I told the other officers. What does it matter anyway? You don't think I attacked Stella? She's never set foot in this flat to my knowledge and clearly she wasn't here when I got into a fight with . . . the cat.'

Huldar changed tack. 'We understand you've lost your

temper on several occasions at your daughter's school. Behaved in an intimidating manner, raised your voice. Were verbally abusive to the headteacher and other members of staff who got in your way. Which suggests that you're in the habit of losing it. And not just with . . . stray cats.'

'No father in his right mind would have reacted any differently. Don't imagine for one minute that I regret making a scene. I'd have done better to blow my top more often, and sooner. The school has shown itself totally incapable of ensuring my daughter a normal, safe environment. What was I supposed to do? Say thanks for the useless service?' The man's jaw muscles continued working furiously after he'd finished speaking.

Gudlaugur cleared his throat. 'Are you on Snapchat?'

'Am I on Snapchat?' Haukur sounded puzzled at first, then it dawned on him. 'Oh, I see. Do you think I haven't heard the news? Of course I know about the messages Stella's killer sent her friends. Am I on Snapchat? Yes. Isn't half the country? Does the fact I'm on Snapchat mean I killed Stella? No. Did I kill her anyway? No. Just because I banged the table a bit at the school that doesn't mean I'm capable of murder. Anyone can lose their temper, the last time I checked.' He bestowed a withering look on Gudlaugur. 'If you seriously think I killed Stella, I feel sorry for you. Because you're barking up completely the wrong tree.'

Gudlaugur was becoming seasoned at last. The man's insults left him unmoved. Of course he'd heard far worse – Huldar had witnessed some of the crap he'd received. It went with the territory. Only recently Huldar had heard a drunk they'd arrested call Gudlaugur a stupid fucking neo-Nazi fascist and a fucking fag with a uniform fetish. On both occasions Gudlaugur had betrayed signs of letting it get to him, but this time he didn't turn a hair. 'Did you follow Stella on Snapchat?'

'What kind of idiots are you? Why would I be following a little girl on Snapchat? Especially a girl who's responsible for spreading filth about my daughter – on that bloody app too. No. I didn't follow Stella on Snapchat. My account is private, I have very few contacts and she's not one of them. Anyway, I can count the number of times I've used the app on the fingers of one hand.'

'Could we see your phone?' Huldar took over smoothly from Gudlaugur. It often worked well to rotate like this, unsettling the interviewee, making them unsure where the next question was coming from. He wished he'd asked Freyja to chip in as well. But it was too late now; she was just sitting and listening in silence. 'If you use Snapchat as little as you say, it shouldn't take us long to run through your account history.'

'You want my phone?' The man unclenched his fingers on the right arm of his chair and moved his hand instinctively to his coat pocket. 'Out of the question. You have no right to demand it.'

'No.' Huldar reminded himself that this didn't necessarily mean the man had something to hide. Personally he wouldn't want to hand over his phone to a stranger either, if only because of the masses of photos, e-mails, texts and other information it contained. Not all of it entirely innocent. 'I can understand that you don't want to give us unlimited access to your phone but would you mind opening Snapchat for us and showing us what you've got on there?'

'No. Out of the question. If you want my phone, you'll

have to get a warrant. I've got personal stuff on there that I don't want you lot sticking your noses in.'

'Does the name Lauga mean anything to you?' Although Huldar would have liked to put pressure on him about the phone, he knew it was pointless. And there would be little to gain from applying for a warrant and getting hold of it that way, since the delay could potentially give Haukur time to get himself a new phone and ditch the old one.

'Lauga?' Haukur thought about it. 'No.'

'What about Gudlaug or Snjólaug? Or any other name ending in -laug?'

'Yes. I work with a woman called Arnlaug. And I have a niece called Sigurlaug. She's eleven. Is she a suspect?'

'The woman you work with – what's her patronymic and what does she do for a living?' Gudlaugur fished a pen and notebook from his pocket. Once a scout, always a scout.

'You've got to be joking?'

'No.' Gudlaugur held his pen ready.

'Er . . . her patronymic's Torfadóttir, I think. She works in payroll.'

While Gudlaugur was making a note of this, Huldar seized the opportunity to ask the man about the bullying his daughter had experienced and Stella's part in it. There followed a long, depressing tale that Freyja seemed the least surprised by. In the course of this inquiry, Huldar had seen a lot of abusive comments he could have done without reading, but even so there were moments when he had to stop himself from interrupting to ask the man if he was exaggerating. Haukur talked at length, hardly pausing for breath, his knuckles white on the arms of his chair. Then suddenly the air seemed to go out of him like a punctured balloon. Relaxing his grip, he lowered his head. 'Things reached rock bottom last spring. It turned out that this boy from the countryside who Adda had befriended through Facebook didn't actually exist. Stella and her mates had invented his profile purely in order to humiliate my daughter. To get her to open up, then use what she'd said to make fun of her.' His knuckles whitened again. 'After that she tried to kill herself.'

'Yes, we heard about that.' Freyja had reported what she'd learnt from the headmistress, but Huldar hadn't been expecting the girl's father to raise the subject himself.

'Oh.' A shiver went through Haukur. He didn't seem to care how they had heard. 'She took some pills she found in the cupboard. A whole handful of all the prescription drugs in the flat. Luckily she threw them up again, but it could have gone badly. Very badly.'

'Was she given counselling afterwards?' Freyja's voice managed to strike a warm, gentle note, without sounding smarmy. Huldar wouldn't be capable of producing a note like that even if he oiled his throat.

'No. We didn't report it. What was the point? No one can do anything. Believe me, we've tried everything. "Don't know, can't, not allowed". Those are the responses I get. Why do you think I went off the deep end at her school? Because of a cancelled Icelandic lesson?'

This time it was Freyja's turn to pull something out of her pocket. It wasn't a notebook but a card that she held out to the man. 'These are the contact details for a psychologist called Kjartan Erlendsson, who specialises in bullying cases. I recommend you get Adalheidur an appointment with him. He might not be able to stop the problem but he can help her work through it. If she's attempted suicide, it's vital she get psychiatric help. If you like, I can ask him to fit her in immediately. He's very sought-after.'

Haukur took the card. 'Seriously? You recommend this guy?'

'Yes. Have you come across him?'

'I have, actually. I went for a couple of sessions with him myself. I was hoping he'd be able to give me some tips for dealing with the situation, but I can't say he was much help.' Nevertheless, he put the card in his pocket, without saying if he intended to follow Freyja's advice. While he was trying to snap his pocket shut, Huldar asked his next question.

'How did you feel when you heard Stella was dead? In light of what you've been telling us.'

'How did I feel?' The man gave a dry laugh. 'To be completely honest, I was relieved. Not exactly pleased, but relieved. It was an odd sensation because I knew I should be shocked, but I just couldn't make myself feel it.' He scanned each of their faces in turn as they sat watching him, waiting for him to go on. 'But I didn't kill her.'

'Where were you on Sunday evening?' Although Huldar thought the man sounded convincing, his word alone wasn't enough. People could lie very persuasively. It didn't take any particular skill, just a powerful desire to get away with something.

'I was at football practice. Old boys. We practise every Sunday evening from seven to half past eight. Afterwards we went to the pub. If you like, I can give you the names of the other guys. I'd rather you didn't start ringing them all, but if that's what it takes to get you lot off my back, it'll be worth it.'

Gudlaugur jotted down the details of the three men as

Haukur read them out from his phone. He held the screen tilted away from them. It was hard to guess why, unless it was just paranoia. Gudlaugur closed his notebook. 'What about your wife? Where was she on Sunday evening?'

'My wife?' The man was startled. 'You don't think she's involved in this? Are you crazy?'

'Where was she?' Huldar took over. 'I don't suppose she was at football practice with you?'

'Er . . . she was at home.' Haukur seemed to search his memory, then repeated, more confidently: 'Yes. She was at home.'

'Can anyone confirm that?'

'Confirm it? No.'

'What about your daughter? Adalheidur? Was she at home too?'

'Adda? I think so. So they should be able to vouch for each other.' He sounded a little unsure. It was as if he'd remembered something he was unwilling to share with them. He opened his mouth, revealing a glimpse of teeth, then closed it again. Firmly.

'Does your wife have short hair?' asked Gudlaugur. 'Have you got a recent picture of her?'

'What's her hair got to do with it?' The little self-control Haukur had displayed up to now had vanished. His gaze flickered rapidly around the three of them, alighting most often on Freyja, who he plainly regarded as his most likely ally. 'My wife has nothing to do with Stella.'

'Does she have short hair?' Gudlaugur persisted doggedly.

'Yes. Is that a crime?' Haukur asked, then swung his head back to Freyja. 'What the hell is this? Don't you even know if you're looking for a man or a woman?'

Freyja didn't answer, just repeated Gudlaugur's question: 'Have you got a picture of her?'

'Yes, on my phone. But you're not having it.'

Huldar saw no reason to pursue this. They could easily track down a recent photo of his wife online – unless she was the only woman in Iceland not on Facebook. 'Right, I reckon we're done here. We've established that you were at football practice and your wife was here with your daughter. Possibly. Or perhaps alone.' Huldar clicked his tongue. 'Or somewhere else entirely.' He prepared to stand up. 'I think we've got all we want. For the time being.'

The cigarette didn't taste right. Maybe it was the dreary surroundings of the yard behind the police station; maybe it was the tender roof of his mouth where he had burnt himself on a toastie from the new microwave in the cafeteria. Either way, Huldar carried on puffing. After all, that was why he was out here in the biting cold.

He desperately needed to think. The buzz of activity in the department had risen to new heights, which made it hard to concentrate at his desk. He needed peace and quiet to pin down his thoughts. The visit to Adalheidur's father hadn't clarified anything beyond confirming that the man had something to hide. The same applied to the nurse, Ásta. His mind shied away from the thought that Gudlaugur was also being secretive. The trouble was that most people had something to hide. If only the public knew how little the police cared about minor transgressions when a murder investigation was under way. Not to mention when a young person was missing, feared dead.

There was definitely something dodgy about Haukur. When

Huldar recalled their conversation, it was like watching a film on his tablet when the wifi stuttered, causing the image to become suddenly pixelated. Why wouldn't he show them his Snapchat account? If he'd received or sent anything incriminating, it would already have vanished. He would hardly keep something like that on file. All Huldar could think of was that he wanted to hide who he was following.

But phone calls to Haukur's friends had confirmed that he had indeed been at football practice the evening Stella was attacked, and, assuming his three friends weren't all lying, he could hardly have slipped away, except to go for a leak at the pub afterwards. The police hadn't got hold of his wife yet, but the hairs found in Stella's fist could conceivably have been hers, going by the pictures of her online. However, the same pictures showed that she wasn't nearly tall or broad enough to have been the person in the CCTV footage from the cinema.

They'd identified another glimpse of the killer, this time as he was aiming his phone at the kiosk where Stella was serving. Again, he had been careful to keep his face hidden. They assumed he had taken a photo of Stella, though this couldn't be confirmed. The incident was easy to miss, like his entry during the interval. No wonder the detectives hadn't spotted him the first time round. It was hard to pick him out in the milling throng in the foyer, especially since they had been specifically looking for a man in a dark anorak rather than an overcoat.

They still hadn't found a shot of him sneaking behind the advertising display and guessed that he had done so during the crush when people were pouring back into the main auditorium. But at least it was clear that Stella could have done nothing at the cinema that evening to provoke the man to a frenzied attack since there had been no interaction between them.

One of the details they needed to look into was what had happened to his overcoat. The cinema had been searched in the immediate aftermath of the attack but with no result. All that had been found was a scarf and two non-matching gloves under the seats in the auditoriums. The crime-scene team hadn't been on the lookout for a coat, since they hadn't known about it at the time, but a garment that large couldn't have escaped their notice, so the assumption was that the man had been wearing it under his anorak, with the coat tails bundled up underneath. That would have made him look bulkier than he really was, which left a question mark over his actual build. He could be as thin as Haukur, or Adalheidur's mother, for that matter. The only problem was that both were shorter than the killer appeared to be.

But the biggest question preying on all their minds was who and where was victim number one?

Huldar took a final drag, then stubbed out his cigarette and pushed it into a nearby bin.

Chapter 26

'I've requested permission to run the DNA profile of the hair through the deCODE database. Running it through CODIS didn't produce any results.' Erla was looking fed up. The piles of paper on her desk were mounting ever higher. If things went on like this, her mouse and keyboard would soon be engulfed, and there'd be no room even for a coffee cup. 'I argued that the hairs could be from a victim we haven't yet found, victim number one. And that they'd ended up in Stella's fist in the killer's car. I pointed out that if we had a name, we might be able to save the woman in question, if she's still alive. But mainly I'm hoping the name will lead us to the killer.'

'Right.' Huldar couldn't think of anything more intelligent to say. The fact that permission hadn't instantly been refused was a clear sign that the investigation was going nowhere and management were getting desperate. And no wonder. Four days had passed since the attack on Stella and statistics were not on their side. As a rule, you'd expect to get the murderer in your sights within twenty-four hours; generally as soon as the body was found. Unlike their counterparts in big cities abroad, Icelandic murderers were normally still standing over the body when the police arrived. Not always, though. And these were the tough ones to crack. Huldar didn't think they stood much chance of getting the go-ahead for the deCODE search. It was an obvious course to try but he couldn't think of a single example of the police being allowed access to the genetics company's database. It probably contravened all sorts of privacy laws, or they'd be using that option every time they got their mitts on some DNA. 'Any chance you'll get the green light?'

'Not much. Unlikely – but not impossible. Isn't that our new motto?' Erla closed her eyes and exhaled wearily. 'The Data Protection Authority will have the final say. Apparently they refused permission in connection with a paternity case where the father was deceased, on the grounds that the subject hadn't given permission for his DNA to be used for anything other than genetic research. I'm just praying they'll overlook that consideration this time, seeing as a person's life could be at stake. That's why I made a big deal about the possibility that the hair came from victim number one.'

'Fingers crossed,' said Huldar. Then, after a moment, 'By the way, what's happening about the nurse? Are you still looking at her?'

Erla fiddled with the papers in front of her. She didn't seem particularly interested in their contents, just leafed through them distractedly as she talked. 'Nope. I've halted the checks on her for the moment. I can't justify them based on nothing more than a gut instinct. But that may yet change. Something's bound to turn up that links her to one or other of the kids.'

Huldar merely nodded. But he thought he knew what was behind this uncharacteristic decision. Erla usually followed her own convictions, come what may. But he'd heard the whispering doing the rounds in the department, the empty gossip about the nature of her interest in the nurse. Totally absurd – but then gossip didn't require any basis in reality to spread like wildfire. Or to be resurrected. Back before Erla had become head of department, before the station had been abuzz with her one-night stand with Huldar and the subsequent sexual harassment inquiry, plenty of people had reckoned she was gay: she had short hair, did a man's job and wasn't willing to jump into bed with every member of the team who gave her the come-on. No further evidence needed.

Huldar didn't for a second believe there was any truth in this but that was irrelevant. Her position was shaky, that's what had got the rumour mill going again; her team were no longer worried about keeping on the right side of her. All the muttering about her sexuality felt so last century; it just showed what a dysfunctional workplace CID was. Homosexuality wouldn't have been considered an issue in most offices these days; certainly nothing to gossip about. But that was beside the point. If it wasn't her sexual preferences, her colleagues would have found something else to bitch about: a drink problem, a gambling habit, you name it. It was a pity their relationship was too fragile for him to point this out to her and urge her to ignore the whispering.

'I happen to know that Ásta's on evening shift for the next few days,' he said. 'If you don't object, I'd like to drop by the hospital later and try having a word with her there. It might jolt her into opening up. No one wants a visit from the cops at work. I thought I might wear my uniform – to leave her colleagues in no doubt about what I am. But first, I've got a proposition for you.'

'What's that?' Erla asked unenthusiastically.

'How about you and me go and pay a visit to the father of the boy Egill was bullying? It'll give you a chance to escape this mountain of paperwork for a while and get some fresh air at the same time.' To his surprise, she didn't immediately dismiss the suggestion. 'Maybe it'll turn out that Stella and Egill knew each other after all – maybe without actually realising it. Most of the abuse they doled out online was under aliases. Their victims could have clubbed together and attacked Egill. Who knows? The boy's dad could have found out about the bullying and wanted to put a stop to it.'

'You've got to be kidding.'

'No. Not necessarily. Everything about this case is so bizarre that who's to say the solution isn't just as unlikely?' Huldar waited, giving her time to think. When it seemed she was going to refuse him, he added: 'Perhaps the link to Egill is just what the girls were afraid we'd uncover.'

'No. We know what that was.'

'What?' Huldar hadn't heard.

Erla rooted around on her desk, then pulled over some papers from the top of a pile. She handed them to Huldar. 'They've just unearthed this.'

Huldar skimmed through what turned out to be the printout of a Facebook page. Adalheidur's name appeared under the picture of a pair of enormous boobs in a ridiculously skimpy bra. Nothing else was visible: head, limbs and torso had all been cut off. Next to her name was the e-mail address: *fuckmegood@gmail.com*. 'What the hell?' he asked. Leafing through the following pages he saw more photos: some were normal shots of Adalheidur fully clothed, others were of headless, semi-naked female bodies in a variety of sexual positions. They were accompanied by conversations between her and other users apparently discussing the cost of various sex acts. He looked up, momentarily confused. 'Christ. Is

Adalheidur selling herself? Stella and her mates too, maybe?'

Erla reached for the papers and replaced them on top of the pile. 'It's not what it looks like. We can safely assume Adalheidur has nothing to do with it. The IT guy says he found a link to the page when he was going through Stella's browsing history. He couldn't get in at first but eventually he tracked down the username and password of the fake profile Stella had set up for Adalheidur. She'd used it to register her with this prostitution page on Facebook. Although it's a closed group, he managed to access it using the fake details. The girls had also created that e-mail address for her, so interested parties could get in touch. It takes real fucking ingenuity to dream up something that cheap.'

Huldar gestured to the pages. 'You don't have to be a genius to see that the pictures don't match. Adalheidur's face doesn't appear in any of the nude shots.'

'No, but come on, Huldar; I don't need to tell you that it's the norm to put up tit or arse shots that don't belong to the woman in question. The punters don't seem to care.'

'And?'

'Nothing as yet. We're trying to trace the men who got in touch with Adalheidur on this page or via the e-mail address Stella set up. Almost all the punters have fake profiles but IT are working flat out to identify them.' Erla shrugged. 'Who knows? Maybe one of these guys freaked out when he discovered he'd been taken for a ride and decided to get even. For all we know, Stella could have used the information to blackmail them. There's no evidence of that yet, but it's anyone's guess what we'll find if we dig deeper.'

Huldar was silent while he digested this theory. 'So what's Egill's link to all this? Did he create a profile for someone on this page too?' All the information he'd got from the IT department, before interviewing Egill's friends, had involved abusive comments and a few posts that could be classed as direct threats. Nothing to do with porn or prostitution.

'That's still unclear. Nothing's been found, but they're going over his computer again with that in mind. After all, there are plenty of pages for rent boys as well.'

'Hmm.' Huldar had nothing further to contribute at this stage. It would be premature to speculate. 'You're just waiting, then?'

'Yep.'

'So there's no reason why you shouldn't come with me?'

Erla glanced through the glass wall at the open-plan office. Huldar half turned, wondering what had attracted her attention, but couldn't see anything out of the ordinary. His colleagues were all hard at it, most of them in front of their computers or on the phone, some in pairs or small groups.

'OK. I'll come. It'll kill some time.'

On the way out she walked disconcertingly close to Huldar, smiling and chatting matily with him as they passed between the desks. It didn't take him long to twig: of course, she was trying to quash the rumours; give her underlings the impression that the two of them were getting friendly again. To hell with the internal inquiry and to hell with the effect it might have on him.

The door was opened by Ævar's son Davíd, the kid Egill had been picking on. He was noticeably small for his age, much smaller than Egill's friends who'd come in to the police station earlier that day, though they were only a year older than him. He was thin and fair, with a sprinkling of pale freckles on his cheeks and nose. A pair of big blue eyes flickered nervously from Huldar to Erla under an overgrown fringe. The unexpected visit seemed to have made him anxious, though he had no reason to be; they were in plain clothes and there was nothing to suggest this was anything other than a friendly call. While he was waiting for them to introduce themselves, his father called from inside the flat to ask who it was. Erla broke the silence first. 'Hello. Is your father in?'

The boy nodded and called into the flat: 'Dad, there are some people here to see you.'

'What people?'

The boy looked back at them and asked: 'Who are you?'

'Could you just fetch your dad, please?' Huldar didn't want to have to tell him why they were there. The boy disappeared inside and they were left staring down a short hallway. The walls were bare and there was nothing to see but a row of pegs for outdoor clothes, a few pairs of shoes and a coat stand. None of the usual hall furniture: no chest of drawers, bench or chair. A single unshaded bulb hung from the ceiling. Huldar guessed the man must have moved in recently. That would fit with the information he'd dug up that Davíd's parents were divorced. In fact, he hadn't expected to encounter the boy there, having taken it for granted that he'd be living with his mother.

The man who came to the door looked belligerent. He had dark hair and was wearing a white T-shirt and jeans and holding a sandwich, obviously in domestic mode. Huldar noted his build: tall, broad-shouldered and muscular, the complete opposite of his son. But not unlike the killer in the CCTV footage. The man gripped the door-handle as if he was about to slam it in their faces. 'Can I help you?'

'Yes, you can. We'd prefer to have a word in private, though.' Erla's gaze slid past him to Davíd.

Ævar turned and shooed his son back inside. Then he looked back at them. 'What's this about?'

Erla explained who they were and said they'd like to talk to him about Egill's disappearance. Instead of asking them in, the man asked, 'Who's Egill?'

'The boy who's been bullying your son. He's missing and we're trying to find him. Haven't you seen the news?'

The man shook his head. He still showed no signs of letting them in. 'You don't think he's here?'

'No,' Erla answered shortly.

'Well, what then? I know nothing about it. Neither does my son.'

'Where were you on Tuesday evening?' Huldar would rather have built up to this gradually but felt it couldn't wait. He wouldn't put it past the guy to shut the door on them. If they had to insist on finishing the interview down at the station, it would only give him time to prepare his story.

'Tuesday evening? Why?' Then it seemed to dawn on him. 'Hang on a minute. Is that when this Egill went missing?'

'Yes.'

'And you think I had something to do with that?' The man looked at first astonished, then angry. 'Why the hell would I have snatched him?'

'Where were you on Tuesday evening?'

'Er, I . . .' The man frowned, thinking. 'Oh yes, I was at my archery class.'

'What time did it start and how long did it go on?'

'From eight to nine. But I hung around chatting with some

of the others afterwards, so I probably didn't leave till about half past nine.'

'Where are these classes held?'

Ævar gave Huldar the street name but couldn't remember the number, not that it mattered since there probably wasn't another archery club in the city, let alone on the street in question.

'Can anyone confirm you were there?'

'Yes. Everyone who attended. There were nine or ten of us – I think. I don't know the other members well enough to have their numbers or anything but the club must have a list of those registered for the class. And I can tell you the first names of a couple of the people I was chatting to afterwards.'

Huldar duly noted these down. 'What about before eight? Where were you then?' According to the original files they'd obtained from Snapchat, the videos of the attack on Egill had been made at half past seven the evening he vanished. So the man could conceivably have attacked him at seven and been at the archery club by eight.

'I was here. At home.'

'Alone?'

'Yes, alone.'

'I see.' Huldar's gaze wandered down the bare hallway behind the man. 'What about your son? He wasn't here?'

'No. He was at his mother's. If I say I was alone, I mean alone. Not alone with another person.' The man had flushed, probably from anger.

'We couldn't see your anorak, could we?' Huldar pointed at the coats hanging on the pegs behind the man.

'My anorak?' The man looked disgusted but reached out and took down a large, blue jacket, not unlike the one the attacker had been wearing. But when he held it out, they saw that it didn't have a hood. They examined it anyway, noting that although it was a bit grubby, there were no traces of blood on it. Huldar handed it back and thanked the man.

Ævar took the anorak and chucked it on the floor behind him. 'Why the hell would you think I'd taken the boy?'

'We've seen some of the things he wrote about your son online. You could have lost patience and decided not to wait for the problem to go away by itself.'

'How about doing your homework next time?'

'What do you mean?' Erla was clearly annoyed by the way Huldar had been steering the conversation.

'That boy doesn't bother my son any more. He's no longer part of Davíd's life. We took the decision to move him to another school last month. There are other, less drastic ways of dealing with bullying than abducting kids.' The man stepped back from the door in order to close it. 'I advise you to look somewhere else. The boy's not here.'

Before Huldar had a chance to point out that Egill's most recent posts about Davíd dated from that weekend, the man had slammed the door in their faces.

They stood there, staring blankly at the wood.

Chapter 27

Security was surprisingly lax at the hospital. Huldar slipped in through the ambulance entrance, nodding to the man on duty, who let him pass without comment. Perhaps he looked like a patient. He was unshaven and dishevelled after working flat out on the investigation all week and had dark circles under his eyes to rival Erla's. At the last minute he had changed his mind about the uniform; he was too tired and couldn't be bothered to put it on. Besides, he would be heading straight home after this and didn't want to draw his neighbours' attention to his job. They'd almost forgotten about it, which gave him a break from their endless requests to investigate who'd been in the dustbin store or what had happened to the post that had gone missing from the mailboxes.

Despite being in plain clothes, he was allowed to wander through the hospital unchallenged. In his search for a lift, he soon found himself lost in a maze of passages. From time to time he encountered a member of staff but not one of them took any notice of him. They all seemed to be in a hurry and looked as tired as he felt. Evidently, if he wasn't clutching at his heart or writhing on the floor in the throes of an epileptic fit, he was none of their business.

Eventually he came across a lift.

When the doors opened on the correct floor, he was met by the characteristic hospital smell of disinfectant mixed with drugs,

sick people and bad food. Huldar wrinkled his nose and shuddered. The moment he pushed open the door to the ward, the
smell intensified, now accompanied by a low electronic bleeping.

Apart from that it was quiet. This was a welcome change
from the depressing noises you often got outside visiting
hours. As he entered the ward, he hoped fervently that he
wouldn't end his days with a long stay in hospital, though
the odds of that were not in his favour. Still, come to think
of it, the alternative was little better. If he died young, it
would almost inevitably be in an accident or involve something
else sudden, which meant he might end up on the pathologist's
slab. His mind shrank away from the thought.

The nurse in reception jumped when Huldar tapped on the
high desk. Behind her, through a glass partition, he could see
a bank of large screens displaying graphs and numbers. They
reminded Huldar more of a financial institution than a
hospital, as if the health service had rented out space in the
ward to a firm of stockbrokers as a way of supplementing
their income. The woman looked up, startled, from the papers
she had been poring over. It wasn't Ásta but then he'd realised
that before he knocked; her hair was dark, with grey roots
at the parting. 'Good evening.' He smiled, trying to project
an aura of 'normal', since he could tell from the woman's
wide-eyed gaze that she had taken him for a fairly presentable
junkie on the hunt for drugs.

'Can I help you?' She put down her pen. 'Are you here to
see a patient?'

'No, actually. My name's Huldar Traustason and I'm from
the police. I'm looking for Ásta Einarsdóttir. I gather she's
on duty this evening.'

'Yes, that's right.' The woman got up, her curiosity roused, as Huldar had hoped it would be. Coming out from behind the desk, she added: 'Ásta's with a patient at the moment. Would you like to wait in the kitchen? I can offer you a coffee. Or some juice.'

Huldar, picturing a faded plastic jug of diluted orange muck made from concentrate, hastily accepted a coffee. The nurse offered him a seat at a tiny kitchen table, fetched him a cup from the cupboard and filled it with black coffee. The room was so cramped that the woman could barely turn round and Huldar had difficulty folding his legs under the table. He felt like Alice in Wonderland after swallowing the 'Eat Me' cake. He was also embarrassingly aware of the smoke clinging to his clothes from the quick cigarette he'd sneaked outside.

'Here you are.' The woman handed him the cup and sat down opposite him. She had to twist sideways on the chair as no more legs would fit under the table. 'Can I ask what this is about? Does it involve the hospital, since you've come to see her here?'

'I just need a chat with her about a case we're investigating. It has nothing to do with the hospital. I only came here because I was sure of finding her and I assumed she'd need to sleep during the day tomorrow. I promise not to distract her from her duties for long.'

'We'll cope. Though I'd advise you not to try catching her during the day shift. That would be quite a different story.'

Huldar nodded and took a sip of scalding coffee. 'No, of course not. I wouldn't dream of it.' He took another sip, allowing the silence to fuel the woman's curiosity.

He had to hand it to her: she resisted the temptation for an uncomfortably long time. Huldar was beginning to think he'd have to say something, comment on the weather or the plans to move the domestic airport from neighbouring Vatnsmýri to a new, out-of-town location, when suddenly she cracked. 'What is this case, anyway? Excuse me being nosy, but Ásta's such a lovely person that I can't imagine her getting mixed up in anything illegal. Are you absolutely sure it's not connected to her job? I ask because of that nurse you lot hauled through the courts for no good reason a couple of years ago. People here are still on edge about it, especially in wards like this one where deaths are inevitable.'

'I promise you it has nothing to do with the hospital.'

'Good.' The woman seemed satisfied with this until she realised it hadn't got her very far. Huldar could teach her a thing or two about interrogation, such as not asking several questions at once, since that gave the interviewee a choice about which one to answer. But there was no putting her off. 'What case is it, then?'

Huldar smiled and took another mouthful of coffee. 'It involves a mobile phone.'

'A mobile phone?' the woman said incredulously. 'You mean they make you work evenings and night shifts just because of a phone? Was it stolen?'

Again, she had inadvertently given Huldar a choice of questions to answer. He went for the last one. 'It's connected to an incident that's rather more serious than theft.' He was surprised Ásta hadn't told her colleagues. To him, that would have been the normal reaction of someone with a clear conscience. It wasn't as if people like Ásta received a visit from the police every day. If she had nothing to hide and the phone had been dumped in her letterbox by chance, you'd have thought she'd have mentioned the incident during her coffee break. 'You mean she hasn't told you about it?'

'No, I have no idea what you're talking about.' At that moment a light-bulb seemed to come on in the woman's head. 'Hang on a minute. It's not connected to the murdered girl, is it? The one in the news? Wasn't there a mobile phone involved?'

Huldar adopted a poker face. 'I'm afraid I can't comment.'

The woman couldn't hide her disappointment. 'No, I don't suppose you can. Though take it from me, Ásta can't possibly be mixed up in that. Her job is to save lives, not kill people. Only last Friday she saved a man's life by giving him CPR in the hospital car park on her way home from her shift. And that's just one example. There's a long list of people who owe their lives to her.'

'I don't doubt for a minute that she's a good nurse. Honestly. This is just a formality and it's up to her whether she tells you about it or not. Though I'd kind of assumed she'd have discussed it with her colleagues. But maybe you two haven't been working together recently?'

The woman frowned. 'Yes, we have actually.'

'What's going on?' Ásta appeared in the doorway, a forbidding expression on her pretty face. Clearly, Huldar was the last person she wanted to see sitting there chatting to one of her colleagues. She wrung the disposable rubber glove in her hand. 'What are *you* doing here?'

'I came to have a chat with you. I thought it would be more convenient than disturbing you at home since you work shifts and I'm never sure when you'll be asleep.' His smile did nothing to mollify her since it was so obviously fake. She must know he wouldn't have thought twice about waking her up if it was necessary.

'I've already answered all your questions. Several times.' Ásta avoided the eye of the other woman, who was still sitting, embarrassed, at the little table. 'This is neither the time nor the place to go through that nonsense again.'

Huldar untangled his legs from under the table and stood up. 'Shall we step outside the ward for a minute? I promise it won't take long.' His intention wasn't necessarily to extract answers so much as to unnerve her and leave her in no doubt that they still had her in their sights.

Ásta gave an infuriated sigh. 'You can have five minutes.'

They seated themselves on a sofa in the area by the lifts. Ásta planted herself at one end, Huldar at the other, to avoid sitting uncomfortably close.

'You've got four minutes left.' Ásta folded her arms in the instinctively defensive posture of someone who wants to put up a barrier between herself and the person she's talking to. She was still wringing the rubber glove.

'Has anything come back to you?' Huldar draped one arm over the back of the sofa, purely to annoy her, and her face tightened. 'You've had a bit of time to think about it now. Perhaps you've remembered something.'

'No. Nothing's come back to me because there's nothing to remember. What do I have to do to get through to you? Do you want me to make something up?'

'No. For God's sake, please don't do that.' Huldar spread himself out a bit more. 'Just tell me the truth. We both know you know more than you're letting on.'

Ásta narrowed her eyes angrily, then unexpectedly smiled. 'You reek of smoke. I advise you to drop by the cancer ward on your way out, if you want to see how you'll end up. It's a sobering experience, I can tell you.'

Huldar met her fake smile with one of his own. 'Sweet of

you to be concerned about my health but that's not what we're discussing here. We're talking about the murder of a young girl and the disappearance of a boy, which you're withholding information about. I find that pretty incredible, given the way your colleague has just been singing your praises. She says you saved a man's life only a few days ago, yet here you are, refusing to say a word when you could save a young person's life. That takes some bloody nerve.'

The blood mottled Ásta's cheeks. Dropping her gaze, she looked away and stared silently into space.

Taking this as a sign that he'd found a chink in her armour, Huldar increased the pressure. 'Maybe you'd like to see some pictures of the treatment the girl was subjected to? Or the boy? You might find it of professional interest. You could tell me how long the boy's likely to live after the injuries he received. Maybe then you'd understand why we haven't got time to go running round after people who refuse to help us.'

Ásta was still staring into space but her profile was now fretted with pain and he thought he detected a hint of fear as well. He was well aware that we have a tendency to read what we want to into other people's reactions, but he reckoned he'd finally got through to her, especially when her jaw relaxed and she opened her mouth.

'Your five minutes are up.' She got up and stalked off, leaving Huldar alone on the sofa.

There were few other cars about. Huldar had been driving the streets for nearly an hour now. After his unsuccessful attempt to grill Ásta he had felt restless. There was no question of going home and flopping in front of the TV, not while he knew the missing boy was out there somewhere. What was he supposed to watch? A cop show from America where his job was done by geniuses? Or the Nordic version in which the cops were collapsing under the weight of their own failings?

Though, in the event, watching TV wouldn't have achieved any less than this aimless driving around town. Of course, he hadn't kidded himself he was going to find the boy, since an intensive search had already been made of the Greater Reykjavík area. In fact, the hunt was still going on, in case the boy had been moved. But sometimes you just had to go tilting at windmills, to appease your conscience. And his endless, slow circling hadn't been completely in vain. He was now convinced that there was no obvious location in the capital area where a living person could be held prisoner for any length of time. Whatever cul-de-sac or one-way street he crawled down, everywhere there were signs of life. Houses and flats stood in tight ranks, either side by side or in clusters. Even the building sites abandoned in the wake of the financial crash were bustling neighbourhoods today. The new construction sites that had replaced them showed every sign of busy activity and were no doubt swarming with hordes of machine operators, tradesmen and labourers by day. It was also apparent that business was booming in the industrial estates, retail parks, riding stables and all the other neighbourhoods he passed through.

Wherever you looked, the city was thrumming with life; there was no sign of death or decay.

Of course, it was always possible that one of the private houses had a windowless cellar with walls through which no shouts or screams could penetrate. However slowly you cruised by, you couldn't spot something like that from a car window. But building inspectors in the capital area had compiled a list of houses with cellars of this type and, though it had been a major undertaking, they'd all been checked out.

It would be different if Egill was dead. For one thing, the search for him wouldn't feel like a ticking time bomb. Mind you, it would be much easier to hide a corpse in a built-up area than a live human being with functioning vocal cords. Only temporarily, though. In a heated space, the stench would soon become as big a problem as calling for help would. All phone calls to complain about bad smells were now being monitored, whether they were made to the police, to council offices, the fire brigade or utility companies – everywhere they could think of that people might report a problem of this kind. But no complaints had been received, apart from one call that had resulted in the bust of a small illegal still in a high-rise flat.

Huldar yawned, then inhaled deeply, breathing in a stale reek of smoke as he had been chain-smoking while he drove. Reaching for the overflowing ashtray, he tried in vain to close it. Ásta's words about cancer came back to him and he grimaced, then felt frustrated yet again that he hadn't shouted after her as she stomped away, to ask if she'd remembered yet where she knew Gudlaugur from. But he knew that even if she had, she wouldn't have told him.

He sat at a red light. His car was the only one waiting at the big junction and Huldar was aware of a sudden sensation almost of loneliness as he drummed his fingers on the wheel. There was no one waiting for him at home: no wife, no dog, no cat. Not even a confused goldfish in a too-small bowl.

It was high time he settled down. Found himself a woman and made an effort for once to hold on to her. He didn't have to look far. It was Freyja he wanted. Perhaps partly because she wasn't interested in him. It made her more of a challenge, and victory would be the sweeter in the end. The lights changed to green and he turned for home, his mood lifting at the thought.

Chapter 28

Freyja stared at the exercises the teacher had marked. She hadn't been at the lecture when he'd handed them back to the students so she'd had to fetch them from a special pigeon-hole for slackers. Seeing what he had written on the first page, she was relieved. She wouldn't have wanted her fellow students to read his comments. In red he had scrawled: *Unless you're working in some other number system than base ten, I advise you to see your tutor.* Below this was a large zero, underlined twice and followed by three exclamation marks. Briefly she wondered if zero was a better mark in another number system and this was just the lecturer's little joke, but a quick online search confirmed that zero is always zero, regardless of what base you're counting in.

She stood there with the exercises in her hand, gazing around her at the big university building. It was a wonderful place, a refuge from the daily grind, a place dedicated to learning. She remembered the delightful feeling of buying the thick course books and stationery back in the autumn. The books had smelt of a new beginning, an opportunity to start over and do things differently this time. Become a business-woman who worked in exciting foreign cities and bought her food from small specialist shops. It was a pity she'd overlooked the obvious flaw in her plans: wherever she moved, whatever aspect of her life she changed, she would never be able to escape herself. And it was time to face up to the fact. The exams were looming and if she were honest, it was unlikely she would pass a single one.

There was no getting away from it: embarking on these studies had been a bad move. She wouldn't be any happier as a businesswoman than she was as a psychologist. For one thing, she hadn't the slightest interest in business. She'd do better to face up to her issues than bury herself in textbooks about a subject that held no appeal for her, in search of that elusive sense of fulfilment.

Business studies wouldn't help overcome her worries about Baldur and little Saga, let alone rescue her finances, at least not for years. She would have to find another way. Freyja sighed and took one more look around the building. Then she went over to the bins by the entrance, tossed in her home-work and walked out of the university for the last time as a student.

Her wretched car refused to start at first, which she put down to its wish to linger a little longer on campus and relish the camaraderie of being among cars of the same calibre. Although most students seemed to drive around in new-looking models that worked, there were a number of old bangers in no better nick than Baldur's. She would miss them too. Still, looking on the bright side, it was the last time she'd be faced with sarcastic comments scribbled in red.

The car finally coughed into life and, to a grinding metallic lament, she pulled out of the parking space and drove away.

Her first stop would be the Children's House, to inform her boss that she was back full time, a task she wasn't looking forward to at all. It was humiliating to have to admit defeat, especially since her colleagues had been sceptical about her plans from the start. In retrospect, it was obvious why. They'd known her well enough to see that she wasn't cut out for a job that revolved around facts and figures rather than behaviour and emotions. But she had chosen to ignore the fact, and now here she was, crawling back with her tail between her legs.

In the event, the director proved very understanding and didn't for a moment rub Freyja's nose in her failure. Instead, she invited her to grab a coffee and bring it along to her office. Freyja felt guilty for even entertaining the idea that the woman would be anything other than kind. Every time her boss said something encouraging, she hid her sheepish expression in her coffee cup.

Nothing was more surprising than when people treated you better than you felt you'd deserved.

'Moving on. How's it working out with the police? Everybody happy?'

Freyja nodded, relieved at the change of subject. Having to be grateful all the time quickly became wearing. 'Yes, I think so. Unfortunately the investigation's not getting anywhere but that has nothing to do with me. It just means that my contribution has ended up being fairly minor.'

'As long as you react promptly and do all they ask of you, we can hold our heads high. You know better than most how vital it is to keep the police on side. Your role finishes today, doesn't it?'

'I'm not sure if they were including the weekend. But seeing how little I've achieved, I feel I owe it to them.' Freyja wasn't actually expecting to hear from the police. The truth was that she needed the weekend to reconcile herself to returning to full-time work at the Children's House, and was afraid that if she said she was free, her boss would put her on standby. Weekends were invariably when the worst cases came in, cases involving such appalling mistreatment that they couldn't wait until Monday. After several months' break from these shifts, she needed time to prepare herself mentally. Like Baldur's car, she felt she needed to get started nice and slowly, in first gear. Besides, she'd promised Saga's mother she'd look after the little girl on Saturday and there was no way she was attending a callout with her in tow.

The director slurped her coffee. 'How are the poor kids doing? The ones you've been interviewing? It's tough losing someone close to you in your teens. They make enough drama out of much less at that age. Are they getting grief counselling?'

'Yes. It's been offered to those who need it.' Freyja put down her empty cup. 'It turns out there's a bullying angle, so it's not entirely straightforward. Not all sweetness and light.'

'Oof. I'm no expert but I know those cases can be ugly. Much worse than when I was young, though you'd never have thought it possible at the time.' She looked thoughtful. 'Have you been advising them on bullying? I'm not sure that's such a good idea. The Child Protection Agency employ people who are better qualified in that area than you.'

'No, I haven't been asked to step in or anything. The purpose of the investigation isn't to tackle bullying. But I consulted a guy who was at university with me, who's an expert on the subject, just to make sure I'm up to date.'

'Oh? Who's that? Anyone I know?'

'His name's Kjartan and he has a practice in town. I'm not sure if you know him.'

'What's his full name?'

'Kjartan Ýmir Erlendsson.'

'Oh, yes. I know him. He's married to my friend's cousin. I understand he's up to his ears in bullying cases.'

Freyja made an effort to control her features. 'Isn't he divorced? Or in the middle of a divorce, rather? I got that impression from something he said, but I could have misunderstood.'

'Divorced? Good heavens, no. They're happily married. Or at least they were last weekend when my friend went round for dinner.'

'Then I must have misunderstood.' Freyja smiled smoothly and rose to her feet. 'I should be going if I want to be ready for a possible callout.'

Freyja reckoned she'd managed to take her leave in a reasonably composed manner, successfully disguising her fury. Why did she have to end up with a total shit every time she went out looking for what, on the face of it, wasn't really asking much – just a little companionship and sex? It wasn't like she was so desperate that she'd jump on the first man who offered.

She was just trying to coax her car into life again when Huldar rang to request her presence. He didn't know what had hit him when she swore at him before he could even explain what he wanted. But it made her feel better.

Gudlaugur bore the brunt of her irritation with men, unfair though this was. He'd never done anything to her other than be unnaturally polite.

It seemed Gudlaugur had been put in charge of interviewing Stella's friends. Erla had ordered Huldar to join her in questioning the men who'd taken the bait and tried to pay for sex with Adalheidur. Apparently, this had come up after he'd rung Freyja, so it had nothing to do with how gruff she'd been with him on the phone. Realising that Gudlaugur was bound to think her bad temper was caused by disappointment at Huldar's absence, Freyja tried to pull herself together.

'We know you were involved, Bjarney. Your friends have all admitted it. So it would be in your interests to do the same.' Gudlaugur hesitated, then added more gently: 'I mean, if you *were* involved.'

Freyja winced. He wasn't the right man for this. He was too shy and retiring, and didn't seem able to interpret the girls' complicated reactions and at times puzzling answers. She had intervened when she felt it was unavoidable, but tried not to tread on his toes. Gudlaugur's problem was that he wanted to keep everybody happy. She longed to whisper in his ear that in circumstances like these that simply wasn't possible.

'I wasn't involved. Not directly. You know, not really.' The girl was the last to be questioned and it hardly seemed worth listening to her trotting out the same story as all the others. No doubt this interview would end in floods of tears as well. Then again, this girl, Bjarney, had been Stella's best friend, so there was a possibility she might actually know more. Whether they could prise it out of her was another matter. 'We didn't mean to cause trouble. We were only messing, you know. It was just jokes. I knew about it but I didn't do anything. It wasn't my idea. But, like I said, it was just jokes.'

The same excuse as Egill's friends had given. 'Joke is hardly the right word, Bjarney.' Freyja put on a suitably stern expression. 'We don't need to tell you how serious this is. Stella's dead and a boy who's a year younger than you is missing. If you're not being honest with us, you'd better do some hard thinking about what kind of person you are. You see, this is going to come back to haunt you further down the line, so it would be best for you to come clean now. Get it off your chest and, I can assure you, you'll feel much better. Keeping bad secrets eats you up inside. Like a piece of fruit full of maggots. You know, it looks normal on the outside, but if they're allowed to gnaw away inside, it shows up on the surface in the end. You wouldn't like that. Not a pretty girl like you.' Freyja noticed that Gudlaugur was licking his lips nervously, unhappy with what she was saying, but she didn't give a damn.

The girl was looking shaken, so Freyja's words must have had the desired effect. 'My dad told me I had to insist on a lawyer if you were mean. Can I have one now?'

Freyja let Gudlaugur answer this. 'We're interviewing you as a witness, Bjarney, not as a suspect. Witnesses don't need lawyers. Besides, they don't come cheap. It would cost you an arm and a leg to call one out. Are you sure your dad's happy to pay that?'

'Er . . . I dunno.' Bjarney faltered. 'But, like, I'm sure he'd pay to stop me going to jail.'

Gudlaugur frowned. 'Why should you go to jail, Bjarney? We don't suspect you of having done anything to Stella. We just want you to tell us all you know about this prostitution website. The man who attacked your friend could have been linked to it. Perhaps he was angry when he found out Adalheidur's profile was fake.'

Freyja felt compelled to continue in the role of bad cop. 'If so, you never know, he might come after the people who helped Stella too. Surely it's better for you if the police catch the guy?'

The girl slumped lower in her chair. She was wearing the same waist-length jacket as the last time Freyja had seen her, with the same long scarf around her neck. She'd dug her hands into her pockets when she sat down and they'd remained there ever since. As she sank lower in her seat, her jacket rode up until it looked as if she had no neck. 'I don't want to get into trouble? Because of Mum and Dad, you know.'

'I think what will matter most to your parents is whether you can help us find Stella's killer. Even if they're a bit cross at first, they'll get over it. It'll be better than if they found out you've been keeping secrets. That would make them a lot angrier.' Gudlaugur reached for the water jug and filled the girl's glass, although she had declined his offer of a drink. 'I can promise you that.'

Bjarney stared blankly at her glass. 'Do you promise I won't, like, go to prison?'

'You're too young to go to prison. If the crime was very serious, some other solution would be found.'

The girl raised her eyes to Gudlaugur's face. 'What do you mean by very serious?'

'Well, murder, of course, and rape, which I don't suppose is relevant in this case. Arson – starting fires, where there's a threat to human life – that sort of thing.'

'I haven't killed or raped anyone. Or set anything on fire. I didn't really do anything, honest. It was all Stella.'

'All what?' Gudlaugur leant towards her, one eye on the recorder to make sure it was working. 'What did Stella do?'

'It was her idea to put Adalheidur on that site. I didn't think it was right but I didn't dare say anything. Stella used to get, like, really mad if you didn't agree with her? She made up an e-mail address for the fake profile as well. I just sat beside her and watched.'

'We know that, Bjarney. Your mates have already told us. They were there too, remember?'

'Not always. Not the time we got the e-mail from that guy. He'd already put a creepy message on the porn site, saying he wanted to meet Adalheidur. We just thought it was funny, you know. But the stuff in the e-mail was disgusting. He was a real perv.'

'Who's this man you're talking about? Lots of men posted on the Facebook site and sent e-mails.'

'I don't know his name. His e-mail address was something stupid, like Mr Lover or something tragic like that.'

'We've seen the messages, Bjarney. We accessed the inbox.'

Bjarney flinched and dropped her eyes to avoid Gudlaugur's stare. 'Not the messages from that guy. 'Cos Stella deleted them. Even our mates didn't know about them. Not about all of them, anyway.'

'What exactly happened? What was in the messages she deleted?' Gudlaugur leant closer again, from excitement this time.

'She . . . the thing is . . . Stella wrote back to this man and told him where Adalheidur lived. Pretended to be her, you know, and they made a date and everything. And agreed how much he should pay.' Bjarney peeped up at them both through her lashes before continuing. 'He was supposed to pay twenty thousand krónur. We found out from a porn site that that's what people are charging.'

'Then what?'

'He replied and said he'd be there.'

'How long ago was this?'

'Um, about a month.'

Gudlaugur nodded. Freyja felt it best not to interfere now that he was getting somewhere. 'What happened then? Did he go round to her place? Or did you send him somewhere else?'

'We sent him round to her place.' The girl was almost whispering now. 'Afterwards he went mental. He sent this scary message saying he was going to get even with us.' She lowered her voice so much they could barely hear. Gudlaugur had to ask her to repeat it for the recorder. 'I mean, suddenly he knew Stella's name and everything.'

It didn't take a genius to guess where that information had come from. Adalheidur must have worked out who was responsible when the man turned up at her house. 'What exactly did he say about getting even?'

'Just that he would. Get even, I mean. But Stella tricked him.'

'Tricked him?' Gudlaugur sounded as surprised as Freyja was feeling at the turn the story had taken. 'How?'

'She found the IP number he'd sent the messages from. She googled the instructions, you know. Her boyfriend's brother works for an internet company and he found out where the IP number was registered. So she got hold of the man's name and address. And she looked up his wife's name in the telephone directory.'

'Then what?'

'She e-mailed him saying she'd tell his wife if he didn't pay up.'

'How much?'

'Fifty thousand. Afterwards, she wished she'd asked for more. He'd definitely have paid.'

'What was the man's name?'

'I don't know. She wouldn't tell me.' Her voice betrayed a hint of resentment. 'I think, like, she was scared I'd try to get money out of him too? But I never would of. Anyway, I never saw any of it. We went out for a meal, like, once, and Stella paid. But that was all. She kept the rest and spent it on stuff for herself. Like clothes.'

'So she got the money? How? Did she meet the man?'

'Yes. She made him meet her at Hlemmur. He turned up and gave her the money in an envelope.'

'Are you sure? She wasn't just making it up?'

'No. I'm sure. Because I went with her, she made me – for safety? I sat on a bench and pretended not to know her. In case he went for her. But he didn't do anything, he just handed her the envelope. Then he spat on the floor, right by her feet.'

'Can you describe him?'

'Er . . . yes. I think so. He had a black eye.'

'A black eye?'

'Yeah, like really bruised.'

Gudlaugur pushed back his chair and stood up, asking the girl to come with him so they could take down her description. He explained that instead of temporary things like his black eye or what he was wearing, she should focus on describing things that would stay the same, like the colour of his eyes and hair, his build and whether he was fat or thin. She didn't seem to understand what was meant by his build, and pointed out that a person's hair colour could change. Freyja, taking in her dyed mane, saw what she meant. If being brunette became fashionable tomorrow, this girl would be dark-haired by evening.

As they left the interview room, Freyja spotted Huldar

escorting a man towards them, presumably one of the 'creeps' who'd contacted Adalheidur and was on his way to be inter-viewed by Erla.

Bjarney stopped dead, clutching Gudlaugur's arm and pointing. 'That's him,' she whispered frantically. 'That's the guy. The creepy guy with the black eye. That's him.'

Chapter 29

The man sitting across from Huldar and Erla was called Arnar Björnsson. It had finally hit home that he was backed into a corner – a dark, lonely corner with no way out. His upper lip was beaded with sweat and he kept trying to wipe it off with damp fingers. His cheeks were unnaturally red, his eyes twitching, and his hands, which he hid in his lap when he wasn't wiping his lip, were shaking badly.

Huldar was elated. He didn't feel an ounce of pity for this desperate, middle-aged man. He couldn't stand sex offenders, could never find within himself the slightest sympathy or understanding for their actions. While he had a pretty colourful history himself when it came to sexual partners, it wasn't rocket science: if a woman was unwilling or wouldn't do it without being paid, it meant she was out of bounds. Simple as that.

Arnar sniffed and Huldar had to work hard to keep the contempt out of his expression. This man wasn't just suspected of trying to buy sex from a schoolgirl but also of brutally murdering Stella and attacking Egill. They hadn't yet managed to establish any link to the boy but it was only a matter of time. He must have crossed paths with Egill through the porn site Stella had registered Adalheidur on, or something similar. Perhaps Egill and Stella had known each other after all and conspired to blackmail Arnar together, without telling Bjarney.

Or there could be a completely different explanation. It didn't matter: they'd caught the evil bastard.

'Where's Egill?' Erla repeated yet again. Finding the boy, alive if possible, was top priority right now. 'I'm going to keep on asking until you answer.' Erla's gaze went to the clock on the wall, then back to the man. 'We're authorised to interview you for six hours at a stretch and we've only been at it for one. That's five to go. When I get bored, I can have a break and get someone else to take over. Go for a coffee while you're stuck here. When the six hours are up, you can go home, but we'll call you back for another interview the moment your statutory rest period is up, and question you for another six hours. And we'll keep on like that until you answer. So let's try again. Where's Egill?'

'What about my human rights?' The man squirmed in his chair. 'You can't interview me for all that time without giving me something to eat. Can you?'

Huldar permitted himself a grimace. What a pathetic loser. But that was often the way. People guilty of the most vicious acts towards others often turned out to be yellow-bellied cowards when they found themselves alone and outnumbered. They got their kicks from picking on the weak. No doubt it made them feel big. What adult male couldn't play the tough guy with children or teenagers? Huldar sat up tall to make the most of his height and folded his arms over his chest to show off his biceps. The wimp in front of him seemed to shrink even further. 'Answer her question. Where's Egill?'

'I've no idea who you're talking about. I swear. Like I told you, I must have got a computer virus that accessed that porn site. It had nothing to do with me. And I never went near any Stella. Or anyone called Egill either. I'd never do anything like that. I'm married. Why would I pay for sex? And from a boy, too?'

The ball passed back to Erla. 'Don't ask us. You're not here to ask the questions. That's our job. Your job is to answer. And don't give us that bullshit about a computer virus. You must take us for a bunch of idiots. Let me remind you that we have a witness who saw you hand over the money to Stella as payment for her silence. Are you saying that was the virus? What, did it morph into human form or something?' Erla did a good job of emulating Huldar's pose, despite her lack of bulk. 'Anyway, leaving that aside for a minute, we've got more urgent matters to discuss. Like where's Egill?'

The man's eyes flickered from side to side and he ran his tongue over his lips again, just missing a big bead of sweat. 'The only Egills I know are a bloke I worked with three years ago, a friend from school and a cousin of mine in Eskifjördur. How many times do I have to tell you that? I've never met the Egill you're looking for, let alone attacked or abducted him.'

'We know you're lying. Just like you're lying about never having met Stella.' Huldar's eyes bored into the man's face. 'Where's Egill?'

'I've just answered that. You've got to stop asking me the same questions all the time.'

'Where and who is number one?' Huldar switched to the other question they'd been asking ever since they'd sat down.

'Am I under arrest?' Another nervous lick of the lips. 'If I am, maybe I should get a lawyer. In fact, yes: I want a lawyer. I'm not saying another word until he gets here. I've answered all your questions anyway. You just keep going on and on about the same things.'

'You're not under arrest. We're simply taking a statement

from you. At this stage you're still only a witness and we haven't decided whether to elevate you to the status of an official suspect. If we do, and if we arrest you, you can have a lawyer present. But only suspects get lawyers, not witnesses.' Erla spoke slowly and clearly, presumably for the benefit of the recording. Huldar didn't know if her argument was water-tight legally speaking, though she'd cited the law correctly. In fact, the correct procedure would have been to interview Arnar as a suspect and let him have a lawyer present. But if he was the man they were after, it was unlikely anyone would criticise their methods. 'Where's Egill?'

The man groaned, clasped his head in his hands and ran his fingers through what remained of his hair. 'I know nothing about any Egill. And I had nothing to do with the murder of that girl Stella.'

'Then tell us why you didn't get in touch with us when you read in the papers that she'd been murdered. Her name's been published, so you must have realised that you'd had dealings with her. Didn't it occur to you that the fact she'd blackmailed you might be important information? Even if you're as inno-cent as you claim, it must have crossed your mind that she could have tried the same with other men. Or didn't you give a damn?' Erla's face couldn't have expressed any more distaste if the contents of a slurry tanker had been emptied out on the seat opposite her.

'I . . . I . . .' The man gulped, then seemed to gather up the tatters of his manhood. In a firmer voice, he repeated: 'It was a computer virus. I knew nothing about that porn site. Your witness must be muddling me up with someone else. I'm nothing special to look at; there are hundreds – thousands – of other blokes who look like me.'

'Where's Egill?' Erla bent forward across the table. 'Where's Egill?' When, instead of answering, the man merely clamped his lips into an invisible line, she caught Huldar's eye and jerked her head as a sign that they should step outside. Then she informed Arnar that they were going to suspend the interview briefly; he'd do well to think things over while they were gone.

When they emerged, their colleagues looked up eagerly. Everyone knew there had been a breakthrough in the investigation. Huldar guessed some of them envied him the chance to take part in the initial interview of the suspect. It was always a big event.

Erla waved at Jóel and the guy sitting next to him to take over the interview. Their orders were to repeat ad nauseam: *Where's Egill?* If Arnar showed any signs of cracking, they were to fetch her and Huldar, otherwise she'd be back to take over again in fifteen minutes.

Huldar seized the chance to go outside for a smoke. He knew it was better to be dying for nicotine during an interview – it sharpened your performance, made you more impatient – but he couldn't hold out any longer.

The weather was as good as it got at this time of year: freezing hard, with a cloudless sky and not a breath of wind. As he leant against the wall, basking in the sunshine, he spotted Freyja leaving the station and called out to her in a great cloud of steam. When she saw it was him, she didn't look too thrilled.

'How did it go with Bjarney?' Huldar stubbed out the barely smoked cigarette, and strode over to intercept her.

'Well. She's positive he's the guy Stella arranged the meeting with.' Freyja raised her eyes to the blue sky, as if searching for a storm cloud to provide her with an excuse to cut this short. But her luck wasn't in. 'Gudlaugur did a good job. Though actually I was expecting you.'

Huldar grinned broadly. 'Aw, did you miss me?'

She pulled a face. 'No. Expecting something and looking forward to it are quite different things.'

Huldar didn't let this get to him. Her sniping paled into insignificance next to her rudeness when he'd rung to ask her to come into the station. 'We believe we've got the right guy. So this is probably a good moment to thank you for all your help. You were right about the bullying, though Stella's death was only indirectly linked to it.'

'What about the boy? Has the man told you where he is?'

'No. But he will.' Huldar felt able to speak with some confidence. Erla was planning to use the break to consult a lawyer and her superiors about the most effective way to make the arrest. Her idea was to use the full six hours they had for taking Arnar's statement, then release him. Give him a chance to step outside into the fresh air, get a lungful of freedom, then arrest him on the steps. That would also give them time to apply for a search warrant before he could go home and destroy any evidence. Huldar was sceptical about the chances of these tactics meeting the approval of the lawyers, but no doubt the top brass would be on side.

'Any hope of him being found alive?' Freyja asked.

Huldar's smile faded. 'Only a very faint one. With any luck a search of his house will turn up something that'll lead us to the boy – if the man doesn't come clean of his own accord.'

Freyja nodded and started looking around, obviously keen to get away. 'OK, well, good luck. I really hope it works out. Sometimes the impossible happens.'

'Yes.' Any minute now she'd be gone. This might be the last time Huldar saw her for ages. 'Speaking of the impossible, how about we celebrate the successful conclusion of the case? Are you busy this weekend? Or next weekend? Or one evening next week, if that suits you better?' He was coming across as desperate, but too bad. He'd do anything to get his foot in Freyja's door.

Her expression was unfathomable. But when she finally spoke, there was no room for misunderstanding. 'I'm busy. This weekend, next weekend, and every weekday as well. Forever.'

'The weekend after that, then?' Huldar smiled ruefully but she didn't respond in kind, merely said goodbye, wished him luck again, and turned to go. But instead of walking away, she hesitated, then turned back again and gave him an appraising look while he stood there like an idiot. 'Have you got any smart clothes?'

'Er . . . yes.' Huldar wasn't sure if Freyja would agree with his idea of smart. She could be talking about black tie, for all he knew. 'How smart are we talking?'

'Smart smart. A suit. Not your old Confirmation outfit or some shabby old-fashioned number you keep at the back of the wardrobe or that you'd borrow from your granddad. No elbow patches or tweed. No brushed velvet either, or checks.'

Huldar nodded each time she vetoed an item. When she finished her list, he reckoned he could fulfil these conditions. 'Yes, actually. My sister got married in August and I was sent out to buy myself a suit for the reception. It's very smart.' He grinned. 'At least, it doesn't feature anything on your list of banned items.'

'Then are you free on Saturday evening to come to a party

with me? I intend to stay for precisely one hour. Not a minute longer. After that I'm going home.' Freyja seemed to have difficulty getting the words out.

'I'm game,' Huldar said.

'Don't you want to know what sort of party it is?'

'Nope. Couldn't care less.'

'OK. I'll be in touch.' Without another word she walked off.

Fifteen minutes dragged into half an hour, then an hour. Erla hadn't got the meeting with management and the departmental lawyer out of the way quite as briskly as she'd hoped.

She'd been ordered to drop all the games and arrest the man immediately. It was evident from the foul mood she was in that they'd torn a strip off her for even dreaming of doing things differently. They'd also chosen that moment to inform her that they wouldn't be requesting permission from the Data Protection Authority to access the deCODE database, on the grounds that it was unlikely to be granted, which would look bad for the police. Erla was spitting mad after the meeting, biting the heads off anyone who dared speak to her and snubbing everyone else. Huldar came in for his fair share of abuse but he couldn't have cared less. Nothing could dent his good mood now that he'd got a foot in the door with Freyja. How it had happened was a mystery to him, but he wasn't going to let that spoil his pleasure.

'Arseholes!' It was hard to tell whether Erla was talking to herself or expected Huldar and Gudlaugur to back up her opinion of the lawyer and her bosses. 'Stupid, fucking arseholes. Now he'll get himself a lawyer and that'll create a delay. How can the thick bastards not grasp how urgent this is? We had three and a half hours left to grill him as a witness.'

'I know.' Huldar felt he'd better agree, though he could understand the attitude of the guys upstairs. If there was even a hint of doubt about whether a party should be interviewed as a witness or a suspect, they were supposed to treat them as a suspect. That way the person was ensured their statutory rights, including the right to a lawyer. 'Arseholes, the lot of them.'

Erla frowned suspiciously. Clearly he hadn't sounded convincing enough. 'Ready?' He nodded and she looked at Gudlaugur. 'You too?' Gudlaugur nodded in turn. 'Not a word from you, though, unless you think some detail from your interview of Bjarney could help us. In that case, give me a nudge and whisper it in my ear.'

'OK.' Gudlaugur shifted awkwardly.

From the other side of the door they could hear the muffled sound of Jóel's voice asking half-heartedly where Egill was. When they walked in, he looked relieved to see Erla, no doubt bored to tears after repeating the same question for an hour, but his pleasure soured the instant he clocked Huldar behind her. Arnar appeared indifferent to the changeover. He looked dazed, like a man who's been put through a spin cycle.

'Thanks. We'll take over now.'

Jóel and his partner got up immediately and walked out without a word, Jóel deliberately bashing his shoulder into Huldar as he passed. Huldar ignored him, silently resolving to pay him back in kind as soon as he got the chance.

Erla informed Arnar that he was under arrest on suspicion of having murdered Stella and abducted Egill. The interview got no further because Arnar immediately demanded a lawyer. Clearly the barrage of repetitive questions hadn't completely robbed him of his wits. Erla closed her eyes, apparently counting to ten before opening them again. There was a screech as she shoved her chair back from the table and stood up.

Her look of fury vanished, however, when the phone rang in her pocket as she was walking out of the door. The conversation was brief and Huldar and Guðlaugur lingered for fear of getting into her bad books again if they abandoned her. The moment she'd finished, she told them, her face grim, that they'd traced the owner of the hair found in Stella's hand. Unfortunately, the information had done nothing to improve the situation. If anything, it had made matters worse.

Chapter 30

Photocopy of a handwritten letter, entry no. 3 – posted on blog.is by a blogger going by the name of Laufa.

Making a friend at last wasn't the only way my life improved after I started secondary school. Before that, Mum and Dad had let me have the old TV for my bedroom after they bought a new one. I got a DVD player too and no longer had to spend my weekends feeling depressed about my life. Instead I soon became obsessed with a certain kind of film. What they all had in common was that they happened in space and the characters never set foot on this horrible planet. Star Wars was my absolute favourite, because although the men, women and robots were constantly at war with each other, no one ever had to face their enemies alone. Everyone had allies, and they were fighting proper battles, not spitefulness and name-calling. If you haven't experienced that sort of thing, you might not realise that physical pain is nothing compared to mental suffering. You can even use pain to forget the agony in your heart for a little while. A single razor-thin cut can grant you several minutes of peace from the pain in your head. The scar's a small price to pay.

One thing that was worse about being a teenager, though, were the summers. Before, I used to have them to myself but now Mum and Dad wanted me to get a summer job with the city council. The result was that I ended up working alongside the same kids who used to pick on me at my old school. Nothing had changed. It was me against the crowd again – everything I said, everything I did, everything I wore sucked. I was stupid, ugly and dumb. By this stage I'd started to believe they must be right and I gave up trying to hold my head high. My place was to give in and turn the other cheek.

It wasn't until the last year of secondary school that my friend came along and everything changed. Suddenly I wasn't alone any more. She didn't seem to think there was anything wrong with me, and though she did comment on my clothes and hair, she meant it kindly. I'd had enough experience by then to tell when people were being mean. She didn't seem to notice that I didn't say much and let her do all the talking. I just listened and gazed at her, enjoying spending time with someone who thought I mattered, even if it was only as an audience. And an admirer. On the rare occasions when I said something myself, she was nice and understanding, though you could tell from her face that she found some of the things I said a bit weird. It's hardly surprising since I had no experience of talking like an equal to someone my age.

Looking back, I don't regret the months we had together. They were worth it, though the pain came back afterwards, worse than before. Because now I had something normal to compare it to. But in my case nothing good lasts forever. I should have realised that. Stupid, ugly, useless me.

If I'd been cleverer, I'd have guessed what was happening when my friend came to talk to me during break. She only did it because no one else would talk to her. But even if I had realised, I wouldn't have cared. Finally someone wanted to have something to do with me. I couldn't have cared less *what the reason was. The gang that hated me were amazed at first; they didn't say anything, just whispered to each other, like they didn't know what had hit them. It was like they realised they'd lost their power over me. Their insults bounced off me, they no longer hurt, and the other mean stuff they did to me didn't bother me as much any more.*

To my mind they were like a swarm of flies – annoying but not bad enough to drive you indoors. They didn't take kindly to this change but I was on cloud nine and too happy to notice the approaching storm.

Adam wasn't allowed to stay long in Paradise, so why did a pathetic loser like me think I had any right to?

Chapter 31

'Come *on*. She must have been on Facebook. Something has to come up if you google her.' Erla was standing behind Huldar. Feeling her hands tightening on the back of his chair, he hoped she wouldn't snap it.

'Nothing's coming up. You can see for yourself. One entry in the Athletics Association track records from nearly thirty years ago, when she was eight. If it's her.' Huldar leant away from the screen so Erla could check the results for herself. 'I've spelt the name right, as you can see. There's just no info about this woman online.' The back of his chair protested under Erla's wrenching grip. 'She seems to be the only person who's ever had that name. Not surprising, really: Laufhildur Brá Mardardóttir – bit of a mouthful.' He twisted round, waiting for Erla's reaction.

'How's that possible? Everybody has something about them on the internet. Could she have deleted her online presence?'

'Don't ask me.' Huldar was as baffled as Erla. He couldn't remember ever having encountered this situation before.

'Try entering her name in the system again. If she or somebody close to her has taken the trouble to wipe her history from the internet, she must have something to hide.'

Huldar did as he was told, though he knew it wouldn't achieve anything. He wasn't suited to the role of secretary and cursed himself for having jumped in ahead of Gudlaugur at the computer when Erla asked them to check out Laufhildur, the owner of the hairs that had been found in Stella's fist. 'Nothing. Same as before.'

'For fuck's sake,' Erla growled.

'Could she be victim number one?' wondered Gudlaugur, who was standing next to her. He broke off quickly when he realised he'd been thinking aloud.

'Use your bloody brain – she'd have been reported missing.' After a pause, Erla qualified this. 'Unless she lives alone and doesn't have any contact with family or friends. Or have to report to an employer – if she has one.'

'If she does, we can find out where she works from the tax office,' Huldar pointed out. 'They'll know if she's on benefits, too, or if she's a student.' Erla didn't appear keen on this suggestion. She'd hoped to gather information on the woman as discreetly as possible, which would have been easy in most cases. Few people could live for thirty-five years without leaving a digital footprint.

'Open the National Register window again.' The entry containing the woman's date of birth popped up on screen. Her legal residence was down as a block of flats in the Breidholt district. According to the telephone directory, she'd never had any sort of phone registered to her name, which also struck them as peculiar. Frustratingly, it meant they couldn't check under her landline to see if she was living with anyone. She wasn't recorded in the National Register as married or cohabiting, though that didn't necessarily mean she'd always lived alone. But there was no record of her having any children.

Huldar waited as Erla and Gudlaugur contemplated this minimal information again. 'Why don't we try her parents? Or her father, rather. Her mother died seventeen years ago.'

'Sixteen years ago,' Gudlaugur corrected. Gritting his teeth, Huldar pretended not to hear.

'OK, try the father.' Erla let go of the chair-back and began gnawing her thumbnail instead. 'Check the police database first.' When they drew a blank there, Erla ordered Huldar to google him. Little of interest came up: the man wasn't on social media, so all that appeared were results linked to his job and the information that he'd been on the board of a shooting club about twenty years ago. He worked for a large software company where his position as a general programmer seemed rather humble for a man of sixty, unless his age counted against him in the IT world.

'A computer programmer.' The way Erla said it, he might have been commandant of a prison camp. 'So he shouldn't have any problems with Snapchat.'

'No, probably not.' Huldar decided not to risk annoying her any further by pointing out that a five-year-old could master Snapchat; she was already near the end of her tether. 'What do we do now? Ring the guy and ask about his daughter?'

Erla shook her head irritably. 'No way. What if he wants to know why we're calling?'

She was right and the three of them were silent, momentarily stumped. The method by which they'd identified the DNA was unorthodox, to say the least. The pathologist had, on his own initiative and without authorisation, run the DNA profile through the National Hospital's database of paternity tests. It appeared that Mördur had had doubts about his daughter's paternity after she was born. According to the pathologist, it was almost impossible that the hair could belong to anyone but Laufhildur, given that she didn't have an identical twin.

'We can't approach the guy without inventing a plausible excuse,' Erla continued. 'He's bound to ask what's going on if he suspects it's not above board.'

'What if we refuse to answer?' Gudlaugur was rewarded with a poisonous look. He was too inexperienced to realise that although this tactic might work with the woman's father, Erla would almost certainly be required by her superiors to provide an explanation for her interest further down the line, and she couldn't refuse to answer them. But revealing their source was out of the question as it would have serious repercussions for the pathologist. He'd taken a big risk for them, on the grounds that it might just save Egill's life, and possibly those of other victims as well. Having performed the post-mortem on Stella, he knew better than anyone how desperately important it was that the perpetrator was caught. And perhaps there was an element of guilt as well, that nothing useful had emerged from her autopsy. The correct response would have been for Erla to treat his information as if she'd never received it and simply go on vainly hoping that her bosses would change their minds about applying for permission to run the DNA profile through deCODE's database, a request that was no more likely to be granted than before.

'Just let me think a minute.' Erla suddenly became aware that other members of the investigation team had started to eye them with interest. She and Huldar only had to stand next to each other to get heads turning, so muttering conspiratorially like this was bound to raise eyebrows. 'You two take over from here. I've got to deal with the paperwork relating to Arnar Björnsson's arrest. Go round to Mördur's workplace and see what you can find out without arousing suspicion. You'll just have to concoct a cover story for yourselves.' She locked gazes with Huldar. 'Can I trust you not to screw this up? I don't want anyone else involved at this stage. It's vital the guy doesn't find out that his daughter's a potential victim – if that's what this is about. Though it's possible her hair just happened to be on the floor of the cinema.'

Huldar closed the windows on the computer screen, one after the other. 'Relax. We'll think of something.' He just hoped one of them would have a brainwave in the car.

The receptionist didn't look up from her phone until Huldar coughed and asked: 'Is Mördur Jónasson in, by any chance?'

'What?' The woman blinked from peering at her tiny screen. 'Who did you want?'

'Mördur Jónasson.'

She tapped the name into her computer. 'He's not in, I'm afraid. He's off sick.' She looked up again, more alertly this time. 'Can someone else help you? Einar, for instance?'

'Einar?' Huldar hesitated, wondering whether to grab this opportunity or leave. The story they'd concocted on the way there wouldn't stand up to much scrutiny. 'Er . . . no. It doesn't matter. But could you just tell me if we've got the right mobile number for Mördur?' He read out the one they had. When they'd tried it, all they'd got was a recorded message announcing that the phone was either switched off or out of reach.

'Yes, that's the right number,' the receptionist said. 'I can send him a message if you like.'

'No, thanks. We'll try him again later.'

She looked down at her screen again. 'Actually, he's been off sick for a while. I'd recommend you talk to Einar instead.'

Huldar, changing his mind about leaving, leant over the

high reception desk and asked in confidential tones: 'Do you happen to know what's wrong with him? Is it serious?'

The woman shook her head. 'I'm fairly new here so I don't know him. But I can see from the computer that he's been off sick for weeks. The person down as the contact in his absence is Einar.'

'Then maybe it would be a good idea if we had a word with him. If he's free.'

'Well, he's green, so he should be.' Huldar didn't ask what this meant, just waited for her to call Einar.

When the man finally appeared, they stood up and shook the hand he extended to them. Huldar asked if they could have a private chat. He didn't want the receptionist to hear what they had to say, though she was mesmerised by her phone again and seemed to have forgotten all about them.

Einar showed them into a tiny meeting room which contained no chairs, only a small round table at standing height. The walls were decorated with framed posters featuring inane motivational statements about teamwork that were supposed to be clever. Whoever had come up with them had obviously never worked for the police.

'I have to admit I'm a little surprised,' Einar said. 'I thought we'd informed all our clients that Lárus has taken over Mördur's projects. I'm terribly sorry if you got left out.'

'We're not clients.' Huldar tried but failed to find a comfortable position, resting his elbow on the ridiculous meeting table. It forced them to stand embarrassingly close together, making him feel stupid. They'd have been better off talking to Einar in reception. 'We're from the police.'

'The police?' The man's head jerked back a little. 'I'm afraid I don't understand.'

'There's no reason why you should. We need to get hold of Mördur as a potential witness in a case we're investigating. His car was parked near the scene of the incident in question and we were hoping he might have seen something that could help us. He's just one of a number of people we're eager to talk to.'

'I see.' The man seemed relieved. Huldar and Gudlaugur were too: it looked as if they were going to get away with their cover story.

'We thought we'd try his workplace when we couldn't get hold of him on the phone, but the receptionist told us he's ill and has been on leave for some time. I just wanted to know if it was serious because in that case we might as well cross him off our list. It's not that urgent and there are other potential witnesses we can talk to instead.'

Einar looked grave. 'I'm afraid he's very ill. I don't have any information about his present condition, but he went on sick leave nearly two months ago. He'd been working part time for just under a year when he was diagnosed with cancer and under-went a difficult operation, followed by radiotherapy and chemo. If you like I can ask the head of HR if she knows anything.'

Huldar thanked him and Einar turned away while he made the call, creating an illusion of privacy, though of course they could hear every word. After a brief conversation he rang off and turned back. 'Bad news, I'm afraid. She thinks he's either about to have another operation or he's just had one. Either way, he's in hospital.'

Once they were back in the car, Huldar's first action was to ring the National Hospital and ask about a patient called Mördur Jónasson. He thought he'd misheard when the oper-ator told him which ward Mördur was in. 'Sorry? Isn't that

Cardiology?' The woman said it was. When Huldar asked why he wasn't in Oncology, she said it wasn't her job to decide where patients were allocated beds, and, with a terse goodbye, she cut him off.

Huldar met Gudlaugur's eye. 'He's in Ásta's ward.' He slammed the car into reverse, screeched out of the parking space and drove off at a speed unbefitting a policeman.

Chapter 32

The same nurse was on duty as on his visit the previous evening, and her face clouded over when she saw Huldar. The ward was busier this time, with staff dashing in and out of the rooms. It was no surprise that a police investigation didn't count as a priority in this setting. People fell ill, were injured and died every day, and they needed caring for, regardless of whether a crime had been committed.

'Ásta's not on duty this evening.' The woman had stepped out from behind the reception desk after Huldar rapped on it. She stationed herself in the middle of the corridor with arms folded, deliberately blocking their path. She was wearing a lilac tunic with the blue hospital laundry mark and white trousers to match. Her breast pocket appeared to be on the point of tearing off, weighed down as it was by a heavy watch and numerous pens and other instruments that Huldar couldn't identify. Nor could he identify what had caused the dubious splashes on the woman's face. Probably just as well. 'You'll have to come back tomorrow morning if you want to talk to her. Or go round to her house instead of interrupting us in the middle of our duties.'

'It's not actually her we've come to see.' Huldar couldn't decide whether it was good or bad that Ásta wasn't on duty. He supposed it depended on the nature of the information they managed to extract from Mördur. If it proved useful, they'd call Ásta in for questioning that evening, before she knew what had hit her. But if they got nothing out of him, it would be better to have her present, if only to witness her reaction to their visit. With part of his brain, Huldar registered Gudlaugur's obvious relief at the news that Ásta wasn't there. 'We need a word with one of your patients.'

'Oh?' The woman's eyebrows shot up. The change in her manner since the previous evening suggested that Ásta had given the police a less than flattering report after Huldar had left. 'What's his name?'

'Mördur Jónasson. We understand he's a patient on this ward.'

The woman's expression didn't soften at this. 'May I ask what exactly's going on?'

'No.'

'Oh. Well.' She unfolded her arms. 'I'm sorry to disappoint you but Mördur's no longer with us. And since there's nothing more I can do for you, I'll have to ask you to leave. We're rushed off our feet.'

Huldar controlled his frustration with considerable effort. 'We're aware of that. If you could just let us know where he's gone, we'll get out of your hair.'

'I'm sorry but I couldn't tell you.' The woman didn't appear in the least sorry. 'Except that wherever he's gone, it's either uncomfortably hot or a much better place than here. He died' – she consulted the watch pinned to her breast pocket – 'an hour and fifteen minutes ago. You're just too late.'

Huldar was blindsided by this news, but Gudlaugur took over. 'What happened?'

'Cardiac arrest. There was nothing we could do.'

Neither Huldar nor Gudlaugur knew what to say to this.

The nurse, interpreting their silence as a criticism of the hospital, became instantly defensive. 'These things happen. He was suffering from heart failure as a result of chemotherapy and complications caused by an infection following his heart attack at the weekend. On top of that, he had advanced lung cancer. His time was up. We did all we could but it wasn't enough. It's not the fault of the treatment he's received here, if that's what you think.'

'We didn't mean to imply any such thing.' Huldar forced himself to answer politely while inwardly cursing their bad luck. Fuck, fuck, fuck. Why the hell couldn't they have got hold of his name earlier? 'Was he conscious this morning?'

'Yes and no. He's been in and out of consciousness ever since he was brought in.'

'When was that?'

'Last Friday evening.'

'And he's been here the whole time since then? He never left the hospital at any point?'

The woman smiled. 'No. Believe me. He couldn't even get out of bed to go to the toilet. We're talking about a very sick man.'

'You're sure?'

'Yes, I'm quite sure. No one leaves here without our knowledge.' She waved at the large screens Huldar had noticed the previous evening. 'The patients are all hooked up to monitors and their readings are displayed here. If they pulled out their tubes and wandered off, we couldn't fail to notice.'

Huldar was silent, his mind working furiously. How the hell could this man or his daughter be connected to Stella or Egill – if they were connected? 'Did Ásta look after him at all?'

'Yes. As did the other nurses on the ward. He wasn't her particular responsibility, if that's what you mean. Though, given the circumstances, she may have been more invested in him.'

'The circumstances?'

'She saved his life on Friday evening.' The woman regarded Huldar in surprise. 'I told you that yesterday, didn't I?'

'I don't remember.' He had a vague memory of her going on about how great Ásta was but couldn't recall any of the details. 'What exactly happened?'

'Ásta gave him CPR. Out in the car park. She kept him alive until someone heard her calling and fetched help. Like so many people, he'd sensed something was wrong and driven himself to A&E. It was sheer luck that he didn't collapse behind the wheel – and that Ásta saw what was happening. If she'd left a few minutes earlier or later, the man would have died alone in the car park. It's not unusual for people – especially men – to react foolishly to the first signs of a heart attack. They don't like ringing for an ambulance in case it's a false alarm. As if anyone would care about that.'

'Did they know each other?'

'No, not at all. Why do you ask?'

'No reason. But they talked, didn't they? After he was brought in here?'

'No more than anyone else. Like I said, the man was mostly out of it, and Ásta's not the only nurse around here. If anything, she had less to do with him than the rest of us.'

'Oh? Why was that?'

'He kept making such a big deal about thanking her for saving his life that she got fed up with it. Every time he came to, he would ask for her. He didn't seem to remember that he'd already thanked her repeatedly. It all got a bit much for Ásta and the rest of us, because we're extremely busy, as I said, and don't really have time to stop and chat to patients, especially if they insist on endlessly rambling on about the same stuff.' The woman checked her watch again. 'And the same applies to the police. If there's anything else, I'll have to refer you to Ásta and request that you talk to her outside the hospital.'

Huldar and Gudlaugur were obliged to step aside as a bed was wheeled past containing a patient whose grey face suggested he didn't have long to live. They were silent while the group went by, unsure what was appropriate in the circumstances. As they turned to watch the bed's progress down the corridor, the nurse grew visibly impatient.

'Right, are we done here? Can I get back to work?'

'One last question. Did his daughter come to see him? Or any other visitors?'

'No, not that I remember. But I don't keep track of all the visits as I'm not always on duty.' She looked at them both in turn, then, relenting slightly, said wearily: 'I suppose you'd like me to check for you?'

Huldar thanked her and prepared to wait while she consulted her colleagues. But the nurse said she wouldn't be talking to anyone until the staff gathered later to prepare for the handover, so they would just have to be patient. She asked for a phone number and after Huldar had given her his card, almost shoved them towards the exit.

Huldar turned just before they reached the doors. She was still standing there as if to make sure they were really leaving. Her expression, when she saw him coming back, was distinctly frosty.

'You don't happen to have someone listed as next of kin, do you? Someone to be contacted in case of emergencies? We're trying to get hold of his daughter's phone number. If you could check for me, I promise we'll leave.'

The woman let out an exasperated sigh but did as he asked. When she came back, the number she gave them was Mördur's brother's. It was better than nothing. Perhaps he would be able to put them in touch with the elusive Laufhildur. Huldar was beginning to wonder whether she'd moved abroad without informing the authorities. Maybe changed her name too. It also crossed his mind that she might have returned to Iceland recently, for reasons that might not bear examination.

The three of them were sitting in a car behind the police station, Erla in the driver's seat, Huldar beside her and Gudlaugur in the back, leaning forward between them, his elbows resting on their seats.

Erla was reluctant to discuss Mördur and Laufhildur in the office. She still hadn't come up with a plausible excuse to explain her interest in them to the rest of the team and had decided that meeting in the car like this would be less likely to arouse suspicion. Huldar disagreed but kept his mouth shut. Although it was only 5 p.m. it was pitch dark outside and as Erla had switched on the light in the car, the three of them were on display like goods in a shop window. The moment someone stepped outside for a smoke they could be sure tongues would start wagging – possibly about a threesome this time.

'And you say he was positive he didn't know Stella or Egill and that, as far as he was aware, his brother didn't either?' Erla's eyes were fixed on the windscreen and she was gripping the steering wheel.

'He was adamant. Of course, he couldn't be a hundred per cent certain that Mördur didn't know them, but he'd never heard him mention their names.' Huldar could have done without having to make that phone call to the brother. It turned out that the hospital hadn't got round to informing him of Mördur's death, so Huldar had been forced to break the news.

'Were they close?'

'According to him they were. But how close can brothers be if they live on opposite sides of the country? He lives in Akureyri and Mördur lived here in Reykjavík. Apparently they rarely met up but they talked on the phone once a month. Does that count as close? Anyway, the brother was pretty upset to hear Mördur was dead. Said he'd had a tough time of it. His wife had been diagnosed with MS when their daughter was little and had gone progressively downhill until she was completely incapacitated by the time she died.'

'And he said there was no point talking to the daughter?'

'No. None at all. He was reluctant to discuss her. All he said was that she'd had a serious accident in her teens that had left her unable to speak. Mördur cared for her at home until it became obvious that he was losing his battle with cancer. In the end he admitted defeat and got her a place at a group home for the disabled. He thought it was the best solution as he'd still be around for a while to help her adapt to her changed circumstances. According to his brother, she moved in there fairly recently. Incidentally, I did learn one interesting fact from our chat. He never once called her Laufhildur but referred to her the whole time as Laufa.'

'Laufa?' Erla frowned, not following him. Then the penny dropped. 'Laufa – Lauga!'

'Bingo.' Huldar would have held up his hand for a high five if the situation hadn't been so deadly serious. 'Is there any chance that our mystery caller said Laufa, not Lauga?'

Erla thought for a moment. 'Maybe. I'd need to listen again. But it's possible.'

'Doesn't that solve our problem, then?' Gudlaugur brightened up. 'Now we can say we want to check her out as a result of the tip-off. No one's going to cast doubt on the importance of that phone call for the investigation.'

Erla threw him a withering look. 'Yeah, great. Why don't you take it to management? Explain that we can't find any Lauga or woman whose name ends in -laug but we have managed to dig up the only woman in the country called Laufhildur. She happens to live in a group home and can't talk but we're convinced she's relevant to the case.'

Gudlaugur had no reply to this. Erla took up the thread again. 'So what next?' She moved the wheel inadvertently and the snow crunched under the tyres. 'Hadn't you better visit the home? Did the brother know what it was called?'

'He said it didn't have a name. Apparently they're not allowed to give these places names any more. He'd heard the address but couldn't remember it.'

'Well, it shouldn't be too difficult to find out.' Erla let go of the wheel and ran her hands through her hair. 'The only problem now is how I'm going to explain our interest in this woman.' She looked at Huldar, then twisted round to search Gudlaugur's face. 'Any bright ideas?' They shook their heads. 'Shit.'

'Want me to ask Freyja? She should be able to access the social services database. Laufhildur ought to be registered there if she's living in a group home. We wouldn't need to fill Freyja in on the background, just ask her to do the search discreetly.' Huldar braced himself for the inevitable shitstorm. He knew it was a brilliant solution; the only question was whether that would be enough to outweigh Erla's antipathy towards Freyja.

Erla stared out of the windscreen again, her face hard. 'No. Let Gudlaugur do it.' She twisted round to the back seat again. 'Got that?'

Gudlaugur nodded. He could hardly have failed to hear in the cramped confines of the car. Turning back to Huldar, Erla told him to stay within reach in case she needed his help with interviewing Arnar Björnsson. The plan was to start the next round of questioning the moment the lawyer showed his face. The poor sod hadn't exactly picked the cream of the crop when he pointed to a name at random on the list he was shown. The lawyer in question was approaching retirement and rumoured to be getting a bit forgetful these days. He could hardly be trusted to keep track of what his clients had been accused of. However, since this was extremely convenient for the police, no one had commented on Arnar's choice.

'Does that mean you only want one of us to go to the group home, then?'

'We'll see. I'll let you know.'

When it became clear that no one had anything else to contribute, Erla switched off the ceiling light. They got out and the empty yard echoed with the slamming of car doors.

Chapter 33

From the living-room window Freyja watched her neighbour reeling across the road. His shabby anorak was unzipped, revealing a T-shirt emblazoned with fruit that would have been better suited to drinking cocktails on a tropical beach than a can of beer in the middle of a snowy Reykjavík street. The man skidded on the icy ground, slopping his drink. Freyja half expected him to fling himself down on his hands and knees and start eating the snow where the beer had landed but instead he paused halfway across, emptied the can down his throat, then chucked it on the ground. Freyja wasn't bothered about the litter; before long one of the other occupants of the building would be out there, scavenging the can for the deposit. It was that kind of place.

Earlier that morning she would have been filled with gloom by this reminder of how she'd come down in the world but now she simply took it as yet another incentive to do something about her life. Something realistic that didn't involve a complete career change and a new start. It needn't be that drastic. She was healthy, she'd got the education she'd always wanted and did a job that suited her and that she was good at. This was a sound basis to build on, so there was no reason why she shouldn't be happy with her lot. The problem was that she'd allowed her life to fall into a rut, from sheer laziness. But things were going to change. Her mission now was to find herself a flat that suited her better than this dump, throw herself into her work and recover her former position. When Baldur got out, she would take him under her wing and help him find his feet. For Saga's sake, she was even prepared to share a flat with him at first, to make sure he didn't take the fast track back into the gutter. Then he could sell this place or rent it out to tourists. There must be foreigners out there desperate enough for a bargain that they wouldn't turn their noses up at it.

She fully intended to reassess her love life too. Shelve her search for a good man and let him find her. Hunting for a mate was probably like trying to remember something: it wasn't until you stopped trying that things started to happen. Desperation was a turn-off. Thank God she'd been spared from making a terrible mistake with that idiot Kjartan. Up to now she had managed to stick to her principles about not sleeping with married men.

She hadn't picked up when he'd called; hadn't felt like talking to him, though she had every intention of ringing him in due course to give him a piece of her mind. But first she wanted to prepare what she was going to say, and maybe run through it a few times, just to make sure she didn't end up swearing or hurling insults at him. She still hadn't got the wording quite to her satisfaction and was beginning to think she shouldn't even mention his lie about getting a divorce. Surely it would be more devastating to his ego to say she'd heard on the grapevine that he was a bit disappointing in the sack, so she felt she could do better? Then leave him to fret over where she could have heard this. She didn't for a minute believe that she was his first attempt at adultery.

The really galling part was that the bastard had tricked her into saying she'd go to the class reunion with a plus one. Humiliated by the thought of having to either turn up alone or announce at the last minute that she couldn't go, she had resorted to inviting Huldar along. On the face of it, the solution was a satisfactory one: he was a good-looking guy and those who didn't know any better might even think she was lucky. But on second thoughts the plan hadn't been so clever after all. Her invitation was bound to have been interpreted as flirtation. She'd done her best to make it crystal clear that this was a one-off but she feared it would only encourage Huldar to start bombarding her with phone calls and messages again.

It just showed how heavily the past still weighed on her. She was prepared to do anything to show her former class-mates – though show them what? If she turned up with Huldar on her arm, they would at least realise she was capable of attracting a man. But that was pathetic, as well as being far from the truth. She would do better to show them that she was comfortable in her own skin. And that they could get stuffed. But that was a harder message to convey, especially since she was afraid she would be too ill at ease in their company to make the desired impression.

Freyja heaved a sigh. At least she wasn't going to turn up with Kjartan and run the risk of bumping into someone who knew his wife. Then she would really have sunk to new depths in their eyes.

Turning away from the window, she contemplated her open laptop. Up on screen was a draft of the report she had promised Erla. The contents were still very sketchy; in fact, all it consisted of were half-finished introductory sentences for the sections she intended to include. It didn't help that the bulk of the information was derived either directly or indirectly from Kjartan. Being constantly reminded of him ruined her concentration. It also bugged her that she'd recommended him to poor Adalheidur's father. If Kjartan was that dishonest, he could hardly be a good therapist – or so she tried to persuade herself. The thought that his lies were bound to affect his professionalism made her feel a little better. But it couldn't be helped; she could hardly ring the girl's father and retract her recommendation.

Freyja went over to the coffee table and closed the over-heated laptop. The fan seemed to groan with relief at no longer having to cool the clapped-out machine. It probably wouldn't be called on again until tomorrow morning as Freyja didn't think she would achieve any more tonight. She had gone over to the window to see if the weather was good enough for her to take Molly out, in the hope that the bracingly cold air would wake up her brain, but now she realised it would be pointless.

The report might not even be needed. The police had caught the guilty man, the sex pest who Freyja had seen with her own eyes when Stella's friend had identified him at the station. At first sight, the man hadn't looked particularly dangerous; quite the opposite, in fact: he'd resembled the kind of sheepish middle-aged bloke whose worst crime was leaving his dirty coffee mug in the sink at work. And although she knew that appearances could be deceptive, she couldn't shake off the suspicion that they'd got the wrong man. He'd looked shifty, but that could be because of his disastrous attempt to pay for sex, a crime of which she had no doubt he was guilty. But in the brief time she'd seen him, he hadn't come across as someone who was hiding a secret as big as murder. He had looked everyone in the eye, had blinked a normal amount and not too fast, his head hadn't been constantly jerking round, and his arms had hung down naturally at his sides, with no twitching or fidgeting. It had been obvious that he was a bit nervous, but instinct had told her that here was a man who was confident that he could blag his way out of trouble; who regarded himself as the victim rather than the guilty party.

Freyja resisted the urge to ring Huldar and hear the latest on the investigation, though she was bursting with questions. Had the man confessed, even told them where Egill was? Had he revealed the identity of victim number one? Surely she had the right to be kept informed? After all, she had pointed them towards the bullying angle.

Her phone lay on the table beside the laptop, almost daring her to pick it up. There were now three calls she either wanted or needed to make: one to Kjartan to give him hell, one to Adalheidur's father to take back her recommendation, and one to Huldar.

This train of thought touched something deep in her consciousness. Something to do with a phone call. But what? However hard she racked her brain, the memory remained tantalisingly out of reach. Trusting that it would come back to her if she stopped pursuing it, she pushed the thought away, picked up her phone and selected Huldar's number.

When he didn't answer, she tried Gudlaugur, who picked up at the first ring. Clearly he didn't have her number stored in his phone as he seemed to regret having answered the moment he heard who it was. He was tight-lipped about the investigation, fobbing her off with the comment that they were making progress and hopefully things would be clarified soon. Freyja, tiring quickly of his evasions, interrupted him mid-sentence to ask if Huldar was there. He told her he wasn't, then became even more deliberately vague when she asked where he was, though he did offer to pass on the message that she'd rung.

Freyja was thoughtful after their conversation. Gudlaugur had been open and chatty when she'd said goodbye to him after their interview of Stella's friend Bjarney. He was perfectly aware that she'd known what was happening in the inquiry at that point, so why was he answering in monosyllables now?

As she'd suspected, the moment she stopped trying to remember it, the thing relating to a phone call that had been niggling at the back of her mind came back to her. Going into the bedroom, she dug around in the pile of clothes on the chair until she found the trousers she'd been wearing during the visit to Stella's school on Monday. Sure enough, in the pocket was the scrap of paper bearing a telephone number that she'd torn off the poster on the school notice-board. After watching Adalheidur and her father drive away, Freyja had gone back inside and read the notice. It wasn't very informative; it merely asked if you or anyone close to you had been the victim of serious bullying. If so, help was at hand. There was no other information, just a fringe of tear-off phone numbers.

Freyja smoothed out the tatty piece of paper. Perhaps it was a psychologist, like Kjartan, who specialised in bullying. If so, it would be handy to be able to refer to him or her in the report and leave that bastard Kjartan out altogether. After all, she only had his word for it that he was the top specialist in Iceland. Well, that and all the results including his name that had come up when she'd googled the subject. But that didn't tell the whole story; there might be other experts who avoided the limelight. All she'd need was an hour with this person: she had the questions to hand and already knew most of the answers.

However, when she rang the mobile number, it was either switched off or had no reception. Frustrated, she tried tapping the number into the telephone directory in the hope of finding out the person's job title. If it turned out to be some amateur, she could chuck the scrap of paper away.

The number turned out to belong to a man called Mördur Jónasson, a software programmer. She put down her phone, glad not to have got through to him. Looking back at the directory, she wondered why a man who worked in a logical profession like IT should have involved himself in as emotional and irrational an area as bullying. Perhaps he was a former victim himself or had a child who suffered from the problem. After all, it was rife in the country's schools and workplaces.

Curious now, she tried entering his name into the search engine. The results were oddly sparse and not one of them was linked to bullying. The more she thought about it, the stranger it seemed that an IT expert should have chosen to stick an old-fashioned poster on a noticeboard rather than advertising online. All she could think of was that the act of abandoning technology might be a means of reconnecting with the world of the emotions.

While she was puzzling over this, her phone rang. It was a friend trying to lure her out on the town and she dealt with the conversation quickly, not letting herself be tempted by promises of a happy hour on cocktails or Hot Shots. It wasn't that she didn't want to go out and have fun but she was determined to be at her absolute knock-out best the following evening. If she went out tonight and got lucky, she'd be a wreck until Sunday at least: with bloodshot eyes, a woozy head and – who knows? – maybe even a sore neck from too much sex. Turning up in that state could hardly be classed as 'showing them'.

During the brief conversation, Freyja felt a sudden impulse to tell her friend the truth. Confide in her about how important this class reunion was for her and why. But she couldn't bring herself to do it. In the eyes of her friends from sixth-form college she was one of the cool kids. If she hinted that she hadn't always been part of the in-crowd, they might start looking at her differently. Seeds of doubt would be sown in their minds and everything she did, said or wore would be called into question in future. Unless, of course, they proved to be just as kind and understanding as they'd always been. But no, she couldn't take the risk. So much of our experience of people is based on preconceptions. Up to now, they had assumed she was cool, not a sad frump like the girls at her secondary school had unanimously agreed.

Her phone rang again and Freyja didn't even check the screen before answering. It must be one of her friends, wanting her to change her mind about coming out this evening. But no, it was Gudlaugur, who took forever to come to the point, twice apologising for bothering her, and wittering on about why Huldar hadn't yet returned her call, without actually explaining anything. In the end she lost patience and asked bluntly what he wanted.

'I was wondering if you could access the Child Protection Agency computer system, though technically speaking it's the weekend.'

'Er . . . yes, I should be able to. I can access most of its records through my computer at work. What are you looking for?'

'Information about a woman. From when she was a child – or a teenager, to be more precise.'

'Who is she?'

'She lives in a group home.'

Freyja rolled her eyes. 'It's going to be a little tricky to find anything based on information that general. Do you have anyone specific in mind?'

'Oh, yes, yes, of course, sorry. Her name's Laufhildur.'

'Laufhildur?'

'Yes. Laufhildur Brá Mardardóttir.'

'Did you say Mardardóttir or Hardardóttir?' Freyja thought she must have misheard. 'Mördur's daughter' . . . It wasn't that common a name. Was it possible that this was the daughter of the man she'd just been trying to ring? If so, the coincidence was extraordinary.

'Mardardóttir. We need to know if she cropped up on the children's services radar about twenty years ago. We also need the address of the group home where she's currently living. She moved in recently but no one seems to have got round to informing the National Register yet.' Gudlaugur paused a moment and, when he resumed, his voice had dropped to a murmur. 'But your search must be absolutely confidential. You mustn't discuss it with anyone. Do you think you can do that for us?'

Freyja was pretty sure she could.

Chapter 34

The boy was dead. Of that there could be no doubt. His head had rolled sideways and his eyes were open, fixed blankly on the door. Perhaps he had been hoping in vain that someone would break in and save him. But now those eyes gave the appearance of staring at him accusingly as he stood in the doorway, his nose buried in the crook of his elbow. He'd remembered a torch this time and when he shone it on the boy's face he noticed that there was something wrong with his eyes, a dark red welt running right across them, as if they'd been swapped for cat's eyes that had been turned on their side. And what he had taken for a shadow on one cheek transpired, when he looked closer, to be a large bruise that hadn't been there last time. Death showed little respect for the physical remains of the deceased.

He went inside and dragged the door shut behind him, still breathing through the sleeve of his coat, partly to avoid the smell so he didn't start retching and partly so he wouldn't inadvertently spread any DNA when he breathed out. His fears were probably groundless but he wasn't taking any chances. Just because he hadn't heard of the police nailing any suspects thanks to particles of saliva carried on their breath, that didn't mean it wasn't possible. If he was in charge of the police, he'd make damn sure they withheld information like that from the public. Anyway, he avoided the known pitfalls, wearing disposable rubber gloves and a swimming cap hidden under his hood. He had no intention of leaving any hairs or fingerprints at the scene.

He became aware that he was standing with his back pressed against the door, as if his body was baulking at going any nearer the dead boy. But he had to do it; he didn't have a choice. Bracing himself, he took one step towards his macabre goal. The sooner he got it over with, the sooner he would be out of here. Able to breathe freely, dispose of his clothes and try to act normally for the rest of the evening. He'd read up on how memory worked and was planning to stay awake for most of the night. That way he was more likely to forget the details. The memories would still be there but he wouldn't be able to access them, or so he understood. Sleep was needed to tidy them away and create the connections necessary for recalling them. But he didn't want to picture the dead boy every time he closed his eyes for the rest of his life: some things were better forgotten.

He made his way to the back where the boy was lying and clamped his torch in his armpit. For what he had to do next, he would need to lower his elbow from his face. Instead, he pulled the neck of his jumper over his nose, taking care to breathe sparingly and only through his mouth. Then, removing a small plastic ziplock bag from his pocket, he pulled out a tuft of hair and bent down. He swallowed, taking as deep a breath as he dared, and took hold of the boy's icy hand. The fingers were stiffer than he'd been expecting, which gave him a jolt. Was he not dead after all? Was he resisting? But then, remembering that corpses stiffen after death, he applied a little more force to prising the boy's fist apart. Fortunately the rigor mortis wasn't advanced enough for this to result in a sound of snapping or cracking. He laid the tuft of hair in the boy's palm, then closed his fingers again, one at a time.

Straightening up, he put the bag back in his pocket, then fetched the boy's phone from his breast pocket. It was an expensive model, more expensive than his own. Too expensive to belong to a teenager who clearly didn't look after it. There was a hairline scratch across the screen, from corner to corner, and it was unbelievably battered, considering how recently this model had come on the market. Only someone who was confident of being given a newer, upgraded model if he damaged it would treat his possessions like that. It was a kind of luxury he himself had never known.

Before switching on the phone, he hesitated, reminding himself that he had to act fast. Take a picture, send a Snap, place the phone beside the boy's body, then get the hell out of there.

He smiled grimly at the smeary screen and the smudges left by the boy's fingers where he had pressed them against the phone to unlock it. Just as well the kid didn't use facial recognition, given how smashed up his features were. He counted slowly to three, feeling all his muscles tense. The instant he switched on the phone, its location would be traced, as had been clear from what happened on the path on Öskjuhlíd. He didn't want to be anywhere near the place when the police arrived. In hindsight, he regretted that phone call: he'd only eluded them by the skin of his teeth. It hadn't been part of the plan but he'd panicked when the media didn't publish the material they'd been sent. He'd just wanted to be sure of pointing the police in the right direction. But all deviations from the original plan were unwise; not only the phone call but also the fact that he'd allowed a delay before

Egill's body was found. That was the bloody boy's own fault, though: he hadn't been able to risk them finding him alive.

One, two, three. He switched on the phone, holding his breath while it started up. It seemed to take an inordinate length of time but it was probably only a few seconds. Then he aimed the camera, taking care to get the boy's face in focus, even if it did take slightly longer. He didn't want to have to take another if this one came out blurred. The picture appeared instantly, those eerie cat's eyes staring at him from the screen. With trembling fingers, he shared it on Snapchat, sending it to all the boy's friends.

The message took an agonisingly long time to send and he began to worry that the 3G connection wasn't good enough. But finally it went, the picture of Egill's body winging out into the ether in the form of an electromagnetic wave. After that, he laid the phone on the floor, pocketed his torch and got himself out of there. There was no need to lock the door this time but still he paused to check that it had definitely clicked shut. It would mess up the plan if someone got a glimpse inside before he was well out of sight.

Then he walked away, taking the longest strides he dared to without drawing undue attention to himself.

He would never come back. At last it was over.

Now the process of forgetting could begin.

Chapter 35

The group home was located in an ordinary residential street and didn't stand out particularly from the neighbouring houses apart from being a little bigger and having noticeably more parking spaces outside. Huldar could understand this arrangement. No one should be condemned to living somewhere that resembled a state institution. It wasn't good for the soul.

Huldar parked beside a beaten-up wreck that reminded him of Freyja's car. The only other vehicle in the drive was a motorbike. From what Freyja had told Gudlaugur, the place was home to six residents, who required a fair amount of care. She'd failed to dig up any details about Laufhildur's accident but had found information relating to her move and an explanation of why her case had been processed so quickly. Apparently people often had to wait years to get their adult children into a group home, but Mördur's personal circumstances as a widower with a terminal illness, who had, moreover, shouldered the burden of caring for his daughter for far longer than most, had justified the speedy turnaround.

When Gudlaugur passed this on to Erla, she decided he should go to the home and take Huldar with him. Arnar's interview had been delayed by the non-appearance of his lawyer and was now unlikely to happen until tomorrow. Huldar was at a loose end and Erla couldn't send anyone else as they still hadn't cooked up a sufficiently plausible story to explain their interest in Laufhildur.

Though you could say that Freyja had provided one on a silver plate.

As usual, however, Erla was dismissive of any information that came from Freyja, saying it still didn't sufficiently explain the police's interest in Mördur and his daughter. Huldar and Gudlaugur could hardly object since it was true that the explanation wouldn't stand up to much scrutiny. Though, to Erla's credit, she did ring Adalheidur's headmistress to ask about the notice. The woman was at home, in the middle of cooking supper. She vaguely recalled having seen the poster but that was it. A phone call to Egill's headmaster proved more productive. He clearly remembered the notice appearing on the wall by the entrance shortly after term began, because he'd had it removed on the grounds that only notices about school business were permitted in the building. He had a feeling that two or three of the phone numbers had been torn off before he was made aware of its existence, and although he couldn't be sure who had been behind it, he'd assumed it had been someone messing about. After all, they didn't have a big bullying problem at his school.

As Huldar and Gudlaugur left the station, Erla had still been debating whether to ring Adalheidur's head again to request access to the school so the police could confiscate the notice as potential evidence. They had set out in a hurry before she could make up her mind, for fear of being landed with that job as well. The visit to the group home had to take priority. If they couldn't find out anything about Mördur there, they would have hit a brick wall. The nurse from Ásta's ward had rung Huldar to tell him that Mördur hadn't had any visitors. Not a single one. The man seemed to have been a recluse.

Snow was falling gently, the flakes melting the moment they touched the ground in the car park and on the path leading to the house. Geothermally heated pipes had obviously been installed underneath to keep the area clear for the residents. Gudlaugur knocked and after a lengthy interval, the door opened. The expression on the face of the young woman standing there almost made the wait worthwhile. She was unusually diminutive and had to tilt her head back to see their faces. Rarely had Huldar been so aware of his and Gudlaugur's height. He regretted not having taken the time to shave that morning. It would have been better to turn up in uniform too, but neither of them had thought of it. The upshot was that Huldar looked more like one of the men he spent his days pursuing than a guardian of the law.

'Good evening.' Gudlaugur smiled at the woman and Huldar followed his example, but far from reassuring her, their smiles prompted her to half close the door again. 'We're from the police. Could we have a word with you or whoever's in charge of the home?'

The woman's face radiated suspicion. 'Have you got any ID?' she asked through the crack.

Huldar fished his out of his pocket and presented it to her. She bent forwards to inspect it carefully, then, her suspicions allayed, opened the door properly.

'We're here about Laufhildur. Am I right that she lives here?' Huldar entered what turned out to be a spacious hall.

'Yes.' The woman waited for Gudlaugur to come in as well, then closed the door behind them. But she showed no sign of allowing them any further inside. 'Has something happened?'

'Her father died earlier today. I don't know if anyone's informed you yet.' Huldar assumed not, since this was probably a job for Mördur's brother, who didn't know the address of the home, let alone the phone number.

The woman drew herself up. 'No. We hadn't heard.' She sighed heavily. 'We were wondering why he hadn't been round. I suppose it was connected to his illness?'

'Yes.' Huldar left it at that, assuming that someone more qualified than him would explain the precise cause of death to the staff. 'Did he visit often?'

'Every day. Sometimes twice a day. Though he did warn us last week that he was going to be busy, so we shouldn't expect to see as much of him. But we didn't know it was because of his illness.' The news seemed to be taking a while to sink in. She shook her head, sighing again. 'I can't say I look forward to breaking it to her.'

'We can do that if you like. We need to talk to her anyway, if possible. But we've been told she's in a bad way and can only express herself with the help of aids?'

'Laufhildur?' The woman looked surprised. 'Did no one tell you that she doesn't see anyone? Only her father, though the carers can go in if she opens the door to us. No one else – including the other residents – is allowed in. That was stressed to us when she arrived. Apparently she's so agoraphobic that she never leaves her room. She even wanted her windows blacked out. We drew the line at that, obviously, but we do try to respect her wishes as far as we can by limiting unnecessary contact and avoiding putting any pressure on her to come out. I think those were two of the conditions for her coming to live here. Not that anyone's tried to see her since then. Her father was her only visitor. And now you.'

'May I ask why?' Huldar asked, disconcerted. 'Is it connected to her accident? To be honest, we know next to nothing about her situation.'

'Oh.' The young woman's eyes widened. 'Oh.' Looking from one to the other, she saw that they were waiting for enlightenment, and that just saying 'Oh' wasn't enough. 'I don't know exactly what's true and what isn't, because I've heard different stories. I mean, her father claimed it was an accident but I've heard it whispered that it was attempted suicide.'

'Did she suffer brain damage? Or paralysis?' During his years on the beat Huldar had attended the scenes of a few failed suicides. The consequences could be devastating.

'I gather she suffered some kind of brain damage, but she hasn't been assessed since she finished her treatment following the accident. She's supposed to be evaluated in due course but they decided to wait till she'd settled down here and come to terms with the move. As I mentioned, she doesn't want to see anybody, and that applies to doctors and other health workers as well. Though of course we'd make an exception in an emergency. But we keep our contact with her to a minimum, in accordance with her wishes.'

'I have to say it all sounds rather unorthodox to me.' Huldar tried to suppress his irritation over the odd embargo.

'Yes and no. Not in light of her injuries. You see, she shot herself. Either by accident or design. But either way I'm sure she didn't mean to rip off the lower half of her face.'

'Rip off her face?' Gudlaugur looked shaken.

'Yes. Her lower jaw's missing. And her tongue. That's why she can't talk.'

'Christ.' Huldar tried and failed to picture it. Suppressing his curiosity, he merely asked if it couldn't be sorted out with modern plastic surgery, by grafting on a new jaw or replacing it with an artificial one, for example.

The woman shrugged. 'Maybe. But it wasn't possible at the time. Her face was just patched up without its bottom half. You never know, she might be persuaded to explore the options now that she's living with us. I really hope so. I haven't seen her face but I gather it's a pretty shocking sight.'

'So you haven't been allowed into her room?'

'Oh, yes, sure. But she wears a mask.'

Huldar and Gudlaugur nodded uncertainly.

The young woman picked up on their confusion and added, on a more upbeat note: 'As I said, we're hoping things are going to start looking up. Though her father wanted nothing but the best for her, maybe he wasn't the ideal person to look after her. She hasn't received the treatment she should have had. I don't doubt for a minute that she was the one refusing to meet other people, but he should have consulted a specialist.'

'Are you saying she never once left the house in the two decades following the accident?' Gudlaugur's eyes widened in disbelief.

'No, apparently not. I gather there was a fenced-in decking behind their flat, so she could go out for some fresh air, but she never mixed with other people. Her father paid to have a garden entrance put in for her here and the same kind of fenced-off decking built. That was another of his conditions for her moving in. I expect he intended the arrangement to remain unchanged but we've got other ideas in the long run. The fact he's passed away may ultimately be a good thing.'

Huldar and Gudlaugur were both silent and the woman fidgeted, as if uncertain what to say next. Then she clapped her hands and offered to check if Laufhildur would agree to meet them, seeing as they were from the police. 'Though of course I can't guarantee anything.'

Waving her tiny hands at their feet, she added that there was no need for them to take off their shoes. Then she showed them into a large lounge area where several residents were watching television. None of them took any notice of the visitors but remained glued to the frantic action on screen. Asking them both to wait, the woman disappeared down a corridor. They heard a distant knocking, then the sound of a door opening and the woman saying something, though they couldn't make out the words over the noise of the TV. A few moments later she returned, looking surprised. 'She's willing to see you.'

As they followed her down the corridor, she filled them in on the rules. 'Though Laufhildur can't talk, she understands plenty, so be tactful. If you don't mind, I'd like to be present, because I've got quite good at interpreting her body language and mood. If I say we need to call a halt, I mean it. I don't want her upset. OK?' They nodded. On the way, the woman stuck her head into a small coffee room and asked the young man sitting there to stand in for her at reception. He raised his eyes from his phone and got to his feet, showing a total lack of interest in the visitors.

Laufhildur's door was halfway down the corridor. It wasn't numbered like a hospital room but had her name on it, spelt out in colourful wooden letters, presumably courtesy of her father. None of the other doors were labelled in that way; in fact, they were all different, presumably to avoid an institutional feel. The woman tapped lightly, then, without waiting for an answer, opened the door and ushered them in.

Laufhildur's living space was more like a big hotel room than a flat; larger than your average bedroom but smaller than the few studio apartments Huldar had seen inside. It contained a large bed, a tiny kitchen corner, a two-seater sofa, a compact sideboard and a small wardrobe that wouldn't have met the needs of any woman Huldar knew. In addition there were shelves full of books and a large television tuned to the same channel that the residents had been watching in the lounge, though the quality was terrible, the pixels so large you'd have thought it was Minecraft. Yet, despite the limited space, Huldar reflected rather ruefully that it was homelier than his own flat.

Two large *Star Wars* posters hung over the bed, while on the sideboard and here and there on the walls were framed photos all featuring the same little girl and smiling woman. Two healthy-looking pot plants decorated the window sill and there was nothing institutional about the curtains, which were drawn back although it was dark outside. The view from the window and garden door consisted of nothing but a high fence, presumably the one enclosing the decking. Next to the rows of books on the shelves were figurines and ornaments more suited to a young girl than a woman in her thirties. Perhaps they were relics of her former life, before the accident that had completely cut her off from the outside world.

Huldar's gaze didn't linger long on the furniture or decorations. Instead, it was drawn to a wicker chest that stood against the wall, its lid open to reveal a collection of masks. He recognised several, including the Guy Fawkes one used by the Anonymous group, the *Scream* mask, a red-eyed number from the *Saw* franchise, a green Ninja Turtle and a white stormtrooper from *Star Wars*. And then there was the shiny black Darth Vader mask. He had an odd sensation that it was looking at him, daring him to pick it up. Huldar coughed but there was no need to nudge Gudlaugur, who was examining the chest and its contents with equal fascination. Next, they both turned their attention to Laufhildur herself.

She was sitting on the edge of her bed, straight-backed and quite still. She was a large, big-boned woman, but what immediately caught Huldar's attention was not her build but the mask she was wearing. A chalk-white face, black hollows around the eye slits, blood-red lips and scars extending from both corners of the mouth. The whole was topped with fake green hair that was combed back over the head. He was face to face with Batman's arch-enemy, the Joker. The situation was so grotesque that his mind went momentarily blank and he just stood there, gawping like an idiot.

The young woman who had accompanied them into the room didn't seem remotely fazed. Taking a remote control from a cloth bag that hung from the headboard on the bed, she switched off the TV, replaced it, then said to Laufhildur: 'These are the policemen I was telling you about.' The woman lowered her voice as she turned to Huldar and Gudlaugur. 'I'm afraid they have some bad news for you.'

Huldar drew himself up. 'Hello, Laufhildur. My name's Huldar and I'm from the police.' He could see that she was watching him through the holes in the mask but it was impossible to tell if her eyes were friendly. Instinct told him they weren't, but that didn't necessarily mean anything. It could just be the bad associations conjured up by the Joker.

'Like she said, I'm afraid we've got some bad news.' Huldar paused. His dread of what he had to say next had nothing to do with the weird situation he found himself in. After the

Yrsa Sigurdardóttir

three previous occasions on which he'd been required to notify someone of the death of a close relative, he had vowed never to do it again if he could possibly help it. He coughed, trying out the words in his head, but he couldn't come up with anything this time either. Better men than him had lost their tongues in circumstances like this. Best keep it simple. 'I'm terribly sorry to have to tell you that your father's dead, Laufhildur. He passed away in hospital earlier today.' He paused, unable to decide whether he should add anything, and if so, what.

Laufhildur watched him, the mask hiding all expression. She must be heart-broken. The news had turned her world upside down and nothing would ever be the same again. 'I'm terribly sorry, but he'd been very ill.' Huldar hadn't a clue whether she'd known about her father's cancer. After all, what good would it have done to tell her? She would probably have been worse off knowing that something bad was going to happen. Personally, he wouldn't want to be told if the plane he was travelling in was about to crash into a mountainside.

Laufhildur kept her gaze fixed on his. He was beginning to wonder if she'd understood when he noticed something glistening in the corner of her eye. It was a tear that swelled and swelled until it disappeared from sight under the mask. He didn't think he'd ever seen a bigger tear in his life.

The young woman seemed to have noticed as well because she went and fetched some loo paper from the en-suite bathroom. She left the bathroom door open and Huldar noticed the same air of homeliness in there as well: a pink towel hanging by the sink, a soap bottle of the same colour on the side, and a collection of necklaces draped over a hook beside the mirror. But something was missing: there were no cosmetics, no face creams or make-up. He'd been in enough women's bathrooms to realise how unusual this was. But of course this woman had missed out on many things more remarkable than the opportunity to slather herself in beauty products. Laufhildur took the loo paper from the woman but made no move to dab her face. Instead, she scrunched it up in her fist. A peculiar noise emerged from behind the mask.

'What is it, Laufhildur dear? Is there something I can do for you?' The young woman reached out to take her hand but Laufhildur snatched it away. Then she turned her head and pointed to the small sideboard. Seen in profile like this, the mask didn't quite conceal her facial disfigurement. Where her earlobe ended there was nothing but a mass of scarring where the skin had been pulled tight under her cheekbone, and below that nothing but the dark hollow where her jaw should have been. Gudlaugur elbowed Huldar and pointed unobtrusively at Laufhildur's head. At first Huldar thought he was drawing attention to the disfigurement, but then he realised it was something else. Just above her ear there was a small bald patch where the skin was redder than on the ear itself.

The young woman straightened up and went over to the sideboard, watching to see where Laufhildur was pointing. She touched the drawers one after the other until Laufhildur started waving more agitatedly. 'Is there something in this drawer?' Laufhildur nodded. The woman opened the drawer and rooted around inside, then took out a white envelope and held it up to Laufhildur. 'Is this what you mean?'

Laufhildur, alias the Joker, nodded and the woman gave her a kindly smile. She came over and handed Huldar the envelope. 'There you are. I recognise the writing. It's from her father.'

A single word was written in blue biro on the front of the envelope: *Police*. No address or any other indication that the envelope was meant to be posted. Huldar was reluctant to touch it but had no choice but to pinch it between thumb and fingernail before the woman could handle it further. 'Thanks.' Gudlaugur, cottoning on, pulled out a clear plastic evidence bag from his coat pocket. The bag was too small, which left half the envelope sticking out, but it would have to do.

'Could you excuse us a moment?' Huldar asked Laufhildur out of politeness. It was her home, after all. 'We're just stepping out to the car but we'll be right back.'

The young woman answered for Laufhildur, apparently no more thrown by their sudden departure than she had been by the discovery of the envelope.

Once in the car, Huldar removed a pair of tweezers from the small toolkit in the glove compartment. Donning a pair of latex gloves, he removed the envelope from the evidence bag. It wasn't sealed, so he carefully drew out the letter it contained, ignoring Gudlaugur's protests that they ought to take it straight down to the station.

The phone rang in his pocket but, ignoring that too, Huldar delicately unfolded the letter and began reading. The ringing stopped and he was distantly aware of Gudlaugur's phone starting up instead. He continued reading while Gudlaugur answered and had just finished the densely written page when his partner tapped him on the shoulder. 'That was Erla on the phone. They've found Egill's body. She wants us to go straight there.'

Huldar sat there without moving for a moment, his eyes unfocused. What the hell? Turning to Gudlaugur, still holding the letter in the tweezers, he said: 'Mördur claims responsibility for the murders. He doesn't name any names but it's clear what he's referring to. He says he did it to show his countrymen once and for all that bullying is a deadly serious matter. Because nothing else had worked. Jesus Christ.'

'What? But he was in hospital.'

'It gets worse. He says he killed all three of them. Three!' Huldar clenched his jaw. So there was a victim number one after all.

Gudlaugur was lost for words. Huldar handed him the tweezers, asking him to put the letter back in the envelope. Then he started the car and backed out of the drive. Unfortunately there wouldn't be time to say goodbye to Laufhildur or her carer. But it didn't really matter since the police would be back all too soon.

Chapter 36

The mood at the scene was subdued. Despite knowing that it was almost impossible Egill would be found alive, they'd been unconsciously nursing a faint hope, which had now been brought crashing down to earth. The news that there was a third victim out there had only deepened the air of despondency. Hardly anyone spoke.

The boy had been found in a shipping container. The location had been revealed when his phone suddenly appeared on the system and a Snap of his dead body was sent to all his friends. As might be expected, the kids, who made up most of his contacts, had been unable to resist the temptation to view the picture. In the wake of this, the police had been inundated with calls. Most of those who got in touch wanted to know if this meant Egill was dead, a question the police refused to answer. They didn't need to: the boy's face in the picture said it all. They made an exception when Egill's father rang, though. It was deeply regrettable that he'd contacted the police before they'd had a chance to notify him, but it couldn't be helped. The officer who took the call was quick to forward it to Erla, who was tight-lipped afterwards about what had been said.

The twenty-foot insulated shipping container stood in an enclosed paddock near a poultry farm on the outskirts of Mosfellsbær, a small town located thirteen kilometres north-east of Reykjavík. The land was registered as grazing, though there were no horses to be seen nor any sign that they had been pastured there the previous summer; the grass had been left to grow unchecked and there were no piles of dung visible under the thin layer of snow. By the time Huldar and Gudlaugur arrived, the police had tracked down the owner, one Eiríkur Gestsson, but when they got hold of him, it transpired that he had rented out the field the year before. The name of the tenant was all too familiar: Mördur Jónasson, Laufhildur's father. How Erla had managed to control her face at that point Huldar couldn't imagine. She had seen no option but to grasp at the lifebelt Freyja had thrown her earlier that day, claiming that she'd come across the name in connection with a notice at Stella's school. She explained that she'd already sent Huldar and Gudlaugur to check out the man in question, so the team was awaiting their arrival with a degree of eager impatience they were quite unaccustomed to these days.

Thanks to the contents of the letter, they didn't disappoint anyone.

Like Huldar, Erla had been unable to wait until she got to the station before reading it. She'd grabbed the envelope half hanging out of its evidence bag and stormed off to her car. The rest of the team had clustered around Huldar and Gudlaugur in the hope of illumination. Huldar decided to lighten the demoralised atmosphere by telling his colleagues that Mördur had confessed to the killings in his letter. When he saw how they brightened at this news, he was forced to disappoint them by adding that there was no way this could stand up: the man had been incapacitated at the time of the attacks. At this, the faces of those present fell again and with a dispirited air they drifted back to their allotted tasks.

Huldar and Gudlaugur were left standing alone in the open, exposed to the biting wind, like the horses for whom the pasture was intended.

'Shall we take a look inside?' Gudlaugur spoke in a low voice, though they were alone out there. He surveyed the rusty container. Forensics had propped one of the doors open with a tripod. The dry stalks of grass poking up from the snow cast long shadows over the ground in the glare of the flood-lights that had been set up inside.

'You can, if you like. I can live without it.' Huldar slapped his coat in search of cigarettes and felt the packet in his breast pocket. He'd have to go over to the fence to smoke so his ash wouldn't contaminate the scene for Forensics. As far as he was concerned, the greater the distance between him and the container, the happier he'd be.

Instead of heading for the open door, Gudlaugur dithered. 'Who do you think will get a bollocking for failing to search it?'

'No one in particular. You can hardly blame them. The container's invisible from the road because the poultry farm's in the way, so I doubt anyone noticed it. And I expect the smell from the farm would have confused the dogs if they had any with them.' Huldar fiddled impatiently with his cigarette. 'I don't suppose they did more than a cursory search of the farm itself. There must be several people working there and they'd be unlikely to club together to hide a corpse. I don't suppose the search party thought it was worth wasting precious time on it, any more than on other busy workplaces. Sadly. If they had, they might have spotted the container in time.' Huldar didn't mention that he himself had driven past and discounted the farm for precisely these reasons. But this wasn't the only place he had overlooked and doubtless not the only one the search parties had ignored. The appeal to the public to check around their homes and workplaces had probably created a false sense of security.

Huldar smiled at Gudlaugur with genuine warmth for the first time since Ásta had planted doubts about him in his mind. 'But at least *we*'ve avoided a tongue-lashing for once.'

Gudlaugur finally moved towards the container, looking slightly more cheerful now. But Huldar couldn't shake off his depression, weighed down as he was with fatigue and sadness at Egill's fate. When he reached the fence he lit his cigarette at last, leant his head back and blew a stream of smoke into the sky. He was still standing like that when Erla appeared beside him.

'What kind of fucking bullshit is this letter?'

'I don't know.' Huldar sent another cloud of smoke heavenwards. 'According to the nursing staff, he was on the ward when both kids were attacked. Hooked up to monitors, so they'd have noticed if he'd gone AWOL.'

'Where's his phone? We need to get hold of it ASAP. Maybe he rang someone else after he had his heart attack and asked them to take care of the killings.'

Huldar glanced down at her. 'I don't know what kind of people you hang out with but there's no one in my address book who I could casually ask to take over a couple of murders for me.'

'Not even one of your sisters?' Erla reached out for his cigarette and took a drag.

'Since when do you smoke?' Huldar watched her exhaling amateurishly.

'I don't. Apart from the odd one when I drink. Or when

I'm freaking out.' She took another drag, though she didn't appear to be inhaling. When she handed back the cigarette it was smoked down to the filter, which was glowing orange. 'He mentions three murders. If it wasn't for those bloody numbers we could have celebrated the fact he'd only managed to nail two out of the three. But no one kills in the order two, three, one.'

'Why not?' Huldar stubbed out his cigarette on a fence post. 'Would that be stranger than any other aspect of this case? The man's crazy enough to cut down kids in the flower of their youth.'

'Oh Christ, don't start getting poetic on me.' Erla was gazing over at the open door of the container. 'They're about to bring him out. The poor kid.'

'What does the pathologist say? Has he been lying there dead since Tuesday?'

'No. He died less than twenty-four hours ago. They should have a more accurate time of death after the post-mortem, though just how accurate we'll have to see. Anyway, that's irrelevant since the pathologist is pretty confident the boy died of the injuries he received on Tuesday evening. He can't find any signs of violence inflicted subsequently.'

Huldar hastily interrupted to forestall a detailed description of the difference between old and new injuries. 'Are you telling me he was lying there alive for forty-eight hours, maybe even calling for help?'

'If he did try to make a noise, it wouldn't have carried far. He was in a very bad way. Even I could see that. Anyway, it wouldn't have done any good. No one could have heard him. The container's too far away from the chicken farm. We've questioned the security guard and he insists he didn't hear anything. He says the hens cluck all day long so you can't hear anything else. As they're layers, there are no windows in the sheds, which means none on the side facing this paddock and the container. Apparently, they control the hens' sleeping and waking hours with artificial lights. In the evenings and at night, when the lights are off and they're asleep, there's not much to do, so no one has any reason to go outside. Of course we'll talk to the staff who work there on the day shift but I think we can rule out the possibility that any of them heard Egill. There's a chance someone might have noticed any comings and goings in the vicinity of the container, though.'

'Maybe.' Huldar doubted it. He'd learnt over the years that with some investigations everything went like clockwork and with others nothing went right. This case definitely fell into the latter category. Mördur's death just before he and Gudlaugur arrived at the hospital was the clearest proof of that. 'Do you want me to go to the hospital and find out what happened to Mördur's phone? His daughter isn't going anywhere and, apart from her, he's got no family except a brother up north. I'm betting his stuff's still unclaimed.'

Erla appeared to consider this as she watched two men carrying a stretcher over to the container. They tapped on Gudlaugur's back to get him to move out of the way, then disappeared inside the steel crate. 'OK. That'd be good. You won't be any use here, if I know you.'

It was a fair comment and Huldar didn't protest. 'What about Mördur's flat? Is there any reason to delay searching it? I could help with that as well, if you like.'

The wind turned and wafted over a throat-catching stench from the poultry farm. Huldar made a face but Erla didn't react, her sense of smell dulled by the menthol cream she'd smeared under her nose before entering the container. 'As soon as I'd read the letter I rang the clerk of the court on duty but he didn't see any reason to drag a judge out of bed. Told me to wait till tomorrow morning; put a guard on the flat tonight. I tried to argue that it couldn't wait but the jumped-up little prick wasn't having any of it. But after I hung up, I started wondering if we actually need a warrant. He lived alone. And he's dead.'

Huldar regarded her in surprise. 'Er, yes. I'm pretty sure we do.'

'Really? Do dead people have a right to privacy? Can't we just go and search the place? It's not like he's going to care now.'

Huldar pushed himself upright from the fence and turned to face her. 'Had enough of being a manager, have you?'

'No. Yes. I don't know.' Erla was still looking at the container, avoiding Huldar's eye. 'I'm sick of all the petty bureaucracy. Like now – just when things are finally moving, some twat of an official throws an obstacle in my path. I've had it up to here with that kind of crap.'

'If you're not sure you want to wave goodbye to your job, you'd better forget that idea p.d.q. From what I remember, the law makes no distinction between the living and the dead when it comes to privacy.' Of course Erla knew this as well as he did, if not better. Lack of sleep over the last five days must be taking its toll. 'Post a guard so no one can get inside tonight and we'll apply through the right channels in the morning. If we go in without a warrant, they'll crucify you. The circumstances don't meet the criteria of imminent destruction of evidence, so you can't hide behind that excuse.

The man's dead, after all. Incidentally, I recommend you apply for a warrant to search Laufhildur's room while you're about it. She's big and strong enough to have been the perpetrator in the CCTV footage. The staff at the group home may claim she never goes out, but she has her own entrance. I don't know how she'd get around without attracting attention, but she may have found a way. After all, she's got a Darth Vader mask and for all we know she may have a blood-stained anorak rolled up in her cupboard.'

Erla took time to digest this, her gaze still fixed on the container. 'No clerk of the court is going to bother a judge for a warrant to search a group home for the disabled at this time of night. He'll just tell me to wait till tomorrow.'

Huldar had to be satisfied with that, though personally he would at least have tried. But he was in no position to go over her head.

'The person who killed Stella and Egill must be alive,' Erla went on. 'If the information from the hospital is correct, it can't possibly have been Mördur. So right now I'm more worried about his flat. There's a risk the killer, whether it's his daughter or someone else, will go round and remove any incriminating evidence.'

'So put a guard on the flat as the clerk suggested.'

The container creaked as both doors were pushed fully open to make room for the body to be brought out. They watched in silence. Neither would be attending the boy's funeral, so this was the closest they'd come to paying their respects. Mourners tended not to appreciate the presence of the police, seeing them as nothing but an uncomfortable reminder of the horrific events that had led up to the funeral. The stretcher-bearers walked slowly, taking care not to stumble on the rough ground in the dark, under the watchful eyes of the team who'd been working on the corpse. The technicians clustered around the entrance to the container, silent like Huldar and Erla. Gudlaugur, still standing outside, was quiet too. As the stretcher passed them, Huldar stared at the white shape under the sheet, struck by how slight the boy had been, how far off adulthood. All that was visible was one white hand protruding from under the sheet. Erla appeared to be transfixed by the sight. Once the stretcher had passed, she broke the silence. 'He was clutching some hairs in his fist. Just like Stella.' She said nothing further and Huldar didn't ask any questions. They waited until Egill had been loaded into the ambulance. When the slamming of the rear doors had stopped echoing in their ears, Erla turned to Huldar and picked up where they'd left off. 'What if the first victim's at Mördur's flat? Possibly still alive?'

Huldar heaved a sigh. She wasn't going to let it go, so it was up to him to save her from herself. However strained their relationship was, the prospect of a new boss held no appeal for him. Christ, it could be Jóel, for all he knew, and then he might as well start clearing his desk. 'Say I go and fetch Mördur's belongings from the hospital and they just happen to include his house keys.' Erla's eyes narrowed. 'Then say I happen to take a swing past his place on my way home and think I spot a light and movements in the window. I suppose I'd have to check out the situation to make sure it wasn't another victim or the perpetrator come back to dispose of the evidence. Wouldn't that be convenient?' He paused, and meeting her eye saw a glint that hadn't been there for ages. 'Just an idea.'

She grinned at him. 'Get your arse over to the hospital. I'll delay posting that guard on the flat.' She gave him a matey slap on the shoulder, rather harder than necessary. 'I knew I could rely on you.'

Huldar knew the way to the cardiology ward like the back of his hand by now. As on his previous visits, no one paid him any attention when he walked in through the A&E entrance, but perhaps that was understandable this time. He strode in like a man who knows exactly where he's going.

All was quiet on the ward apart from the usual irritating bleeping. The corridor was empty and the lights were out in the rooms. He didn't recognise the nurse on duty and couldn't decide if this was good or bad. The woman he'd dealt with last time would probably have raised objections, fed up with the constant interruptions. But at least he'd have been spared the necessity of explaining why he was there. This wasn't easy as he was limited in how much he could reveal, but luckily the nurse turned out to be one of those rare creatures who still trusted the police implicitly and accepted what he said without question. He had to suppress a smile of triumph as she disappeared into a storeroom in the corridor, then reappeared with an unmarked plastic bag. It took all his self-discipline not to look inside until he was back in the car.

Once there, he pulled on a pair of disposable gloves and tipped out the contents on the passenger seat, having first spread plastic over the seat to prevent contamination. He had bags laid out ready for each piece of evidence. This wasn't quite by the book: he should have taken Mördur's property straight down to the station and handed it over to Forensics. But it wasn't the first time a detective had interpreted the rules rather loosely and it wouldn't be the last.

Mördur's clothes made up the bulk of the contents: jeans, vest and shirt, socks and underpants. Huldar felt the trouser pockets but they were empty. So was the breast pocket of his shirt. He crammed the clothes into two bags and sealed them. There was a wallet, too, but it didn't contain anything of interest: a thousand-krónur note, credit card, debit card, a new, unused strip of bus tickets and several credit card receipts. When he unfolded them, they appeared to be perfectly innocent; the sort of thing Huldar carried in his own wallet. Groceries, petrol, fast food. The only difference was that Huldar's wallet was also stuffed with receipts from the bars of Reykjavík.

After he'd replaced the contents of the wallet and sealed it in a plastic bag, there was nothing left on the seat but a new-looking mobile phone and a bunch of keys. The phone had run out of battery. Huldar turned it over in his hands. He had a charger that would fit it and could have plugged it into the car socket but decided against the idea. Forensics would be able to detect that he'd tampered with it and such behaviour would be hard to justify. So the phone went into a bag as well. Apart from the keys, there was nothing left on the seat.

There were five keys on the ring. One was recognisably a car key, and there was another small one that looked as though it would fit a padlock, possibly the one on the shipping container. The other three appeared to be house keys. No two were the same, so one could conceivably fit a storeroom, workplace or other space the man had access to. They'd find out in due course. Before replacing the bunch on the seat, he tried locating the man's vehicle in the hospital car park by pressing the fob. There was no sound of beeping. Not even when he got out and held the key up to his chin to use his head as an aerial, which was supposed to double its reach, and pointed it in different directions. Still no joy.

Not a sound, not a flashing light anywhere.

He drove up and down the car park with his window open, repeatedly pressing the fob. Either it had run out of juice like the phone or the car was parked out of range.

Frustrated, Huldar set off for Mördur's flat. Erla must be getting impatient for news. Yet there was something niggling at him, something connected to his visit to the hospital. Perhaps it was just the worry about having to explain to management how he had happened to be passing a flat all the way out in Breidholt while ostensibly driving the short distance from the hospital to the police station. He'd just have to hope the matter was never raised or that people were so relieved about the case being solved that they were prepared to overlook this minor detail.

It was almost impossible to find any free parking spaces outside the block of flats but eventually Huldar managed to squeeze in between two other cars.

The flat was on the ground floor. One of the keys fitted the entrance to the block, another the flat itself. The front door was unusually wide, much wider than the other doors on the corridor. He guessed this was because Mördur's wife had been an invalid, confined to a wheelchair.

Huldar turned the key in the lock, pushed open the door, then reached inside and switched on the light. His hands, still encased in the rubber gloves, felt sweaty and clammy. Poking his head through the door, he sniffed warily. To his immense relief, there was only a smell of stale house, made up of countless indefinable elements. He'd been prepared for much worse.

Instead of closing the door again and heading back to the station, Huldar decided, now he'd come all this way, that he might as well do a circuit of the flat. He carefully removed his shoes in the hall and touched as little as possible as he padded around what turned out to be a very ordinary home. Most of the furniture was made of dark-stained wood, and there was a lot of velvet upholstery. It reminded Huldar of his grandparents' house. He couldn't resist the temptation to step outside onto the fenced-in decking to see with his own eyes the few square metres that for two whole decades had been Laufhildur's only access to the great outdoors. The space turned out to be much smaller than the exercise yard in a prison. He went back inside and continued his exploration of Mördur's bedroom, the sitting room and adjoining dining room without discovering anything of interest.

Until he opened the door to Laufhildur's room.

Huldar took out his phone and rang Erla. She'd have to have another go at getting a search warrant. There was no time to lose. He'd never in his life seen so much evidence in one place.

It was a real smorgasbord.

But on the rare occasions when a smorgasbord of evidence had turned up like this, it had almost invariably been specially prepared for the police, as Huldar knew from bitter experience. It wasn't the evidence that held him transfixed, though, so much as the bedroom window; the window that more than anything else bore silent witness to the misery and isolation that Laufhildur had chosen in preference to braving the outside world in her disfigured state. It had been blacked out with paint.

Chapter 37

Huldar wasn't the only one who turned up to work dishevelled and desperate for caffeine. He'd only slept for four hours, in addition to the half-hour it had taken him to drop off. Usually he had no problem conking out. But last night he had tossed and turned, alone in his double bed, trying not to obsess about the case and all the material he'd found in Mördur's flat. Even his attempt to distract himself by thinking about his upcoming date with Freyja hadn't worked.

'Erla's looking for you.' Gudlaugur, being younger, wore his lack of sleep better. He'd gone home around the same time as Huldar, shortly after the items from Mördur's flat had started arriving at the station.

It had taken a maddeningly long time to secure a search warrant and while Huldar was waiting at the flat for his colleagues, he had passed the time by examining everything he could without disturbing the evidence. In the end, tired of being on his feet, he had gone out to the squad car for a smoke. He could expect a reprimand for that, but as an infringement it paled into insignificance next to the fact that he'd entered Mördur's flat without permission. As yet no one had commented on this. Last night they had all been too high on adrenaline to think of anything but itemising and examining the evidence, but no doubt they'd sober up as the day went on. Then he could expect to be hauled up in front of the senior command or the departmental lawyer. Fuck it. He'd just have to let it wash over him; pretend to be ashamed of himself while focusing on the prospect of his evening with Freyja. It was a trick he'd learnt as a kid when he was always getting into trouble.

Huldar sat down and switched on his computer. He didn't ask Gudlaugur where Erla was; she'd come and find him if it was urgent. 'Where's the evidence? Still with Forensics?'

Gudlaugur stood up to see Huldar over his monitor. 'Part of it. Only some of it's been processed but they've made copies of the lot. Erla's had them hung on the walls of the incident room. It's worth a look.'

'Thanks but no thanks.' Huldar had already seen most of it. A succession of weird ramblings, the justifications of a madman plotting to kill teenagers who bullied other kids, with the express aim of putting an end to the problem once and for all. And, at the same time, of taking revenge on the world for the fate his daughter had suffered after being bullied as a kid. Total insanity. Nowhere in any of the printouts of his crazy outpourings that had been strewn over the floor of his flat was there the slightest hint that he shouldered any of the blame for his daughter getting hold of a gun. Yet it was pretty evident that the weapon had been his as he'd been on the board of a shooting club at the time and stood down shortly after the accident. Much easier to blame the whole thing on other people. Easier and no doubt less painful.

To carry out his plan, Mördur had managed to dig up the names of several school bullies, including by putting up notices in schools, and, with the help of some careful detective work, had amassed detailed information about each one of them. After that he had created a table in which he awarded them marks to work out who was the most deserving of punishment. The greatest number of points was reserved for those cases where the victim had tried to commit suicide, with bonus points if the suicide was successful. Credit was also given for stamina: the longer the bully had kept up the pressure on a particular individual, the more points he or she earned. Then there were points for involving other kids; the more likes or hurtful comments the bullies got on their posts about the victim, the higher the marks. They also went up the list based on how multi-faceted their attacks were and how many social-media platforms they used. The more vicious the bullying, the more points they scored. Destruction of a human soul: *douze points*.

It was no surprise to find Stella and Egill high up the list. Not at the very top and not marked out in any way, but near the top, in second and fifth position. There were ten names in all. 'Have we established that the other kids on this list are alive?' In the bin under Mördur's kitchen sink Huldar had spotted some packaging and, when he pulled it out, his blood had run cold. The picture on the box was of a big, heavy-duty knife that obviously wasn't designed for the kitchen. Since the attacks on Stella and Egill had been carried out with a blunt instrument, he wondered if the knife had been reserved for the first victim. There was no sign of it anywhere in the flat.

Gudlaugur nodded. 'Yes. They checked first thing this morning and none of the kids are missing.'

'So none of them are victim number one?' Gudlaugur shook his head but Huldar wasn't convinced. 'Are they absolutely sure they contacted the right people? Some of those names are pretty common.'

'They're the right kids. He had so much information on them in his database that there can't be any doubt.'

'What about his phone? Have they finished going through that yet?'

'No, not yet, but a couple of things have come to light.' When Huldar made it irritably clear that he was fed up with having to prise the answers out of him, Gudlaugur elaborated. 'For one thing, he had a Snapchat account that he deleted. His username was *Just13*. God knows what that means. We've submitted a request to the company for the records of who he exchanged Snaps with and who he followed. The snag is that his account was deactivated on Thursday and it's possible that Snapchat does a regular clean-up. If so, all the information about him has probably vanished. Which means that if he sent Snaps instead of just lurking and spying on what the kids were doing, they've almost certainly disappeared. Assuming the recipients opened them.'

'What about his home computers? I noticed both a laptop and a desktop computer.' The laptop had been open on the kitchen table beside a half-drunk cup of tea and a stale piece of bread and cheese with a bite taken out of it. Having seen how tidy the rest of the flat was, Huldar took this as a sign that the man had been intending to return home. The tea had struck him as incongruous. Irrational though it was, he'd have expected a murderer to drink something a bit more hard-core, like black coffee or whisky.

'They're going through them now. I overheard someone saying he'd installed a Tor search engine, both on his phone and on the computers. If I've understood right, that allows you to erase your digital tracks, though it's not impossible to retrieve the information. It also looks as though he had access to the records of a psychologist who specialises in bullying cases, since some of them turned up on his laptop. Though whether the man gave them to Mördur or he managed to access them illegally is unclear. They're going to call the psychologist in for questioning. They're also sorting out a warrant to confiscate Mördur's work computer, though that's a bit more complicated as it's the property of his employer.'

Huldar doubted Mördur would have been any less cautious when using his work computer than he was with his home ones. It wasn't the first time Forensics had got their hands on a machine where the user had been trying to hide their tracks, though usually the people they dealt with were amateurs, not experienced programmers like Mördur. If anyone could operate anonymously online, presumably he could. 'Who's the psychologist?'

'Kjartan. I think his second name's Erlendsson.'

Huldar was fairly sure this was the man Freyja had recommended to Haukur, Adalheidur's father. He made a mental note to ask her about this, since it was yet another link. If he remembered right, Haukur had said he'd been to see the psychologist himself and hadn't been that impressed. 'What about his car? Any sign of that yet?'

'Yes, it was found this morning, parked on Fjölnisvegur. They've brought it in and Forensics are inspecting it for biological traces. If they find any evidence that Stella or Egill was in the car, we'll have to talk to the hospital again and establish exactly how bedbound Mördur was. Perhaps he managed to trick the monitors he was hooked up to. After all, he was an IT expert. We'll also need to check if anyone else could have used the car while he was lying on his deathbed.'

Huldar called up a map on his phone, unable to remember exactly where Fjölnisvegur was. When he typed it in, he saw that the road lay to the north-west of the hospital, in the opposite direction from Breidholt. Why on earth would Mördur have parked there if he had been in a hurry to get from his flat to Cardiology due to chest pains? Perhaps this theory was wrong; perhaps he hadn't been coming from home at all, or his imminent heart attack had confused him. 'Do you know if the car was badly parked?'

Gudlaugur shook his head. 'No. But there are photos of it on the server. What are you thinking?'

'Not sure. I was just wondering what sort of state he'd been in and which direction he'd been coming from. Do we have any idea?' He opened the case folder on the server and examined the photos that had been taken earlier that morning. The first few showed the interior of the vehicle, revealing that nothing of interest had been found there. The only extraneous object in the front was an empty soda-water bottle. On the floor behind the driver's seat was another exactly the same, and an empty supermarket bag. The seat-back pocket contained a first-aid kit from the Scouts. The back seat was empty. No sign of the missing knife.

Finally there was a picture of the car taken from the outside. It was a people carrier, the sort of vehicle no self-respecting man would buy himself out of choice and Huldar couldn't help wondering why Mördur had picked it. Then he noticed the blacked-out rear windows and large space in the back where an extra row of seats had been removed. Convenient for moving bulky objects, like wheelchairs . . . or bodies.

Leaving these details aside, the photos showed beyond a

doubt that the car had been neatly parked. It didn't jut out into the road and was well between the lines, which, considering its length, was quite a feat. Especially for a man supposedly suffering from acute chest pains. 'You'd have thought he worked as a driving instructor on the side.' Huldar leant back in his chair while Gudlaugur came round to study the photo. 'He managed to park like a pro, regardless of the pain he must have been in.'

Gudlaugur agreed, with reservations. 'Actually, people can behave oddly when they're having a heart attack. When my granddad got chest pains he started shifting the furniture around the living room. He'd have died if my gran hadn't worked out there was something wrong and called an ambulance. I'm sure he'd have taken care over the parking too if he'd driven himself to hospital. But who knows, maybe someone else parked the car, after Mördur was admitted. An accomplice, for instance.'

Out of the corner of his eye Huldar saw Erla emerge from the interview room. She looked as exhausted as the reflection that had met him in the mirror on his way up in the lift. 'Any idea when Erla went home last night?'

'Did she go home?' Gudlaugur turned to watch Erla as she went into her office. Instead of the usual strut, her walk was slow, even a little wobbly. 'I doubt it. When I left she was talking to the guys responsible for searching the group home. Not that there was any point since apparently they drew a blank. Laufhildur's coat was clean, though it hadn't been washed recently. Besides, it was red, and a completely different style from the killer's anorak. The Darth Vader mask looked clean too, but they took it anyway and sent it to Forensics. I hear the guys were seriously spooked by having to work under the evil eye of the Joker. They still had goosebumps when they got back. Erla was still at work then and I reckon she's been here ever since.'

Huldar stood up. 'Oh, for Christ's sake.' He didn't explain, but then he didn't have to.

He marched straight across to Erla's office. For once his colleagues didn't bother with the snide comments and stupid sniggering. Even Jóel ignored him. They were all too busy. Even the limping Kári, who wasn't known for his diligence, was bent over his desk, looking unaccountably red-cheeked and chastened.

Huldar didn't waste time knocking, just barged in and shut the door behind him. Erla's reaction was all the proof he needed that she was wiped out. Instead of glaring at him, she looked up blearily from the computer, slack-jawed, as though doped up on sedatives. 'What?'

'How much sleep have you had since Sunday?'

The dopey look became even more exaggerated as she tried to think. 'I don't know. Plenty.'

'Plenty?' Huldar had never seen her desk so buried in paperwork. Clearing a stack of documents off the visitor chair, he plonked himself down. 'I'm betting that *plenty* doesn't apply in this case. You need to go home and get some kip, even if it's only four hours.'

Erla rolled her eyes under their heavy lids. 'No chance. I can't. Do you know what I'm up against? I've got that sleazebag Arnar Björnsson in the interview room, suspected of the murders that Mördur Jónasson claims to have committed. But Mördur's dead and it's becoming increasingly clear that he didn't kill anyone, and to make matters worse we're still missing victim number one. On top of that I've got the press on my back – they've got wind of the fact that we've found Egill's body and have a man in custody. The news has already hit the online sites. And as if that's not enough, Egill's dad keeps calling, freaking out and demanding to know who we've arrested. Egill's post-mortem's due to start in an hour. Then we've still got to question a whole load of people to find out who Mördur's accomplice was, as well as processing the data from Forensics on his phone, computers and car. We also need to keep management informed and supply the lawyer with the material he needs to apply for all the warrants necessary to keep the inquiry going. And, to cap it all, we've got a woman with half her face missing, who seems to have been the main reason for the killings, judging by her father's crazy ramblings.' She broke off and took a deep breath that changed into a yawn halfway through. 'Just when the fuck am I supposed to go for that rest?'

Huldar gave up. It was pointless trying to give her any advice. 'Can I go and have another word with Ásta?' he asked instead. 'It's just too much of a coincidence, Mördur being on her ward. We can't ignore the fact that she had access to his phone and car keys. If he had an accomplice, she'd be the ideal candidate. If nothing else, she was in a good position to tamper with the monitors he was hooked up to, so he could slip out of the hospital unobserved. Perhaps he invented his illness or it was a conspiracy between them. What do I know? But she's mixed up in it somehow. She has to be. There was nothing random about the fact that Stella's phone was put through her door.'

Erla frowned, her brain working sluggishly. 'Couldn't he have got his accomplice to shove it through Ásta's letterbox? Maybe he took against her for some reason after meeting her at the hospital. Maybe she was rough with him, or rude.'

'Do you really think he'd play a nasty trick like that on the woman who saved his life? I don't buy it. Besides, there are too many elements that don't fit.' He took out his phone and showed Erla where Mördur's car had been parked, pointing out that a man who was having a heart attack would be unlikely to drive past the hospital car park and leave his car further away, on a side street. 'If he hadn't died, I'd have thought his heart attack was a total fabrication.'

Erla was studying his phone screen thoughtfully. 'Is that possible? Could someone actually fake a heart attack and con the doctors and nursing staff?'

Huldar had already checked this out. 'No. The heart releases an enzyme into the bloodstream during a cardiac arrest. They can measure it. But maybe Ásta could have tampered with the results; substituted a blood sample from another patient, for example. She'd have had plenty of opportunity. There are patients in every imaginable state on the ward and I don't suppose they'd have blinked an eyelid at another blood test. Lots of them must have cannulas too, so she wouldn't even have needed to use a needle.'

Erla looked up and stared at him, her eyes bloodshot. 'Why, for fuck's sake? What would be the point of getting himself admitted on false grounds? If they were in cahoots, I can't see what that would have achieved. Especially if he was planning to take the rap anyway. Plots don't come any stupider than that. Besides, you seem to be forgetting that he died. He must have had something wrong with him if the hospital says the cause of death was heart failure. Unless you believe Ásta was capable of swapping bodies. Or of killing him herself.' She shook her head.

Huldar took back his phone and stuck it in his pocket. 'I haven't got any answers yet but maybe I can get her to talk. She knows she's on our radar. She may be starting to panic. If we put pressure on her, she'll keep having to tell more and more lies until in the end she trips herself up. I'm the ideal person to go after her because she can't stand me – it'll make it harder for her to concentrate on making stuff up. Best-case scenario, I'll get answers to some questions; worst, I'll see what makes her jumpy. That often tells its own story. For example, it'll be interesting to see how she reacts when she hears that we've actually arrested a man for the murders. If she's Mördur's accomplice, that should at least get a reaction out of her.'

Erla considered this for so long that Huldar was afraid she'd fallen asleep with her eyes open, but finally she gave a weary sigh and told him to go ahead. Before he could stand up, she added: 'I forgot to mention another piece of the puzzle that's just fallen into place. That idiot Kári knocked on my door earlier to tell me that hearing about Laufhildur this morning jogged his memory and now he knows what caused his déjà vu in the car park where we found Stella. Twenty years ago he was on duty when Laufhildur tried to kill herself in the exact same spot. The reason there was nothing about it on the police database or anywhere else is that he never got round to finishing the report afterwards; it slipped his mind. His words, not mine. That's why there's no paperwork. All he can remember is the horrific scene when they arrived and how traumatised the girl from the shop was after hearing the shot and finding Laufhildur. Apparently there was a suicide note but of course he's forgotten what it said apart from the fact that it was very long and made for depressing reading. Which is fuck-all help. They're scouring the basement for the case files but I don't believe the old sod filled out a single form. He's a fucking waste of space. I thought he was just burnt out but it sounds like he's always been totally incompetent.'

Huldar was less interested in Kári's ineptitude than in what he'd told Erla, presumably in the expectation of praise. He guessed she'd torn a strip off him. 'What on earth was Laufhildur doing behind that shop? They were living on the other side of town in Breidholt at the time.'

'Search me. She'll have to tell us that herself. Which reminds me of yet another thing I've got to do – bring Laufhildur in for interview. That should be interesting, given her alleged agoraphobia. I suppose there'll be something about the suicide attempt in her medical records but I doubt we'll be allowed to see them. She's not under suspicion herself and the search of her room didn't turn up anything of interest. She doesn't have a smartphone and her crappy old laptop came up clean. Also, the staff at the care home are adamant that she never leaves the building. Until something proves them wrong I'd say her involvement is zero. I mean, it's hard to picture someone as broken as she is committing a brutal murder.'

There was nothing more to say. Huldar got to his feet. As he was leaving, he paused in the doorway to ask if he could take Gudlaugur along. Although he was more than capable of tackling Ásta on his own, he wanted to see if Gudlaugur's presence would remind her where she knew him from.

Erla said yes in an absent voice, then asked, before he could leave: 'Are you hassling me about getting enough sleep because I'm a woman, Huldar? Would you give a shit if I was a bloke?'

He smiled, shaking his head. 'Erla, if you were a bloke you wouldn't feel the need to drive yourself into the ground. You'd be getting your eight hours every night.'

Without waiting for her response, he went back to his desk and told Gudlaugur they were paying a visit to Ásta. He suppressed a grim smile when he saw the young man's dismayed reaction.

Chapter 38

It was one of those beautifully clear frosty winter days, without a breath of wind. The snow creaked underfoot as Huldar and Gudlaugur walked up to Ásta's house, past a small, rather lopsided snowman standing alone in the middle of the lawn. The grass showed through where the snow had been rolled into a large ball, suggesting it had been made that morning. Huldar hoped the two little girls had gone out with their other mother. It was much harder to talk to people with their kids around, even if they weren't in the same room. The thought that they might be listening tended to throw him off his stride. As Gudlaugur, looking pale and subdued, was ringing the bell, it occurred to Huldar that it might have been wiser to bring Ásta into the station. But it was too late now.

Predictably, it was one of the daughters who opened the door to them. The older girl – Huldar had forgotten her name. She clung to the door-handle, peering through the narrow opening, her cheeks still scarlet from playing outside in the cold. Her hair was tied back in a ponytail but tousled on top, as if she'd recently pulled off a woolly hat. Now, though, judging by the glitter that appeared to have been liberally sprinkled over her head, sleeves and front, she was in the middle of some Christmas art project. Huldar had received his fair share of such creations from his nephews over the years. The parcels would emit a puff of glitter when opened, and the stuff was as hard to clean off as if you'd been tarred and feathered. 'Is your mummy in?'

'I've got two mummies.' The girl's face was stony. She wasn't wearing her patch this time and one of her eyes pointed off to the side when she looked at Huldar. 'You're cops. You should know that. You've been here before.' It wasn't surprising the girl recognised them as they'd changed into uniform to underline the official nature of their visit and, hopefully, bring home the gravity of the matter to Ásta.

'Of course. Sorry, silly me. I meant your mummy Ásta. Is she home?'

'Yes. Wait a minute.' She closed the door in their faces but they weren't bothered. Not being let in was par for the course in their job.

The door opened shortly afterwards, this time to reveal Ásta, with her two daughters close behind, the younger girl as sparkly as her big sister. Ásta's cheeks were even redder than theirs, but Huldar guessed that was from anger rather than cold. He was right.

'Why are you two back?' she snapped. 'I thought we were done?'

'We can talk to you at the station if you prefer. It's not a problem.' A barefaced lie, designed merely to frighten her.

Ásta ran a hand through her curly fair hair, drew down her shapely brows and hesitated. She appeared to be weighing up whether it would be better to invite them in or have to explain to her family why she'd had to leave the house in the company of two police officers. 'Come in, then. But please make it quick, and keep your voices down. My wife's asleep. She was on night shift.' She told the girls to go to their room and when they protested, spoke sharply, and reminded them not to make a noise. The older girl scowled at Huldar, evidently blaming him for disrupting their Saturday. He nodded at her and grinned, but she stuck out her tongue, then whirled round and ran off down the hall.

They stepped inside, Gudlaugur ducking his head to hide his face from Ásta while they were taking off their shoes. He needn't have bothered: she was far more preoccupied with checking behind her to make sure the girls didn't come back. She showed them to the kitchen, ushering them past the living room where Huldar saw open cardboard boxes of Christmas decorations. A scent of pine testified to the presence of a Christmas tree, though he couldn't see it from the hall. He reflected that if his suspicions about Ásta proved correct, the family might as well close the boxes, throw away the tree and kick down the snowman in the garden. There wouldn't be much festive cheer with one of the mothers in custody.

'Mind the girls' paintings.' Ásta flapped a hand ungraciously towards the chairs at the kitchen table, which was covered in Christmas cards, scissors and glue. Glitter was strewn over the surface and sparkled on the seat pads as well. While they sat down, she closed the kitchen door and stood with her back to it. 'Are you here to ask me about Stella again? If you are, I can save you the trouble, because nothing's changed: I don't know her and I've never met her.'

'Thanks.' Huldar pushed his chair back from the table to protect his uniform but couldn't move far because of the wall. 'Actually, we're here to ask you about Mördur, the patient you allegedly gave CPR to in the hospital car park just over a week ago.'

That wrong-footed her but she recovered quickly, folding

her arms across her chest and thrusting out her chin. 'What about him?'

'It seems he was involved in the case we're investigating. The murders of Stella and now Egill. As you may know, the boy's body was found yesterday evening.'

'Yes, I saw the news.'

'Then perhaps you also saw that we've arrested a man on suspicion of Stella's murder?' Huldar watched her intently as she leant against the door to ensure that the girls couldn't come in. But her reaction wasn't what he'd been expecting. Instead of looking guilty, she appeared relieved. Her pupils dilated and she opened her mouth in a long breath.

'No, I wasn't aware.' She didn't add anything or ask who the suspect was, as Huldar would have thought natural. 'Did you come here to tell me that?'

'No.' Huldar tried to lean back, hindered by the wall. 'We need to ask you some questions about Mördur Jónasson, as I said.'

'What about him?' She glared at Huldar with a sudden look of her older daughter. Perhaps she'd stick her tongue out at him as well.

'There are some question marks over the way you saved Mördur's life and the fact that Stella's phone was put through your door, given what we now know about his connection to the case. Doesn't it strike you as odd that a man who owed you his life would want to implicate you in a murder?'

'Don't ask me what was going through his head. I can only repeat that I haven't a clue why the phone ended up in our letterbox. Mördur was already seriously ill and helping him in the car park only put off the inevitable. I can't believe he could have had anything to do with the case since he was bedbound all last week. I think you must have got your wires crossed.'

'Well, you're wrong about that.' Huldar pulled a piece of paper out of his pocket, unfolded it and laid it carefully among the glue, scissors, glitter and coloured paper. It was a printed map of the National Hospital. 'Would you mind showing us the exact spot where you encountered Mördur?'

Ásta detached herself from the door, came over and picked up the map. Biting her lower lip, she turned it this way and that, as if unable to work out what was what. Huldar pressed her. 'It only happened a week ago. You must be able to remember.'

'I'm trying to get my bearings.'

He guessed she was playing for time, trying to work out why the location mattered and whether to tell the truth. 'If you've forgotten, we can ask the people who came to help you. We'll need to talk to them anyway, to confirm your story.'

Ásta looked up from the map, then replaced it on the table and pointed to the car park near the entrance to the Children's Hospital. She seemed to have suddenly oriented herself. 'I parked here. He appeared on foot and collapsed around about here.' She moved her finger a fraction to indicate a point only a few metres from the place where she claimed to have parked. 'Of course, I can only say roughly. I can't remember exactly which space I parked in or where he collapsed. But I'd only taken a couple of steps from the car when I spotted him.' She raised her eyes to Huldar, waiting for his reaction.

To up the tension, he pretended to consider this, though he didn't need to. The place Ásta had indicated didn't fit at all with the route Mördur would have taken if he'd been heading straight from his car on Fjölnisvegur to A&E. 'When you first noticed him, was he clutching his chest or showing any other signs of distress?'

Ásta appeared to give this some thought but again Huldar suspected that she was merely trying to work out which answer would serve to shut him up and convince him that she'd been drawn into the matter by pure chance. 'Er . . . I can't remember exactly. It was dark, of course. I think he was looking a bit strange, but he just sort of crumpled up almost as soon as I caught sight of him so I didn't have a chance to observe him any more closely.'

'I see.' Though actually he didn't: there was no rational explanation for what the man had been doing there, unless he had come to find Ásta. 'Had you maybe agreed to meet there? Did you know him?'

'No, he was a total stranger. It was a complete coincidence. I certainly didn't have some secret assignation with him, if that's what you're insinuating. If I had, why on earth would I have arranged to meet him in the car park right outside my workplace?'

'We're trying to find a plausible explanation. The man's linked to the murders. You save his life. By complete chance the phone belonging to one of his victims finds its way into your letterbox. You have to admit it looks suspicious.'

'I'm a nurse. I know nothing about solving crimes. I thought that was your job.'

Huldar ignored this, asking instead: 'Is it possible to induce a heart attack?'

'Induce a heart attack?' Her face expressed astonished incomprehension. Then it hardened and Ásta clenched her jaw for a moment before continuing. 'Are you implying that that's what I did?'

'I'm just asking. Is it possible or not?'

'I'm sure it is. The method would depend on whether the person in question had a predisposition. I haven't a clue how you'd do it to a healthy individual but it wouldn't necessarily take much if the person had arteriosclerosis or coronary heart disease. The first thing that springs to mind is epinephrine, which is given to patients suffering from anaphylactic shock. It might cause a heart attack in an individual who's at risk. But you must be insane if you think I'd do something like that.'

Gudlaugur, who'd been running his finger through the glitter on the table, paused and looked up for the first time since they'd sat down. 'Was a blood sample taken when he was admitted?'

Ásta stared at him in surprise, as if only now noticing him. 'Yes. Of course.'

'Did they test it for epinephrine or any other substances?'

'No. They wouldn't have screened for that, at least not under normal circumstances. Possibly for other substances, if the patient had been suspected of taking something, but as far as I know, that wasn't the case in this instance. But I went home so I don't know exactly what they did or what tests they requested. You'll have to speak to the staff in A&E.' She looked from Gudlaugur back to Huldar. 'I didn't induce his heart attack.'

Huldar didn't react and Gudlaugur turned his attention back to the table.

'Could you – or anyone else – have disconnected Mördur from his monitors and claimed that he was going for tests or something?'

'Why would anyone have done that?' Without warning,

Ásta stepped across the kitchen and put her ear to the door. Then she turned back to Huldar, clearly relieved that she had imagined whatever she thought she had heard. 'And, before you ask, no, I didn't do anything like that. Mördur was lying in his bed the entire time, apart from when he was sent for tests. Neither I nor anyone else falsified the requests.'

'But if somebody had, Mördur would have been free to go wherever he liked instead of undergoing tests somewhere on the premises. Wouldn't he?'

'Yes, theoretically. But he wouldn't have made it far. If you don't believe me, ask anyone on the ward. Talk to his doctor. Or do you think the entire hospital staff is involved in a conspiracy?'

Huldar continued his policy of ignoring her questions. 'We're examining his phone and assume that'll clarify things. Did he have access to it and, if so, did he use it?'

'I wasn't on duty the whole time and even when I was, I had other patients to attend to. But I think I remember seeing the phone on his table a couple of times and at least once – maybe twice – in his hand. Though most of the time he was asleep or out of it.'

'But he had it with him and could theoretically make calls. What about internet access?'

'The hospital has wifi that anyone can use. And there's a 3G connection too. So he could have gone online if he wanted.'

'What about his car key and house keys? Both were among his belongings. Could anyone have got hold of them or were they kept in a locker?'

'Anyone could have got hold of them. The patients have cupboards in their rooms for personal items, like clothes, but no one goes poking around in them.'

'Did he have a room to himself?'

'Yes.'

'So it would have been easy for someone to get into his cupboard while he was asleep, if they wanted to?'

'Yes. But no one would have. What kind of questions are these?' Ásta's indignation appeared to be genuine. 'I suppose next you'll start accusing us of stealing the rings off the fingers of dead patients?'

'No.' Huldar persisted: 'Did you know he had a daughter who's in a bad way after a suicide attempt?'

'All I knew was that he was a widower. We have more than enough to do without speculating about our patients' private lives.' Ásta spoke quickly, darting a sideways glance at the clock on the wall above Huldar's head. 'Are you nearly finished?'

'Just a couple more things. Did you ever hear Mördur mention Stella or Egill by name? Or possibly a third teenager? In his sleep, maybe?'

'No. He did nothing like that. Not in front of me or anyone else, as far as I know. Don't you think I'd have told you if he had?'

There was a silence. Huldar was trying to digest what had been said and, more importantly, what had been left out. On the way there he had thought it possible that Ásta was Mördur's accomplice. Now he wasn't so sure. If she had been, surely she wouldn't have thrown cold water on the idea that Mördur could have slipped out of the ward? She'd have wanted to make sure all the blame fell squarely on him. And she'd have claimed that he had his phone constantly in his hands. Her relief on hearing that they'd arrested a suspect didn't fit with that theory either.

But if she was as innocent as she insisted, why was she so reluctant to answer questions about giving Mördur CPR in the car park? Her behaviour wasn't consistent with what he was used to from those who had nothing to hide. It didn't make sense.

Before he could decide what this meant, his phone rang.

Erla was on the line. He stood up as he answered and went over to Ásta as a sign that she should move. For a moment it looked as if she was going to block his way, then she stepped aside. He closed the door behind him, leaving her alone with Gudlaugur, who had looked alarmed when he realised what was happening.

Out in the corridor he listened to Erla gabbling that they were to come back to the station immediately. She had started talking almost before he could say hello. 'What's happened?'

'Snapchat has sent us the information about the usage on Mördur's account. It seems they keep the records of customer accounts for thirty days after they deactivate them, in case they change their mind or they closed them by mistake. So they hadn't destroyed the data, though everything Mördur sent or received has vanished as it had already been viewed. He had quite a lot of friends, all teenagers, apart from his brother. But on closer inspection one of the teenagers' accounts appeared to have been set up under a false name. And guess what?'

'What?' Huldar heard stealthy footsteps from the corridor leading to the bedrooms and moved into the hall so he wouldn't be overheard. He guessed that Ásta's daughters had lost patience and sneaked out of their room.

'One IP address associated with the account was assigned to Haukur Stefánsson. Adalheidur's father.' Erla paused for breath. 'There's a meeting in half an hour. I want you two there with your ears open. You're not to barge in halfway through. Understood?'

'But . . .'

'Huldar. Listen to me. No bloody "but"s. That nurse is obviously of secondary importance. We'll have plenty of time to talk to her later. Get your arse down to the station right now.' She hung up. There was nothing to be done but obey.

Ásta's daughters had taken up position outside the kitchen, face to face, ears pressed to the door.

'Hey! What are you doing?' They whipped their heads round, terrified, and Huldar pulled an angry face to heighten the effect. 'Shouldn't you be in your room?'

They didn't answer, just stared at him with wide eyes, the elder squinting worse than ever, then fled past him down the hallway. When the younger girl bumped into him in passing, she left glitter on his trousers. Christmas was coming early this year.

Huldar tapped on the door in case Ásta was still standing on the other side. He didn't want to knock her over. But she was by the sink with the tap running, a glass in her hand. He didn't seem to be interrupting a conversation as he'd expected. His announcement that they had to leave brought her head round fast, and Gudlaugur glanced up equally quickly from the table. It was hard to tell which of them was the more delighted.

Once they had their shoes on and were walking out of the door, Ásta suddenly spoke from behind them. 'Now I remember where I recognise you from.' Unlike Gudlaugur, Huldar turned round. He waited for her to go on, a little taken aback by the spiteful look on her pretty face. 'You were at that meeting, weren't you? You sat next to me.'

Huldar nudged Gudlaugur who kept his face stubbornly turned towards the road. So Huldar asked: 'What meeting was that, Ásta?'

'The general meeting of the National Queer Organisation.' She was speaking to Gudlaugur's back. 'When they held the vote about extending membership to the BDSM community, remember? At the time I wondered if you were gay or one of those BDSM guys.' She leant against the doorframe. 'Which is it?'

As Gudlaugur continued to ignore her, Huldar realised that he'd been led into a trap, following Ásta's script as if he were her puppet. He'd have done better to shut up and keep walking. Angrily, he turned away from her malicious smile, nudged Gudlaugur and headed for the car.

It wasn't until he'd pulled out of the street that he unleashed his fury on his partner.

Chapter 39

Huldar and Gudlaugur made it to the meeting just in time, their colour still heightened. They'd had a blazing row in the car, which had continued until they were forced to abandon their quarrel and race inside to avoid a reprimand from Erla. Huldar hadn't a clue whether he'd managed to get across what he'd wanted to say – that he couldn't give a toss who Gudlaugur chose to love or how he got his sexual kicks.

It was the secrecy that he found unforgivable.

That's what really stung. The implication that Gudlaugur had Huldar down as one of those cops who only ever mentioned homosexuality to mock it. He felt he was better than that, and he was hurt and insulted that Gudlaugur hadn't just told him the truth, sparing him all that irritation and anxiety about what exactly had been going on between him and Ásta. In hindsight, though, Huldar saw that he'd gone too far and he was now longing to prod his partner in the shoulder and apologise. Instead, he had to wait impatiently for the meeting to end, his thoughts in such a turmoil that he couldn't concentrate on the finer points of Erla's briefing.

But he did grasp that the plan was to bring in Adalheidur's father, Haukur Stefánsson, for questioning. Erla's theory wasn't that far-fetched: that Haukur and Mördur had struck a deal whereby Haukur would get his revenge on his daughter's tormentor and Mördur would take the blame. He was dying anyway, so he had nothing to lose. But his heart attack had put a spanner in the works and the plan had gone wrong. What exactly was in it for Mördur nobody knew; perhaps money for his daughter, or a promise that she would be taken care of after he died. Huldar thought the latter a more likely motive. It wasn't as if money would make much difference to Laufhildur's wellbeing, and Adalheidur's father was unlikely to have much to spare.

The only snag was that Haukur had an alibi for the evening of Stella's attack: his three friends had confirmed that he'd been with them at football practice and in the pub afterwards. The police had initially regarded their statements as sufficient but now things had changed and they would have to speak to every single member of the team. If they all insisted that Haukur had been present, it would be necessary to consider other possibilities, including whether his wife, or a friend or relative, could have carried out the attack. It was thought unlikely that he would have involved his daughter but sooner or later she would have to be questioned as well.

Now they were waiting. The entire team were at their desks, killing time with tasks that required little concentration. All their thoughts were preoccupied with the message that had been sent via Mördur's reactivated *Just13* account to Haukur's fake teenage Snapchat account after the meeting. The message was simple: a short text asking if he was the suspect being held in custody. There had been some heated discussion before they'd arrived at this decision. People had disagreed over the wording and whether it was strong enough to incriminate Haukur if he answered.

In the end, Erla had got her way, arguing that the other suggestions ran the risk of making the recipient suspicious.

'Have you disposed of the body?' was shot down on these grounds. You only had to look at the online news to know the answer to that, so the message was bound to sound a warning bell for Haukur. Equally, Erla thought it a bad idea to ask about victim number one.

To complicate matters, they had no idea how the two men had communicated, whether it was via private text messages, video clips or photos with captions, for example. They decided to send an image that was as neutral as possible but unequivocally linked to the murders. There were as many suggestions for the photo as for the text, but in the end they went with one showing the three numbers, using the same font as in the notes found in connection with the attacks on Egill and Stella.

The message was sent off and everyone crossed their fingers. That was almost half an hour ago now and there was still no sign of an answer. Every minute that passed increased the chances that Haukur had seen through their trap. At least that appeared to be the consensus of those present, judging by how often they glanced at the clock. Just as often – if not more often – their eyes turned to Erla's office, where she was sitting with a member of senior management. Mördur's phone lay on the desk between them and neither seemed able to take their eyes off it. The rubbish that had covered her desk before was now piled in messy stacks on the floor, so nothing would distract them.

Huldar turned back to his computer. It showed nothing of interest. There were more productive ways of using the wait than trawling through the last two years' worth of Mördur's credit card transactions. He stood up, looking over at his partner who was pretending to be absorbed in examining bank transfers. 'Gudlaugur . . . Gudlaugur.' The young man didn't react. Huldar didn't dare risk raising his voice since the last thing he wanted was to attract the attention of his colleagues. For once, though, he'd probably get away with it since they were entirely focused on waiting for an answer to the Snapchat message. Gudlaugur would have to march through the office at the head of the Gay Pride parade before anyone noticed him.

'What?' The young man finally snapped. His colour was still high and he was frowning. 'I'm not prepared to discuss it any further.'

'I understand. I just wanted to say sorry. Look, I couldn't give a toss about how you live your life. I was just angry that you thought I would. I hope we can be friends again, and I promise not to say another word on the subject if you don't want me to.' He didn't make the mistake of repeating what he'd blurted out in the car about *being in the closet*. The comment had caused Gudlaugur to go completely apeshit. If Huldar hadn't been so worked up himself, he'd have taken in what Gudlaugur had been saying. But it was only during the meeting that his words had sunk in: Gudlaugur didn't see himself as in the closet just because he chose not to discuss his sexuality at work. As he pointed out to Huldar, none of his colleagues found it necessary to state their sexual preferences, so why the hell should he have to make a declaration about his? Especially given the macho atmosphere in the office. He didn't want people whispering and laughing the moment he turned his back.

'Anyway, I just wanted to apologise,' Huldar struggled on. 'I overstepped the mark when I said you should have confided in me. It won't happen again. How you choose to live your life is entirely up to you.'

'Up to me?' Gudlaugur gave him a weary look. 'It's not something anyone chooses, if that's what you think.'

'No. I realise that. I put it badly. You know I'm no good with words. Assume I mean well, even if it doesn't come out that way.' Huldar smiled at him but his smile wasn't returned. 'And I'm not prejudiced.' During the meeting he had been hastily reviewing his behaviour over the last eighteen months or so, since Gudlaugur started work there. Had he ever told a gay joke or made a disparaging remark about homosexuality? It wasn't like him, and after racking his brain he was fairly sure he hadn't. Though the same couldn't be said of certain other members of the team. He couldn't imagine what it was like to have to listen to that kind of crap, day in, day out, with no chance to respond. Personally, he knew he'd have lost his rag more than once.

Before Huldar could flounder any deeper into the mire, Gudlaugur turned away. Not to his computer but to look across the office. People were moving. Some were on their feet. It wasn't only the lower ranks who were looking excited. Erla and the senior officer were both standing up too, Erla with the phone in her hand, both their eyes glued to the small screen. Then they locked glances and exchanged a few words.

After this, Erla came out and informed the department that a reply had been received and that Haukur Stefánsson was to be brought in for questioning.

No one could fail to notice when Haukur arrived in the company of two police officers. Conversations broke off, people removed their headphones, dropped their papers, let go of their computer mouse or hurriedly ended their phone call. No one wanted to miss this.

Huldar watched the man stumbling along between the two policemen, cutting a pathetic figure. When he first came in, he scanned the office nervously, but seeing the interest his arrival had attracted, he lowered his eyes and continued with bowed head to the interview room. He almost oozed guilt.

The door closed behind him. Erla disappeared through the same door a moment or two later, accompanied by that bastard Jóel. Huldar feigned indifference but it was no good. He hadn't dared leave the office to get changed in case something happened in the few minutes he was gone; the suspense had been too great. Perhaps the glitter on his trousers, jacket and shirtsleeves had ruled him out. It was important to be able to intimidate the interviewee, but a disco cop wouldn't exude much menace. The upshot was that he had to wait like everyone else while Jóel enjoyed a front-seat view.

The waiting was as hard as the wait for an answer to the Snapchat message had been. Only the most dedicated smokers stepped outside and even then Huldar noticed that these trips were more widely spaced than usual. People restrained their coffee cravings for longer too. He himself tried to pass the time by concentrating on the credit card transactions, with mixed success. Mostly his thoughts were on the interview.

No lawyer had appeared. And only once was there a development, when Erla came outside, leant against the wall, closed her eyes, took a deep breath, then went back in, totally ignoring all the enquiring faces turned her way. Huldar hadn't a clue what this meant but assumed it didn't bode well.

Since then, more than half an hour had passed.

In the meantime Huldar had run out of things to do. He had scrutinised every single transaction on Mördur's credit card in search of any link to the case. Having dismissed hundreds, he was left with only four possibilities. A purchase at a toy shop that could have been the Darth Vader mask, another at a DIY shop, the third at a sports shop and the fourth at a shop selling outdoor gear. Apart from that, the transactions recorded business with petrol stations, super-markets, ice-cream parlours, pizza places, cinemas and monthly direct debits to utility companies, the lottery and that sort of thing.

Huldar stood up and stretched. Gudlaugur was still sulking. He hadn't given him so much as a glance since the conversa-tion Huldar had been hoping would clear the air. Since he was obviously useless at making up with people, he decided not to bother trying again but to resort to the back-up plan, which was to let time heal the wound. Though, he had to admit, this method had proved singularly unsuccessful during his short-lived relationships with women.

Without warning, the door of the interview room opened and Erla and Jóel emerged. Huldar lowered his arms mid-stretch and tapped Gudlaugur's monitor to alert him. Erla and Jóel walked over to her office without exchanging a word. She closed the door behind them and they had a brief conver-sation, after which Jóel came out again, crimson in the face and fuming. As he stormed back to his desk, Erla let her gaze travel round the room. It paused on Huldar and she beckoned, without giving any indication of whether he should be pleased or alarmed. He decided to be pleased.

Erla told him to sit down and explained that she wanted him to take Jóel's place. In spite of the dark shadows under her eyes and the limp hair, she radiated a renewed vigour and had no problem summoning up the familiar look of contempt. 'The guy's totally fucking useless. I don't know who he thinks he is. He keeps taking over the interview, butting in and throwing his weight about like he's in charge. I've half a mind to send him out to Miklabraut to count the drivers using their phone at the wheel.'

'He can't count that quickly or that high.' Huldar rolled up his sleeves, feeling the adrenaline start to course through his veins. 'So, what's the situation? Has Haukur admitted anything?'

'Not yet. I haven't got to the Snapchat message, just asked if he knows anyone called Mördur. He denied it but he flinched when he heard the name. I haven't told him Mördur's dead either, or asked him straight out about the murders of Stella and Egill. But he knows exactly how serious it is, though we're still tiptoeing around the big questions. It was only by some fucking miracle that Jóel didn't give the game away. That's why I wanted to get rid of him; I was afraid he wouldn't be able to hold back much longer. Management was clear that the moment we confront him or reveal what we've got on him, I'll have to inform him he's under arrest. Then he'll insist on a lawyer and that'll delay the whole process. I want to wear him down first. I reckon it won't take long. He's simmering nicely. Maybe he's already cooked through.'

'Got you.' Huldar was chafing at the bit to get stuck in. It was a role that suited him but he would have to be careful not to tread on Erla's toes when things heated up. He didn't want to get thrown out like Jóel.

'One more thing before we go in: management are pretty pissed off about you entering Mördur's flat. For some reason they're all jittery about the search-warrant business. The judge who got dragged out to OK it has complained. He doesn't seem to have swallowed the story we cooked up for the clerk about why you went in. I tried to argue with them but I'm afraid you can expect a slap on the wrist. Nothing major, just enough so they can claim they've taken measures.' Erla tried to look upbeat but was clearly on edge. Yet again Huldar was being expected to take one for the team. When he didn't react, she added hastily: 'But no one's twigged about the DNA profile and Laufhildur, thank Christ. They still haven't seen through the story about the notice at the school. If they do, there'll be a real shitstorm – for the pathologist. We owe him big time.'

'No worries.' Huldar slapped his knees to show his eagerness to get down to work. 'I'm not about to grass on him and I'm not bothered about being disciplined. Though I'd prefer to postpone that till Monday.' His main worry right now was that he wouldn't get away from work in time to go home and change before his date with Freyja. But he couldn't tell Erla that. 'Shall we get cracking?'

'Yes. You go in. I'm going to grab a coffee.' She got to her feet and tried to fluff up her hair but it instantly fell flat again.

As Huldar headed for the interview room, he took the time to bestow a nod and a smile on Jóel, who instantly dropped his eyes to his computer screen.

Haukur looked no less glum as he sat alone, staring unseeingly at the bare walls of the interview room. In front of him was an empty glass that he was clasping in both hands, as if it were a lifeline. He glanced up as Huldar greeted him and sat down across from him. The man released his hold on the glass, his hands shaking as if it was freezing in the room. 'Can I go now? I've answered all your questions and I need to get home. My wife's waiting for me. And my daughter. I don't want to worry them.' He met Huldar's eyes briefly before lowering his gaze to the glass again. Huldar said nothing and they sat there in silence until Erla reappeared with a steaming cup of coffee, her face hard as nails.

'Right. Sorry about the wait.' She took a notepad from under her arm, chucked it on the table and sat down. Then she sipped her coffee, put down the cup, folded her arms across her chest, leant back in her chair and studied Haukur without saying a word. Huldar copied her posture, but couldn't inject the same level of disdain into his sneer.

'I was just asking if I could go now? I think I've answered all your questions.' The man searched their faces anxiously. It was almost depressing to watch the spark of hope fading in his eyes. 'Can I ring my wife?'

Erla reached across the table and switched on the recorder. Then she reclined in her chair again, her eyes boring into Haukur's face. 'Are you sure you don't know any Mördur?' She spoke in a monotone, her voice like ice and quieter than usual. 'Think carefully before you answer.'

'No. None. I've already told you that.' Haukur licked his lips. 'If you want, I can give it to you in writing.' It didn't sound as if he was being sarcastic.

'Don't bother.' Erla blew out through her nose, then turned her head to Huldar. 'I reckon we should bring in his wife and daughter. They might know Mördur.'

'They don't know him any more than I do.' The man tried in vain to hide how desperate he was to prevent this. His forehead was shiny; his eyes flickered nervously.

'You can't be sure of that. Can you?' Erla smiled coldly at him.

Suddenly the man seemed to perk up slightly. His back

straightened and he no longer looked quite as pathetic. 'Why can't I go? Why don't you bring in this Mördur you keep banging on about and ask him if he knows me?'

Erla didn't reply. Huldar knew exactly what she was thinking. Was this the right moment or would it pay to spin things out a little longer? Her nostrils flared, then her face returned to normal and she smiled. 'I'm afraid that won't be possible. You see, Mördur's dead. He had a heart attack. He was admitted to hospital but died in spite of their best efforts.'

Haukur drew a sharp breath and didn't say anything for a long moment. He seized the glass again, pulled it towards him and weighed it in his hands. 'Well, there's no point saying I'm sorry, is there? Because I didn't know the man.'

'Don't you want to know when it happened?' Erla's gaze was trained, unblinkingly, on Haukur's face.

'I can't see how that concerns me.' He dropped his eyes to the glass.

'He had a heart attack just over a week ago. After that he was bedbound right up until he died. Bad luck, eh?'

Haukur blenched. His Adam's apple moved up and down convulsively. The glass rattled on the table and he let go of it, sticking his shaking hands under the table instead. 'I didn't know him.'

'That's strange. You see, I think he knew you.' Erla seized the opportunity, while the man's eyes were lowered, to shoot a glance at Huldar. She winked at him, her lips drawn back in a savage smile. It was time to go for the jugular. Then, turning back to Haukur, she leant forwards over the table. 'Mördur was lying on his deathbed from Friday evening last week. There are any number of witnesses who can confirm it. He couldn't go anywhere; not to the cinema, not to the suburbs to pay a visit to a teenage boy. Do you understand where I'm going with this?' She broke off, giving Huldar a sign and he obligingly reached across the table and grabbed Haukur by the chin, forcing his head up to meet Erla's eye. 'We've got Mördur's phone. The weird thing is that a short time ago you answered a message from him. Under a fake profile, granted, but don't worry, we can prove it's yours.' Erla flashed a smile at Haukur. 'It's a pity you didn't know about his illness then. It's particularly sad for Stella and Egill. You know, I'm not sure you'd have gone ahead and killed them if you'd known that the person who was planning to take the rap was out of the game. Or am I wrong? Would you have done it anyway?'

Still gripping the man's chin in his hand, Huldar watched the hope dying in his eyes. Up to now Haukur had kidded himself that he was going to get away with it; that he'd be able to talk his way out of trouble. But now, as all the escape routes were closed off, his false sense of security was ebbing away.

Erla told him he was under arrest and read him his rights. Huldar watched his growing bewilderment, and when she told him he would shortly be taken to the cells, after a body search, it was all over for him. He closed his eyes and his face slackened, the picture of defeat.

Then he opened his eyes and searched their faces for understanding. 'Have either of you got kids?'

They shook their heads, their faces deliberately expressionless. His confession was just around the corner.

It wasn't until two hours later that Huldar escaped for a cigarette. Haukur had chosen not to wait for a lawyer and had gone ahead and made his confession without taking legal advice. Although this went right against his own interests, it was extremely convenient for the police. Erla raised a perfunctory objection, just enough for it to be recorded on tape that she had done her duty. But, to her credit, she did insist that Haukur picked a lawyer, who was duly informed. While they were waiting, the suspect proved quite willing to talk, and as time wore on it became obvious why. The matter was more complicated than they'd realised and if things went on this way, there was no prospect of Huldar getting home in time to change before his date with Freyja. Too many questions remained unanswered. He'd be lucky to make it on time if he went straight to her place from the station, and he wondered if he could get away with wearing his regulation police trousers and shirt if he left off the jacket.

His jacket was hanging on his chair and he hurried over to fetch his cigarettes. He was just fishing for the packet when Jóel came over and perched on the desk by Gudlaugur, who pretended not to notice either of them.

Jóel picked up a stapler and played with it as if he'd never seen such a wonder of technology before. 'Got a threesome going in the interview room?'

'Oh, shut your face, Jóel.' Huldar tried another pocket in search of his lighter. He hadn't the patience to listen to his colleague's bullshit right now. 'Get lost and stop bothering people who are working.'

'Working? Who's working?' Jóel took offence at the silence that greeted this comment. 'What the fuck's that on your jacket? Is that the latest fag fashion? Who's been sprinkling you with fairy dust? Erla? Or the suspect?' He turned to

Gudlaugur and noticed that he was sparkling too. 'Ah. Of course. Your little poof of a partner.'

Huldar ripped the lighter out of his pocket with such force that he tore the lining. He threw a glance at Gudlaugur who shook his head irritably and carried on working. Though Jóel couldn't have a clue about his sexuality, it must be insufferable to have to hear it bandied about as an insult. Huldar placed his cigarettes and lighter carefully on the desk, while weighing up his options. According to Erla, he already had a bollocking coming to him from management. What would another breach of discipline matter?

Gathering himself, Huldar sprang at Jóel and they went crashing to the floor together, rolling over and over among the desk and chair legs. Every blow Huldar landed felt so cathartic that he barely noticed when Jóel hit him back. At last, a release for all the pent-up rage caused by the constant snide remarks, the sniggering and backstabbing. It felt fantastic.

What's more, he was definitely getting the upper hand by the time the fight was broken up. And the reluctant smile on Gudlaugur's face was worth any amount of hassle.

Chapter 40

Saga seemed content on Huldar's lap. Not that her face was split by a grin or anything – her perma-scowl was still firmly in place – but Freyja knew her well enough by now to tell when she was pleased. The little girl had gone to him of her own accord. It was the first time Freyja had ever seen her take an interest in another person when she was babysitting her. Usually, Saga behaved as if the two of them were alone in the world.

The child was clutching a soft toy, a black bat with flappy wings, to which she had developed a great attachment. Cute, cuddly teddy bears and bunnies were treated with the same indifference as strangers. She kept shoving the toy in Huldar's face and he reacted without fail as if it was the most amazing thing he'd ever seen.

'Her mother should be here any minute.' Freyja looked apologetically at Huldar who'd got the bat's wing slap in the middle of his swollen eye again. He didn't wince or seem to mind, which was surprising given how sore it must be. He hadn't wanted to talk about how he'd acquired the black eye, just said it had happened at work and that was the reason he'd been able to get away early. Otherwise he was looking good, freshly shaven and cleaned up. He was even smartly dressed – too smartly in fact – but fortunately the effect was offset by his black eye. He was far better-looking than that idiot Kjartan. Her stomach contracted at the thought of him. She'd finally worked up the courage to ring him about an hour before Huldar turned up, ready to give him a piece of her mind, but he hadn't answered. So she'd sent him a text instead to say she'd rather he didn't come, but had received no reply. Suddenly she was afraid he hadn't seen her message and would turn up on her doorstep, expecting to escort her to the party. While she'd have no problem confronting him and telling him where to go, she didn't want Huldar witnessing the incident. She couldn't bear the thought of him knowing that she'd almost been made a fool of by a married man.

'I'm in no hurry.' Huldar made a face at Saga who instantly made one back at him. 'Would you like to hear more or am I holding you up?'

Freyja closed Saga's bag. Huldar had turned up earlier than arranged, so she still had to sort out the child's few belongings. Saga's mother wasn't due to pick her up until just before Huldar had been supposed to arrive, so Freyja had been forced to get ready while she was babysitting. It was either that or greet him in her dressing gown with a towel round her head. She'd managed to grab a quick shower by putting Saga on the bathroom floor, surrounded by saucepans that she could bang with a wooden spoon to her heart's content, undisturbed by the splashes from the leaking shower cabinet. Molly had watched morosely from the doorway. After that, Freyja had got dressed and put on her make-up, her stomach knotted with fear, when usually she'd have been full of happy anticipation about going out. Whatever his faults, it was actually good to have Huldar there for moral support while she was waiting for Saga's mother. That way she didn't have time to dread the upcoming reunion.

Having something to talk about really helped to distract her too, so Freyja had welcomed it when Huldar started bringing her up to date with the inquiry, though the subject was hardly suitable for children. 'Go on. It's better hearing it from you than reading the sanitised version in the news.'

Huldar pinched Saga's nose. She waited, as still as a statue, eyes shining with excitement, to see what would happen next. He twisted it gently as he went on updating Freyja about the investigation, which sounded as if it was drawing to a close. 'As I was saying, Haukur, Adalheidur's father, has confessed to murdering Egill but not Stella. He swears he had nothing to do with that and claims he has no idea who was responsible. According to him, it was Mördur who organised the whole thing, provided what was needed – the anorak, baseball bat, mask and shipping container – and timed the attacks so Haukur would have a solid alibi for the night Stella was killed.'

'And it was all done through Snapchat?'

'Yes. Almost all of it. Though they met up originally, presumably so Mördur could satisfy himself that he could rely on the guy. Haukur alleges that Mördur rang him from an unlisted number nearly three months ago, and turned out to know a surprising amount about Adalheidur's problems. He told Haukur he could help by unconventional methods and that sounded good to him. At the time, Haukur said he'd become so infuriated with the system for the way it had failed Adalheidur that he was prepared to do anything. He says Mördur started off by dropping all sorts of hints, without going into any details about what form his help would take. That's how Mördur got Haukur on board. He claims he thought at first that it would involve making anonymous threats.'

'Anonymous threats?'

'Yes, or something along those lines. Haukur assumed Mördur was planning to scare the living daylights out of Stella and maybe slap her about a bit. That sparked his interest. Enough to make him carry on meeting the man, anyway. By the time Haukur finally learnt about the real plan, he was so psyched up that he agreed to take part anyway. Mördur had sworn it would put an end to the ordeal Adalheidur had been going through. It was like choosing who had the right to live: his daughter, who hadn't hurt anyone, or Stella, who was a good way to destroying her. Mördur kept rubbing it in that Adalheidur had tried to kill herself and warning Haukur that one day she would succeed. Or end up like his own daughter. He showed Haukur pictures of Laufhildur before and after the accident, which knocked him sideways. You know, she's the woman you looked up for us, the one with half her face missing.'

Huldar blew gently in Saga's face and she screwed up her eyes and nose, then waited eagerly for him to do it again. She'd been following what they said so intently that Freyja was almost afraid she could understand the words. Which was absurd, of course.

'Anyway, the deal was that Mördur would have Stella done away with and take the blame himself. In return, Adalheidur's father was to kill the bully in a different case, which he had no link to, and Mördur would shoulder the blame for that too. And also for a third killing he was planning, which doesn't seem to have been carried out. Since Mördur knew he was dying, he didn't care about being seen as a murderer.'

'Wow. Some deal.' Freyja kept an eye on Molly, who was sidling closer to Huldar and Saga, prepared to shut her out in the hall if she started growling at the guest. But the dog just lay down by his feet with a grunt. 'The man must be seriously screwed up, to put it mildly, to have agreed to a deal like that.'

'He claims he got cold feet. Had serious doubts. But every time he was on the point of backing out, something would happen to remind him how unendurable his daughter's life was. Either it was Mördur deliberately rubbing it in or him noticing what a wretched state Adalheidur was in. He was haunted by the photos of Laufhildur and terrified that something like that might happen to her. In the end he says he stopped trying to suppress his rage and abandoned common sense. After that, there was no turning back. But he regretted the whole thing after he attacked Egill and couldn't bring himself to put him out of his misery. Instead, he left the dying boy in a shipping container in the Mosfell district, according to plan. He just locked the door on him, hoping he'd be dead by the time the person who was to take over from him came to fetch his body.'

'How incredibly noble.' Freyja tried not to think about the dying boy. 'Is that what happened?'

'He doesn't know. He didn't see Egill again. The plan was that a different person would dump the bodies, to confuse the police. Haukur was sent to fetch Stella's body and leave it in the car park behind the convenience store. The idea was that the obvious suspect – the parent of the bully's main victim – would have a watertight alibi for the time the murder was carried out. Mördur arranged early on that his other killer would murder Stella on a Sunday while Haukur was at football; and presumably the other killer has a regular appointment on Tuesday evenings. That way, even if we did make the bullying link, the right parent would have an alibi. And Haukur was to say he'd been doing something on his own at the time he fetched Stella's body from the container and moved it to the car park. They were hoping we wouldn't question people too thoroughly about moving the bodies of the kids they clearly couldn't have killed. Which, I have to admit, was what happened in his case. We focused entirely on the attacks.'

Huldar poked his tongue out at Saga who closed her eyes with pleasure at the attention. Then he looked back at Freyja, pretending not to notice the bat as it whacked his face. 'The idea was to con us into believing there was a single perpetrator, as the murders were so similar. Apparently Mördur gave Haukur access to the *Just13* Snapchat account so he could send Egill threatening messages. I'm guessing he did the same for the other accomplice so he or she could scare Stella. Everything was set up to point to a single perpetrator. It would be enough for each killer to have an alibi for the other murder, because our attention would naturally be focused on Mördur as soon as he marched into the police station and confessed to the whole thing. On top of that, his flat was crammed with evidence to implicate him in both cases, so it would have been hard to come to any other conclusion.'

'Why didn't Mördur call a halt?' Freyja could feel her jaw sagging in disbelief. 'When he realised his plan had gone wrong. Couldn't he have warned the men?'

'Yes, he could.' Huldar pretended to grab at the bat and Saga snatched it perversely away. 'He took the answer to that with him to his grave. Personally I reckon he realised he wouldn't be leaving the hospital alive. But he didn't want to die without seeing his plan through, so he abandoned Adalheidur's father to his fate. Presumably the other killer too, though we've yet to catch him. Haukur says he began to suspect something was wrong when he got a Snap ordering him to stick Stella's phone through the letterbox of the nurse I told you about. He was to use it first to send a picture of Stella taken at the cinema, presumably by her attacker. Anyway, dumping the phone like that that hadn't been part of the plan. Originally, Haukur was supposed to send a Snap, then leave the phone by her body in the car park. We've no idea why Mördur changed his mind but hopefully things'll be clarified shortly.'

'Where did Haukur get Stella's phone from, if he didn't kill her himself?' Freyja watched as Huldar pretended for the fourth time to snatch the bat away from Saga. She hoped he realised the little girl was capable of playing this game for hours on end without getting bored.

Huldar made a disappointed face when he missed the bat again. 'He fetched it from the place where he was supposed to leave Egill's phone – a small polystyrene box hidden under the shipping container. That was agreed beforehand. The box was at the scene where we found Egill's body, but we didn't know if it had any connection to the case. It was empty by then, of course. And phones don't leave biological traces.'

'But hang on a minute – wasn't Adalheidur's father outside the school when the phone was dumped? How could he have driven from there to the Mosfell district, then to the nurse's house and back again before the meeting ended? It's not like it lasted long.'

'He'd already fetched the phone earlier that day, on Mördur's orders, so he didn't have to drive all the way out of town. Ásta lives quite close to the school and there wasn't much traffic, but even so he says he only just managed to make it back in time after chucking the phone through her letterbox. Then, as soon as he'd dropped Adalheidur off at home, he drove all the way back to the Mosfell district to fetch Stella's body from the container and dump it in the car park behind the shop. He hadn't dared to fetch it by daylight or risk keeping it in the boot of his car until after dark.'

'I still don't get why the bodies were removed from the scene after the attacks. Surely that just made the logistics more difficult and created all kinds of extra risks?'

Huldar gave up on the bat and started bouncing Saga up and down on his knee as he continued the story. She had to hang on to the toy for dear life so as not to drop it on the floor where Molly was lurking, waiting for her chance to seize it and make off with it to some quiet corner where she could chew it up. Like Saga, the dog was indifferent to cute teddies, showing interest only in the black bat with its little white fangs.

'Mördur wanted it that way,' Huldar explained. 'While the entire country was gripped by the drama, he meant to turn the spotlight on bullying. He didn't explain to Haukur in any detail, just said he was going to send some material to the newsdesks, starting with a blog designed to promote a debate about the repercussions of bullying. He was going to make it clear that the letters were connected to the abduction of the kids and that the victims' fates depended on the pieces being published. Which wasn't true, of course – it was just a ploy to get the media to run them. But it didn't happen. Maybe because he didn't have his computer with him in hospital, only his phone. Either he was too ill to send the letters to the press or he had no way of sending them that couldn't be traced.'

'And Adalheidur's father didn't suspect anything when no letters appeared?'

'No. He just assumed the press had refused to publish them and forwarded them to the police instead. We've got them now. They were found at Mördur's flat. Though I doubt they'd have been published even if he had sent them. The text's far too abusive. No better really than the stuff I've seen in cases of cyberbullying. The man doesn't seem to have grasped that his sick quest for revenge reduced him to the level of the very people he wanted to punish. Made him much worse, in fact.'

Freyja nodded. People had an unbelievable ability to rationalise the most appalling actions. Everyone was guilty of this to some extent, though not usually with quite such lethal consequences. Not many of us are capable of facing up to our own imperfections, dishonesty, unreasonableness or foolish mistakes. It's far easier to blame other people or circumstances beyond our control. 'Why didn't Mördur kill the kids himself? Or do you think he did actually kill Stella? Is that why you haven't arrested anyone for her murder?'

'No, he definitely didn't kill her. He was in hospital at the time. And according to Haukur, even before the heart attack, Mördur would have been too weak to do it himself. The bodies would have to be dragged some distance and he didn't have the strength. Though maybe that was just an excuse. Maybe he was secretly afraid that when it came to the crunch he wouldn't be able to go through with the brutal acts he'd been fantasising about. Though, having said that, it's clear he didn't have second thoughts when he came face to face with his own mortality in hospital, because he went on sending messages to Adalheidur's father from his deathbed.'

'So you believe there's another murderer still on the loose, maybe even more than one, planning further attacks? Couldn't Haukur shed any light on their identities?'

'He claims not to know. One possibility's Ævar, the father of the boy Egill was bullying. We've interviewed him and I have to say I've met gentler characters. He's down at the station now. But we didn't find any clues at Mördur's flat about the identities of the other members of his sick little club. He was careful about that. We do have the names of the people who rang the number he put on his notice and we'll be talking to each of them individually. When I left the office they'd also hauled in a psychologist for questioning. I rang Gudlaugur just before I came out and apparently it's Kjartan Erlendsson, the guy you recommended to Adalheidur's father.'

Huldar didn't seem to notice that Freyja had turned pale. So that was why Kjartan wasn't answering his phone. Struggling to appear normal, she cleared her throat and asked in rather a high voice: 'How's he linked to all this?'

'Mördur had files belonging to him on his computer. Confidential patient records. We still don't know whether he handed them over to Mördur voluntarily, maybe for money, or whether Mördur broke into his computer and stole them. But Kjartan's being questioned as a suspect. So far he's refusing to talk, insisting he's bound by confidentiality. He's demanded a lawyer, so he's being held in the cells until one turns up. Of course, until Kjartan agrees to talk, he's also a possible candidate for one of the killings. He's an expert in bullying. Maybe he'd had it up to here with the scale of the problem and thought he could do something more drastic to tackle it than sitting on his arse listening to the victims.' Huldar fell silent for a moment, then asked awkwardly: 'Is he by any chance a friend of yours?'

Freyja managed to control her face. 'No, God no. Nothing like that. I hardly know him.' A simple no would have been more convincing but she couldn't help herself. There would be no question now of any reference to him in the report she was intending to finish tomorrow. She coughed. 'How did he get mixed up with Mördur?'

'No idea. But we'll find out eventually – if he *was* mixed up with him. He may just have had his files stolen. Gudlaugur says they're suspicious because all the files contain references to aggressive tendencies of one kind or another. In other words, they weren't chosen at random. For example, they found notes on Adalheidur's father in which it's clear the man was struggling with violent thoughts as a result of his daughter's situation and might be capable of anything. They believe Mördur approached Haukur as a result of this information. There's also stuff about Davíd, the boy Egill was bullying. At one point the notes mention that his biggest worry was that his father might attack his main enemy – Egill. The boy describes his fear that this would only make the situation worse. Anyway, regardless of how these records ended up in Mördur's hands, it looks as if he didn't just rely on his notice but also hunted through the files in search of potential accomplices. It was quite a smart move since people are more likely to open up to therapists. The big question now is whether the psychologist himself is an innocent dupe or a cold-blooded killer.'

Freyja didn't trust herself to say a word. Although Kjartan

had proved to be a real slimeball, she found it hard to picture him planning a murder. He seemed too smooth somehow.

'We'll be tying up the loose ends over the next few days. Mördur had the names of ten victims of serious bullying but I don't believe for a minute that he'd have entrusted ten parents with the plan. We're working on the assumption that he started with a longer list and whittled it down to those who were most likely to carry it through, then dismissed the rest. There's a good chance that the person who was supposed to do away with victim number one simply lost their nerve. We'll soon find out.'

'So Adalheidur's father, Haukur, is the man you've arrested?'

Huldar smiled and started bouncing Saga, who was getting bored, again. 'No, actually. That's Arnar Björnsson, the man who tried to pay for sex with Adalheidur. It turns out Stella sent him round to her house and her father answered the door. The stupid sod mistook him for her pimp and unsurprisingly Haukur beat the crap out of him. He'll be released and his case will be referred to the State Prosecutor's office. I hope he'll be charged with attempting to pay for sex with a minor, but sadly I doubt anything'll come of it.'

Freyja nodded, not knowing what to say. The case was so sordid. Her own problems seemed trivial in comparison. Huldar was silent too; he seemed to have run out of things to say. He had stopped bouncing Saga on his knee and was gazing at Freyja. From the smile playing about his lips it seemed he liked what he saw, but then she had made an effort to choose an outfit that really suited her, accentuating all her best features. Not for Huldar, but out of a determination to out-glam all the other women at the reunion. From their profile pictures on the Facebook reunion page, that shouldn't be too much of a stretch. Still, never mind. Nothing must ruin the message she wanted to convey: eat your hearts out, bitches – you peaked too early.

The doorbell rang. Freyja buzzed Saga's mother in and, while she was on her way upstairs, took the little girl back from Huldar. As she bent over, he gave in to the temptation to peer down her low-cut dress. He could feel his cheeks flaming and couldn't understand why; it wasn't as if he hadn't seen her breasts before. Had had a much better view of them, in fact.

Freyja hurried to the door, encumbered by Saga and a pair of vertiginous heels. She let Fanney in, having given up trying to conceal from her how she lived. Fanney had grown so dependent on Freyja's help that, apart from turning up her nose and casting disapproving glances around her the first time she saw the place, she'd carefully refrained from any comment. And by now she knew better than to react to anything she saw in the squalid block of flats, even when she'd entered the house at the same time as another resident who was so high on drugs that he mistook her for an angel. Afterwards she had kept dusting down her coat where he had repeatedly stroked it on their way up the stairs.

'Gosh, you look smart.' Fanney took back her daughter so Freyja could dig out the child's outdoor clothes. 'Sorry I'm so late.'

'That's all right.' Freyja rummaged around among the coats on the rack, searching for Saga's other glove. She found it lying on top of a pile of shoes, soaking wet – no doubt from Molly's slobber, as the dog had a habit of chewing the child's socks and gloves like gum and spitting them out when she got bored. Freyja handed the disgusting object to Fanney.

Saga's mother made a face as she took the soggy wool gingerly between finger and thumb but next minute her face broke into a radiant smile. She had spotted Huldar who had just appeared in the doorway. 'Hello!'

'Hi, I'm Huldar. I just wanted to say goodbye to Saga.' He grinned at Fanney, then bent down to the little girl. Saga shook his hand with a grave expression. He patted her on the head, then straightened up, said goodbye to Fanney and vanished back into the living room. Freyja couldn't help noticing when he bent over that there was something sparkly in his hair. To her horror, she realised it was glitter. What on earth had he been thinking?

Freyja smiled coldly at Saga's mother who was expressing her approval of Huldar by raising her eyebrows and giving a thumbs up. Not a word about the black eye or sparkly hair. At least that boded well for the impression he'd make this evening. Freyja wasn't planning to stay long anyway, certainly not long enough to give Huldar a chance to reveal his true nature.

Huldar tried to make small talk in the car but received so little response that in the end he gave up. Freyja used the opportunity to check her appearance in the mirror, reapplying her lipstick and making sure not a single hair was out of place. She was grateful she wasn't driving herself as it would have ruined her entrance to turn up in her brother's rust-bucket.

Huldar switched off the engine outside. He studied her, seeming to pick up on the fact that something was wrong. She was sitting rigidly upright, her eyes fixed on the community centre. The muffled sound of a pop hit from her early teens floated out to them. The song hadn't improved with time. 'Something wrong?' Huldar peered out at the building as if he expected to see flames rising from the roof. That wasn't so far off the mark: her teenage hell awaited her inside.

'Want me to drive up to the door?' He gestured at her shoes. 'I'm not sure I'd get far in those.'

'No, this is fine.' Freyja still couldn't bring herself to open the door. She turned from the ugly building to Huldar. He gave her an awkward smile and for a moment she considered telling him why she was rooted to the spot. The moment passed. She pulled the sun visor down again, met her own gaze in the mirror, then slammed it up.

Then she nodded at Huldar, opened the door and got out. Ready for battle.

Chapter 41

Photocopy of a handwritten letter, entry no. 4 – posted on blog.is by a blogger going by the name of Laufa.

In the end the other kids at my school realised they weren't getting under my skin like they used to. So they changed their tactics. They started sucking up to my friend, the friend who was everything to me and nothing to them. It started so gradually that I didn't see where it was going. The most popular girls started talking to her from time to time, while I hung back at a safe distance, watching and waiting patiently for her to return to me. I never asked what they'd been talking about or what she thought of them. I knew they were way cooler, way more fun than me. It started happening increasingly often, and lasting longer each time, and my friend got more and more excited when they appeared. Little by little she began to withdraw from me, had less to say when we stood together during break, kept darting glances over at the group of girls who seemed to be having a much better time than we were. I spoke less and less. The only times I could relax with her were when I dropped into the shop where she worked two evenings a week. The shop was in her old neighbourhood, so there was no risk of any our classmates turning up there. I hung around by the counter, listening to her talk and agreeing with everything she said but adding little myself.

Nothing I had to say mattered.

It was as boring and pointless as I was.

Then one day it was all over. I was left standing alone in the corner of the school playground again, just like in the old days. She didn't come over to join me after a quick chat with the other girls as she usually did.

Instead, she went off with them.

I never took my eyes off the group, so I couldn't fail to notice when they all turned round as one and stared at me, saying something that was obviously bitchy, then giggling and turning away again. The first time, my friend was careful not to smile and kept her eyes lowered. But the more often it happened, the more she copied the crowd and in the end she became one of them. She was no longer on my side. I was alone again.

Too pathetic even to be able to hold on to one friend.

Now that I'd finally learnt what companionship was like, I felt even more miserable than before. But things were about to get worse. At the end of yet another horrible day at school, my former friend came up to me as I was putting my books in my bag deliberately slowly, to be sure I'd be the last to leave. She started talking to me while the other girls waited out in the corridor. By then she'd been ignoring me for about a week. I didn't suspect anything, just cheered up and felt stupidly happy. She invited me to come round and see her at the shop that evening and said she was sorry for being so unfriendly – she'd make it up to me. She added that I should dress up because we'd be going to a party afterwards with some of her old school friends.

It was the first and last time I was ever invited to a party.

I got Dad to leave work early and drive me to Kringlan so

The Absolution

I could buy a dress. The woman in the shop helped me pick one out because I had no idea what was in fashion. I thought my reflection looked so cool in the changing-room mirror. I borrowed some of Mum's make-up and she watched me putting it on, advising me from her wheelchair. By then she'd lost the strength in her right hand so she couldn't help me. But after a few failed attempts the end result was OK. Like me, my parents were happier than I'd seen them for years.

Dad dropped me off in the car and I smoothed down my dress before going into the shop. I thought it was a bit strange that there were so many customers in there but they all had their backs to me. But the moment I opened the door and caught my so-called friend's eye, I realised something was wrong. She looked away, ashamed. I'd rather not go into what happened next but basically a bunch of kids from our school had turned up, ready to make fun of me for being so stupid as to believe that anyone would invite me to a party. They pushed me about and humiliated me. They laughed at my dress, lifted it up at the back and insulted me. They needn't have bothered. I didn't need anyone to tell me how crap I was. I was well aware of that already. I'd known for a long, long time.

I got out of there in the end and went home on the bus. I couldn't hide what had happened from Mum and Dad – my face was too swollen from crying. The sadness and anger in their eyes were the final straw. My existence was no good to anyone. All I did was make things worse at home, though they were bad enough already thanks to Mum's illness.

The decision was easy after that. I hope Mum and Dad will understand that the world will be a better place without me. I know where Dad keeps the key to his gun cabinet and

I've already chosen the most powerful one. I've measured it against myself and although the barrel's long, I should be able to get it in my mouth and still reach the trigger. I've chosen the time and place too. The car park behind the shop where my so-called friend works.

I'm going to do it this evening, while she's there.

Finally, I want to ask my mum and dad to try and understand my decision. And to remember the important thing, which is that the world will be a much better place without me. I'm looking forward to the moment when everything goes black.

Please take this letter to them after I'm dead.

Yours,

Laufhildur

Chapter 42

A new song was booming out as Freyja and Huldar entered the hall. She had left her coat on the rack outside; he was still wearing his jacket. She paused, surveying the room and breathing in a cloying smell of alcohol. Some of the guests appeared to have drunk more than others; those who had downed the most were reeling around the dance floor with a wildly distorted sense of the impression they were making. Most of the faces were familiar, though they looked more careworn these days and in many cases fleshier. Everyone seemed to be making a big effort to pretend they were having fun, as if afraid that otherwise the spell would be broken and grim reality would intrude. Whereas Freyja saw the hall and the guests for what they were with a sudden cold clarity. No longer cool. No longer smart. Just terribly ordinary.

Huldar leant over and whispered: 'Have we come to the wrong place?'

She shook her head.

'Then why are we standing here instead of going in?'

Before she could answer, she saw the old classmate she'd run into at the supermarket charging towards them. He was red in the face, his top button was undone and his tie was askew. In his haste he slopped his beer and Freyja shuddered when he paused to lick it off the back of his hand.

'Wow! Great that you're here. I was told you were coming

but I thought maybe you'd changed your mind.' The man stopped right in front of Freyja, ignoring her companion. She shrank back towards Huldar, away from those glazed eyes.

'Come on, come inside. We're all having a crazy time.'

Freyja squeezed out a smile, her eyes scanning the room again. Unfortunately some of the others seemed to have noticed her arrival and faces were turned to the entrance, printed with surprise. The men appeared pleased, the women less so. This was the final confirmation, had she needed one, that she was looking good.

'Are you ready to party?!' The man lurched out of time to the music, slopping more beer from his glass. This time he didn't even notice and Freyja was spared the sight of him sucking his sleeve. 'Come over and join us. We're all thrilled you could make it.' He bellowed at the ceiling: 'Let's rock!'

Freyja caught Huldar's eye. He gave her a conspiratorial grin. As a policeman, he must have encountered more than his fair share of piss-artists. Looking back at her pickled former classmate, she discovered that she didn't hate him, any more than she hated any of the other people there. What was the point? But that didn't mean she felt any desire to embrace them. She hadn't come here to vent her anger, but neither had she come to make up with anyone or forgive them. It was enough to put it all behind her. With this revelation it was as if a heavy burden had been lifted from her shoulders. She smiled at the man, who beamed back. 'You know what? I'd have cried with joy if I'd been invited to join you lot back in the day. But now I think I'll pass. We've got somewhere else to go this evening.' She turned to Huldar. 'Shall we head off?'

'OK. Up to you.' Concealing his surprise, Huldar turned to go, throwing the guy a nod in parting. The man was left standing there, apparently casting around for something to say that would make her change her mind. Freyja didn't give him the chance but made her escape into the fresh air as fast as her heels would allow.

'What just happened?' Huldar pulled his thin jacket around him. 'Please tell me that was an old boyfriend.' He grinned at her.

'No. Believe it or not, he thought he was too good for me.' They were met by an icy blast of wind and she realised she'd forgotten her coat on the rack. With a sigh, she decided to come back for it tomorrow. There was a risk it would be spattered with vomit and reeking of smoke after someone had mistakenly grabbed it on their way outside for a ciggie, but anything was better than ruining the effect of her exit by scuttling back inside, shame-faced, to fetch it.

'So, can I buy you a drink anyway?' Huldar slapped his hands together, optimistic as ever. The offer was actually quite welcome; after all, she had good reason to celebrate. But his expression suddenly changed. 'You forgot your coat. Want me to get it for you?'

Freyja thanked him, wrapping her arms around herself to ward off the biting wind. There was no way she could walk downtown like this. But when Huldar reappeared with her coat in his hands, something had changed. He was wearing his policeman's face; frowning, eyes narrowed. 'Look, would you mind if I dropped in at the hospital on the way? I promise to be quick.'

She saw no alternative but to agree. The drink could wait.

It was growing stuffy in the car by the time Huldar finally re-emerged from the exit by A&E. He was carrying a bulky, dark anorak with a leather collar, which he hadn't had with him when he'd disappeared inside half an hour ago, saying he'd be back in five minutes. As he got into the car, she noticed that he was wearing rubber gloves of the kind surgeons use. 'Sorry. It took a bit longer than expected.'

'Do you usually leave your coat there? And where did the gloves come from?'

'I got them from the ward. And the coat was Mördur's, not mine.' Huldar patted the pockets. 'It suddenly hit me when you were standing there without a coat on that there was no anorak or jacket among his things when I collected them from the hospital. But the weather was freezing the evening he was admitted, so he must have been wearing one.'

'What happened? Did they forget to hand it over?'

'Not exactly. He was taken straight to A&E after his heart attack in the car park and they removed his coat there. Later, when he was moved to the ward, the anorak got left behind in A&E. By the time somebody noticed it, the shift had changed and no one knew whose it was, so they sent it to lost property. That's why it took me such a long time. I had to go through a mountain of stuff to find it.'

'Are you sure it's the right one? Every other person in Iceland has a jacket like that, and just about every tourist too.'

'I'm sure.'

'How?'

Huldar drew a socking great Rambo knife from the front pocket. 'There's no way this belonged to anyone else. I found the packaging from one of these in the kitchen bin during the search of his flat, but no sign of the knife itself.' He turned the blade over in the glow of the ceiling light. 'It looks unused.'

'Why did he take a knife with him to hospital?' Freyja stared, shocked, at the cold flash of steel.

Huldar returned the knife to the pocket and continued his inspection of the coat. In the outer breast pocket he found a small bag containing a clump of pale-grey hair, torn out by the roots, and a scrap of paper that he held up to the light as well. 'Looks like a car registration number.' He replaced the hair and paper without further comment and continued his search. From an inside pocket he removed a folded piece of paper and carefully opened it to reveal a single large number printed in the middle: 1. 'So . . . It looks like he wasn't taking himself to hospital because of chest pains after all. He was on his way to kill his first victim, but the heart attack stopped him in his tracks. That explains why he was coming from such an odd direction.'

'Who was the intended victim?' Freyja tried to imagine what it would be like for the person in question to learn how narrowly they'd escaped and what it was that had saved them. She bet they wouldn't be donating to the Heart Association again in a hurry.

'No idea.' Huldar searched the pocket for anything else and discovered a bundle of pages, which he unfolded to reveal a densely written text. He read it through in silence, then, telling Freyja to grab some latex gloves from the glove compartment, he handed the pages to her. 'It's Laufhildur's suicide note.'

Freyja recognised the text almost immediately. 'I've seen this before. When I was searching online for material about bullying a blog page came up, which featured a scan of this letter.' She leafed through the pages. But I only saw part of it; the last pages hadn't been posted.' She read them, then handed them back to Huldar. 'Well.'

'Well, indeed.' Huldar put the pages back in the anorak pocket and took out his phone. While Freyja gazed unseeingly at the illuminated hospital reception, he made a call. Freyja could hear the surprised reaction of the person at the other end, who seemed to think Huldar had been sent on leave. Judging by how quickly Huldar cut him off, this couldn't be a reference to overdue holiday. Huldar asked him to look up the owner of the car registration number he'd found, but the man at the other end refused as Huldar was officially suspended. Huldar snapped at him to put him through to Erla then, and there was silence at the other end.

They waited.

Huldar got out to smoke, the phone still clamped to his ear, while Freyja looked down ruefully at her party dress and shoes. She hadn't got all dolled up to spend the evening hanging around in a hospital car park. Outside, Huldar was now engaged in a heated argument.

When he got back in, he broke it to her that her dress wasn't going to a bar after all.

'I'm afraid I've got to go back to the station. I've been suspended.' It was impossible to read from his expression what he felt about this. He seemed preoccupied above all. 'But they told me the identity of the car owner. It's a woman who's mixed up in the case. She works here at the hospital. The only plausible explanation is that Mördur was on his way to meet her. She was almost certainly supposed to be victim number one.'

'The nurse?' Freyja tried to cover up her disappointment

at missing out on their drink. Still, the trip to the bar would almost certainly have ended in disaster. No way would they have stopped at one drink. And after that it was a foregone conclusion that they'd end up in bed. 'I thought Mördur had it in for school bullies. Teenagers.'

'Maybe I'm wrong, but she's around the same age as Laufhildur. She could have been the ringleader of the kids who bullied her. Or the friend who betrayed her. At any rate, one thing's clear: we need to get hold of her ASAP and grill her until she comes clean.' Huldar brightened a little. 'By the way, that psychologist, Kjartan, has been released. Apparently Mördur was one of his clients and offered to design a program to help him keep track of his appointments. Our IT guys reckon the program may have contained a code that allowed Mördur free access to the man's hard disk. Anyway, he's no longer on the list of suspects.'

Freyja didn't react. She wouldn't have minded if Kjartan had had to spend a night in the cells. 'What about Davíd's father? Do they think he was involved?'

'Yes.' Huldar smiled at her, clearly relieved. 'He's on the point of signing a confession to Stella's murder. The news of Mördur's illness knocked him sideways like it did Adalheidur's dad. He saw that the writing was on the wall. Though Erla tells me he'd already started panicking before he was brought in. Apparently Egill was still alive when he came to fetch his body from the container. And he got nervous when none of the material Mördur was supposed to send to the press was mentioned in the news. To make matters worse, there appeared to be only two victims, not three as planned. It was him who rang the Red Cross to make sure we heard about Laufhildur, in case Mördur had changed his mind about taking the blame

379

for the whole thing.' Huldar let out a long breath. 'So the pieces are all falling into place now.'

He started the car and prepared to back out of the space, but catching sight of her as he turned, he suddenly paused. 'I still owe you a drink. What about tomorrow evening?'

Freyja shook her head with a faint smile. 'Sorry. Just drop me home and we'll call it quits. The drink wasn't a very good idea anyway.' It wasn't just fear of ending up in bed with Huldar that was putting her off. She simply wasn't in the mood any more, haunted by the thought of the suicide note and the way life had treated Mördur's family. Of course it didn't for a minute justify what he'd done, but at least it made it easier to understand.

For once Huldar didn't try to hide his disappointment. He drove her home in silence and said a curt goodbye without pestering her to change her mind, as she'd expected. He was angry, perhaps with her, but more likely with someone else.

As she stood watching his car depart down the street, she felt a twinge of sympathy for the woman he was on his way to interview. She certainly wouldn't be getting the kid-glove treatment.

Ásta tucked the duvet firmly around her daughter, kissed her on the forehead, then reached for the lamp on the bedside table. The eye patch was hanging from the pink lacy lamp-shade, the stark contrast oddly charming.

'But . . .'

'No buts. It's long past bedtime.' Ósk had waited up for her, no doubt worried about what her mother was doing at the police station so late in the evening. She had been woken by the knock on the door and was terrified when Ásta was told she would have to go with the two police officers. One was that Huldar who wouldn't leave her alone. He seemed pleased about dragging Ásta away, though his pleasure had faded a little when Ósk appeared.

'Close your eyes. You can't go to sleep if they're open.' Ásta brushed her fingers softly over Ósk's eyelids. She still had her coat on, having come straight in to see the girls after spotting her daughter at the window. 'Follow your sister's example.' Sól was fast asleep on the other side of the room, lying as if she was playing at being a starfish, with the duvet kicked down at her feet. The girls didn't have to share a room but had chosen to themselves, preferring to keep the other as a playroom. It wouldn't be long before that changed, though, as the age gap was beginning to show. They quarrelled over what to hang on the walls and Thórey's suggestion that they each choose a wall had ended in a fight over who got which one.

It was such a relief to be able to worry about this kind of trivial everyday problem again. The past week had been pure hell but the nightmare was finally coming to an end. Ásta hadn't been able to concentrate on anything, either at work or at home, but there was no chance of faking illness when you had a doctor in the house. Anyway, Ásta hadn't dared to risk it in case Mördur resorted to doing something drastic if he discovered that she was deliberately avoiding him. The man was utterly ruthless. If he had no qualms about killing kids, he wouldn't have hesitated to ruin her life. He'd have taken pleasure in it.

The curtain billowed out and fell back. Remembering that a storm was forecast, Ásta closed the window. As she did so, she peered outside, still feeling the need to reassure herself that no one was lurking in the shadows. It would take a while for the fear to die down, now that she was safe. *If* she was safe. Until the news got out that Mördur was dead, one of his henchmen might still be after her, as he'd threatened.

Ásta dropped the curtain and turned back to Ósk. Her daughter hurriedly closed her eyes but wasn't quick enough. Ásta caught a glimpse of blue irises, one in the middle, the other pointing off to the side. But she pretended not to notice, just leant against the wall and decided to wait for the little girl to fall asleep. Her concern at her daughter's wakefulness was only a pretext; really, she was just putting off the moment when she got into bed with Thórey. Her wife was bound to wake up and start interrogating her about what the police had wanted. Ásta was dreading the inevitable confrontation. She was prepared to sleep on the sofa if that would put it off until morning.

She would have to make a clean breast of things to her wife – just as she'd been forced to with the police. She hadn't lied; she'd told them the truth as far as it went, hard though that had been. It had proved even harder than she'd imagined when rehearsing what to say in the car on the way there, but then she doubted anyone would enjoy having to show themselves in such a negative light. During the taking of her statement, she had avoided the eye of that detective Huldar. He had done nothing to hide his opinion of her for her role in Laufhildur's fate. The policewoman in charge of the interview had been a little more understanding. Though not much.

Anyway, she was free of the police now. For good. She'd confide in Thórey about what she'd told them and hope she'd encounter more understanding in her eyes than she had in theirs.

She'd begin the story as she had at the police station, with Mördur's heart attack. How she hadn't suspected a thing when the lean, older gentleman had suddenly collapsed in front of her in the car park. His name hadn't rung any bells, hadn't triggered any memories of the teenage Ásta, a person with whom she had long since severed all ties and would rather never have to think about again. She was a completely different person now; an adult, who lived her life in peace and harmony with all. A grown woman, focused on what mattered most: the wellbeing and safety of her family. Before, she had only ever thought about one thing: herself. Her own little life and whatever minor drama was at the centre of her world at any given time.

Of course, her teenage years hadn't been easy, but then no one's were. She wasn't unique; lots of gay teenagers went through a major crisis when they discovered their sexuality. It was especially hard because it came at the height of adolescence, at a time when most kids just want to fit in with the crowd. Opinions, appearance, weight, height, taste, hair, clothes, shoes, even shoe size – nothing must be different from the sacred norm. It had been desperately hard to discover one's homosexuality at that age. So she had been over the moon when she was suddenly invited to join the elevated ranks of the popular clique at her new school. All it had taken was for them to open the door a tiny crack and she had rushed up to them with her tongue hanging out, ready to sell her soul for the privilege of being one of them.

Her conscience told her now that this was no excuse. She had been a real traitor to another outcast, and the fact that she had been admitted to the inner circle did nothing to excuse her behaviour. Few gay kids took part in bullying as self-defence. She'd just been weak, that's all. Not bad. Not really. If she had truly been a bad person, she would still be bad. You couldn't just shake off something like that. At least, that's how she chose to look at it.

Thórey might provide a sympathetic ear for these reflections, but the police had been dismissive, merely telling her to stick to the point. It had been enough for them to know that she'd forgotten all about Laufhildur once her former friend had vanished after the accident with the shotgun. Ásta hadn't even been given a chance to correct this impression by explaining that she hadn't stopped thinking about her, just that it no longer happened every single day. Laufhildur only flashed into her mind on the rare occasions when she saw young people with serious injuries at the hospital. Then she would freeze. It was horrific to have been the cause of such terrible suffering to another human being.

That was why there had only been one possible response – to block out the incident from her mind. Pretend it had never happened. She refused all shifts in the orthopaedic ward or at the Children's Hospital. She stuck to caring for senior citizens in the cardiology ward, only agreeing to do extra shifts there or in geriatrics. That way she reduced the risk of being reminded of the incident. The suicide attempt and the gory aftermath in the car park behind the shop were kept locked away in a compartment at the back of her mind.

Right up until an older man came walking quickly towards her in the car park, only for his face to contort and for him to crumple up on the ground in front of her. She'd have done better to step right over him and go on home.

None of what she'd told the police was a lie. Every word was true. She just hadn't told them the whole story. They'd seemed satisfied by her explanation, though, and didn't ask any further questions once she'd finished. Apparently they believed her when she claimed that she'd been acting strangely because all the talk of bullying had raked up painful memories that had filled her with shame, and that when Laufhildur's name finally came up she'd denied that she knew her out of sheer panic. They'd also accepted her claim that she hadn't twigged when she heard Mördur's name, because her friendship with Laufhildur had been brief and had ended such a long time ago. That was no lie. She hadn't known who he was at first.

The only time during the interview that she'd been required to put on an act was when the policewoman told her they believed Mördur had been on his way to attack her the evening she'd saved his life. She had gasped at the news, putting a hand over her mouth. She must have been convincing because the interview had been wrapped up soon after that, though doubts had remained in Huldar's eyes.

But he couldn't begin to suspect that Mördur had confided in her.

She was tortured by regrets. If only she'd left Mördur to die on the tarmac, she would never have found out what he'd come there to do, and the girl and boy would have been allowed to live. None of it would have happened if she hadn't looked in on him the following day to see how he was doing, if she'd managed to avoid tending to him before he died. But, as she'd told the police, the penny hadn't dropped when she saw his name. It had all been too long ago and when she thought about Laufhildur, it was always by her first name. At first she had merely smiled when the man gripped her hand as she stood by his bed. But his grip was so hard that it hurt and her smile had faded. People as ill as him weren't usually that strong. But hatred had lent him strength. He jerked her close until she could smell the stench of death from his mouth, too astonished to resist. Death dripped from his words as well, from the threats and the demands he made of her.

The strange thing was that she had believed him, never once doubting that he meant what he said. He brought up Laufhildur straight away and that was enough to get her attention. She took in the whole thing, grasping at once that it had been no coincidence she'd been there when he had his heart attack; he had come to find her. He told her he'd been lying in wait for her, to make sure she didn't make it home from work alive. He was going to kill her in a belated revenge for Laufhildur. Fatally wound her, then drive her to a shipping container where she'd be left to die alone. Ásta had hardly been able to breathe when he told her this.

In retrospect, it was a miracle she hadn't cried out when he went on to describe how, long ago, he'd found out that she was to blame for what happened to his daughter. Laufhildur had given a clear account of it in her suicide note. It didn't matter that she had deliberately left out Ásta's name. It hadn't been hard for him to guess. His voice quivering with hatred, he told her how he'd dreamt of revenge, dreamt of seeing her suffer like the vermin she was. When she realised that he didn't have long to live and that when he was gone Laufhildur would lose her only support, he had decided to take action. That way he felt he could die at peace with himself. In the process, he would do others the favour of drawing attention to bullying and its consequences. He told her too that the gentle Laufhildur who hadn't wanted to name

Ásta in her letter had long gone. In her place was a far more vindictive person who had supported him all the way. Few things had pleased his daughter more than the thought of Ásta, alone and forsaken, in her death throes. While he was speaking, Ásta's knees had almost given way. She felt a despairing urge to smother the man with his pillow but resisted it. He was dying anyway.

Although it had been his illness that made him determined to quit the world in style, it had in fact saved her life. His heart hadn't been able to cope with the tension that had built up as he was lying in wait for her. He'd ignored the sharp pain in his arm and chest that had intensified the more agitated he became. He wasn't the first person to ignore the warning signs. When Ásta appeared, he had charged towards her but the effort had proved too much.

Ásta had had an unbelievably narrow escape. Now she would just have to take care until any of Mördur's remaining accomplices learnt that he would no longer be able to shoulder the blame for anyone else. He had boasted that he had several people working for him and threatened to send them after her if she didn't keep her mouth shut and obey his orders.

When she left his room she hadn't believed for a minute that he had men working for him, but that changed when Stella's phone turned up at her house. He boasted to her next day that he'd arranged it. But by this stage, she was in no position to go to the police. He had already made her charge his phone for him and send a Snap to a user on his list of friends, claiming he was too weak to do it himself. If she didn't help him, he'd threatened to tell anyone who stuck their head into his room what kind of person she was, how she'd treated Laufhildur and what had happened as a result.

At the time this had seemed the worst thing imaginable. She couldn't bear to think of her colleagues giving her sideways looks, as they were bound to do, however many excuses she made, however hard she tried to explain. But she'd had absolutely no idea then that he'd planned Stella's murder, or that the Snap he'd made her send had given the green light for the attack. Her original worries paled into insignificance in comparison. She'd unwittingly helped him attack a girl who was the same age as Laufhildur had been. So now she had the cruel fate of two young people on her conscience.

It couldn't be undone. She'd sent the message on Snapchat and although she'd kidded herself that it was harmless, she'd known better, even as she was sending it. She'd bought herself some respite at another person's expense. And as if that wasn't bad enough, she'd done it again in Egill's case. She'd also agreed to keep an eye on Mördur's phone, which was lying on his bedside table, and give him a nudge whenever he received a message. Each time she tried to persuade herself that it didn't matter. He'd have done it himself anyway and got her into trouble as well. She had to think of herself and her family. Besides, she owed him a debt, there was no denying the fact. These acts she performed for him were her pathetic attempt to buy his absolution.

But it was all over now. The police were satisfied and hopefully Thórey would be too, eventually. One day she'd have to forgive herself as well. Cling to the thought that she'd only been one link in a much longer chain of events. Just as she had been all those years ago. Her role in Laufhildur's story hadn't really been that big; she'd simply finished off what years of relentless cruelty by others had started. The same applied to Mördur's crimes. All she'd done was press 'Send'.

And keep her mouth shut. There's no way she could have known about Stella or done anything to save her. As for Egill, she'd just have to push away the thought that she could have prevented his death if only she'd opened up and taken the consequences. But she mustn't think that way. She was no more than a pawn, an instrument in the hands of fate.

Just as she had been no more than a pawn in the hands of Laufhildur's enemies. Those girls hadn't really been her friends. They'd only invited her into the fold because she'd befriended Laufhildur and, in order to be successful, bullies had to isolate the victim. Once Laufhildur was out of the picture, Ásta was no longer needed and she had been unceremoniously ejected again. When she went back to school after several days' absence while she was trying to recover from the horror of the scene behind the shop, they'd turned their backs on her. She found herself out in the cold again after only the briefest spell in the warmth.

Sól murmured in her sleep and kicked the duvet against the foot of her bed. Ásta knew there was no point tucking her in again; the little girl got so hot in the night that it would be thrown off before she even closed the door. Ósk, on the other hand, felt the cold and liked to sleep with the covers pulled up over her head. Funny how different children could be, despite the same genes and the same environment, and only being a few years apart in age.

'Mummy.' Ósk opened her good eye as she whispered this.

'Go to sleep.'

'But it's important.'

'It'll keep till tomorrow morning. You need to sleep now.' Ásta went over to the bed and smiled at her daughter. It was over. The whole thing. Now she could concentrate on what mattered: on the girls, on Thórey and on her job. Laufhildur, Mördur, bullying and all that stuff belonged in the past and could stay there.

'But I don't feel good.' Ósk opened both her eyes, which were now glistening with tears.

'What's the matter?' Ásta sat down on the side of the bed and stroked her daughter's hair.

'The other kids say I'm ugly. That I've got someone else's eye in my head.'

Ásta took a deep breath. 'Well, they're wrong. You and your sister are the most beautiful girls in the world.'

'They say I'm stupid. Stupid and ugly. They say I'm a stupid, ugly pirate. No one wants to play with me and María didn't invite me to her birthday party and Gunna didn't either, and the boys spat in my hair during break.'

Ásta's hand stiffened in the act of stroking her daughter's hair. She squeezed her eyes shut but it didn't help. The tears started pouring silently down her cheeks. She'd been given a chance to repay her debt to Laufhildur, to make a clean breast of things and save two young people from a horrible, premature death. But instead of taking it, she'd only bought herself a brief respite from the debt. And now it seemed that the person who was going to have to pay was Ósk.

The only consolation was that the police would never be able to link her to the crimes.

'And Mummy . . .' The little girl hadn't finished. Ásta wiped away the tears she didn't want her daughter to see, before turning back to her.

'What?' She managed to sound normal.

'There was a strange person in the garden earlier. I saw them from the window.'

'There's no one in the garden, Ósk. I checked just now and there's no one there but the snowman.'

'But there *was* somebody there.'

Ásta felt a pang. Her daughter might be right. Few people knew of Mördur's death yet. Now that she came to think of it, he'd let her off pretty lightly. Was it possible that he'd sent someone after her, as a parting gift to Laufhildur? Surely he didn't expect his daughter to avenge herself?

Ásta stood up and went to the window again. She tore the curtain aside with a shaking hand. But the garden was empty and there was no one to be seen. All was as it should be. All apart from the snowman, which was now wearing a gruesome mask.

A mask with green hair.